makeover

makeover

by
Shannon Guymon

Bonneville Books
Springville, Utah

This is a work of fiction. The characters, names, incidents, places, and dialogue are products of the author's imagination, and are not to be construed as real.

ISBN 13: 978-1-59955-081-7

Published by Bonneville Books an imprint of Cedar Fort, Inc., 2373 W. 700 S., Springville, UT, 84663
Distributed by Cedar Fort, Inc. www.cedarfort.com

LIBRARY OF CONGRESS CATALOGING-IN-PUBLICATION DATA

Guymon, Shannon, 1972-
Makeover / Shannon Guymon.
p. cm.
ISBN 978-1-59955-081-7
1. Mormons—Fiction. I. Title.

PS3607.U96M35 2007
813'.6—dc22

Cover design by Nicole Williams
Cover design © 2007 by Lyle Mortimer
Edited and typeset by Kimiko M. Hammari

Printed in the United States of America

10 9 8 7 6 5 4 3 2 1

Printed on acid-free paper

To Matt, my inspiration

chapter 1

"You have got to be kidding me," Sophie said to no one in particular as she watched the man she had waited faithfully for search the crowd, glance over her quickly, and then settle on a gorgeous brunette, who walked quickly toward him, extending her hand immediately.

Sophie's mouth dropped open as Blake passionately gripped the woman's hand.

"You have got to be kidding me," she whispered again, shaking her head in an attempt to make the scene before her disappear. She lowered the sign she was holding, realizing too late that Elder Blake Donovan wasn't interested in her welcome. He was much, *much* more interested in the welcome he was getting from the tall, glowing beauty.

She felt a comforting hand rest on her shoulder, and she looked up to see Blake's dad looking down at her with compassion.

"Probably some convert going to BYU or something. You know how these missionaries are when they get home. They still have their minds on the work. Come on, let's go welcome him home properly," he said and urged her forward, sign and all.

Sophie felt the presence of Blake's mom on her other side as they walked forward. Blake's mom and dad had been like her second family. They had assumed, *as she had*, that she was pretty much their daughter-in-law. Sophie looked up at Dorie Donovan and was comforted by the scowl on Dorie's face as much as by the hand of Blake's dad on her shoulder. Everything was going to be okay. What was she thinking?

This girl Blake was staring at so intently must be someone he had baptized. There was no other explanation. Really, there couldn't be.

"Hey, Elder Donovan! Welcome home!" Jack Donovan boomed out, startling his son and the woman standing so close to him.

The two stepped apart, and the spell between them seemed to be broken. Blake grinned and ran the rest of the way to his father, throwing his arms around him, hugging him tightly for what seemed like years. Sophie watched as Blake then hugged his mother. And then, it was her turn. Blake looked at her, and his smile seemed to falter slightly. Sophie ignored the pain constricting her heart and smiled brightly up at him.

"Welcome home, Blake," she said softly, waiting to see what his cue was before she moved in for the physical contact of a handshake.

Blake winced but then forced a smile.

"Sophie, wow. You came to the airport. That was really nice of you. You shouldn't have done that," he said, finally holding his hand out to her to shake.

Sophie stared at Blake's extended hand and felt her smile turn stiff and painful. *I shouldn't have come to the airport? To welcome home the elder I waited faithfully for, for two years? The reason I didn't even look at another man for two years?*

Sophie took a deep breath, reached her hand out, and firmly grasped Blake's hand.

"Of course I came, Blake. How could you think I wouldn't?" she asked.

Blake ran a hand through his bright blond hair and glanced over his shoulder at the tall, dark-haired girl standing to the side, listening to everything that was being said.

"Um, anyway. Mom, Dad, I want you to meet someone," he said, turning and motioning for the girl to come forward into the small circle.

The girl walked confidently toward Blake, beaming at everyone. Sophie stared at her and felt diminished with every step she took toward them. Not only was she tall, almost as tall as Blake, but she was completely, classically beautiful. Glossy mahogany hair that Sophie knew instinctively had never been touched by chemicals. Her complexion was porcelain, no freckles in sight. And her eyes were a cool shade of green.

"Hi, everyone, I'm Bailey," she said.

Dorie and Jack looked at each other with raised eyebrows before politely introducing themselves to the girl who stepped closer to Blake.

Blake stared down at her, beaming as if she were the best show-and-tell he'd ever had.

Sophie cleared her throat, knowing her life was slowly going down the toilet but wanting it spelled out for her just the same.

"So how do you know Blake, Bailey?" she asked in a strangely ordinary voice.

Bailey turned and looked at her, as if she had just noticed her.

"Oh, didn't you know? Blake, you shouldn't have kept it a secret. Blake and I are getting married," she said, blushing sweetly.

Even knowing it was coming was no preparation for the blow. Sophie's face went white with shock, and her legs felt weak. She stared up at Blake in horror and watched as he looked down at his feet, not meeting her eyes.

Jack glared at his son and put his arm around Sophie's shoulders, bracing her. Dorie stared in horror at her son.

"Blake, how could you?" Dorie said and stepped closer to Sophie.

Blake looked up at his parents in surprise, realizing that their reaction wasn't what he'd had in mind. He glanced at Bailey in confusion, as if wondering if his parents were blind. Couldn't they see how beautiful she was? It wasn't as if he'd had a choice.

"Mom, Dad, what Bailey said is true. I don't know what Sophie has told you, but I'm guessing she's exaggerated some things. I'm in love with Bailey, and we'll be getting married as soon as possible. I guess I should have told you sooner, but I thought it would be a fun surprise."

Sophie stared at Blake as if she were seeing him for the first time. *She'd exaggerated their relationship? Him begging her to wait for him and promising her the biggest wedding Mount Timpanogos had ever seen was exaggerating their relationship?* Sophie felt light-headed and realized she was starting to hyperventilate. She clumsily stumbled over to the group of chairs closest to her and sat down, bending her head forward and trying to breathe slowly. She immediately felt Dorie's hand on her back.

"Honey, just concentrate on breathing in and out. Just ignore Blake and that girl. Don't faint on us, Sophie. Stay strong," she said.

Sophie tried to nod but felt too weak. She breathed in and out and felt the black popping bubbles behind her eyes start to recede. She raised her head five minutes later, hoping Blake and Bailey were gone, only to find Jack, Blake, *and* Bailey standing right in front of her, staring at her as if she were some kind of science project.

"Um, Sophie. I was just talking to my dad, and I apologize for saying that you had exaggerated our relationship. I can see how that would upset you. I hope that you can be happy for Bailey and me. It would mean a lot," he said, his blue eyes glowing sincerely.

Sophie dragged in one more deep breath and closed her eyes, wondering how she had gotten herself into this mess and how in the world she could get out of the airport with her dignity. She opened her eyes and smiled first at Jack and then at Dorie. Then she stood up shakily and gave Jack and Dorie both a fierce hug.

"Jack, Dorie, these last few years have been wonderful. You've been the perfect parents to me. I will always love you for the kindness and love you've shown me," she said sincerely, with a hint of tears in her voice.

She turned and speared Blake with eyes that had turned a bright, molten gold.

"Blake, all you had to do was let me know that your feelings for me had changed. You wrote me a three-page letter just last week. One little sentence. That's all you had to do. And you were too chicken to do it. So, no. I don't think I will be happy for you," she said and picked up her purse and her welcome home sign and walked away. She shoved the sign she had worked on for two hours the night before into the nearest trash can and paused to pull her purse strap over her shoulder. She smoothed her hair out of her eyes, thrust her shoulders back, and held her head high. Sophie Reid was a pro at putting on a happy face for the crowds. She'd done it before, and she'd do it again. But being happy for Blake and Bailey was so far beyond her that the thought made her giggle. Happy. For them. Sophie laughed all the way out of the airport and barely reached her faded red Jeep before the tears started pouring out in earnest. Two years of her life wasted. Gone forever. She shoved her key in the ignition and jerked out of the parking lot quickly. Blake owed her two years. And he was going to pay for them.

chapter 2

Sophie made it to Alpine in forty-five minutes, surprising her mom and all the clients in the beauty salon by running to her mother and bursting into fresh new tears.

"What in the world are you doing here?" Candy demanded, patting her daughter's back. "Was Blake's plane late? Did he miss his flight?" she demanded.

Sophie raised red eyes to meet her mother's, not caring who was listening. "Mom, there was another girl there! He ignored me, and when he finally noticed me, he told me that he wanted me to be happy for him and this girl because they're getting married soon! He told everyone that I had exaggerated our relationship and that I shouldn't have even come to the airport," she sputtered, crying softly on her mother's shoulder.

The salon broke out into furious whispering. Sophie heard a few people say, "I cannot believe him," and a few more say, "That little punk!" She'd be a liar if she didn't admit that it was a comforting background noise.

"Honey, you just sit down here and tell me from the beginning what happened. We'll work through this," Candy said, with a few tears slipping down her own cheeks.

"Mom, I hate him! He humiliated me. After all I've done for him. I never even looked at another man for two years, and he meets someone *on his mission*! Ooh! I hate him!" she said passionately and then leaned her head on the counter.

When she looked up again, she and her mother were surrounded by every woman in the salon. As she wiped her eyes, she noticed that the Relief Society president, Sister Murphy, was there, obviously getting a perm. Sister Martin, the bishop's wife, was there, with half her head foil wrapped. And on and on. Everyone would know by the end of the day about her and Blake. Sophie sniffed and looked down to see a tissue being shoved in her hand. *Everyone.* That meant the relatives would know. Sophie felt ill and laid her head down again as the reality of the situation draped itself around her. It was all over. Her dream marriage to the most perfect man in Alpine would now never happen. She had been dumped. She looked up at her mother and saw the look of complete understanding in her eyes. Like mother like daughter.

"You know what? I feel the need for Dimitri's pizza coming on," Jacie said, taking her cell phone out and dialing.

Sister Murphy moved to Jacie's side and added an order of bread sticks. Sister Martin put in an order for some root beers, and they were set. Sophie felt some of the tension leave her shoulders as she stared around the small but ultra chic salon. Here were the people who cared about her. The feelings and emotions of everyone surrounding her were thick with concern and compassion. She felt like she was being covered in a thick blanket of love.

"Sophie, you get that letter out that you always keep in your drawer. You know the one, where he tells you he loves you and that he wants to be with you forever," Cathy said, still cutting away at Sister Bennion's light gray hair.

Sophie looked up at her mom, and her mom shrugged with a grin. *Why not?* She leaned over and pulled open her drawer. It was full of letters from Blake. She grabbed the thickest letter in the back corner and pulled it out, feeling new tears seep out her swollen eyes. Blake had written this to her when he had been out for six months.

She slowly smoothed the letter out and read aloud.

"Dearest, loveliest, most beautiful Sophie," she began. She was surprised when a giggle slipped out. Wow, Blake sounded so lame all of a sudden.

"Please put me out of my misery and promise me that you will wait for me. Please, Sophie, please promise me that you will only think of me. If you will prove your faithfulness to me, I will make it up to you. You will have the biggest, most wonderful wedding Mount Timpanogos has ever seen."

Sophie lowered the pages in her hand to her lap and frowned. She looked up at the spellbound group around her. Even Cathy had stopped cutting. Sophie was surprised to see a few tear-filled eyes. Her mom looked almost as bad as she did, her eyes getting redder by the second and her skin turning white and blotchy.

"Well, you tell me. Did I exaggerate my relationship with Blake to his parents? Was I an idiot to show up at the airport?" Sophie demanded angrily of the small group of women surrounding her.

All of the ladies shook their heads in unison and angry chatter erupted.

Sophie threw the pages down on the counter and swiveled the chair around.

"I was the biggest idiot Alpine has ever seen," she said fiercely, running her hands through her painfully straight hair. She hadn't worn her hair naturally wavy since she'd started dating Blake almost three years ago. She hadn't done a lot of things since she started dating Blake.

"Sophie, you are not an idiot. Blake is the idiot if he thinks he can find a girl better than you," Sister Frandsen said, pounding her wrinkled, age-spotted fist on the arm of her chair.

"Thanks, Sister Frandsen. But trust me, I *am* the idiot. And he already found a girl better than me. You should see her. She's beautiful. Tall, gorgeous, and just plain perfect," Sophie said sadly, slumping down farther in her chair, feeling ill just thinking of Bailey.

"I just don't understand, Sophie," Candy said shaking her head and pulling curlers out of Sister Murphy's hair. "I know you got a letter from Blake just last week. And it was thick just like they've always been. Why didn't he just tell you?"

Sophie leaned her head on her hand and gazed over at her mom.

"That's the most painful thing of all. He could have told me and he just didn't. If he'd really cared about me, he would have said, 'Hey Sophie, look, things have changed and I don't think you should come.' But he didn't. He could have spared me the pain and the humiliation, but he was too gutless. He just talked and talked about all the people he was going to miss. The last six months of letters haven't been as romantic as the first year and a half, but I thought that was just him really getting into the missionary work, you know? But it wasn't. Blake is a selfish coward. A heartless, selfish coward, and I'm glad I found out now, instead of ten years down the road," she said and then winced, looking guiltily over at her mom.

Candy frowned, keeping her head down. Sophie's dad had left them ten years ago when she had been a shy little eleven-year-old. Candy had been devastated and humiliated. And everyone had known it.

Sophie sighed and leaned her head back, closing her eyes. She half listened to the sounds of the pizza guy arriving and everyone getting their plates of food. She finally looked up to see Jacie standing in front of her, staring at her sadly.

Jacie had been Sophie's best friend since kindergarten. She was a tall, gorgeous blonde, with a wide streak of sarcasm and humor. Everyone looked at her and thought she was sweet as honey, but Sophie was one of the few people who knew the real Jacie. She didn't let many people past the pretty packaging, but once she did, they realized she was a very smart, cynical, but kind-hearted person. Sophie loved her like a sister.

"Man, Sophie, you're killing, me you're so sad. It makes me want to scream. But you're nice, just like your mom. You're going to let that jerk get away with it. If it were me, I'd be out getting revenge," she said and took a ferocious bite of pepperoni pizza.

Sophie frowned up at her friend. "You know, Jace, I'm not feeling that nice right now. You never know," she said.

Jacie raised an eyebrow and took a swig of root beer.

"Yeah right. I'll believe it when I see it," she said and flounced away. Sophie smiled, knowing her friend was furious on her behalf. She knew how many dates Jacie had cancelled just to go to the movies with her because she didn't want her friend to be alone on a Friday night.

As the clients left the salon one by one, they all stopped by Sophie on their way out and patted her shoulder, giving her hugs and words of encouragement. The bishop's wife, Sister Martin, was the last one to leave. She looked in the mirror one last time and fluffed her now glossy raven-colored waves and then walked over to where Sophie was slumped in a puddle of misery.

"Ah, now this isn't the Sophie I remember from girls camp! Perk up, young lady. I want to see a smile! See, now doesn't that feel better?" she demanded.

Sophie lowered her frozen stiff lips from the smile position and sank even lower in her chair.

"You know, you're just like your mom. Now, Candy handled her little situation with grace and dignity. I'd be surprised if you didn't end up this new girl's maid of honor. You're just a sweetheart. You can't help it," she said and then glided out the door.

Sophie had never been more depressed by someone in her life. She had sat back and watched as her mom had suffered silently through all the gossip and talk that had erupted when Tanner Reid had left her for a younger, richer woman. She'd seen her mom's face when she'd run into her father's new wife, Julie, at the store or seen her eating lunch with one of Candy's old friends. Sophie had seen Candy smile through it all.

Sophie licked her dry lips and clenched her fists. She didn't feel like smiling. She didn't feel like making it okay for everyone. Maybe she wasn't like her mom after all. Sophie looked over at Jacie sweeping the hair up around her stall. Jacie'd never stand for a man humiliating her without making him pay for it. Why should she? What was it about Sophie that said, *Hey, world! Dump on me!*

Sophie stared morosely at her reflection and tried to figure out what it was about her that had Blake turning to someone else. He had picked a girl the complete opposite of her. Was it her hair? She'd straightened it faithfully for him after he'd made a comment one time about how if he had curly hair like her, it would drive him crazy. So she'd changed. Was it the color of her hair? The reddish brown was a little different from all the blondes and brunettes walking around. He'd never said he preferred dark brown. But if he had, would she have dyed it? She didn't know the answer to that. She looked at all of her features. Large, light brown eyes, with dark lashes. A small straight nose and an ordinary mouth with full lips. And one small dimple in her right cheek. Her mom had always told her that she had a heart-shaped face. There was really nothing spectacular about her. Men never stopped in the streets and stared or anything, but they didn't hide their eyes and look away either. She knew she wasn't ugly. So what was it? Why did he do it? There was no reason. That was the answer. Blake was a complete and total jerk. Period. And he deserved to be punished.

Sophie sat up straighter in her chair and felt a little bright light go on inside. Maybe a little revenge wouldn't hurt. Maybe it would even feel good. Two years of dateless, hope-filled nights good.

Sophie jumped out of her chair and walked over to her friend's station.

"You've got one more customer today, Jacie," Sophie said, plopping down in the bright white plastic chair.

Jacie paused and put the broom down, walking in a circle around Sophie, with a small smile on her face.

"Don't tell me you're going to let the inner Sophie out to play. She hasn't been here in a long, long time."

Sophie wiggled her head and smiled. "I never liked straight hair anyway," she said.

Jacie snorted. "You sure thought you did for the last three years. Or was that a Blake thing?" she asked with an evil twinkle.

Sophie rolled her eyes and sat back firmly in the chair, grabbing a drape and slinging it around her shoulders.

"It just so happens that straight hair *was* a Blake thing. I'm ready to do the Sophie thing again. Give me back me," she said to Jacie and smiled when she heard Jacie and Candy cheering.

"Give me back me," she whispered to no one in particular and closed her eyes as she felt a small part of herself return.

chapter 3

The next day was Sunday, and Sophie lay in bed as long as she could. Blake would be giving his homecoming talk in church. People would have to get to church early just to get a seat. *Maybe I should go to the singles ward,* she thought, covering her face with a pillow. She'd never been before. She hadn't wanted to tempt herself, so she'd stayed in her home ward. She even had a calling as the CTR 7 teacher. She couldn't let her kids down. But after church, she'd have a talk with the bishop and let him know she'd be going to the singles ward from now on. It was definitely time to get a social life.

She stumbled out of bed and took a quick shower. She started to rush through her hair and makeup like she always did on Sunday, but stopped suddenly. Everyone there was going to be looking at her, knowing she had been dumped at the airport just the day before. They would be expecting her to look pale and sad and pathetic. *Not today,* she thought, slowing down and taking her time.

She used the diffuser Jacie had given her the day before and sent her naturally wavy hair into the next level. Wild and curly. Jacie had given her a few light golden highlights around the face and chunky layers all over to give her waves a lift. Sophie smiled at her reflection. There she was. And to think she'd taken so much time every day straightening her hair. And for a man who had been half a world away. Sophie winced at her stupidity. She had been so sure that her life was going to be great. She had been so certain that she would be different from her mom.

Sophie sighed and started her makeup. At the salon, she was always the one people called to have their makeup done for pictures or for parties and weddings. For the last two years, though, she'd barely put any makeup on. Why bother? But things were different now. She finished fifteen minutes later and stepped back to look at her work. She grinned at herself. She looked fantastic. Gone was the pale girl with the super straight hair. The girl looking back at her looked alive. She looked ready for anything.

Sophie walked with determination toward her closet. She ignored the classy cream suit she had bought especially for Blake's homecoming talk and grabbed a knee-length summery skirt in bright blues and greens instead. She reached for the matching silk shirt that tied in the back and quickly put the outfit on. She ignored the conservative flats and picked up an old pair of high heels. Blake had always liked her to dress a certain way. *Boring.* Sophie winced as she realized she had been transforming herself into Blake's idea of the perfect woman for the last two years. *What an idiot!* she scolded herself for the thousandth time.

She walked over to her bedside table and grabbed her scriptures. She was ready. And after a late-night trip down to Maggie Moo's with Jacie, she knew what to do. Jacie called it her Five Steps to the Perfect Revenge. Step one, make the man regret his decision.

Sophie glanced in the hallway mirror before entering the kitchen and felt better. She was the complete opposite of Bailey in every way. Where Bailey was dark, Sophie was light. Where Bailey was tall and elegant, Sophie was short and curvy. She'd make Blake remember why he'd fallen in love with her to begin with. And then she'd laugh in his face.

"Hey, Mom," Sophie said and leaned down to kiss her mom on the top of her head.

Candy was reading her scriptures and eating a bowl of oatmeal, like she did every day.

Sophie grabbed some toast and made a couple scrambled eggs.

"You and Jacie were sure out late last night," her mom said, not looking at her.

Sophie turned away from the stove and glanced at her mom.

"Yeah. You've been used to me being home early for the last two years. Not anymore, Mom. I've got some living to make up for."

Candy raised her eyebrows and looked up from her scriptures.

"Now hold on just a minute. Just because Blake did what he did, doesn't mean it's okay to start being wild," she said

Sophie laughed and grabbed the salt and pepper.

"Oh, Mom. You know me better than that. But it will be weird to start dating again. Last night, Jacie took me to Maggie Moo's, and we talked for a long time. We have decided to get my life back where it should be. Blake free. And first things first, a little revenge to jump start things," Sophie said in a menacing voice.

Candy put her spoon down and turned to look at her daughter.

"You will do no such thing, Sophie Reid," Candy said in a shocked voice.

Sophie slid her eggs onto her plate and walked over to sit at the small round table with her mom. She took a bite of eggs and smiled before looking up to catch her mother's eye.

"Oh yes I will. Just because you didn't, doesn't mean I'm not going to," she said in a quiet, firm voice.

Candy cleared her throat and looked down at her nails.

"You don't know what you're talking about, Sophie. Revenge will get you nothing. It won't get you Blake back. It won't make you happy. It won't do anything but turn you into a bitter, mean person."

Sophie put her fork down, no longer hungry. She poured herself some orange juice from the pitcher on the table and took a small sip.

"Look, I'm not going to go pop his tires or egg his house or prank call him at three in the morning. That's not what I'm talking about. I'm talking about The Five Steps to the Perfect Revenge. Step number one is making the man regret his decision. Now does that sound so evil?" she asked.

Candy frowned. "Well, not really. I guess. Just don't . . . don't do anything you'll regret. Okay?" she pleaded.

Sophie got up and put her plate in the sink before answering.

"I have too many regrets right now as it is. I should have done what Jacie did and dear John-ed my missionary when he was in the MTC. That girl is brilliant."

Candy rolled her eyes and got up from the table. She walked over and put her arms around Sophie, hugging her tightly.

"Honey, I know today is going to be hard on you. You don't have to go today, if you don't want to. I'll teach your class for you if you want," she said.

Sophie hugged her mom back just as tightly and smiled.

"How can he regret dumping me if he doesn't see me? Nope, the easy way out is not part of the plan. As a matter of fact, I plan on seeing quite a bit of Blake in the future."

Sophie smiled and went to brush her teeth before leaving for church. She was actually looking forward to it.

chapter 4

"No! Not in the back. We're sitting right in front, right in the middle. And by the way, you look incredible. Love the bronzer," Jacie said, pulling Sophie by the elbow.

Sophie cringed as everyone turned to stare at her with pitying frowns. It was fine to be brave and strong at home. But being brave in the chapel was a whole different story. As soon as she and Jacie had walked in, she spotted Blake and Bailey surrounded by a small crowd of people, laughing and smiling.

Sophie couldn't help it; she had to stop and just look at Blake for a moment. He was so good-looking. Tall and blond, just like a J. Crew model. He was grinning and gesturing with his hands. He looked so alive and so happy. For two years, she had thought of no one else but him, and here he was, further away from her than he'd ever been.

Jacie pushed Sophie forward into the chapel before she could start drooling. Jacie gently dragged her toward the front and pushed her toward the very middle. They were surrounded by two families on either side of them, but Jacie didn't care. Her fast track to the perfect revenge cared nothing for comfort. Or the sound of crunching Cheerios.

Sophie sighed and placed her bag on the floor by her feet. When she looked up, she could see Dorie squeezing into the pew in front of her and making her way toward the middle. Sophie's eyes went wide at the sheer amount of people the woman was pushing aside just to get to her.

"Sophie, honey. I've been waiting for you. I just wanted to invite you to the luncheon at our house after church. I insist that you come.

You kept me sane for two years while Blake was away, and you wrote him every week and sent him care packages every month. You should be there, Sophie. I insist on it."

Sophie's mouth dropped open in horror. The airport had been bad enough. What would Blake do if she did show up? Tell her how much his future children with Bailey would appreciate her getting lost? No thanks.

"Um, I don't . . ." was as far as she got before Jacie jumped in.

"Sister Donovan, we'd be happy to come. We wouldn't miss it," Jacie said with a large smile.

Dorie glanced at Jacie and smiled gratefully.

"Oh good. I'll just tell Jack. He was worried that after yesterday, you wouldn't feel like coming. But I knew you would come. You're part of the family," she said and squeezed back out of the pew.

Sophie's shoulders slumped, and her public smile slipped five notches. Jacie put her arm around her shoulder and leaned her head down.

"No crying. Now knock it off. That family part was a hard hit, but shake it off. Get that smile back in place now, before you start looking pathetic and dumped. That's right. Let's see that dimple. Good! Now head up and glance around slowly, left and right. Smile at anyone who is staring at you. Perfect. Now when we get to Blake's house after church—" Jacie said, but stopped when her toes got stuck under Sophie's heel.

"How could you do that to me? Now I have to show up at Blake's house? Are you my best friend or not?" Sophie whispered furiously.

Jacie shrugged and reached for her ChapStick.

"What's rule number one, Sophie?" she asked, smiling at the child beside her.

Sophie frowned and fidgeted with her scriptures.

"Make him regret his decision," she said sullenly.

Jacie smiled and patted her arm.

"Good girl. Now, this is the perfect opportunity. You have a lot going for you. You have past history. All you have to do is use it as a weapon. Wield it like a sword. Fire it like an arrow. Shoot it like a gun. You know what I mean," she said.

Sophie closed her eyes and wished she had taken up her mom's offer to substitute for her today. She could be at home right now, soaking in a bubble bath. But no, she was here, trying to begin her five steps to the ultimate revenge or whatever it was. Out of the corner of her eye, she saw Blake walk past on his way to sit on the stand.

"It's go time," Jacie whispered fiercely.

Sophie sat up straighter and smiled demurely. She had practiced in the mirror, so she automatically knew she didn't look defeated, dumped, or the very worst, devastated. Jacie had pounded it into her head just last night. If she showed Blake how devastated she really was, then his ego would get too much of a boost. But if she looked like a caring friend, then the door remained open for the revenge part. He would be curious. And he would be thinking of her and hopefully not Bailey.

Jacie squeezed Sophie's arm to let her know that Blake was looking at her. That had been the game plan. A squeeze equaled interest. Now, she had to barely turn her head and look right at Blake, smile serenely, and then look back at the bishop. She turned, put her face in position, and looked. Blake was staring at her in a bemused way, as if he were finally remembering who she was. He looked confused and a little unsettled. *Good!* Sophie thought and turned to look at the bishop again. This went on until it was Blake's turn to talk.

Sophie couldn't help noticing the way his suit fit over his shoulders and the confident way he smiled at everyone. She sighed and remembered why she had fallen so hard for him. So hard that she had promised to wait two very long years for him. *Because he was perfect in every way.*

"Stop it!" Jacie whispered. "This isn't the time to go all gooey. This man humiliated you in front of hundreds of people at the airport, and let's not forget his fiancée. Now stick to the plan and stop staring at him like he's a piece of chocolate cake."

Sophie turned and glared at Jacie but did as she was told and looked serene through the whole talk. Even when he thanked the ward for all of the support and letters and packages. She knew for a fact that 99.99 percent of those letters and packages had come from her. And yet, he didn't mention her even once. *Total serenity.*

After sacrament meeting, Sophie went through the motions as she taught her class and kept everyone in control during singing time. But when the clock struck twelve, she knew it was fight or flight. She could run down her mom in the parking lot and beg for a ride home or go with Jacie to the homecoming luncheon. Sophie bit her fingernail as she tried to decide what to do.

Jacie grabbed Sophie's arm and pulled her toward the parking lot. *Too late.*

"You know, I'm going to have bruises tonight because you keep dragging me everywhere. You're acting like some FBI agent with a felon. Personal space, Jacie. Look it up."

Jacie snorted and led her to her black Chevy Avalanche. "Just get in. You had that *I'm flaking out* look and you know it."

Sophie shrugged. She probably did. "Okay, so what's the game plan for the luncheon?" she asked as Jacie drove out of the parking lot.

"Easy. Stay in his vicinity the whole time, but just out of reach so he sees you but can't talk to you. Then when we get ready to leave, go up and give him a big hug. You can hug him now, since he was released by the stake president this morning. So give him a big hug, and maybe even a kiss on the cheek. Say something like, 'It's good to have you home.' And then walk out. So easy," she said with what was supposed to be an encouraging smile.

Sophie flipped down the mirror and frowned at her reflection before reapplying her lipstick.

"What about Bailey? What if she comes up to me and wants to start something? I just don't think I can handle her, Jacie. Not today," Sophie said quietly.

Revenge was all good and fun, but underneath it all, Sophie's heart was still broken, and hearing all about Blake's mission had brought back so many memories. All she wanted to do was go home and cry on her mom's shoulder. But that just wasn't part of the five steps to really cool revenge.

"Just leave Bailey to me," Jacie said. "She won't know yet that I'm your best friend. I'll do a little investigating and protect you at the same time. But that means I won't be able to stick by you."

Sophie smoothed down her skirt and pushed her now curly hair out of her face.

"I'll survive. Let's just get through this. Maybe then we can move on to step number two."

Jacie pulled up to Blake's house and turned the car off. "Honey, I don't think you're ready for step number two."

Sophie got out of the car and walked beside Jacie up the long stamped concrete pathway to the oversized, glossy wood doors.

"What was number two? I can't remember now."

Jacie smiled. "That's because you were snarfing down ice cream like nobody's business. Next time take notes. Geez. Number two is make him jealous. And if you see any good-looking men here, then get started on that. The five steps to the perfect revenge can be moved around. He probably has tons of ex-companions who will show up."

Sophie groaned and rang the doorbell. "Two years of fasting and now the feast. And I don't even feel hungry," she said pathetically.

Jacie laughed and pounded on the door. "You're hungry. You just don't know it yet. There's nothing like one or two rebounds to get you back in the game. Look at me. I dumped Bryan and I've never been better. For the last two years, I've dated tons of guys. I'm completely happy," she said, frowning at the door.

Sophie stared at her friend. She'd dear John-ed Bryan while he was in the MTC and hadn't heard from him since. Bryan was getting home from his mission in a few weeks. Maybe Jacie wasn't as over Bryan as she thought she was.

"Someday you're going to have to tell me why you dumped him," Sophie said as the door suddenly swung open.

Bailey. Gorgeous, perfect, relationship-ruining Bailey.

"Well hi there. I didn't expect to see you here today," Bailey said with a pitying smile.

Sophie ground her teeth and moved forward to push her way past Bailey when she felt a restraining hand on her shoulder.

"Hi, Bailey. I've heard nothing but good things about you. I'm Jacie, a friend of Blake's," Jacie said and shook Bailey's hand warmly.

"Well, please come in, Jacie. I know Blake is looking forward to getting caught up with all of his old friends," she said and stepped aside for Jacie.

Sophie started to walk forward only to have Bailey move back in place. Right smack dab in the middle of the doorway.

"Explain to me why you're here," Bailey said with a smile so cold, Sophie felt a shiver.

"I was personally invited by Dorie. You know Dorie, Blake's mom? She insisted I come, since, and I quote, *I'm part of the family*," Sophie said, her cheeks starting to turn red in anger.

Bailey glared down at her and moved aside without saying another word. Bailey might have Blake, but she sure didn't have Jack or Dorie yet. They were still Sophie's.

She caught up with Jacie in the living room, and before she could say anything, Jacie blurted out, "She is one scary chick. Sorry I couldn't do more back there. She was determined to make her point."

Sophie found an empty chair and plopped down. "Yeah, well I made my point too."

"Sophie!"

Sophie turned to see Jack and Dorie bearing down on her in unison. She jumped up to hug them both.

"You look so gorgeous, Sophie. I love your hair. Come in the kitchen and help me," Dorie said, pulling her past Bailey.

"Sister Donovan, is there anything I can help you with?" Bailey called out sweetly.

Dorie barely turned her head and said, "Why, Bailey, you're a guest. Just have a seat and relax. Sophie is the only one who knows how to do the punch just right. Old family secret."

Sophie smiled as Dorie deftly put Bailey in her place. Dorie had cemented what Sophie had just thrown at her. Bailey was a guest, but Sophie was part of the family. But she was still sane enough to realize that without Blake, Sophie's place was anywhere but here. And Bailey might have a hard road ahead with Blake's mom and dad, but she had Blake. End of story.

"Sophie dear, will you grab the ginger ale out of the fridge and get the white grape juice out of the freezer? I really am behind," Dorie said.

Sophie smiled and started making the punch, feeling as if she were right at home. She'd spent so many nights here with Dorie, she'd lost count. Dorie had spent the last two years teaching her how to cook all of Blake's favorite meals. She would miss Dorie so much. She suddenly felt a tear course down her cheek and tried to wipe it away.

"Oh, honey," Dorie said, not missing anything, and ran to put her arms around Sophie.

"Dorie, I think I'm going to miss you the most," Sophie said through her tears.

"You won't be missing anybody if I have anything to do about it. Blake's being a little twit, but once he realizes what's what, you'll be right back where you should be. With me!" she said with a warm smile.

Sophie sniffed and pulled away, to see Blake standing across the room, looking at her. She turned quickly and went back to making the punch. He couldn't have heard anything. But he would have had to have been blind to have missed the love between his mother and his ex-girlfriend.

The next hour went by quickly as she forgot about Jacie's plan and concentrated on helping Dorie get all the food out. She did notice Blake staring at her every now and then, but she turned away and busied herself with another chore.

Jacie came up to her toward the end and took her by the hand.

"Listen, we gotta go now, because I have to be back at my house in half an hour. Lance is coming by to hang out. So get ready for your big good-bye scene. You've been playing it perfectly so far. If you can carry this off, you will be the queen of revenge."

Sophie grinned and slipped off Dorie's apron. She followed Jacie into the living room and saw Blake immediately. With Bailey glued to his side.

"Uh, Mayday. Bailey alert. Get rid of her, or I'm not getting near him," Sophie said quietly.

Jacie sighed but walked right up to Bailey and took her by the arm, saying something about helping Dorie out with the rolls. Bailey almost ran to the kitchen. Sophie took a deep breath and walked up to Blake.

"Hi, Blake," she said, staring up into his bright blue eyes.

"Hi, Sophie. Thanks for helping Mom out so much today. I know she appreciates it," he said

Sophie shrugged and smiled. "I would do anything for your mom, Blake. She's the best. Well, I've got to be going. So, anyway, welcome home," she said in as friendly a manner as she could manage.

Blake smiled down at her and shocked her when he said, "What about a hug for old time's sake?"

Sophie smiled back and leaned forward, putting her arms around his neck and holding him tight for a few seconds. A few warm, lovely seconds. *Mmm. Heaven.*

Sophie heard Jacie clearing her throat loudly and let go. She was surprised when Blake didn't get the hint and let go too. She backed up, and he was forced to let his arms fall to his side.

"You still wear the same perfume," Blake said quietly, just for her to hear.

"Yeah, it's the one you gave me for Valentine's Day," she said and then turned to leave.

"Hey, Sophie, maybe I'll call you tonight," Blake called out.

Sophie stopped in her tracks and traded a shocked look with Jacie. She turned slowly to face Blake and stared at him.

"Blake, I don't think that's a very good idea. I was under the impression that you're engaged," she said, noticing that everyone in the room looked toward the door in case Bailey came back. She noticed Blake did too before answering.

"Well, it's complicated. I've been talking to my mom and dad a lot since yesterday, and maybe Bailey and I are moving too fast. I'm just really confused right now. I could use a good friend," he said with an imploring look in his eyes.

Sophie closed her eyes and looked away to break his spell. She was spared from having to answer by the reappearance of Bailey in the doorway. Bailey took one look at her and glared. Sophie knew when to retreat. She turned and walked as quickly out of the house as she could without saying another word to Blake.

chapter 5

"Sooo?" Sophie said as soon as they got in the car.

Jacie grinned and pulled out into the street before answering. "Well, Bailey's going to BYU now, and she's majoring in early childhood education. *Of course.* That's so she can teach school and support Blake after they get married. Now, they met, as you know, while Blake was on his mission. She was a sister missionary in the same district. She went home six months after Blake arrived, and they've been writing ever since."

"Oh," Sophie said in a small voice and looked out the window. Jacie frowned and looked over at her friend but went on anyway.

"So from what Bailey says, they started out as friends but things just got serious through their letter writing. He just barely asked her to marry him a few months ago. Although why a guy would propose through the mail is beyond me. *Loser.* But she thought it was great. She's planning on a fall wedding. Right here in Alpine too. Her family isn't LDS, and they live in California. They've pretty much disowned her since she joined the Church four years ago. She works part time on campus to help pay her bills. So she's pretty much doing it all on her own. I hate to say it Sophie, but if it weren't for her stealing Blake, I might actually like her. And from what I can tell, she really is in love with him. Sorry."

Sophie winced and looked down at her lap. "Good old Dorie and Jack. They must have put a lot of pressure on him last night. I kind of feel bad for Bailey now. Nobody likes a flake for a fiancée. If I ever fall in love again, it's going to be with a man who's so in love with me, he doesn't even look at other girls. Or write them. What a mess," she said sadly.

Jacie looked over at her curiously and pulled into Sophie's driveway.

"You're not backing out of the perfect revenge by Jacie, are you? You going soft?" she asked.

Sophie pushed her hair out of her eyes and looked at her friend.

"I don't know. Blake wasted two years of my life. I kind of feel like he deserves to pay for that. But does Bailey deserve it? I honestly don't think he ever told her about me."

Jacie winced. "Well, actually, she did know about you. But Blake always told her that you were like his best friend. He told her there was nothing romantic about your relationship."

Sophie took a deep breath and got out of the car but leaned her head down before shutting the door. "Yep, the revenge is still on. I'll call you later, okay?" she said and watched as Jacie drove away.

Sophie opened the door to her house and practically ran for her bedroom. She just needed a little rest, a little quiet, a little time to get used to the events of the last two days. And especially to get over the fact that Jacie's plan was working with alarming precision. Blake wanted to call her tonight? The thought should have sent bright beams of sunshine through her heart, but for some reason it didn't. And that was possibly what was bothering her the most.

"Don't even think about it," Candy called out from the kitchen.

Sophie sighed but veered back toward the kitchen and her mom's open arms. She sat on her mom's lap, just like she did when she was little. She towered over her mom now, and she looked like Buddy sitting on his elf dad's lap in the movie *Elf*, but that was where she needed to be. She laid her head on her mom's shoulder and felt the comforting back rub almost immediately.

"Honey, I hate to tell you this, but you're expected at the relatives' house in half an hour."

Sophie slowly raised her head and looked her mother in the eyes, hoping this was her idea of a joke. No deal. Her mother never joked about the relatives. Who could?

"Please don't make me go, Mom. I'm almost twenty-one years old. I can make up my mind where I go and who I see. I keep telling you I've disowned those people. Why does no one listen to me?" she whined and stood up, heading for the fridge for something wet without five gallons of sugar in it. *Aaahh. Fresca.*

"You're absolutely right, Sophie. It's up to you what you do, but just know that if you don't show up, then your grandmother will be calling, and then your aunt will be calling, and then who knows what. They might actually show up here."

Sophie snorted and grabbed a straw out of the pantry.

"Oh, then you'd think my dear old dad would be concerned? Not hardly. He only has me show up at these events to say hi as briefly as possible, and then everyone thinks he's a loving devoted father and not some scumbag who left his family and became the biggest loser in Alpine."

Candy didn't say anything but just looked at Sophie with her eyebrows raised. Sophie sighed in exasperation. "Mom, why did you stay? Why in the world didn't you take me and hightale it back to Richfield? We could have lived near Grandma and Grandpa and Uncle Danny and Aunt Janie and all of my cousins. Now those are relatives. People who care about you and are nice to you. What do I have here? This is not right," she said sadly.

Candy closed her eyes, almost as if she were in pain, and shook her head slightly.

"Sweetie, it wasn't an easy decision. Don't you think I wanted to run back to Mom and Dad and my brother and all my friends? You don't know how many times I thought about doing just that. But I couldn't. It wasn't to torture you or to ruin your life. It was because they'd gotten rid of me so easily. I didn't want them getting rid of you. I couldn't let them get away with forgetting about this amazing, beautiful person we'd created together. Every time you go to these horrible family get-togethers, it gives your father a chance to look at you and see his daughter. I will never let him forget you. Never."

Sophie stared at her mom and knew how close she was to tears. She walked over and kissed the top of her mom's head and leaned down to hug her.

"Okay, I can understand that. But today of all days. I'm exhausted. I'm beat and worst of all, I'm dumped. I can barely face them on a good day. And today is not good."

Candy patted her daughter's hand and smiled sympathetically. "I know exactly how you feel, but I know if you don't face them, it only gets worse. But it's up to you. You're right—you're too old for me to tell you what to do. So what are you going to do?" she asked with a smile.

Sophie pushed herself away from the table and headed toward her room.

"I'm going, of course, but the mood I'm in, there's no telling what will happen. If Julie even looks at me the wrong way, I'm bound to say something rude. Like, whoever is doing your hair is an idiot and blind in one eye."

Candy laughed and watched Sophie get ready and leave ten minutes later, her heart breaking a little for her daughter. She sighed and started doing the dishes. Everyone had to deal with heartache. And at least all the relatives would get it out in the open. They were merciless. Sophie would either come home beaten, or determined to show them. And if she knew her daughter, beaten was something Sophie would never be.

chapter 6

"Well, you poor little thing," Aunt Lexie said in a voice meant to carry to every corner of the mini-mansion. She heard a soft snort of laughter and winced.

Sophie smiled and tried to ignore her, but Aunt Lexie was impossible to ignore. Heaven knew Sophie tried.

"When Bonnie called and told me everything, well, I was just shocked. I mean, the way you chased that poor boy, we all thought he was a goner for sure," she said, flipping her perfectly cut black bob to the side.

Sophie had to admit the classic bob was the perfect choice for her aunt. It showed off her anorexic cheek bones to perfection. No one would ever know her aunt was pushing forty-five. She didn't look a day over fifty.

"Hmm," Sophie said and looked around for reinforcements, anyone to save her from this verbal flogging. Great, no one. Her grandmother was over in the corner, praising Julie, her father's wife, on her gorgeous garden. *As if she'd done any of the work.* The army of landscapers employed by her dad kept Julie's arms and face pale and perfect.

There were her cousins. Oh *please*, not them. Two of them. And not a heart between them. It had been their job from a very early age to remind her of how poor she was, of how tacky she was, of how unworthy of her last name she was. And the one they liked the best, how much Grandma liked them more than her. Oh, the memories.

Possibly her father? No, he hadn't looked her straight in the eye since she was ten years old. He'd had joint custody of her but had never once taken her for the weekend or out to lunch. He didn't even show up at her high school graduation. He counted these monthly get-togethers as their special time together. Yep, it was very unlikely he would come to her defense at a time like this. Or ever.

And that left her half-brother and half-sister, ages seven and four, Carter and Callie. Out of all the relatives there, she liked them the best. Too bad they cared more for Dora the Explorer and Yugioh than for her.

Okay, so she was on her own. She could either go on the attack or go hide in the corner like she'd done for the past ten years. *What to do, what to do?*

Sophie smiled brightly and said, "Mind your own business, Lexie."

Lexie's stiff face looked surprised for a second but then relaxed into its favorite superior expression. "I guess it still hurts a lot. You should ask your mom for pointers, you know. Getting dumped is something you two have in common. It must be genetic or something."

Sophie's eyebrows went up a fraction but not really in surprise. Lexie was a cruel, mean snake.

"Ah, Lexie, my dear sweet aunt. How like you to know exactly what to say," Sophie said and then placed her glass of water down on the nearest wooden table. No coaster. She hoped Julie's pain at the ugly water spots wouldn't last too long.

"You know, you're acting a little different tonight. You usually hide in the corner, like some pathetic little ghost, but you're actually breathing tonight. You should have gotten dumped a long time ago. It's done wonders for your personality."

Sophie rolled her eyes and picked up her car keys.

"You mean, now that I'm too tired and bored to behave like a polite human being, you see the family resemblance. Sad, Lexie. Really sad."

Lexie actually laughed. "Now there you've gone and done it. I might actually like you now."

Sophie ignored that and walked to the front door. She waved a half-hearted good-bye to everyone and glided toward freedom. She'd given the relatives fifteen minutes, and that was all they were getting today.

"Sophie! You can't go yet. I wanted you to meet my nephew. He's here trying to get our upstairs air conditioner to work. He mentioned he might have met you once before. Just wait a second and I'll go grab him," Julie said and ran out of the room.

Sophie paused with her hand on the doorknob and sighed. She turned to face the crowd of relatives, who were now all looking at her, and pasted on a fake cheerful smile—the one she used for relatives and gynecological exams. Lexie grinned wickedly at her and toasted her silently. Her cousins each studied her with a smirk, and her father and grandmother turned around to find something to do besides look at her. She felt like a monkey at the zoo. Pretty soon they were going to start throwing peanuts at her. She looked down at her bright lime green Fossil watch and waited. In one minute she was gone. Nephew or not. What was she going to say to this guy anyway? *Hey, nice to meet you. Now get out of my way before I suffocate on all of the carbon monoxide my relatives are blowing my way.*

She glanced up and watched with interest as Julie pulled a tall, muscular man into the room. He had dark brown wavy hair and a gorgeous smile. His face was all interesting planes and angles. And his eyes were a dark, warm brown. He walked right up to her with a wide, friendly smile.

"Hi, Sophie. Julie was telling me about you the other day, and I think we've met before," he said, reaching out his hand to shake hers.

She would have remembered this man for sure. Who could forget a face like that?

"Well, why don't you remind me? What's your name?" she asked, shaking his hand, liking the way his hand felt all warm and strong and big.

"Sam Kellen. I think we met about a year ago at a singles dance. The New Year's Eve one," he said.

Sophie frowned. She remembered the dance now. Jacie had dragged her to it, even though she had wanted to stay home and think of Blake and plan the next fifty years of her life, starting with all their children's names. Pretty much what she did every Saturday night. *Pathetic.* And she still didn't remember this guy. How could she have been so caught up in waiting for Blake that she hadn't even noticed this guy? Her stupidity was simply stunning sometimes. Well, moreso lately.

"Um, yeah, you do look familiar now," she said, lying through her teeth. "So how have you been doing?" she asked, noticing that all the relatives were still staring at them. She glared at them over his shoulder. They were obviously listening to every single word. *Rude.* She saw her cousins, Farrah and Daphne, move even closer. Obviously they wanted their introduction too.

"Hey, I'm still working on the AC. Why don't you come outside and talk to me for a minute while I finish up?"

Sophie blinked in surprise. "Why not?" she followed him out the front door and around to the side of the house, where not one, not two, but three AC units were. Mini-mansions took their cooling seriously.

"So," she said as he knelt down and started pulling things apart.

He glanced up at her and grinned. "Hey, I'll take my payment out in a free haircut."

Sophie laughed. "What? Am I missing something here?"

Sam shook his head and grabbed a tool off the grass.

"Julie told me how all your relatives go after you like starving dogs when you come around. I thought I'd rescue you. And no, you're not losing your mind. We've never met."

Sophie grinned and sat down by his side.

"Well, Sam. Thanks, but if you hadn't noticed, I was almost out the door. I didn't need too much rescuing."

"That's not what I hear. Maybe they'll leave you alone about this ex-boyfriend stuff. I'll mention on my way out how beautiful and wonderful you are. That'll stick it to them."

Sophie looked at Sam bent over and busy and frowned. Julie had told him all this stuff? *Julie?* The woman she had tried so hard to hate for the last ten years?

"Wait a second. I'm a little confused. Julie told you all this stuff about me and the relatives? Why?"

Sam didn't look up but kept working. "You know Julie. She's a softy. She has a thing for puppies, children, and lost causes. I'm not sure which one you are, though."

Sophie snorted and leaned back on her elbows. "I'm not sure myself, to be honest, but I'm pretty sure I'm not a puppy. So this is weird, though. I've never met you and you're Julie's nephew?" she asked, looking out at the beautiful view her father and stepmother had of the Alpine valley.

"Well, our family moved to Utah from California about five years ago, but I was on my mission at the time, and then I was at college where I got my degree in construction management. Here's my business card," he said, handing her one out of his jeans pocket.

Kellen Construction. He had his own construction business? *Wow.*

"That's really awesome, Sam. Good for you," she said and handed it back.

He waved her hand away. "Keep it. If you ever know anyone who needs a house built or an add-on, or anything like that, keep me in mind," he said, going back to work.

Sophie shrugged and slipped it in her skirt pocket.

"Well, listen, it was really nice to meet you and all. Thanks for coming to my rescue. You *and* Julie, I guess. Anyway, thanks," she said and got up. She turned to walk away and tripped over his toolbox and did a perfect belly flop onto the grass.

"Holy cow!" Sam yelped and ran to her side. "Man, you went flying!"

Sophie winced and fought down the bright red blush that she could feel spreading all over her face. She was a redhead, after all, and curse the genes all you want, but you just couldn't hide your emotions. Your skin always screamed it to the world. Sam reached down and pulled her up. She winced and limped as far away from the blasted toolbox as she could get.

"Are you all right?" Sam asked, looking at her worriedly.

She looked up at him and paused when he smiled down at her. He wasn't laughing, just kind of smiling.

"Of course. No one's been able to keep Sophie Reid down yet. Although they keep trying," she said darkly, as she realized a group of relatives were staring down at them through the bay window in the dining room. Right above them. Sam turned to see what she was looking at and frowned, realizing that quite a few were laughing out loud.

He took her by the hand and walked her to the street and her car.

"Look, just ignore them. No one gets to pick their relatives, right?"

Sophie pushed her curls out of her face and tried to smile. She just wanted to get out of there. She was about to die from humiliation, and having an attractive man as a witness would only be more embarrassing. It was a vicious cycle.

"Yeah right. Well, looks like I'm out of here. Good luck with your ACs and everything. And tell Julie . . . tell her thanks for me," she said finally.

Sam reached over, pulled a leaf out of her hair, and smiled down at her.

"Are they still looking?" he asked suddenly.

Sophie looked around his very large, broad shoulders and noticed that her cousins and aunt Lexie were standing in the living room now, looking curiously out at them.

"Of course they are. Maybe I should go into a seizure now. They would get a big kick out of that," she said, turning to open her faded red Jeep door.

"Well, we could give them something else to look at. Why don't I give you a kiss good-bye? They sure wouldn't be laughing then, would they?" he asked, completely serious.

Sophie turned around, her mouth hanging open in shock. *What?* She hadn't kissed anyone in two years, and even then nothing but little innocent pecks. Blake had wanted to be as pure as possible before his mission, and kissing was too dangerous, he'd told her over and over. As far as she knew, she kissed like a seventh grader. With braces. And now this man, this complete stranger, was offering to kiss her in front of a window full of vipers—*oops*—relatives.

"Sounds good to me," she said and stepped toward him.

He took her by the shoulders and leaned down. Way down. Wow was he tall! He tilted his head, giving her plenty of time to back out if she wanted to. He slowly dipped his head and kissed her smoothly on the lips. It wasn't a passionate kiss. It was sweet. Very soft and very sweet. He slowly lifted his head, his eyes twinkling down at her.

"That'll get 'em," he said kindly and stood up.

Sophie stared up at him and smiled back. "That was really nice," she said honestly and then blushed again.

Sam laughed and smoothed the hair out of her eyes.

"Any time you need me to keep the wolves at bay, you have my number," he said and turned and walked away.

Huh? Oh! The business card. She slowly got in the Jeep, grinning her head off and drove home. Now, where in the world could she find some wolves?

chapter 7

"You what?!" Jacie screamed in her ear as Sophie drove home. Sophie spent the next ten minutes giggling into the phone, going over every wonderful, exhilarating, embarrassing, exciting moment. She had just kissed for the first time in two years. *Yes!*

When she got home, she went over every detail again with her mom, who looked stunned.

"Julie was nice to you?" she kept saying over and over.

Sophie frowned at her mom and went to the freezer to pull out some ice cream.

"Yeah. I guess so. What do you think?" she asked, scooping out some for both of them. She never ate at the relatives' house if she could help it. Sometimes poison was hard to prove as the cause of death. She watched CSI; she knew.

"Well, I just think that's so interesting. And here, we've kind of had this certain impression of her all this time. Was she being real, or do you think she had some weird ulterior motive?" Candy asked, digging into the Breyer's peach ice cream.

Sophie took a bite and thought about it. Good question.

"Well, I don't know if you're going to believe me—I can hardly believe it myself—but I'm kind of thinking she was being real. And the way Sam talked about her having a tender heart, I'm thinking there might be another side to her. You know, one side, the heartless home wrecker; the other side, kind and normal. Is that possible?" Sophie asked.

Candy sighed and took another bite before answering.

"Well, I haven't hated her for years now, so it might be nice to believe that she's a good person," Candy said truthfully.

Sophie shook her head. "But wouldn't that be weird if Sam ever asks me out; he's her nephew. And he likes her. That could be really weird. But just think of it. Me dating again! That kind of sounds fun. And kissing. Oh, Mom. You've got to try that again. It is so amazing. I felt like asking Sam to kiss me again. But he walked away, darn it."

Candy laughed and pushed her bowl away.

"You know, you might be right. Heck, I'm only forty. Maybe you and I should both start hitting the singles wards. Could you see me dating again?" she asked with a laugh.

Sophie stared at her mom. She was beautiful. Medium height, thin athletic build, and exceptional hair if she did say so. Sophie was the one who added the bangs and the light golden highlights around her mom's face. And her face was so sweet and kind. Who wouldn't love to go out with her mom?

"The question is, why haven't you been dating?" she asked quietly.

Candy frowned and traced a circle on the table with her finger.

"Well, you know how you felt when you came home from the airport, all sad, and depressed and feeling unattractive and what's wrong with me? Well, I felt like that, times a hundred, and to be honest, I'm just now getting over it. The divorce kind of knocked me for a loop. But you know, I think I'm ready. I want to try again. Pretty soon, you'll be gone with your own family and I'll be all by myself. I don't want to be all by myself. I really don't," she said, looking up to catch her daughter's eyes.

Sophie got up from the table and hugged her mom. "Mom, you are right. Let's do it. Let's start dating like crazy. We'll do it together."

Candy laughed and got up to put the bowls in the sink. "Like always."

The phone ringing caught them both off guard. They looked at each other before Candy answered.

"Hello?"

"Hi, Sister Reid, is Sophie there? This is Blake. I really need to talk to her."

Candy looked at Sophie, who was motioning with her hands that no way was she talking to Blake.

"Um, well, Blake. I don't think Sophie can come to the phone right now. She's kind of busy. Can I take a message?" Candy asked politely.

"Just tell her, that . . . just tell her that maybe I was wrong. Maybe I was wrong about a lot of things. I just need to talk to her. Face to face. Tell her that I want to see her tomorrow and that not to worry because Bailey has school tomorrow. Okay?"

Candy sighed and then agreed before hanging up.

"He wants to talk to you in person and not to worry, Bailey has school tomorrow."

Sophie sniffed and crossed her arms over her chest.

"Not in this lifetime. Dump me once, I'm a fool. Dump me again, hah! Like I would ever let that happen again. Nope, Mom. I loved him. I *loved* him. But now I just don't. Sorry, he's on his own," she said

Candy laughed. "Well, how are you going to get your revenge if you take off into the sunset of glorious dating and kissing?"

"Well, I can't remember some of the steps to totally awesome revenge, but I do know that one of them is living well. Being happy without him is the best revenge a woman can have," she said, nodding her head emphatically.

Candy looked taken aback and sat down again.

"I think maybe I need to call Jacie. Maybe I need the five-step program too."

Sophie laughed. "We'll do it together."

chapter 8

Sophie woke up Monday morning not depressed, not happy, but somewhere in the middle. And that was so much better than waking up devastated like yesterday morning. She hurried and took a shower and grabbed a bowl of cereal before heading out the door. She had an appointment at nine with a new client, and she liked to make a good first impression.

She breezed into the salon and waved at her mom, who was already curling Sister Hansen's hair, and Cathy, who was hard at work on Sister Donaldson's nails.

"Is my appointment here? I had to stop and get some gas," she said as she set her purse down at her station and glanced around. Her mom had a strange, strained look on her face.

"What?" Sophie said, frowning.

Candy pointed toward the sitting room, where there were chairs and piles of magazines everywhere. Sophie walked toward the front, in case someone was sitting in the corner. She poked her head around the half wall and saw a petite blonde sitting with her head down and her hands clenched. *Ah, a nervous one.* Sophie smiled and walked over.

"I promise we won't hurt you . . ." she said and then reared back as Julie lifted her head and looked her in the eyes. Sophie felt as if the air had been knocked out of her. *Her father's wife? Here?*

"Julie?" Sophie said but was interrupted immediately.

"I know. I should have warned you, but I didn't think you'd take me if you knew who I was. I didn't exactly lie when I called in last week. I just gave them my full name, Julianne."

Sophie blinked, still in shock. "Okaaay. But why? I mean, do you really want me to do your hair? Seriously?" she asked.

Julie smiled nervously and ran her hands through her perfectly highlighted hair.

"Well, yes. Everyone needs a change now and then. You always look so beautiful, I thought you could help me decide what to do with myself."

Sophie sighed and walked over to look more closely at Julie's hair.

"Well, it looks just about perfect right now. Why don't you come back and have a seat and we'll figure out what you want. Okay?" Sophie said, gesturing toward her station.

Julie smiled and got up, walking quickly toward the chair before Sophie could change her mind.

Sophie exchanged raised eyebrows with her mother and then focused on her new client. She sat Julie down and then ran her hands through Julie's hair. Fine, thick healthy hair. Highlighted to a perfect ash blonde. Simple shoulder length. Why in the world would she want to change?

"So give me a little hint, Julie. What were you thinking of? Maybe some downlights? Maybe some layers and a new style? What do you think?" she asked.

Julie straightened her shoulders and tilted her chin as she stared back at the mirror.

"I don't know, Sophie. I just know when I look in the mirror, I don't like what I see. Help me see something I like," she said quietly.

Sophie paused and stared at Julie. Julie was talking about more than hair here. But why? And why tell her? Sophie shrugged and put a drape around her stepmother's thin shoulders.

"Well, let's start with a few downlights and some layers. We'll go from there, okay?"

Julie nodded her head. "Okay. I trust you, Sophie. Everyone who has you do their hair just raves about how you know exactly what to do for them. Janielle told me the other day, she came to you and said, 'Surprise me,' and you did, and she's never looked better."

Sophie grinned at the memory. She loved it when people trusted her. But her stepmother? She wasn't sure Julie *should* trust her so much.

"Well, it's true," Sophie said. "I can't help looking at people and automatically thinking about how I'd change their hair to make it more flattering for their face and their personality."

Julie smiled shyly. "Go for it."

Sophie smiled back. "Okay, but just remember, you asked for it," she said with an almost evil laugh, causing Julie's face to turn pale.

She walked to the back and mixed her colors and was immediately joined by her mother.

"She wants you to do her hair?" Candy asked in shock.

Sophie glanced at her mother briefly and went back to mixing.

"I know, strange. I think something else is going on, like she wants to talk to me or something, and this was the only way she could figure out to do it. I don't know."

Candy grimaced and reached for a bottle of bright red.

"Slip some of this in there for old times' sake," Candy whispered.

Sophie looked up in surprise and then smiled when she realized her mom was joking. Messing up a client's hair was hitting way below the belt.

"Mom, your appointment's done. Why don't you run over to Kohlers and grab some drinks for the fridge and some snacks and stuff. You don't need to be here. It's too weird," she said.

Candy frowned and straightened the supplies. "Maybe you're right. I feel all jumpy. I can't relax with her here. My next appointment's not until eleven. I'll see you then."

Sophie watched as her mom grabbed her purse and went out the back exit. Wives and ex-wives were never a good combination.

Sophie walked back in to join Julie and immediately got to work with the foil, comb, and color.

"Sophie?" Julie said nervously.

Sophie paused and looked at her in the mirror. "Yeah?"

"I didn't want you to find out from anyone else but me. That's why I'm here today. I'm leaving your father," Julie said sadly.

Sophie paused, her mouth hanging wide open. "Oh my word. I wasn't expecting to hear that. Are you serious?" she asked and went back to Julie's hair.

"Yes, I'm very serious. I've been wanting to leave for the last eight years, to be honest. I think marrying your father was the biggest mistake of my life," she said, tears dripping down her cheek.

Sophie paused and slipped off her gloves. She walked back to the lounge and got a soft drink and some tissues and walked quickly back to Julie, handing both to her.

"Here. Drink something; you look parched."

Julie smiled gratefully and blew her nose before popping the top on the can.

"Thanks, Sophie."

"So, why?" Sophie asked, after putting her gloves back on.

Julie sighed and took another sip before answering. "Well, I'd need to start at the beginning for you to really understand, I guess. When I moved here from California, I had just been crushed by the man of my dreams. I was so in love with him that I couldn't even see straight. It was my birthday, and I thought he was going to give me an engagement ring, but instead he told me he was going to ask one of my good friends to marry him. The whole time he thought we were just being good friends. So I came out here to get away from all the memories and to get over him. I just couldn't be there anymore. When I moved here, your father was assigned to be my home teacher. He was so nice and so charming and always so helpful. After he divorced your mother, he started coming over more often, by himself. He just made life easy for me, you know? So when he asked me to marry him, I said yes. I think at the time I was still an emotional wreck, and just having someone be kind to me, and gentle to me, was like a balm to my spirit. So like an idiot, I said yes. And we got married. I thought after marrying your father, everything would be perfect, but it wasn't. I saw how he treated you, and worse, how he let his family treat you, and it just made me feel cold inside. How could a man treat his own daughter that way? So I decided to leave him after getting my courage up. But then I got pregnant, and I decided to wait and see. Maybe he would change. But he didn't. He never did. I found out two years ago, from an overheard conversation, that he married me for my money. And that's the only reason he did. It wasn't because he loved me. It wasn't because of anything to do with *me*. He just wanted to impress his mother with his bank account."

Sophie tilted her head back and stared at the ceiling, trying to take it all in. Julie was innocent? Julie had been taken in by her father? Sophie's whole world turned on its axis and stumbled to a halt.

"Holy crap," Sophie muttered and grabbed another piece of foil.

"Yeah, that's what I think too. So I started to do a little investigating, and it looks like your dad has been taking money from my accounts and putting it into his personal account that he had set up two years ago and which he never bothered to tell me about. Tanner doesn't know I'm leaving him yet. I've been in touch with my divorce attorney for over a year now. Your dad has really taken a chunk out of my inheritance. I don't know how much I'll come away with. It's going to be messy, I think. But whatever happens, I want you to know that you will always be Carter and Callie's older sister. I'm just sorry that you and I . . . well, that you and I hadn't been closer. It would have been nice to have had someone to talk to."

Sophie frowned and used her comb to part Julie's hair.

"Julie, this is just so weird. Everything I've ever thought about you, well, it just doesn't fit anymore. My mom and I were under the impression that you broke up their marriage. I guess that's why I could never be myself around you," Sophie said, shaking her head.

Julie closed her eyes and rubbed her hands together nervously.

"I think that's the impression Tanner wanted you to have. I had no idea he was romantically interested in me until he asked me to marry him, and that was three months after his divorce," she said.

Sophie sighed, feeling a headache begin to brew behind her eyes. "He came home one night and told my mom that he had fallen out of love with her and that he couldn't live a lie any longer. And then he divorced my mom, and that was the last time I saw my dad. Well, you know what I mean. He kind of turned into a stranger overnight. And we blamed you. For ten years, we've blamed it all on you," she said honestly.

Julie looked up and met Sophie's eyes through the mirror and smiled kindly. "I know."

Sophie finished applying the color to Julie's hair and led her to the dryer. Instead of walking away, she grabbed a stool and sat down at Julie's feet and really looked at her. Maybe Sam had been right about Julie. Maybe she was a softie. So soft that her father had eagerly taken advantage of her while she was still vulnerable from a broken heart.

"So where do we go from here?" Sophie asked, wishing now that she had spent the last ten years getting to know Julie.

Julie frowned, and Sophie noticed new tears falling down her cheeks. She handed Julie two more tissues and got up to get some more.

"I don't know, Sophie," Julie said at last. "That part I don't know. I do know that the kids and I will be moving out of the house and into one closer to the school. I don't want the kids to leave their friends. That's too stressful. So I'll still be around. I just won't be with Tanner anymore. It's time I grew up. I need to be strong now, for my kids and for myself. I know it's the right thing to do. It's just going to be so hard. Tanner and your grandmother can be very domineering."

Sophie snorted and nodded her head. "Do you know what she said to my mom the first time she met her? She took one look at my mom, and she said to my dad, 'It's just as easy to fall in love with a rich girl as it is a poor girl.' My mom just about died," Sophie said with anger in her voice.

Julie laughed a little and shook her head. "I think she was wrong, though. I don't think Tanner can love anyone. He loves money too much. And he certainly never loved me."

Sophie sagged and looked down at her feet. She'd always wondered why her father never loved her. Maybe, just maybe, it wasn't her fault. Maybe he was incapable of loving another person.

"Well, I'm glad you came in and told me, Julie. I really appreciate it. I wish you had talked to me honestly about everything before. We could have been friends or something," Sophie said.

Julie smiled and looked up.

"That's what cowards do. They always wait until the next time, and then the next time comes, and they decide to wait until the next time again. You always looked so mad at me all the time. I'd just shrivel up and walk out of the room. I think it was guilt, though. I felt so bad. After I found out from your mom's friends about how wonderful you and your mom are, I realized that the both of you blamed me for the divorce. Tanner had always told me that your mom was the one who had asked for the divorce because she had cheated on him. Her friends laughed their heads off at that one. I was a real idiot. I believed everything he told me."

Sophie reached over and held Julie's hand for the first time in her life.

"No, Julie, the real idiot is the man who had two beautiful, wonderful women in his life and lost them both," she said honestly.

Julie burst out into fresh tears at that. "Make that three beautiful, wonderful women," she said through her sobs.

Sophie was surprised when she felt her own eyes tear up. Candy picked that minute to walk in and stopped in shock.

"Sophie! What did you say to her? Oh, honey, just ignore Sophie; she's just headstrong. I'm sure she didn't mean it, whatever it was," Candy said, rushing over to Julie's side, glaring at Sophie the entire time.

Sophie laughed, and laughed harder when Julie started laughing. Candy stood there with her hand on her hips, glaring at both of them.

"Was something I said really that funny?" she demanded.

Sophie snorted and leaned over to turn the hair dryer off.

"Mom, you are something else."

"Candice, please don't get mad at Sophie on my account," Julie said. "I'm just an emotional wreck right now. I've been telling Sophie why I'm leaving Tanner," she said with a determined smile on her face.

Candy's mouth dropped open in shock. Sophie grinned and pulled Julie to her feet and over to the sink to rinse her hair. By the time she got Julie back to her station, Candy's mouth had barely closed. Candy then demanded to hear every last detail, and by the end of the hour, Candy, Sophie, and Julie were, strangely enough, friends.

Julie stood up and looked in the mirror one more time. Her hair didn't look so helmet-like now. It moved and looked fun and young. The downlights added dimension and softness and a definite glow to her cheeks.

"They were telling the truth, Sophie. You're a genius with hair. It's hair magic," Julie said with a happy laugh.

Sophie grinned back at her and walked her to the door.

"Listen, this one is on me, Julie. If you can't do your own stepmother's hair for free, then what's this world coming to?"

Julie burst into loud sobbing tears again, and Sophie had to escort her to her car and practically pour her into her seat.

"It's going to be okay, Julie. I promise. And if you ever need anything, please let me know. I could watch Carter and Callie for you sometime if you need me to."

"Thanks, Sophie. Thanks so much. I really needed this today, and you were the best," Sophie said through her tears.

Sophie waved her away and watched her drive down the street. What was the world coming to? she wondered and walked back into the salon to go over every detail with her mom again. When Jacie walked in at lunchtime, Sophie had to go through it for the second time. What had happened to her boring life, she wondered, as she watched Blake pull into the parking lot.

chapter 9

Sophie ran to the back of the salon and hid behind some boxes. No way was she going to talk to Blake right now. She had barely had a chance to digest Julie's divorce drama. Now she was supposed to hear how Blake's mom and dad really thought he should still be with her? No thanks. What girl could be in a relationship knowing it was all because of his parents? *Gag.*

Sophie jumped when Jacie found her three minutes later. "What are you doing?" Jacie asked.

Sophie frowned and held her finger up to her lips. "Not so loud. I don't want him to know I'm here," she whispered.

Jacie raised her eyebrows and leaned against the shelves.

"Uh, hate to break it to you, but he saw your Jeep in the parking lot. He knows you're here, and he also knows you're hiding back here. He sent me back here to tell you that he just wants to talk to you."

Sophie felt like throwing a temper tantrum. She could run out the back and take off before he would even know she was gone. But her keys were in her drawer in the other room. *Dang!* She was stuck.

"Fine!" Sophie snapped and stomped out of the room toward the front of the salon where Blake stood, smiling hopefully.

"There you are! Jacie said you'd only be a minute."

Sophie frowned at him and sat down in one of the chairs by the window.

"Blake, I don't mean to be rude, but what are you doing here? You publicly dump me at the airport, you shove your new fiancée down my throat and everyone else's, and now what? We're supposed to be friends? I don't feel like it. So just leave me alone, okay?" she said as brutally as she could.

Blake's face fell immediately, and he sat down next to her.

"Yesterday at my house you seemed happy to see me again. And when you hugged me, I sort of thought you still wanted to be with me. Mom told me how you were crying in the kitchen over me. I guess I read you wrong. I didn't realize how mad you are," he said, sounding small and confused.

Sophie rolled her eyes and crossed her arms over her chest.

"Well, you'd have to be a moron not to know then, okay? And I hugged you yesterday because you *asked me* for a hug. So what did you want to say to me? Huh? Because I have an appointment in fifteen minutes," she said stonily.

Blake gulped and looked out the window.

"Well, after talking to my mom and dad last night, I've decided to break off my engagement with Bailey. And I just thought you'd want to know," he said, looking at her with a hopeful smile.

Sophie frowned at him. "Okay, let's get a few things straight here, okay? I would never want a guy who didn't want me. You're only here because your mom and dad put you in time out. I'm not totally blaming you, but let's face it. I was the only girl you dated in high school, and you were the only guy I've ever dated. Maybe both of us need to see what else is out there. I do agree with your parents, though. Don't ask Bailey to marry you until you've at least been on a date with her. *Duh!* But, and I'm being completely honest here, I'm never going out with you ever again. I thought I was totally and completely in love with you. I wasted two years of my life waiting for you, only to have you come home and tell me I shouldn't have come to the airport. So honestly, it's been fun knowing you, but it's time to cut our losses. Agreed?"

Blake stared at her as if he were seeing her for the first time. He licked his lips and then looked down at his feet.

"Huh. Well, that's that then. I guess I really screwed up. No second chances with you, huh, Sophie?" he asked quietly.

Sophie looked up at the ceiling, refusing to let her heart thaw.

"Fraid not, Blake. For all it's worth, I do think you're a great guy. Seeing you again, it brings back all the reasons I fell for you in the first place. But you're going to have to be somebody else's great guy now.

Maybe Bailey's, maybe a complete stranger's. Just not mine," she said more kindly this time.

Blake nodded his head and stood up. Sophie sighed and stood up too, walking him to the door.

"Well, I guess this is bye then," he said, staring at her sadly.

Sophie smiled back, wanting their parting to be on friendly terms.

"Yeah, it is. Send me an announcement when you do get officially married. I would love to come to your reception," she said honestly.

Blake sighed and walked out of the building without replying.

Sophie watched him go and felt the presence of someone behind her.

"Man, Sophie, that was quick and harsh. What happened to the five steps of radical revenge? First step, make him regret dumping you; second step, make him suffer; third step, make him jealous; fourth step, make a fool out of him; and fifth step, live well without him," Jacie said, staring at Blake's car disappearing down the road.

Sophie shrugged. "I kind of jumped to the last one, where you just live happily ever after without the guy. I think that was the best step anyway. Yep, I'm ready for your next five-step program. What do ya got?" she said, turning around and trying to smile.

Jacie gave her a half-smile and put her arm around her shoulders as they walked toward the back of the salon.

"Well, I have the five-step program to getting the perfect husband. Or there's the five-step program to having a great social life. Which do you feel like?" she asked sticking a Fresca in Sophie's hand.

Sophie smiled and sat down in her chair, swiveling around to face her image in the mirror. She looked at herself and wondered what it was she was ready for now.

"How about the five-step program to having fun and being happy?" she asked taking a sip.

Jacie shook her head. "Sorry, those are the only two I have right now."

Sophie laughed and leaned her head back on her chair.

"Fine, give me the social life then. From what I can tell, husbands are no fun."

Jacie shrugged and took her cell phone out of her pocket and dialed a number.

"Social life it is . . . Hi, Paul? Hey, this is Jacie. Remember that friend of mine I was telling you about? Yeah, the one with the gorgeous red hair. Well, she's free now. How about a double date this weekend with your roommate? Yeah? Great. Call me tonight and we'll talk it over. Bye," she said and hung up.

Sophie laughed and took another sip. "Jacie, what would I do without you? You're the best friend anyone could ever, ever have."

Jacie grinned and sat down in the chair next to hers.

"Too true."

chapter 10

Sophie spent the next four days busy at the salon. Julie had given her so many referrals that she was working from seven in the morning to seven at night. She was definitely making good money, but she was starting to feel worn out. When Friday arrived, she was looking forward to getting off early and going on a real date.

Sophie finished the last touches of Brinley Smith's updo. Brinley was having her wedding photos taken that afternoon. Sophie grinned with pride as she sprayed the entire creation of whirls and curls with finishing spray.

"Brinley, my beauty queen, you are going to knock 'em dead," she said as the nervous girl smiled and giggled at her reflection.

"Holy cow, Sophie, this is amazing. It doesn't even look like me. I look so . . . so sophisticated and beautiful," she said in awe.

Sophie laughed and twirled her chair around, giving Brinley a hand up.

"Of course you do. You are beautiful," she insisted.

"Now, you promise you'll do my hair for the wedding? Being at the temple at seven in the morning was kind of a bad idea, but we're stuck now," she said imploringly.

Sophie winced at the reminder but nodded her head. "Yes, Brinley. I will be at your house at five sharp in one month. You just be there. No last-minute jitters from you. If I'm getting up that early, so are you."

"Well, well, well. And I didn't think you liked weddings," said a furious voice behind her.

Sophie whipped around and stared at Bailey, who was standing five feet away from her with her hands on her hips and murder in her eyes.

"Uh, Brinley, why don't we settle up later. I think I need to take care of this."

Brinley grabbed her purse and fled with a frown on her face.

"Bailey, what is this all about?" Sophie asked in a calm, neutral voice as she checked to see if Bailey was hiding a gun under her sweater.

"Yeah right. Like you don't know. I'd already bought my wedding dress, you jerk!" Bailey spat at her.

Sophie blinked in surprise and let out a big breath.

"Um, okay. And what does this have to do with me?" she asked, still using a calm, soothing voice. She looked back around her, but she was totally alone in the salon. She was supposed to be getting off at four to get ready for her date with Paul, so everyone else was taking their breaks.

"Knock it off, Sophie. The dumb blonde thing only works when you're a blonde. Now, I just want to know why. Why are you so determined to ruin my life?" Bailey demanded, stepping closer to Sophie.

Sophie bit back a squeak and moved back a step.

"All right. Why don't I get you a drink and we can sit down like two adults and discuss this. Okay?"

Bailey tapped her foot impatiently on the tile floor but nodded and followed Sophie to the back, where there was an old comfortable couch and a TV. Sophie motioned for Bailey to sit and sat down as far away from her as she could.

"Now, what is this all about? Why are you here?" she asked Bailey.

Bailey practically snarled at her.

"Blake called off my wedding because of you! What do you mean, what is this about? Are you dense?" she shouted.

Sophie held her hands up, as if she were blocking a blow.

"Whoa! Wait a second here. Let's get some facts straight. I never bought my wedding dress, but I believe you're the one who ruined my future wedding to Blake. And I have nothing to do with Blake breaking things off with you. If you want someone to blame, then talk to Dorie and Jack, not me. As of last Saturday afternoon, when Blake made it crystal clear that we were done, we were done," she said, backing up further on the couch.

Bailey stared at her, breathing hard and not blinking. Sophie fingered her cell phone in her jeans pocket, wondering if she could dial 9-1-1 if Bailey jumped her.

"Just be honest with me. Are you seeing Blake now? Are you back together?" Bailey asked in a low, pained voice.

Sophie shook her head immediately. "No, Bailey! No. Of course I'm not seeing him. Why would I want to? He chose you over me. Whether you want to believe it or not, I'm not dense. I catch on to things pretty quickly. You won. Hands down, you won. Take your prize and leave. The man kicked me in the teeth and then spoke the next day on Christlike behavior. No thank you," Sophie said, her voice only wavering slightly with fear.

Bailey frowned and studied her, trying to tell if she was lying.

"Well, all I know is that everything was perfect and now that Blake is home, things aren't perfect anymore," Bailey said. "Now he's telling me we need to see other people. Now he's telling me he's not sure if he's in love with me anymore," she said with a catch in her throat.

Sophie winced, hoping against hope, that she wouldn't have to give Bailey a hug.

"All right, buck up, chick. I've had enough tears this week to last me a year. Now if things aren't going smoothly between you and Blake, then frankly, that's between you and Blake. Well, and possibly Dorie and Jack. But honestly, I have nothing to do with any of this," Sophie said.

Bailey sighed and tiredly got up from the couch.

"You know, all I ever wanted was a nice husband, a comfortable home, and a couple kids, give or take. Why is that so impossible?" she asked, not really expecting an answer.

Sophie sighed and got up to follow Bailey toward the front of the salon.

"Bailey, you're talking like you're forty-five and you've never been on a date. Holy cow, you're at BYU, the marriage mart of the Mormons. Why don't you follow Blake's example and start dating? A lot. Have some fun. Don't be so serious. You're beautiful, smart, and . . . uh, well, I don't know you very well. But don't give up on the big dream yet. And next time, wait until the guy gets home from his mission before you buy your dress," Sophie said, trying to be encouraging.

Bailey glanced back at her and tried to smile.

"Thanks. And I'm sorry for coming down here and being so rude to you. I just thought for sure you were the reason Blake had changed his mind. I mean, the strongest force on earth is love. What can get in the way of love?"

Sophie gave in and patted her on the arm as she opened the door for her.

"You'd be surprised," she said and watched as Bailey walked dejectedly down the sidewalk.

Sophie walked back toward her chair and slumped down, shaking her head at the confrontation she'd just had with Bailey. Darn Blake and his pathetic social skills. If one more person walked in today and threw some weird revelation or accusation at her, then she was quitting and moving to St. George. That was it. She was done with Soap Opera Alpine.

The bell on the door jingled, signaling a walk-in. Sophie glanced at her watch. She didn't have an appointment for twenty more minutes. She stood up and walked around the corner to see Dorie Donovan staring at her with a very unhappy look on her face.

"What's gotten into you, Sophie Reid? I told you I was going to fix everything. And I did. And all you had to do was pick up where you and Blake left off. And now where's Blake? He's moving out to live in some run-down apartment by UVSC with some old mission companions. Do I have my son back? Not really. Do I have the girl I hand picked for my daughter-in-law back? No. Am I happy? Heck no," Dorie bit out furiously.

Ah! St. George, here I come. Sophie sat Dorie down and tried to explain to her how she couldn't want Blake anymore after realizing that he hadn't really wanted her.

"Dorie, you know I love you. You know I do. But we can't force this thing between me and Blake. I've spent this last week thinking over our relationship, and you know what? If I'm being completely honest with myself, Blake and I were really just good friends. We never even really kissed. Probably because on some level, we didn't feel comfortable with that aspect of our relationship. That's telling. Of course he fell for someone else. Why would he want to marry someone he loved like a sister? Honestly, Dorie, I truly appreciate everything you've done. I know why you did it. Heck, I dreamed of all the holidays we would spend together at your house, baking and laughing and talking. But those dreams were of you and me. Blake was always somewhere in the background, watching football. And this pains me to say it, but I really think you should give Bailey a chance. The only thing she's done is fall in love with your son. And from what I hear, she could use a good mom like you. Her own mom disowned her because she joined the Church. I will miss you terribly—so terribly, Dorie. you have no idea. My future mother-in-law will probably end up being some cold-hearted woman who turns me to stone every time I get near her. But I want a husband who wants me no matter what anybody thinks or says or does. I want a powerful love. Dorie, I just know you were meant to be someone else's mother-in-law. Not mine, however much I wish things were different," Sophie said.

Dorie sagged in her chair, and Sophie got up to massage her shoulders, like she used to do.

"Hey, perk up, Dorie. Why don't I give you a quick do? My flat iron is hot. I bet Jack is planning on taking you out to a movie tonight. Want to look smokin'?" she asked with a grin.

Dorie looked up and smiled with tears in her eyes.

"Sophie, I don't care if you never are my daughter-in-law. You'll always be a daughter to me," she said and wiped her eyes.

Sophie leaned down and kissed Dorie's check and hugged her tightly.

"That's the best thing I've heard all day," Sophie said and grabbed the flat iron.

chapter 11

Sophie left the salon at four and rushed home to shower and change. She rubbed some leave-in conditioner into her wet hair and let it dry naturally. Instead of curls, she ended up with thick waves. She studied her hair in the mirror, turning this way and that, and smiled. Yep, that was the look she wanted. She was getting tired of the Shirley Temple look anyway. This was a little more sophisticated, and dare she say, maybe a little bit sexy. She grinned at herself and applied a light peach lipstick. She paused as she realized she had only thought of Blake a few times that day. A vast improvement over thinking of him every other minute. She was really getting over him. *Yeah, Sophie!*

Sophie sprayed on a new fragrance Jacie had given her a sample of and nodded. She was ready, and she looked good. Even better, she felt good. She was in a good place, and she meant to stay there. The next person who tried to knock her out of her happiness was going to be knocked right back.

The doorbell rang and she ran to answer it. She checked the peep-hole first. *Blake.* She knew it. He was going to try to knock her out of happy. Well, he could try. She was sticking.

"Blake. What a surprise," she said with zero emotion in her voice as she watched him fidget nervously and smile at her.

"Wow, Sophie. You look amazing. You're wearing your hair like you used to in high school. I always loved your hair," he said, smiling shyly at her.

Sophie blinked. *What?* She'd spent the better part of the last three years damaging her hair with her flat iron daily to make it super straight to impress a man who liked her better with her naturally wavy hair? She shook her head and silently swore to never again try to impress a man by being someone she wasn't. *Whoa. Total mind melt.*

"Okay. Well, thanks Blake. So what are you doing here? I thought we kind of settled everything between us already," she said, looking up and down the street in case Bailey was watching.

Blake smiled down at her, his blond hair gleaming in the sun, and Sophie was almost tempted to invite him in and ask him about his mission. Of course she'd have to cancel her date and then fight off Bailey the rest of her life, but . . . but no. *No! Ugh!* He was not going to pull her in again just to call her in two weeks and tell her that he'd fallen in love with a family home evening sister or something.

"I was just driving by and wanted to know if you wanted to go see a movie or something. Just as friends, of course. I was thinking about you and me, and we were always such good friends. Just because I messed everything up shouldn't mean we can't be friends. What do you say?" he asked, moving in closer and grabbing her hand.

Sophie blinked in surprise a couple times. Blake had never been this aggressive before. Her aunt had been right. She'd chased Blake until she'd got him, and he'd just been along for the ride. But now, it almost felt as if Blake was being the aggressor. So strange. *And yet compelling. . . . Ugh! No!*

Sophie pulled her hand back and smiled at Blake. "You know, I'd have to think about the friend thing. But tonight's out. I have a date tonight, and as a matter of fact, I'm supposed to be at Jacie's right now. So we'll talk later, okay?" she said as nicely as possible.

Blake frowned, looking furious.

"What do you mean you have a date? We were together three years, and now in just one week, you're out with another guy? You have got to be kidding me," he spit out.

Sophie's mouth dropped open at the hypocrisy. She had to be kidding? *She* had to be kidding? Oh no, she didn't.

"Blake? Get out of my life," she said and slammed the door in his face. She locked it for effect and stomped back to her room to grab her purse and lip gloss. She had to be kidding? *Where is that revenge list?* she wondered, kicking shoes and chairs and doors. She felt like throwing something. She felt like kicking Blake! She felt like, she felt like . . . crying. Sophie flopped on her bed and put her arm over her eyes. How could Blake play with her emotions like this? They were best friends for years. She thought she was in love with him, but now she wasn't sure if she ever had been. He'd always treated her with as little passion and romance as humanly possible. And now he was acting all possessive and interested, like he'd never really been before. What was going on?

Sophie's cell phone rang, and she winced at the sound, knowing immediately it was Jacie.

"Get your butt over here five minutes ago!" Jacie's voiced screeched from the phone. Sophie jumped up, fixed her makeup, and then ran for her car. She checked the mirror and felt better. She looked a little pale, but not too pathetic. But Blake had done it. He had knocked the happiness right out of her. And now all she was, was confused. And late.

chapter 12

It's classic male behavior," Jacie assured her. "It's all part of the chase. As soon as you're out of reach, then that's when they want you. Honestly. That's like in Men 101. Please tell me you're not this clueless about guys," Jacie implored.

Sophie rolled her eyes and watched as Jacie applied her lipstick. A beautiful sheer nude.

"Look, I thought you were yelling at me because the guys were here already and I was late. What was the big hurry?" Sophie asked as she went through Jacie's drawer full of nail polish. She picked out a bright green and raised her eyebrows at Jacie.

Jacie grabbed the polish and dumped it in the drawer.

"The best part of any date is when you get to hang out with your best friend before you're picked up. Now, does my hair look good? You're so much better at hair than me. Just fix whatever needs fixing," Jacie said and started applying her mascara.

Sophie sighed, picked up a comb, and started ratting hair here, smoothing there.

"Jacie, I just can't figure you out. You've been working at the salon for years now, but I don't even think you really enjoy it. You hate giving haircuts. You only do the kids, and you hate the smell from doing nails. Why haven't you gone off to college and gotten a degree in, I don't know, accounting?" Sophie asked, smiling at the image of Jacie doing somebody's taxes.

Jacie rolled her eyes and grabbed her eye liner.

"Well, not everyone can have Hair Magic like you. But you're right. I don't really see myself working at the salon forever. It's just until my real life starts. I always thought I'd work there for a few years until Bryan got back, and then I'd get married and be a mom. That's what I want to do when I grow up. I want to be a mom and a wife. I want to join a book club and go walking with all the other moms in the neighborhood in the mornings. I want to have play dates and trips to the library. I want to make cookies and tuck my kids into bed at night. Hair is just something to do until my real life starts."

Sophie tilted her head and looked at her friend. She was dead serious. She was saying what women had been afraid to say for the last twenty years. Wow.

"Well, so why did you dump Bryan then? Why didn't you just wait for him? You're not still in love with him are you?" Sophie asked, raising her eyebrows in surprise.

Jacie winced and paused as she thought about it.

"You know he's going to be back in two weeks. I thought by now I'd be married and have a baby. I thought I would be over him. So over him. But you know what? I'm not. I'm as in love with him today as I was the first time I saw him make that three-pointer at the Young Men's basketball game."

Sophie cleared her throat and went back to teasing and combing Jacie's hair. And Sophie thought her life was complicated.

"So all those guys you've been out with. Nothing? Not one spark? Nada?" she asked, still in shock.

Jacie frowned and grabbed her earrings. "Yeah, it's hilarious isn't it? Me, the know-it-all. I can give you five steps to accomplish anything in life. But I can't figure out my own. The man I love and will always love will be back in town in less than two weeks, and he hates me now. I dumped him while he was still in the MTC. I didn't have the guts to tell him I wanted to date while he was gone. So I told him in a letter and I haven't heard from him since. And every time I see his mom or dad or one of his sisters at the store or at church or something, they give me this evil eye. Like they blame me for the war in Iraq or something. Even if Bryan ever did forgive me and take me back, his family never would. It's just hopeless," Jacie said and surprised Sophie by whisking a tear off her cheek.

"Dang, Jacie. Why didn't you ever tell me what was going on inside that stone cold heart of yours?" Sophie asked with a shake of her head.

Jacie laughed and reached for a tissue to blow her nose.

"Then what would happen to my big tough reputation? I can't let that get out," she said.

Sophie frowned. "But I'm your best friend. I tell you everything. You tell me everything. That's the way best friends work."

Jacie took a deep breath. "I'm sorry. It's a pride thing. You always came to me for advice. How could I let you know I'm a complete idiot who doesn't know one thing about anything to do with life, love, or relationships? And by the way, that five steps to the most amazing revenge was total crap. Made it up right on the spot," Jacie said with a laugh.

Sophie laughed and shook her head. "You know my mom is taking your course on revenge, don't you? About ten years too late, but I'm trying to steer her toward step number five, which by the way is not crap. It's complete wisdom."

Jacie shook her head and picked up a small, handheld mirror to see the back of her hair.

"Yep, you're way better at hair than I'll ever be. Well, we better get going. We're meeting the guys at the restaurant. That way there's no uncomfortable kiss good night."

Sophie followed Jacie out to the car and sat down in the passenger seat.

"You know, Jacie, let's do it. Let's make a five-step plan to get Bryan back. It's not hopeless. Heck, as soon as I did what you said, Blake was putty in my hands. Too bad I don't want him anymore. So don't underestimate yourself. If Bryan is the one you want, then who's to stop you from getting him?" Sophie asked.

Jacie pulled out into the road and headed for American Fork. "You're forgetting about one thing. He doesn't love me anymore."

Sophie turned the radio on and tilted her seat back. "What would you say if it was me who had screwed everything up with the man of my dreams? What would you tell me to do?" she asked with a twinkle.

Jacie smiled over at her and turned the AC on. "Well, I'd have to say something like, 'Buck up little camper. Let's go get yer man,' " she said with a laugh.

Sophie laughed with her. "Then let's do it. Just take yourself out of the equation. Plan this like you were planning it for someone else. And then when you're done, just put yourself back in. Easy!"

Jacie sighed and shook her head. "Lesson number one, my little hair magician. It's always easier when someone else is doing all the work."

Sophie agreed. "So where are we going? You never said."

Jacie smiled, glad at the change in topic. "Ottavio's. You know the one, right off the freeway exit. I've been craving Italian all week. This is going to be amazing. The food. Not necessarily the date."

Sophie snorted and shook her head. "So these last two years of happy dating. Were they worth it? All the restaurants and dances? Would you go back and do things differently?" Sophie couldn't resist asking.

Jacie sighed and let her face fall into such complete sadness that Sophie automatically grabbed her arm.

"In a heartbeat. I'd do anything to go back. I'd trade every stupid dinner, every uncomfortable kiss, every corsage, every movie to just go back and not mail that letter."

Sophie sighed and patted Jacie's shoulder. They rode in silence the rest of the way, both contemplating love and life and why people messed both up so well.

"Come on. Let's forget about it tonight. But tomorrow, you're coming over to my house and you're not leaving until we have a plan. Deal?" Sophie said as they walked into Ottavio's.

Jacie gave her a half-smile and nodded. "No more heartbreak tonight. Just you and me and some truly excellent food. Oh yeah. And a couple guys willing to pay for it all, just for the chance to be in our sparkling, beautiful company."

Sophie winced at her friend's cynicism but followed her in anyway. There was a grain of truth to it. But wow, what would it be like to go to dinner with someone you were so excited to be with, you couldn't care less about the food? That's the kind of date she wanted. Sophie sighed as she saw two very tall, very attractive men standing by the hostess, obviously waiting for them. Maybe tonight was the night.

chapter 13

He was at least six feet tall and had longish brown hair and dramatic dark eyebrows that movie stars dreamed of having. The only thing wrong with him that she could see was that his smile was too big. Like he wanted to make sure everyone saw his perfectly straight white teeth.

"Sophie! It's a pleasure to meet you, and I must say, Jacie did not exaggerate your loveliness at all. You are beautiful," Eric said, smiling blindingly at her

Sophie blushed, not used to such over-the-top compliments. Well, not used to compliments period, to be honest.

"Thanks, Eric. It's nice to meet you too."

"Okay, Eric, knock it off. You're embarrassing her. Come on, our table's ready," Paul said, grabbing Jacie's hand and leading them toward the back. After being seated, they went through the usual info sharing. Paul and Eric were both in law school at BYU. Sophie was surprised at how alike their ambitions were and how completely opposite they were in everything else.

Sophie automatically liked Paul. He was just as good-looking as Eric but not half as flashy. He had medium brown hair, cut missionary short, and light blue eyes with a sprinkling of freckles across his nose. He seemed very calm, intelligent, and kind.

"So are you guys going to start a law firm together?" Sophie asked Eric.

Eric leaned in close, too close actually, and smiled at her.

"Well, that would work if Paul knew what he was doing. He thinks he's going to be a public defender. Now, I, on the other hand, I have my future completely mapped out for success. Corporate law. There's nothing like it. And the money . . . Sophie, the money would make your head spin," he said with raised eyebrows and a firm nod.

Sophie frowned and glanced at Jacie, who just shrugged and shoved more bread in her mouth. Paul tried to steer the conversation toward more general topics, and as long as she kept scooting her chair closer to Jacie's, Eric couldn't lean in too close to her. She liked Eric and everything, but the man had no clue about personal space or that the effect of his great eyebrows were better from a distance.

Jacie poked her hard in the ribs and coughed into her napkin at the same time.

"What?" Sophie whispered, rubbing her side and glaring at her friend.

"Wicked witch number one coming right for us. Hide!" Jacie whispered loudly.

Sophie whipped her head up just in time to see her cousin Daphne walk straight over to their table. Sophie licked her lips and sighed. Annoying date and all, this had been the best evening she'd had in such a long time. Just to be ruined now, by one of her very least favorite people.

"Sophie!" Daphne exclaimed. "You're on a date? Someone revive me. I'm about to have a heart attack. I thought you'd be home still crying your eyes out over Blake. Oh, hi, Jacie. You're here," she said with a smirk.

Jacie rolled her eyes but didn't say anything. Sophie dabbed her lips with her napkin before answering.

"Bye," she said and picked up her water, hoping Daphne would take the hint and get lost. She didn't. Daphne laughed and put her hand on her hip as she smiled. A sure sign she was starting to enjoy herself.

"Well, at least introduce me to your gorgeous date," she commanded, leaning over her to reach Eric's already outstretched hand.

"So are you here by yourself, Daphne?" Sophie interrupted.

Daphne grinned even wider and looked over her shoulder.

"Oh, he's coming. Just give him a minute. And in the meantime, I can chat with you all."

Eric, the idiot, stood up and walked over to an empty table and grabbed a chair.

"If you're Sophie's cousin, why don't you join us?" he offered, dazzling her with his ultra-white smile. Sophie tried hard not to gag. She'd be lucky if he didn't propose to Daphne before the night was over. Daphne had that effect on men. She was a sensory overload. Big blonde hair, big blue eyes, big—well, everything.

Jacie's mouth had opened in protest but made no sound as Daphne shoved herself between Eric and Paul. Jacie and Sophie exchanged pained expressions. There was absolutely nothing they could do but eat fast and leave.

"Oh, here's my date. Sam! Over here. We're joining my cousin. You remember? The one who's so graceful?" Daphne said with an annoying giggle.

Sophie felt her heart constrict and sputter to a halt when Sam walked toward her with a half-smile. She looked from him to Daphne and back again in shock. He asked Daphne out? Sam was on a date with her cousin, the wicked witch of Alpine? The man who had insisted on kissing her to teach her relatives a lesson? She shook her head in confusion and then stared at him again in surprised horror. She must have been completely wrong about him. How utterly depressing.

He smiled at everyone at the table before grabbing a chair and scooting in next to Daphne and Paul. Daphne made the introductions for him, and he shook hands with Paul and Eric, nodded with a smile at Jacie, and then smiled at Sophie, looking slightly guilty and almost embarrassed. She couldn't blame him. If she had been on a date with Daphne, she'd be embarrassed too.

The waiter took Daphne's and Sam's order quickly and brought them out some bread and salads.

"So, Sam, how long have you and Daphne been dating?" Sophie asked with a bright, fake smile.

Sam winced and speared a tomato while Daphne giggled and laid her head on his shoulder.

"Sophie, that's such a personal question. But I will say that Sam is the most romantic man I've ever been out with," Daphne said with a giggle and a flip of her ultra blonde, ultra big hair.

Sophie turned green and took a sip of water. Sam rolled his eyes and leaned slightly away from Daphne.

"Well, thanks, Daphne, but since you're the one who asked me out, I'd have to say that the romance is all one-sided," he said, looking at Sophie.

Sophie blinked and took a bite of her chicken marsala. Daphne frowned at Sam and turned her attention back to Eric, asking him questions about his family and where he was from.

The conversation turned to movies and everyone relaxed again. Jacie was unnaturally quiet, and since Eric and Daphne were now staring into each other's eyes and ignoring everyone else, that left Paul and Sam for her to talk to. Sophie looked at all the food still left on her plate and felt like groaning. Dating just wasn't what it used to be. She remembered going out with Blake and all their friends and all the fun they'd always had. This? This was not fun. This was uncomfortable at best and downright miserable, if she were being honest. Her date was throwing himself at her wretched cousin. The man of her dreams was on a date with said cousin. Her best friend was statue-like. Maybe staying at home with a package of Oreos and a video wasn't so bad after all.

"So, Sophie, are you working tomorrow?" Sam asked her from across the table.

Sophie looked up and met his dark, warm eyes and felt like crying. He was so gorgeous. What she wouldn't have given to have gone on a date with him. But he'd said yes to her cousin. He'd actually gone on a date with her cousin. There was no forgiveness for bad taste like that.

"Yes, but just in the morning. I get off work at twelve," she said, not returning his smile.

Daphne picked up on their conversation and turned a pitying look at Sophie.

"Did you all know? Sophie does hair. Isn't that cute? She's a little hairdresser, just like her mom. It's a family dynasty," she said with a snarky laugh.

Jacie glared at Daphne but didn't say anything, just went on eating her angel hair pasta and garlic sauce. Sophie glared at Daphne but refused to stick up for herself. She wasn't ashamed of what she or her mother did for a living.

Paul wiped his mouth on a napkin and cleared his throat, gaining everyone's attention.

"Let me get this right, Daphne. You think what your cousin does for a living is somehow beneath you? Or beneath us?" he asked with a deceptively kind voice.

Daphne mistook the tone of voice and automatically assumed he was with her on her opinion of Sophie.

"Well, doesn't everyone? I mean, come on. She never went to college. She graduated from high school and went to beauty school and has been working for her mom ever since. And that's her goal in life. To work for her mom the rest of her life, perming little old ladies' hair and giving haircuts. I mean, come on. This is the twenty-first century," Daphne said with a proud tilt of her head.

Paul smiled kindly at her and held up his hand when Jacie started sputtering.

"Daphne, you do seem like a woman of the world. And what is it that you do? Are you a student?" he asked.

Daphne blushed and nodded. "Well, I do take some courses online. I haven't exactly decided what I'm going to do, but whatever it is, it has to be better than doing people's hair," she said with an arrogant sniff.

Sophie was furious. She grabbed her water and contemplated throwing it in her cousin's face. Just watching all of that black mascara and eyeliner drip down into Daphne's pasta would make the wreck that was her date so much better.

"Now, Daphne, I find that so interesting," Paul said. "Here you're obviously making fun of your cousin, who from what I hear is a very hard worker, working from seven in the morning until seven at night sometimes. I bet on average she pulls in anywhere from sixty to a hundred dollars an hour. There's not a lot of people with college degrees who can make that kind of money," he said with a confused look on his face, as if wanting Daphne to explain so he could understand what exactly she was making fun of.

Daphne frowned and licked her lips, obviously trying to dig herself out of the hole.

"Well, honestly, what man would want someone like Sophie for a wife? I mean, look at the three of you. Two of you are going to be lawyers, and Sam already owns his own company. Men like you want women with education. You would want someone with class. You would want someone you could be proud of. No way is that Sophie. I mean, let's face it. Her boyfriend she waited two years for dumped her as soon as he got home and found a girl who was going to school," she said triumphantly.

Sophie felt as big as an ant. She felt completely worthless. Daphne hadn't made her cry in five years, and she sure as heck didn't want to ruin that record. But the tightening in her throat warned her that tonight could be the end of her dry spell.

"Daphne! Come on! How can you say that?" Paul interrupted, pulling everyone's attention away from Sophie and back toward him.

"Obviously, there's something you don't understand about men. I'll use Sophie as an example, since you are. Now, here I am, a returned missionary. I'm in school, and I'm getting ready to graduate in less than a year. I'm looking for a wife who's sweet and kind and who will make a good mother. Sophie, obviously from the way she hasn't gone after you with her fork, is a kind human being. She makes a great living, and if I'm lucky, she could help support me for the next couple of years while I get my career started. And then after we have children, she can work from home if she wants to. You see, if I were looking at Sophie, I'd think she was perfect. There's not one drawback to her. And being a gorgeous redhead doesn't hurt. She's practically perfect," he said, smiling kindly at Sophie.

Sophie gulped and felt some of the pain inside disappear. Why was Paul being so nice to her? And why wasn't he her date?

"Thanks, Paul. You're very sweet," she said quietly.

Sam reached into his pocket and pulled out a business card.

"Paul, here's my card. Call me when you pass the bar exam. I could use a good lawyer like you," he said, slapping Paul on the back.

Paul grinned and grabbed the card. "Hey, my first client."

Daphne glared at Paul and Sam and turned back to Eric, to find he had turned his attention back to Sophie. Sophie breathed a sigh of relief when the conversation turned away from her and all of her faults and failings. The rest of the dinner went by quickly, with Jacie complaining of not feeling well before they could order dessert.

"Well, we'd better go," Sophie said sadly, while on the inside, she jumped for joy. Freedom, so close.

"We'll walk you to your car," Paul said, taking Jacie by the arm.

Eric followed Sophie outside, leaving Sam and Daphne staring at their plates.

Jacie and Paul walked to the other side of the car and said their good-byes, leaving Sophie to stand uncomfortably with Eric. If he was hoping for a good night kiss, he was dreaming.

"Well, Sophie, thanks for coming to dinner tonight. Would you mind if I called you sometime?" he asked, showing her every tooth he had.

Sophie groaned inwardly but smiled up at Eric. "To be honest, Eric, I don't think we really hit if off. But if you'd like my cousin's phone number, I'd be happy to give that to you."

Eric frowned and then looked surprised. And then he smiled for real.

"Actually, I would like that. Thanks for being so cool," he said, reaching for his cell phone and adding Daphne's number. Sophie smiled back at him. He and Daphne would make a striking couple.

"Bye, Eric," she said and watched as he practically ran back to the restaurant. Paul helped Jacie into the car and then walked around to say good-bye to Sophie.

"Hey, Sophie, sorry Eric is such an idiot. And I wasn't kidding in there. I really do think you're amazing. And by the way, Jacie and I are just friends. She thought it would be cool if you and I hooked up. Would you mind if I called you sometime?" Paul asked with a shy smile.

Sophie smiled back, feeling warm inside. Now that would be nice.

"Paul, after sticking up for me the way you did, I would love for you to call me anytime," she said, reaching out to shake his hand.

Paul grabbed her hand and blushed. Sophie was completely charmed.

"Okay, then. I'll talk to you later. Bye," he said and walked back toward the restaurant. Sophie looked up at the still light sky and breathed in deeply. Tonight hadn't been so crappy after all. She grabbed the car door handle and opened.

"Hey!" a voice called.

Sophie turned around, shading her eyes, and saw Sam run out of the restaurant and toward her.

"Hey, Sophie. I wanted to say good-bye before you took off," he said.

He jogged toward her and then instead of coming to her side of the car, went to Jacie's side and opened her door and leaned down.

"Hey, Jacie. Do you mind if I talk to Sophie for a second? I won't be long."

Sophie crossed her arms across her chest and glared at Sam as he smiled and walked back toward her.

"The reason I was asking if you worked tomorrow is because I was thinking I should get my free haircut out of the way," he said with a grin.

Sophie's mouth dropped open. "You have got to be kidding me. You want a free haircut for letting me watch you fix my father's AC and then kissing me? Are you serious?" she sputtered.

Sam grinned down at her. "Deadly. Why do you think Daphne asked me out? She saw me kiss you and immediately wanted to steal my affections away. I think having to endure her company on a Friday night is worth two haircuts at least. But I'm willing to settle for one," he said with a twinkle in his eyes.

Sophie shook her head in disbelief. "You're telling me it's my fault that you're out on a date with my cousin? Oh this is unreal. This is completely unreal. You kiss me, and then never call me, and then blame me for Daphne. Uh uh. No way is this happening," she said, her voice rising in outrage.

Sam laughed and stepped closer toward her. Sophie stepped back but felt her back come up against Jacie's car.

"Hey, you knew my rates from the beginning. I come to your rescue, you pay up with a great haircut. Play fair now, Sophie," he said softly.

Sophie shoved at Sam's chest and came up against rock-hard resistance. He didn't even budge a little bit.

"Look, buddy, I hate to break it to you, but you never rescued me. And tonight, when Daphne was having me for dessert, I didn't hear you make one peep of a rescue. Now Paul, on the other hand, who is going to be calling me, by the way—you know, with a phone, because he's interested in me—he came to my rescue. He rescued me from that witch who is your date. You? Not the rescuer," she said.

Sam frowned down at her and stepped forward, leaving maybe two inches between them.

"Now, Sophie, you're going to hurt my feelings saying things like that. Now I like Paul, and he does have a way with words. That's why he's going to be my lawyer. And here I am. I don't have a way with words. I'm all action. That might be why I'm out here with you instead of inside with your cousin. Now I'm going to show up tomorrow at nine sharp for the best haircut of my life. Do we have an appointment?" he asked in a voice he must use on late subcontractors.

Sophie moved as far away from him as she could get.

"Um," she said but then stopped as Sam grabbed her hand and kissed it, looking at her pleadingly.

"Please?" he asked sweetly.

Sophie sighed and tugged her hand out of his grip.

"Fine! But if you're late, you're out of luck. I'm an extremely busy woman," she said with more irritation in her voice than she really felt.

Actually the thought of seeing Sam the next day was pretty exciting.

Sam grinned down at her and then turned to walk back into the restaurant. She watched him silently go, as her breathing returned to normal. When he had kissed her hand, it had done something strange to her muscles. She couldn't move.

He stopped with his hand on the door and turned back to look at her with a smile.

"See ya tomorrow, Sophie," he said and then disappeared into the restaurant. Jacie got out of the car and opened the car door for her, pushing her into the seat. Sophie stared dazedly out the window, not seeing anything but Sam's grinning face.

Jacie punched her hard in the shoulder and woke her from her spellbinding daze.

"Ouch!" Sophie yelled, feeling herself return to reality.

"Cheating on Paul already and you haven't been on one date. Geez, Sophie. What kind of girl are you?" Jacie demanded with a grin.

Sophie looked at her friend and smiled so big her cheeks hurt.

"Jacie, I'm the kind of girl who has an appointment tomorrow at nine. That's who I am," she said and then rolled down her window and let out a whoop.

chapter 14

"You know, that's a record. Seriously. Being on a date with one guy, agreeing to go on a date with a different guy, and then having your hand kissed by a third guy. Who does that?" Jacie demanded as they pulled into her driveway.

Sophie grinned and got out of Jacie's silver Acura.

"As it turns out, I do. Forget the long jump in junior high. This is the best record I've ever had," she said with a happy giggle. "And to think when Daphne showed up, I thought I was having the worst night of my life," she said.

Jacie followed Sophie over to her Jeep and leaned on the door. "Man, I do not know how you put up with your relatives. Most people have really nice relatives. Yours really do stink. And Daphne is the worst," Jacie said with a glare.

Sophie leaned next to Jacie, and they both looked at the sunset.

"Yeah, I didn't end up with the best relatives out there, but I have to give Daphne credit. She's not the worst of the bunch. That would have to be my father. So, not to change the subject, but where were you tonight? I mean, it was like you just checked out and left me with a table full of people all by myself," Sophie said, turning to glare at her friend.

Jacie closed her eyes and put her arms behind her.

"Sorry about that. I don't know. After our conversation about Bryan, I just didn't feel like being on a date anymore. Lately I've felt guilty for going out with other guys. And as you know, Paul and I are just friends, but still. I just didn't want to be there after all," she said quietly.

Sophie nodded and stared at the sky again. "I can understand that. But dang, Jacie. All you had to do was jump over the table and strangle my cousin. I picked you to be my best friend for certain reasons, and that's one of them," she said, completely serious.

Jacie opened one eye and looked at her, grinning. "I know that, Sophie. And I plan on making it up to you. But look at the positive side. Because I didn't whoop on Daphne, Paul did it for you, and might I add, he did it with a lot more style than I would have. And I do believe, after sticking up for you so passionately, he's now feeling more passionately about you than he might have felt otherwise. Hmmm?"

Sophie laughed and dug out her keys from her purse.

"Yeah, well. Still. Next time I want her decimated, or I want my best friend's locket back," she said, completely serious.

Jacie gave up and threw her arms around Sophie shoulders, hugging her tightly.

"Okay! I'm sorry. Next time she's toast. I'll have her begging for mercy."

Sophie pushed her away laughing and got into her car. Jacie poked her head into the window before she could leave.

"So what are you going to do? You never said. Which one wins? The one who swindles a free haircut out of you or the sweet defender of light and truth?" she asked, obviously voting for Paul.

Sophie picked a CD and slid it in the player while she thought about it.

"Hmm. That's a good one. And the wonderful thing about being twenty and single is that I don't have to make up my mind tonight. I'm going to date and I'm going to have fun, and I'm not going to worry about it. Why is it that women automatically jump toward commitment? I'm taking this slow," she said with a nod of her head.

Jacie grinned and stepped back from the car. "Okay, but when you come over tomorrow to help me plan my operation Get Back My Man, we're starting you on a new five-step program. How to keep two guys at the same time. I'll work on it tonight."

Sophie waved out her window and pulled away without replying. She'd be interested in that plan. It might be fun. On the other hand, it could be dangerous. And she would never want to hurt Paul. He didn't deserve that. Jacie better come up with a good plan. How to keep two guys at the same time and not hurt either one of them. Now that was a plan.

chapter 15

At nine o'clock the next morning, Sam walked into the salon, smiling and looking good. Too good. Sophie breathed in and straightened her shoulders. This was going to be interesting.

"You're right on time, Sam. Why don't you come on back?" she said in a casual voice with a polite, professional smile.

Sam grinned and walked right up to her. "Starting the day with a beautiful redhead. Now that's the way to start the morning off right," he said and bent down to kiss her on the cheek.

Sophie raised her hand to her check and smiled bemusedly. Wow.

"Um, okay. Have a seat, Sam," she said, feeling a blush stain her cheeks.

He sat down and she immediately draped him. She rested her hands on his shoulders. Holy cow he had big shoulders. And the muscles! Okay, she had to focus.

"So do you just want a trim? What do you have in mind?" she asked, hoping her cheeks had cooled off.

"I haven't really thought about it. I usually just have my mom hack at my hair. She's been doing it since I was born. The only time I've been to a barber is when I was on my mission in Korea. So why don't you just surprise me?" he said with a wink.

She ran her hands through his thick hair, feeling his scalp. He had a ton of hair. She'd give him a trendy new haircut. She'd use some of the new product that just came in to flip up the front. Yep, that's what she'd do.

"Do you have to stop?" he asked with a whimper.

"What?" she asked, frowning.

"The scalp massage is worth fifty bucks. Forget the haircut and keep going. I'll give you a big tip, I promise," he said, completely serious.

Sophie laughed at him and grabbed her buzzers. "If you're a good boy, I'll think about a quick scalp massage when I'm done."

Sam sighed but sat up straight and tilted his head down when she pushed with her fingers. Fifteen minutes later, she was back to massaging his head. He was putty in her hands. She gave him an extra five minutes, but then patted his shoulders, signaling she was done. She grabbed some product from the shelf and squeezed a small amount into her palm. She ran her fingers through his now short hair and tweaked it here and there until it looked the way she wanted it to. He looked like a hair model. Beautiful.

"And there you go. All finished," she said with a smile and took his drape off.

Sam looked at himself in the mirror critically and winced.

Sophie frowned. "What? Don't you like it? I think you look gorgeous," she said truthfully.

"Yeah, your cousin will take one look at me, and she'll never give up. You've made me completely irresistible," he said with laughing eyes.

Sophie snorted and grabbed the broom and started sweeping.

"Sam, modesty is a virtue, but if it makes you feel better, I'll really mess up your next haircut," she said primly, not wanting to think of how irresistible he was to females. Especially her cousin.

"Now, how do you want your tip? I could pay you in kisses," he said, standing up and walking toward her.

Sophie raised her hand and shook her head. "Uh uh. I only take kisses as tips when you're under five years old."

Sam laughed and leaned all his weight on one hip and crossed his arms over his chest.

"Well, that leaves dinner then. Why don't I take you out on a real date tonight? You can't call dinner last night with that guy a date. Now when you're with me, you know you're on a date. I'll take you out to the best Mexican restaurant there is. What do you say? You and me and a scalp massage for dessert?" he asked, holding his hands up in a pleading gesture.

Sophie grinned at him and rested her chin on the broom as she considered. Two dates in one weekend? Well, she was making up for lost time, that was for sure. And if she was being honest with herself, she would love, love, love to go out with Sam.

"Okay. On one condition. You're the one giving me the scalp massage," she said with a wicked grin.

Sam groaned and looked down at his feet. "Sophie, you drive a hard bargain. Can we compromise and both get scalp massages?"

Sophie turned her back and finished dumping the hair into the garbage before answering. When she turned around, he was reading the back of a shampoo bottle. She studied him with the morning light coming in through the windows and couldn't believe she was going to go on a date with one of the best looking guys she'd ever met. He was the perfect cure for a broken heart. Now, what was he like on the inside? If it matched his outside, then she was possibly the luckiest person in Alpine.

"Okay. I'll give you a scalp massage," she said as he looked up from the bottle he was holding.

"Now that's what I'm talking about. I'll pick you up at your house around six," he said, putting the shampoo down and shoving his hands into his pockets.

"So how about a kiss good-bye?" he asked with a hopeful grin.

Sophie laughed and shook her head.

"I don't think so, Sam. And just so you know, I never kiss on the first date," she said, frowning. But did Sam? What if Sam had kissed Daphne the previous night? Ugh! Her eyebrows snapped together and she looked at Sam.

Sam laughed and held his hands up. "Wait a second! Innocent until proven guilty. I don't know what you're thinking in that beautiful head of yours, but I'm not guilty."

Sophie crossed her arms over her chest and looked down at her feet.

"I guess I was just curious. Do you kiss on the first date?" she asked, glancing up to see if he looked guilty.

Sam frowned and pulled out his keys from his pocket.

"To answer your question, no. I did not kiss Daphne last night. You're the only girl I've kissed in two months. And that's the way I'm planning on keeping things," he said and walked out the door.

Sophie stared out the window at him and felt a slow smile spread all across her face. She ran to the back of the salon and closed the door to the employee lounge and then jumped up in the air over and over.

Yes! Yes! Yes! He likes me, he likes me, she chanted to no one but herself. She flopped down on the old couch and grinned to herself. She had a date with Sam. And he hadn't kissed Daphne. *Yes!*

She finally picked her happy self up and walked back into the salon just as her mom walked through the front doors.

"And what put that smile on your face this morning?" her mom demanded with a laugh as she put her purse down by her chair.

Sophie laughed and grinned like an idiot. "Sam didn't kiss Daphne," she announced. "And I have a date tonight," she added happily.

Candy grinned at her daughter and sat down in her chair. "Well, look at you go."

Sophie frowned and walked over to her mom's chair, turning it so she faced the mirror and automatically grabbed a brush and started re-doing her mother's hair.

"Now, you have a sly smile on your face. You got something you want to get off your chest?" she asked her mother.

Candy giggled, and Sophie's mouth fell open. Her mother did not giggle. Laugh yes, but giggle like a third grader, no.

"What did you do, Mom?" she demanded, reaching for the hair spray.

Candy blushed and studied her fingers before answering.

"I have a date tonight too," she said as if she were embarrassed by the fact.

"No way!" Sophie yelled twisting her mother's chair, so she faced her. "And when did this happen?" she demanded.

Candy looked up at her daughter and blushed. "Well, you know Cathy's brother? Her younger brother? He's thirty-nine, and well, he's been divorced for about three years. He's the one with that precious little girl he brings in sometimes for a haircut? The blond one, you know. Well, I mentioned to Cathy the other day how I wanted to start dating again, and she just happened to mention how her brother Clyde had said that he thought I was cute or something, and she called him and he called me and he's taking me out tonight," she breathed out quickly.

Sophie grabbed her mom's hands, pulling her out of her chair, and they jumped around the empty salon like two kindergartners playing ring around the rosies for the first time.

"I always wondered why this place was so popular. You sell drugs here, don't you?" a cold, arrogant voice drawled.

Candy and Sophie stopped jumping up and down and looked over their shoulders to see Lexie. Sophie felt the happiness seep out of her as she dropped her mother's hands and turned to face her aunt.

"Mom, why don't you run to Kohlers and grab some drinks for the fridge? I'll take this appointment, and you can take the next one," she said and felt her mother leave the room quickly.

"Why do you always protect her? She's a grown woman, you know. You don't have to send her out of the room. I won't bite," Lexie said with a laugh.

Sophie's back straightened, her face tightened, and her eyes glinted dangerously. Nobody messed with her mom.

"She had to put up with you as a sister-in-law for ten years. She's done her time. Now why are you here? Don't tell me you want a new hairstyle?" she asked, changing the subject and walking to the appointment book, hoping she had forgotten someone's appointment just so she could send her aunt on her way.

"It does say walk-ins are welcome on your sign out there," Lexie stated, walking over to Sophie's station. Sophie wondered how Lexie could know which station was hers, but then she saw a picture of her and her mom stuck in her mirror. Lexie was a lot of things, but stupid was not one of them. Sophie walked over and pulled a drape around her aunt's bony shoulders.

"What can I do for you today?' she asked coldly, looking at her watch. Cathy was due in at ten. If Lexie had just waited fifteen more minutes, Sophie could have pawned her off. But no. Here she was, and she was going to have to touch her aunt. Oooh.

"Well, it's just not fair. Honestly it's not. Julie came to you looking fantastic to begin with, and now she looks ten times better. Standing next to her does nothing for my self-esteem. I want you to do to me what you did to her. I want you to make me look younger. I have an appointment with a plastic surgeon next week. But if you can take five years off Julie, maybe you can take ten years off me. It would save me a fortune, and I do hate pain. So do whatever it is you do," she ordered and whisked her fingers at her as if to say hurry up about it.

Sophie glared at the back at her aunt's head and then sighed. She'd been wanting Lexie to do something different with her hair for years. Her ultra black hair did nothing for her, and it only made her already white skin look deathly. She looked like Morticia Adam's homely stepsister.

"So before I start, tell me why you dye your hair black. Is it a preference?" Sophie asked as she fingered the shoulder-length strands.

Lexie studied her cuticles and didn't look up. "I started to get a few gray hairs a few years ago. I couldn't stand it, so I covered them up," she said as if it were none of Sophie's business.

Sophie sighed. "Okay. I'll do this as long as we agree I'm the one in charge here. I'm going to make some serious changes to you, and you might not like it at first since you're so used to seeing what you're seeing. But I don't want you to sue me or anything. Agreed?" she asked.

Lexie looked up and nodded her head. "Agreed. Just get going. I have a lot to do today," she commanded and picked up a *People* magazine from the stack beside her.

Sophie bit the side of her cheek and looked at the clock. This was going to take some time. She'd have to strip the black gunk off to get to the natural hair color. Then she'd have to condition and then add color back to it and then cut and style. This was going to be a huge undertaking. Boy was her aunt going to pay. This was going to be very expensive. Miracles always were.

Sophie could hear the door open when her mother and Cathy came back into the salon, but she ignored them and concentrated on the task at hand. This was going to be the biggest challenge she had ever faced. And she had to admit, in some small corner of her heart, she wanted to impress her aunt. She didn't know what that said about her, but she didn't have time to analyze herself.

Forty-five minutes later she had her aunt sitting under a dryer with her head wrapped in plastic and some deep conditioner plastered all over her head. She'd need a good twenty minutes at least. She walked to the back and sat down for a few minutes, laying her head in her hands. Her shoulders were bunching up with stress, and she had to admit she was nervous. What she really wanted to do was return her aunt to the way she looked when she was in high school with her natural hair color. She'd seen old family pictures of Lexie and her dad. Sophie had gotten her red hair from her father's side of the family. Lexie did what she could to hide it, but she had the same freckles Sophie did, and she used to have the same reddish hair color too. Sophie got up off the couch and went to look at the color selection. She picked up the red and considered what her aunt would do to her. Would she sue? It would be so worth it. What the heck! Her aunt walking into her salon

and asking her to do her hair and giving her complete control was the chance of a lifetime. She'd do it. Sophie started mixing color and even started smiling, surprising herself. She was starting to have fun. Extreme makeovers were kind of exciting.

She took her bowls back with her and set them down before rinsing Lexie's hair. She sat Lexie back down and started applying the color and foil. Lexie took one look at the bright orange gloop in the bowl, and her nostrils flared in outrage, but she didn't utter one sound. Sophie grinned to herself and started humming along with the music playing over the sound system. She completely ignored her aunt and did her thing. When she was done, she dragged Lexie back over to the dryer, pushed a magazine into her hands, and walked over to see how her mom was doing with Sister Bledsoe.

"Nice color, Sister Bledsoe. Good job, Mom," Sophie said and sat down next to them to chat while she waited for Lexie's hair to process.

Candy raised an eyebrow at her daughter. "I noticed the color you mixed. Are you crazy?" she whispered.

Sophie grinned and nodded her head. "It's in the genes," she said and laughed when her mother grinned at her.

Lexie could hear the women laughing and giggling and sniffed in further outrage. Sophie heard and shrugged it off. Torturing Lexie was a fun little appetizer. The woman deserved so much more than just getting the haircut and color of her life. She could sit and suffer for a little while longer.

Twenty minutes later she took Lexie back over to rinse and then sat her down for the haircutting portion of the style. Without even asking Lexie her preferences, she did the best she could to get rid of the bob and give her aunt a haircut more suited for a forty-five-year-old woman. Long and sexy bangs to soften her forehead and hide the wrinkles. Multiple layers all over. Longer in the front and shorter in the back. She cut and cut, watching with curiosity as Lexie's already pale face turned whiter and whiter. Sophie wanted to laugh but held it in.

She blew Lexie's hair out, adding gel for body and lift, and then grabbed her flat iron, twisting the hair in small sections to give it tons of body and movement. She purposefully kept Lexie's chair turned away from the mirror until she was completely finished. Sophie stepped back and stared critically at Lexie's new hair. Gone was the jet black severe bob. In its place was shiny auburn hair, cut and styled to perfection.

She slowly turned Lexie's chair around to face the mirror and stepped to the side to watch her reaction.

Lexie's eyes widened, and her fingers automatically lifted to touch her hair. Sophie frowned when she noticed Lexie's hands trembling, and stepped forward.

"So, uh, what do you think, Lexie?" Sophie asked, feeling Candy and Cathy move in beside her. For support or backup. Whichever she needed the most of.

"Julie's right. You do have hair magic," she whispered, blinking fiercely at herself.

Sophie's eyebrows shot up when she realized her aunt was trying valiantly not to cry. She had done it! Her aunt loved her new look.

"I look like I did in high school, Sophie. How did you know? I mean, how could you do this? I can't believe it. I really can't," she said in a voice Sophie had never heard before. Soft and grateful and humble. She didn't hear any arrogance or sarcasm in her voice at all. It was a first.

Sophie tilted her head to the side and studied her aunt for a moment.

"You know what would be even better? If I did your makeup. Now that we've gotten rid of that black mess, why don't you let me show you how to do your makeup? When a woman gets older, she thinks she has to use more foundation than she should. It only makes you look pale and washed out and icky. What do you say?" she asked.

Lexie nodded, still staring at herself. She couldn't look away. Sophie dragged her to the station where all the makeup was and sat her aunt down. She cleansed her face first, getting rid of the layers and layers of makeup her aunt thought was necessary. Fifteen minutes later, Lexie's face had color, and her eyes sparkled, and you could even see some freckles. The eyebrows made the biggest difference, though. After wiping off all the drawn on black eyebrow makeup, Sophie brushed on a light brown eyebrow color.

As she did Lexie's makeup, Sophie couldn't resist giving her aunt a little more advice. "You know Lexie, now that you look really good. I've gotta say one thing. Anorexia went out a long time ago. You have got to eat something. The best thing you could do for your face right now is plump it out a little. Your cheeks are looking gaunt. You don't need to look like you're starving to look beautiful. Men love curvy women. I know it sounds strange, but it's the truth."

Lexie just sniffed, but she looked like she was considering what Sophie had said.

Sophie stepped back and looked at a completely different person. She hadn't knocked off ten years from her aunt. More like fifteen. She looked incredible. And with no plastic surgery.

Sophie finished up, twisted Lexie to see the mirror, and saw her aunt begin to tremble again. Her fingers gripped the arms of the chair so hard, Sophie worried she'd break them

"Ah, now stop it!" Sophie said patting her aunt awkwardly on the shoulders. "If you cry and mess up all my hard work, I'm going to be mad," she said with a smile.

Lexie nodded and breathed in deeply, closing her eyes and concentrating on controlling herself.

"Sophie, what you've done for me—I can't express my gratitude. And I know I haven't treated you kindly. You could have given me purple hair and I would have deserved it. But you didn't. You did something amazing. I don't know what to say," she said quietly, looking Sophie in the eyes.

Sophie winced, feeling very uncomfortable. Her aunt's gratitude was something completely foreign. She was much more used to evil. She wasn't sure what to say.

Candy walked over and studied Lexie in the mirror. With her new lighter makeup, the blush on Lexie's cheeks was evident.

"You know, Lexie, I honestly don't think you've looked better. Your husband is going to flip out when he sees you. In a good way," she added.

Lexie smiled and grinned at her reflection. "Thanks, Candy," she said and got up.

"Well, Sophie, since you just saved me twenty thousand dollars, you name your price and I won't even blink," she said, reaching for her wallet.

Sophie calculated everything she'd done and charged her exactly what she would have charged anyone else.

Lexie's eyebrow lifted in surprise, but she wrote the check out quickly and laid it face down on the counter.

"Sophie, I'll say it again. I'm grateful. You are truly a very talented young lady. And I deeply appreciate everything you did for me today. I hope it's okay with you if I start coming to you from now on," she asked.

Sophie paused and then smiled. Why not? She might not like her aunt, but hey. They were family, right?

She and Candy watched Lexie walk out of the salon like a sophisticated runway model and grinned at each other.

"Honey, you are one brave chick. I wouldn't have touched that woman's hair to save my life," she said and picked up the check.

"Oh my gosh!" Candy squealed and turned the check to show Sophie.

Sophie grabbed the check and started squealing too. The check was made out for five hundred dollars.

"Now that's what I call a tip," Candy said with a grin and waved it in the air with a laugh.

"That's what you get when you're as good as you are," Candy said with a proud smile. "What would I do if you ever left the salon and went to work across town?" she asked.

Sophie rolled her eyes and put the check in the till. "Like that would ever happen. We're a team. You and me and a couple of scissors. That's all we need to rule the world," she said.

Candy hugged her daughter and walked with her toward the back of the salon.

"Now does that come in a five-step plan?" she asked. And Sophie smiled.

"Speaking of five-step plans. I've gotta run over to Jacie's before my date tonight. We're working on a new one," she said

Candy grinned. "Of course you are. And by the way, Blake brought some flowers over this morning for you. I put them in some water. They're on the kitchen table. There's a card."

Sophie sighed and grabbed her purse. "I'm out of here. Jacie's going to have to give me a five-step plan on how to get rid of Blake now."

Candy watched her daughter drive away and smiled. Sophie was growing up. She'd be gone soon. But that no longer filled her with fear. She had her own five-step plan for happiness now. And the first step was not being scared to death of dating.

chapter 16

Sophie walked right into Jacie's house without knocking and waved at Jacie's mom, Helen, before walking back to Jacie's bedroom. She'd practically grown up at Jacie's house. She hadn't rung their doorbell in . . . well, actually, she couldn't remember.

Sophie poked her head around Jacie's door. "Hello? Anyone here?" she asked, noticing the lump under the covers move slightly.

Jacie raised her head and stared blearily at Sophie. "Oh yeah," she said and yawned wide enough to split her jaw. "What time is it?" she asked, trying to sit up, and failing laid back down.

Sophie laughed and pulled the blinds up on her window.

"It's almost twelve thirty, you slacker. And you're working from two to six today, so you better get your rear up or you'll be fired. I know your boss and she's hard core," Sophie said, not really kidding.

Jacie put her arm over her eyes and groaned.

"What's the deal anyway? What did you do last night after I left? You look like you haven't even slept," Sophie muttered, leaning over to pick up some of Jacie's clothes she'd flung here and there.

Jacie turned on her side and lifted her head onto her chin.

"I stayed up going through my box of Bryan's stuff. You know, our prom picture. The first valentine card he sent me. Everything," she said sadly.

Sophie sighed and threw the pile of clothes in the corner before sitting down beside her friend.

"And why are you torturing yourself?" she asked kindly.

Jacie groaned again. "I don't know. It's not like I can help it. It's my only connection to him now. It's like I can't breathe anymore now that I know he'll be home soon."

Sophie shook her head and got up to grab some paper and a pen out of Jacie's desk. She turned to a blank page and sat down again.

"Okay. The five step plan for getting *yer* man back. Step one," Sophie said and looked up.

Jacie was staring at her from under her messy blonde bangs. Sophie didn't look like she was playing.

"It won't work, Sophie. I'm not wasting my time or my pride," Jacie said, turning on her back again.

Sophie frowned and leaned closer to Jacie so she couldn't ignore her.

"So you'd rather have your pride than Bryan? *Really?* Because you've had your pride for the last two years, and call me crazy, but I don't think you and your pride like hanging out so much anymore," Sophie said.

Jacie snorted but didn't say anything, so Sophie went on.

"And as far as wasting your time, what exactly is it that you have to do that you can't spend a little time trying to get the love of your life back? Huh? Cause from where I'm sitting—" Sophie was interrupted by a very large pillow, thrown actually very hard at her head.

"Shut *UP,* Sophie! Okay. We'll plan this out. But so help me, if I end up the laughingstock of Alpine, I'm blaming you," Jacie said, dead serious.

Sophie rolled her eyes and grabbed the pad of paper that had been knocked to the floor.

"Hey, *I'm* the laughingstock of Alpine. Remember Blake? It's really no big deal. Trust me, I'm still breathing."

Jacie nodded her head in agreement. Sophie had a point.

"Okay. Step number one. If I were planning this out for you, what would I tell you? Hmmm. What would I say?" Jacie pondered as she brought her knees up to rest her chin on.

Sophie looked at her with her pen poised.

"I'd say something like, 'Why not write him a letter?' " Jacie said with an eyebrow raised questioningly.

Sophie considered. "Well, what about his email address? It's easier and you'd get a response faster. Depending on what his mission rules are, of course, but it's a good start," Sophie said writing it down.

"I could get it from Lincoln. They're best friends. He got back from his mission a month ago. I saw him at Kohlers the other day.

Maybe I'll give him a call," Jacie said, sounding unsure.

Sophie stared at her friend. It wasn't like Jacie to be unsure or shy or scared of anything or anyone. It wasn't like Jacie at all.

"Well, what would I say to him, Sophie? It's been two years. What would I say?" Jacie asked, sounding very small and very unsure of herself.

Sophie sighed and put her pen down. "How about, 'I miss you. I love you. Can I see you when you get home?' " she said.

Jacie sighed loudly and shook her head. "You make it sound so easy. What idiot would say that?" she asked angrily.

Sophie glared at her friend. "Listen, geek. You've wasted two years. Why in the world would you want to waste any more time? Be honest with him, Jacie. Just tell him the truth," she said.

Jacie looked at her friend and bit her lip. A few seconds later, she nodded her head. "Okay. I'll do it. I'll call Lincoln and get his email address. I'll write Bryan and see what happens. Hey, what's the worst that could happen? He doesn't want to see me or talk to me? Heck, that's my life right now anyway. And I hate it," she said sadly.

Sophie put the paper back on Jacie's desk and walked over to give her friend a hug.

"Listen, I want you to get up and shower and eat and get ready for work. You'll feel better. Then call Lincoln. I've gotta go run some errands, so I'll check on you later, okay?" Sophie said.

Jacie nodded and hugged her back.

"Okay. And thanks, Sophie. Sorry I'm such a grouch. I've just been feeling sorry for myself, I guess."

Sophie laughed. "Hey, I was there just a few days ago. Pretty soon it will be you on top of the world and me down in the dumps because of one thing or another. That's just life," she said and waved before walking out.

Sophie got in her Jeep and turned toward South Town Mall. The biggest errand she had to do was to pick out something to wear for her date that night. And with Lexie's ultra-awesome tip money, she could buy whatever she felt like. She hadn't mentioned it to Jacie because she had a hunch Jacie wouldn't have been in the mood to truly appreciate the depth of her excitement about this date. Well, that and Jacie wanted her to go for Paul. She'd just tell Jacie later that night. Maybe.

chapter 17

Four hours later, Sophie was back home, laying her new skirt and top on her bed. She hadn't wanted to go with a dress. Too much for a first date. She didn't want Sam to think she was that excited. Better to play hard to get. The one lesson she had learned from Blake. Don't throw everything you had at the guy all at once. Take things slowly. No need to plan the wedding yet. So skirt it was. But it was so darling. Long denim that was sleek on the hips and then flared out at the bottom. And the top she had picked was perfect. Slim through the waist, but with a modest little tie around on top. Perfect. Now, all she had to do was touch up her hair and makeup and she was set.

Sam had mentioned Mexican, her favorite. But where was he taking her? She had no clue. Heels or flats? Sophie cocked her head, studied the outfit, and thought about Sam. Heels. Definitely. He was so tall anyway; she needed heels just to look into his face.

Sophie spent the next hour getting ready and chatting with her mom, who was busy getting ready for her own date. Sophie and her mom hadn't giggled this much together since she had been a little girl. They were having a lot of fun. Sophie insisted on doing her mom's nails and hair. Her mom was on her own for her makeup, but when they were both done, they stood and looked at each other in her mom's bedroom mirror and couldn't stop grinning.

Sophie slung her arm over her mom's shoulder, feeling a little protective and very proud of her at the same time. Candy had come a long way. She had struggled through her divorce and raised her daughter single-handedly, all the while starting a business. *This guy better appreciate her*, Sophie thought darkly. If just one more guy dumped her, she'd . . . Sophie let the thought slip away. Better to think positive.

"Okay, gorgeous. Now what perfume are you wearing? Something sexy? Something fun? Or something just clean and fresh?" Sophie asked looking through her mom's perfume bottles.

Candy picked up one and then the other. "Oh, I don't know, Sophie. I don't want to seem too sexy. What if he wants to kiss me or something? I think I'd have a heart attack. Why don't we stick with clean and fresh?" Candy said worriedly as the time drew closer for her date to arrive.

Sophie smiled at her mom and picked up *Design* by Paul Sebastian. *A little sexy never hurt anyone*, she thought. She spritzed her mom and pushed her out the door before Candy could figure out what was going on.

"Now, you have your cell phone in your purse in case you need to call me, right?" Sophie asked.

Candy nodded her head obediently and put her phone in her purse.

"Okay, now do you have some cash on you in case this guy expects you to pay?" Sophie asked.

Candy looked worried but checked her pocketbook just to make sure.

"Good. Now if you feel weird, or like something isn't right or you just want to leave, what do you do?" Sophie asked, her hands on her hips.

Candy bit her lip and looked up at the ceiling.

"Is this where I punch the guy, or where I open the car door and fling myself out to safety?" she asked, completely serious.

Sophie laughed. "Mom, I'm glad you watch Oprah, but we're not to that part yet. If you feel weird or like something isn't right, just tell him you're not feeling well and that you need to come home. Or go to the ladies room, call me, and then I'll call you with an emergency in five minutes. Something like that. This is the twenty-first century. You're an intelligent, beautiful woman. Be prepared," she commanded.

Candy nodded but then collapsed in a chair by the table.

"Sophie, now you have me all worried. I don't think I'm going to have any fun," she said sadly.

Sophie winced and sat down next to her mom.

"Well, that's because you have to let me finish. Now that you're prepared for the worst, now let's prepare you for the best. This is a

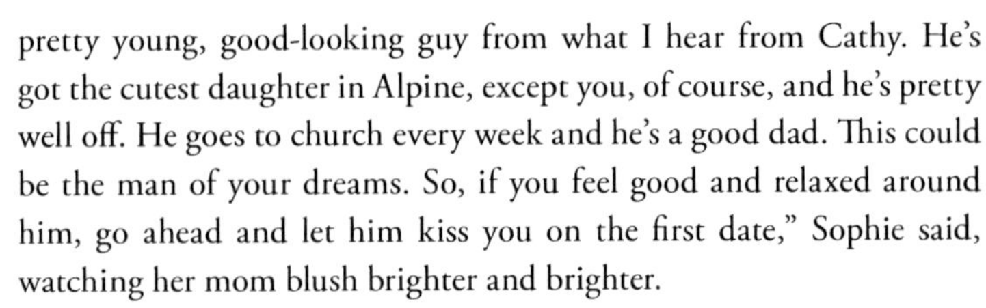

pretty young, good-looking guy from what I hear from Cathy. He's got the cutest daughter in Alpine, except you, of course, and he's pretty well off. He goes to church every week and he's a good dad. This could be the man of your dreams. So, if you feel good and relaxed around him, go ahead and let him kiss you on the first date," Sophie said, watching her mom blush brighter and brighter.

Candy got up to get a drink of water before turning around to face her daughter.

"Sophie, I haven't kissed a man since your father. I think I should cancel. I'm just not ready for this," Candy said, walking toward the phone.

Sophie leapt toward the counter and grabbed the phone away from her mom.

"Mom, don't you dare chicken out. Remember? We're in this together. And I told you how fun kissing is. Probably because I don't have to kiss Blake. But I digress. Maybe Clyde hasn't kissed anyone since his wife left him. Maybe he's so nervous he's green. And what would happen if you cancel on him now? He'd be crushed. Now you just grab your courage by the short hairs and fix your lip gloss. Get the one that tastes like lemonade. It's perfect for kissing," Sophie said with a giggle.

Candy shook her head and laughed. "I know you're teasing me, Sophie, because if you're serious, I'm calling the bishop right now, and you can forget about going out with Sam."

Sophie rolled her eyes but then leaned down and kissed her mom on the cheek.

"Okay, maybe I was teasing you, but still, you gotta trust the expert here; and sadly, that's me. So you go and get that lip gloss before your date gets here," she said with a grin.

"Now when did you get so bossy? I'm the mom here," Candy said but ran back to the bathroom to grab the lemonade lip gloss.

The doorbell rang and Sophie hurried to answer it. It was only five thirty, so she knew it had to be her mom's date. She opened the door to see a man standing on the front porch. He wasn't nervous at all, though. He was smiling confidently. And he looked very nice. Not as tall as Sam, kind of smaller through the shoulders too, but still very nice looking. Dark blond hair, blue eyes. *Nice face really*, Sophie thought. She smiled and invited him in, shaking his hand and introducing herself.

"Hi. I'm Sophie, Candy's daughter. And you must be Clyde," she said.

He laughed, a happy relaxed sound, and said, "I've been wanting to ask your mom out on a date for so long; I can't believe I'm actually here. Is she ready?" he asked, looking excited.

Sophie sighed and felt a burst of happiness for her mom. Clyde was excited to go out with her mom. That was so sweet.

"Here I am, Clyde." Candy said, walking down the hallway toward them.

Sophie watched as Clyde's smile turned into a grin. He pulled a rose from behind his back and handed it to Candy. Sophie loved the romance of it and was proud of her mom when she took the rose and smiled graciously at Clyde. She wasn't flustered one bit. Bravo!

"Sophie, will you put this in a vase for me?" Candy asked, smelling the flower first. Sophie took the rose and nodded without saying anything.

Clyde opened the door for her and took her by the arm. "Let's go have some fun, Candy. What do you say?"

Candy smiled up into Clyde's face and let herself be led out the door. "I can't wait. Bye, Sophie," she said, and then they were gone.

Sophie ran to the living room window to watch as Clyde opened the door for her mother and gently helped her into the car. He ran behind the car to the other side and got in. Sophie grabbed the digital camera from her pocket and took a quick picture of the car driving away. You never knew. If this was the man for her mom, wouldn't they love to have that picture? She would.

She walked back to the kitchen and got a vase out of the cabinet under the sink, filling it with water and putting it in the middle of the table. Perfect.

The doorbell rang again, and Sophie glanced at the clock. It was only five forty-five. Sam was fifteen minutes early. *Strange*, she thought and walked quickly toward the door, smiling as she opened it.

Blake. Why was Blake on her front door step? Again!

"Hey, Sophie. Man, you get better looking every second. Mind if I come in?" he asked, and then walked right past her and into the house, leaving her shocked and her mouth hanging open. She slowly shut the door and turned to see that Blake had walked into the living room and sat down on the couch, patting the seat next to him with a smile.

"Blake, seriously. What is going on here? Did you call Bailey like I told you to?" she asked and then walked toward him, sitting as far away from him on the couch as she could.

Blake smiled at her and moved closer. "Sophie, let's not talk about Bailey. I want to talk about us. I've been doing a lot of thinking lately, and I just think I deserve a second chance here. I mean, I messed up, but a little forgiveness would go a long way. I know you were mad at me. But now that Bailey's gone, let's just give it one more try. I'm not going to give up, Sophie. I can't. When I realized that you were going out with other guys, it just killed me. I can't stand it, Sophie. It was then that I realized that you belong with me. Just give me another chance. And this time I'm not taking no for an answer," he demanded, his blond hair sticking up in strange places and his bright blue eyes gleaming earnestly.

Sophie felt her heart soften a fraction.

"Blake, please stop listening to your mom and dad when it comes to your love life. Have you called Bailey?" she asked again.

Blake shook his head frowning. "Look, Sophie. This has nothing to do with my mom and dad or Bailey. I'm not even living at home anymore. I moved in with some of my old mission companions. I drove up here from Orem just to see you," he said

Sophie bit her lip frowning. This was sounding serious.

"I just can't do this right now. I have a date in like, five minutes. What if I promise to call you tomorrow, okay?"

Blake jumped off the couch and started pacing back and forth. Sophie sat back on the couch, staring in surprise. This wasn't like Blake at all.

"Blake, what is going on with you?" Sophie asked.

Blake stopped in front of her. "What do you expect, Sophie? I screw up everything, and now when I'm trying to fix it, you don't want me to. You just want to go out with other guys. You're killing me! I don't know how much more of this I can handle. I love you," he said desperately.

Sophie shook her head in surprise. Too little, too late.

"If you loved me so much, why did you hook up with Bailey on your mission? Why, all of a sudden, do you think you love me?" she asked.

Blake paused and stared out the window, shoving his hands in his pockets.

"I don't know. I just know I do. I mean, I'm just so used to having you around. And now that you're not, nothing's right anymore. Nothing feels good anymore. I'm miserable. And I just know if I have you back, then I can be happy again," he said sadly.

Sophie pursed her lips. "Blake, I've heard about this happening. It's really very normal. You're just back from your mission, and the world is strange all of a sudden. You don't have your routine anymore. You don't have your companion anymore. And life is just a little too fast and too aggressive. I can see how you might feel safer pulling away from Bailey and getting back together with me. I'm like you're old best friend. Someone safe and someone fun that doesn't put any pressure on you. Especially physically. You know we never had that. But just give it some time, Blake. Let yourself get used to life again. If Bailey scares you right now, take things slow. Heck, go out on a date with her. Hold her hand before you ask her to marry you. But running back to me is not the answer. Not for you, and really not for me," Sophie said firmly.

Blake ran his hands through his hair and his face fell.

"Just give us one more chance, Sophie. Please. That's all I'm asking. One month, to prove that we're still meant for each other," he begged.

Sophie shook her head immediately. "I'm sorry. No," she said firmly.

She got up off the couch and walked toward the front door. As she touched the door knob to turn it, the doorbell rang. She couldn't quite stop from groaning but opened the door anyway. He was right on time.

"Hi, Sam," she said with a half-smile.

"Hey," he said and stepped into the doorway.

Sophie tried to motion with her eyes toward Blake, but Sam wasn't catching on.

"Wow, you look amazing. Are you ready to go?" he asked and then did the unpardonable. He grabbed her hand in such a relaxed and possessive way that Sophie could just feel the tension coming off Blake in waves.

"Get away from her!" Blake yelled as he launched himself off the couch and pulled Sophie away from Sam. With a stricken look on his face, he pushed Sam backward out of the house and down the steps.

Sophie ran out of the house after Blake and Sam, horrified at what Blake was trying to do to Sam, who was huge compared to Blake.

Sam looked surprised at first and then became supremely ticked off.

"You must be Blake," Sam said with a friendly smile, after easily pushing Blake's hands off his shoulders.

Blake was breathing hard, his nostrils flaring and his hands fisted at his side. She could tell he really wanted to fight Sam, either to prove to her how much he loved her, or who knows, just because he was having a bad week and needed to let off some steam. But what a bad choice for a fight. Sam would kill him.

"Blake, please stop. Just go home. Okay?" Sophie pleaded, not wanting him to get hurt.

Blake ignored her and stepped closer to Sam. "Stop asking my girlfriend out. She's taken," he said in an artificially deep voice Sophie had never heard before.

Sam laughed in Blake's face. "Oh right. You dump her at the airport in front of your fiancée, but she's supposed to stay at home pining for you for the rest of her life, waiting for you to come to your senses? That's the most selfish, heartless thing I've ever heard of," Sam said, starting to look even more ticked off.

Sophie opened her mouth to say something but snapped it shut. Sam had a point.

Blake started to grind his teeth. "This is none of your business! You don't even know me. Me and Sophie are getting back together. Now just leave, or you're going to regret it," Blake threatened.

Sam stared at him in surprise. He looked over at Sophie and raised one eyebrow as if to say, Is this guy for real? Sophie shrugged. She had no clue.

"Hey man, if you want to fight, bring it. But if you don't, and you're just looking tough for Sophie, then you're being a real idiot. I'm here to take Sophie out on a date, which she agreed to. She wants to go out with me. Not you. Me. So even if you do punch me or something, she's not going with you. She doesn't want to. Now what's it going to be? You want to leave on your own, or do you want to start something?" Sam said, undoing his buttons on his cuffs and pushing his sleeves up to his elbows. He took his keys and his cell phone out of his pocket and handed them to Sophie without another word.

Sophie knew Blake had never been in a fight in his life, and by the way his face was turning a pale gray, he was just now realizing that. Blake cleared his throat nervously and shuffled his feet.

"I , um . . . I don't want to fight you. I'm sorry I pushed you. I apologize. Sophie, I'll call you tomorrow," Blake said and walked quickly toward his car.

Sophie and Sam stood and watched him drive away. Sam rebuttoned his cuffs and took his keys and cell phone back from Sophie before looking at her and grinning.

"Any more lovesick men hanging around here, obsessed and ready to beat me up?" Sam asked.

Sophie laughed weakly and shook her head. "Not that I know of. Sam, I'm so sorry. Blake's just going though a rough patch right now. He's used to his mission, and now everything is weird for him so he thinks if he gets back together with me, then everything will be all right. He just needs a little time. Thanks for not hitting him, though."

Sam shrugged. "Yeah, his next girlfriend wouldn't be very happy if I messed up that pretty face of his. Wow. I can't even picture you with that guy. What were you thinking? He is so completely wrong for you."

Sophie smiled and walked back toward the house to grab her purse and lock up.

"And why is that?" she asked, turning back to grin at him. "What kind of guy am I supposed to be with?"

Sam grabbed her keys and locked the door for her and then took her hand, walking her toward his truck.

"That guy's still a kid. He's gotta grow up some. You need a man who knows his own mind. Who knows what he wants and goes for it. You need someone like me," he said with a cocky grin.

Sophie laughed but couldn't help a flood of nervousness suddenly pooling around her middle.

"Sam, why don't we go on our first date before we decide anything? Okay?" she asked with a prim nod.

Sam opened the door and helped her up. "Honey, why waste time? If you want something, get it. That's why you're here with me right now. I saw you and here you are. End of story," he said and shut the door, to walk around to the other side.

Or beginning, she thought with a small smile. It was a relief, not having to guess what Sam was thinking. With Blake, she never knew what was going on. Did he want her? Did he want Bailey? Sam just told you flat out. Scary. But a lot less guesswork.

chapter 18

Sophie laughed when Sam drove over the Point of the Mountain to Bajio Grill in Draper.

"This is the best Mexican food in Utah?" she asked, glad she hadn't worn a dress.

Sam grinned and walked around the truck to open the door for her.

"Hey, you can trust my opinion. I'm an expert on Mexican food. I've tried them all out and have come to the conclusion that Bajio Grill is the best," he said, still smiling at her as he opened the door for her.

Sophie smiled and relaxed. She had to admit, a big fancy, formal date would have made her nervous. This was more up her alley. Just being with Sam made her nervous enough.

"You know a lot of people would disagree with you. My best friend, Jacie, is so addicted to Café Rio, she'd argue for hours with you about it," Sophie said, reminding herself that she had to call Jacie when she got home that night.

Sam laid a hand on the small of her back and led her to the end of the line, where the menu was written on the wall.

"Well, now, Jacie doesn't know everything, does she," he said, staring up at the wall, his attention now on his dinner.

Sophie decided on a Mexican pizza with pork, mango salsa, and guacamole. Sam ordered fajitas with lemon chicken. They carried their food to a table in the corner. Sam took their cups and got their drinks for them and brought back the napkins and their forks.

They dug into their food as if they hadn't eaten in days. Sophie paused to breath and looked up with a smile.

"You know what? You might be right. This is really, really good," she said.

"Just don't tell Jacie. I don't want her mad at me," he said and took a sip of his Apple Beer.

Sophie laughed and took another bite. "So tell me a little bit about yourself. I don't know that much, to be honest. You're Julie's nephew. You're a contractor and a returned missionary. What else should I know about you?" Sophie asked as she dabbed her lips with her napkin.

Sam finished his bite and sat back as he thought about it. "Good question. Um, I'm the oldest of six children. I have two brothers and three sisters. I have a brother on a mission right now in Ecuador. My other brother, Trey, is at BYU going to school. He wants to be a teacher. He's a great kid. My little sisters are all still in high school. They're the cutest things you've ever seen," he said, taking out a picture from his wallet.

Sophie smiled at his obvious love for his family and leaned over to see. He held a small picture of three teenage girls in gymnastics outfits, holding up medals and grinning their heads off. They were all tall, blonde, and very muscular. They were gorgeous. Sophie swallowed nervously. What would they think of her? A small town hairdresser. And with not that many muscles to speak of.

"They look incredible, Sam. You must be very proud," she said honestly.

Sam grinned and put the picture back. "Yeah, they're awesome. I feel bad for whoever ends up marrying them though. They're a handful. So headstrong. Those girls could rule the world if they wanted to," he said still smiling.

"Do you see your family much?" Sophie asked, taking another bite even though she was about to burst.

"Every day, most of the time. My family lives here in Draper. My house is just up in Suncrest, so we see a lot of each other. My mom's always coming by and bringing me leftovers or something. She knows I hate to cook. She's a good mom," he said.

Sophie smiled at the thought. "Wow, it's like you have the perfect family," she said, feeling and sounding jealous.

Sam smiled kindly at her and turned the conversation around.

"So tell me about yourself. I don't know that much, except what Julie has told me. Just that your family isn't perfect by a long shot. They sound more like a high school clique than a family," he said with a raised eyebrow.

Sophie laughed at the description.

"Well, you might have a point. As Julie told you, my dad left us when I was ten, and that's when he got together with your aunt. Things weren't that great after the divorce. My mom didn't get any money in the divorce, so she started her own business, doing hair. She's doing really well too. We have clients coming from Lindon, American Fork, Pleasant Grove, and Lehi. We're starting to get a good solid reputation," she said, trying to steer the conversation away from her seriously weird family.

Sam wasn't having any of that, though. "Yeah, your mom sounds incredible. But what about you? How did you handle the divorce and then having to deal with all of your relatives? How did you do it?" he asked curiously.

Sophie sighed and put her fork down and took a sip of her Apple Beer before speaking. She looked at Sam and wondered how someone who came from the perfect family would react to hearing about the strangest family in Alpine.

"I don't know. How do you handle anything? You just keep breathing. You just keep living. Every month I have to go spend an afternoon with my dad and his relatives. It's always the last Sunday of the month, and it's the one day every month I hate. My grandmother is there, and my dad and my aunt and her husband and my cousins. I feel like I'm going into battle and if I get back home alive then I'm doing good. One day when I was twelve years old, I had to go over to my dad's new house, and I was just dreading it. Daphne ran up to me as soon as I got there and told me how Grandmother had flown her and Farrah to Disneyland for a week. And she couldn't wait to tell me all of the details. She couldn't wait to tell me how much Grandmother loved her more than me. And that's just typical. Stuff like that happened all the time. When I was eighteen, I told my mom I was disowning that whole side of the family. I think the only reason I go now is so I can see my little brother and sister. It's not to see my dad, that's for sure," she said with feeling.

Sam looked at her frowning. "Sounds like you have some real issues with your dad," he said with a sad shake of his head.

Sophie glared at him. "Excuse me? Are you judging me?" she demanded, turning red in the face.

Sam blinked and held his hands up. "Whoa there! Whoa! No, I was not judging you. But when you know what it's like to have a great dad and have that unconditional love, then you can't help but feel for people who don't. I'm sorry, Sophie. I didn't mean to hurt your feelings. I'm sure your problems with your dad aren't your fault," he said quickly.

Sophie blushed and took another sip. "Sorry. I guess I am a little defensive. Or embarrassed. It seems like everyone in Alpine has the perfect family. And then there's Sophie Reid. I'm the fly in the pie. Poor little dysfunctional me," she said with a bitter laugh.

Sam frowned again and grabbed Sophie's hand. "Look, Sophie, I'll admit that your relatives aren't the best and they don't treat you well. But there are people out there who have it so much worse than you. Not me, granted. But when I was on my mission, my heart broke almost every day. I felt like coming home and crying my eyes out at the kids I saw and what they had to go through. I'm talking about serious abuse here. Kids whose parents were drugged up and out of control. My companion and I worked the inner city for six months before getting transferred. Your life isn't perfect, but it's so much better than what's out there. You have a mom who loves you and took good care of you. And look at you now. Beautiful, funny, and talented. Someone I really like. You have a lot to be grateful for," he said and then had the nerve to shove more food in his mouth.

Sophie closed her eyes in irritation. He reminded her of a lady in her ward who constantly gave Relief Society lessons about how it didn't matter how horrible your relatives were or what they did to you—you had to forgive them. And if you didn't, then you were a real loser. Which was true to some extent, maybe, but coming from someone who had been raised by a stake president under the best conditions possible, it was just incredibly obnoxious. Whatever happened to "thou shalt not judge"? Sophie sighed and played along with Sam. She was on a date.

"Sorry," she said. "I guess that was a little immature of me. But you wanted to know. You're the one who asked. I'm not saying I don't need my fair share of counseling. I've read the magazine articles. I know I have abandonment issues. I'll probably end up marrying some fifty-year-old guy because I'm trying to marry a father figure or something weird. But hey. That's me. Take it or leave it," she said and laid her napkin on the table.

Sam smiled at her and got up to get a refill. "Hey, I knew what I was getting into when I asked you out. But do I like the boring life? Heck no. I like my food spicy and my women interesting. Not too bent. But interesting," he said with a laugh and walked away.

Sophie sniffed. As if she cared. But as she watched him walk away, she couldn't help a feeling of longing from exploding where her heart was. She'd seen his sisters. Happy, talented, well cared for. That's what she wanted. Okay, not for herself anymore. Gymnastics lessons were out now. But someday when she was married, she wanted that life. She wanted to have a husband and children she could spoil and love. She wanted a normal life with family get-togethers that were fun, not stressful and awkward. Fun. She wanted . . . oops! She'd almost said Sam. Sophie shook her head and tapped her head with her fist. *Knock it off, Sophie! This is your first date. Just because this guy is normal and happy doesn't mean you should throw yourself at him. Slow down!*

Sam sat back down a minute later and finally pushed his plate away.

"I love this place," he said. "You actually get full. I could go to a nice sit-down restaurant, wait twenty minutes for a table, pay a huge tip, and then have to go home and heat up a frozen burrito. Nope, this is the place," he said, his voice filled with love.

Sophie grinned at him and pushed her plate away. "I think I just gained five pounds. But I'll hand it to you. It was good. And if you promise not tell Jacie, I'll agree Bajio is better than Café Rio."

Sam leaned over and grabbed her hand. "I love a woman who agrees with me. It's good for the soul," he said and then took their plates to dump them.

"So now what?" Sophie asked, following Sam back outside.

Sam opened the door and helped her up into the truck before answering.

"Oh, I thought I'd take you back to my place. Give you a tour of my house. I have a great view at sunset. You'll love it," he promised.

Sophie smiled but felt a little bit uneasy. His house? Uh-oh. But she was curious. She'd be interested to see what a single man did with a whole house. She'd seen some of her guy friend's apartments. They were pretty sad.

When Sam was sitting beside her again in the truck, she smiled. "Sounds good. Let's go see your sunset," she said and leaned back in the comfortable leather seat. She put the conversation about her family behind her and concentrated on enjoying Sam's company. She was on a date with a gorgeous man, one who seemed to like her for some weird reason, and now she was getting ready to see a sunset with him. This could not be bad.

chapter 19

Sam drove up the twisting streets, past bigger and bigger homes, toward the top of the mountain. Sophie looked out her window at the view of Salt Lake Valley and felt a catch in her heart. It was so beautiful. So sparkly.

"You must love it up here," she breathed, still staring at the clear night.

Sam laughed. "Just wait until winter. There's snow up here when it's dry down in the valley. And clouds? They love us. On clear nights, though, it's great. But sometimes on foggy days, you wonder if you made the right decision. And then the next night is so beautiful you forget to call the realtor. For the most part, I love it. I feel like I'm king of the hill most of the time. And for the days I don't, I go and hang out at my mom and dad's," he said and pulled into a small subdivision on the right. He drove farther down the road, twisting and turning until Sophie was so confused she knew that even with bread crumbs she'd never find her way back out.

He finally stopped at a house sitting back from the road. It was huge. Lots of brick, rock, stucco, and copper. It was different than most of the houses she was used to, though. The houses up here looked like they belonged in Park City. Tons of wooden beams and artistic touches. This was no cookie cutter house. It looked like a two-story, but when Sam opened the door and pulled her inside, Sophie could see it was a rambler with incredibly tall vaulted ceilings. It was the most incredible house she'd ever been in. It made her dad's McMansion seem so boring.

"Sam, I can't believe this is your house. You really live here?" she asked.

Sam shrugged and threw his keys on the glossy wooden table in the hallway. "It's home," he said simply and walked down the hallway of the entrance and into the great room. Sophie followed, staring wide-eyed at everything in sight.

He must have had a professional decorator, because it could have been out of a magazine. It was that perfect. The walls were a muted brown. She felt like she was surrounded by milk chocolate, but instead of feeling dark and oppressive, the color was warm and comforting. It did have a masculine appeal to it, for sure. Whoever decorated it had decorated it with Sam in mind and no one else. She was sure of it.

Sophie walked slowly into the great room and wasn't surprised to see a two-story rock fireplace. Everywhere she looked there were couches and tables and chairs. On the walls were beautiful pictures. Some religious, some of the red rocks in Southern Utah. Some were blown up photographs of places she had never seen. It was incredible. And then it hit her.

"Oh no. You're rich," she whispered, shocked and a little put off.

Sam laughed and sat down on one of the couches, putting his arm over the back.

"Now wait a second. Why do you sound so horrified? I thought that was a good thing," he said curiously.

Sophie blushed and walked over toward him but sat down in a chair across from him, rather than next to him on the couch. She was too nervous now. She'd never dated anyone rich. She'd been out with two guys before Blake, and she didn't count them. Blake's parents were comfortable, but this . . . this was a whole new level.

"I don't know. I guess when you grow up as poor as me, rich people seem like a different species. Different culture with different customs, and even a different language. Just different," she said with a frown.

Sam studied Sophie and crossed his legs at the ankle.

"Hmm. I see. Well, if it helps, I'll explain a little. My dad's family does have money. As you know from Julie, we all have trust funds. My grandfather owns a publishing company down in California. He publishes things like cookbooks and biographies. But I don't come into my trust fund until I'm thirty," he said.

Sophie blinked. "But you're not thirty," she said in confusion.

Sam smiled. "Hey, I'm a contractor. I build houses. It's a good business in Utah. One of the best actually. But I've earned every penny. I look at this house as a good investment. Sometimes I have business meetings here with clients. They like to see what I can do. It makes them relax. Unlike you," he said looking at her curiously.

Sophie blushed and folded her arms across her chest. She couldn't help that it made her nervous he lived in a Parade of Homes house on top of the mountain. Holy cow.

"Let me turn off all the lights in the house and you can see the sunset better," he said turning to grab a remote control. He pushed a few buttons, and all the lights in the house dimmed. She looked past Sam out the back windows and was transfixed. It was the most beautiful thing she'd ever seen.

"You must love it up here. I would never want to leave," she said softly.

Sam didn't say anything. He turned the lights back on and got up from the couch. "Do you want something to drink? I have everything. My mom keeps my fridge stocked," he said walking away from her toward the kitchen.

"I'll take a Fresca," Sophie said and smiled as she followed him into another work of art. She covered her mouth to cover the gasp and gaped at the kitchen. Granite countertops, Alder cabinets to the ceiling. Travertine tile. It was just too much.

"Please don't show me your bathrooms. I don't think I can take it," she whispered.

Sam laughed and opened the fridge. "I'll take that as a compliment. Here you go," he said and popped the top for her.

She grabbed the can and smiled her thanks.

"Yeah, kitchens are my forte. When you make the woman happy, the rest is easy," he said leaning up against the counter.

Sophie leaned on the opposite counter and smiled at him.

"I apologize for being so shocked, but you have to put yourself in my shoes. This is a little intimidating," she said, smiling apologetically at him.

Sam grinned at her and grabbed her empty hand. "No problem. At least I know you're not going out with me because of my money. Heck, I'll be lucky if you answer my calls now."

Sophie smiled and squeezed his hand back. "Hey, if you can accept me with all of my flaws, I can let this one go," she said with a grin.

Sam laughed and grabbed her hand. "Let's go sit out on the deck. It'll be great. Just you and me and some good conversation," he said.

She smiled and followed him onto his back deck. She stood at the rail and felt him put his arm around her shoulders. It felt good there. Not too scary. Just good. The warm breeze caressed her face and hair, and the fading light touched everything in rose and gold. It was the perfect night.

"This is just too amazing. This is the perfect place for a party. Everyone could come out here and just socialize. How nice," she murmured.

Sam nodded. "I've had a couple, but I've been so busy lately, I haven't had much time for parties."

Sophie leaned into Sam's side and sighed. She could stand out here forever like this.

"I'm a little surprised that you're not married," Sophie said with a laugh, looking up at Sam. "I mean, you're in your late twenties, you're rich, you're smart—and don't let this go to your head or anything, but you're drop dead gorgeous. You should have two kids by now. What's the deal?" she asked with a grin.

Sam smiled down at her and rubbed her shoulders. "Oh you know, just haven't met the right person yet, I guess. I was pretty close to being engaged a couple months ago to be honest. But it didn't feel right. I stepped back and decided I needed a little space. And then I met you," he said tensely looking out over the valley.

Sophie blinked. He had been almost engaged two months ago? That sounded serious.

"So what happened to this girl you were almost engaged to? Does she live around here?" she asked, feeling a little strange all of the sudden.

Sam sighed and took his hand off her shoulder to lean both arms on the railing.

"Sophie, you don't really want to know all this stuff, do you?" he asked, sounding strained.

Sophie stood up straighter. "Yes, actually, I do. I mean, are you still seeing this girl? Are you cheating on her with me?" she asked, horrified at the thought. *Please say no. Please say no!*

Sam glanced at her and frowned. Then he looked away again without saying anything.

Sophie closed her eyes and turned her back on the sunset.

"You are. You're still with this girl. Aren't you? Sam, why am I here?" she asked sadly.

Sam stood up and walked over to the French doors, opening them up and gesturing for her to walk through them. Sophie walked past him and over to a couch. She sat down and waited for an explanation.

Sam walked over to a table with a bunch of pictures of family members scattered on it and picked one up. He looked at it without any expression on his face before walking over to Sophie. He handed the picture to her.

"This is a picture of Tess. She was my girlfriend for almost two years," he said without any excuses.

Sophie gulped and took the picture from him. Of course. Gorgeous blonde. Perfectly straight bright smile. Huge beautiful eyes. Classic. Perfect. His girlfriend.

"She's beautiful. Did you say *was*, as in past tense?" Sophie asked hopefully.

Sam took the picture and laid it down face first on the table. He walked slowly over and sat down next to her.

"When it came time to either marry her or let her go, I told her I wanted some time to myself to decide what I wanted to do. And she said okay, but when she saw me talking to another girl at a friend's party, she freaked out. She got so hysterical I was scared. My friend had to call the police. She started throwing things. She broke two of his windows and she threatened to kill herself." He paused and closed his eyes, remembering. "Let's just say that I'm in a transition stage here. I'm trying to ease her out of my life while at the same time keeping myself and her alive," he said turning to look out the window.

Sophie felt as if the wind had been knocked out of her. Tess was still hanging on to Sam. And what did it mean to ease out of a relationship? Did that mean he was still in the relationship? Sophie shook her head sadly as she thought of a girl so in love with a boy that she'd try to kill herself. She felt her heart go out to Tess.

"Sam, I don't know what to say. That's the saddest thing I've ever heard. I'm still a little confused, though. Does this mean that you're still seeing Tess?"

Sam winced and shoved his hands through his hair.

"It's complicated. No, I'm not dating her, and no I don't kiss her or anything, but yes, I am sort of still involved in her life to a point. I just don't know what to do sometimes. I've been trying to get her to see a counselor or something, but she refuses. I've been setting her up with some of my old college friends who are still single, but nothing seems to work. She'll seem fine for a while but then totally lose it if she finds out from somebody that I've been out on a date. I'll come home and find my house trashed or my mailbox run over, or she'll call some of these girls I've gone out with and tell them horrible things about me, like she's pregnant or that I used to beat her up. To be honest, I haven't dated anyone in two months, because I just got sick of all the drama. But I met you, and I knew I had to take a chance again. Now, I just have to make sure Tess doesn't find out about you," he said darkly, reaching over to grasp her hand.

Sophie looked down at Sam's large strong hand on hers and couldn't help wondering what Tess would think if she could see him now. What would she do? She felt a shiver of dread rip down her spine and slowly pulled her hand away.

"Sam, you can't date anyone until you deal with Tess. I shouldn't even be here right now. What if she came over and saw you and me together? She'd have a nervous breakdown," Sophie said in horror.

Sam looked at her sadly.

"By the time I found out what Tess was like, it was too late. She had even planned our wedding and honeymoon. She went out and bought herself a diamond engagement ring and then showed it to me one night. She said, "Doesn't this look perfect on my finger? I told her to immediately take it off, and that's when I tried to break up with her. Ever since then, I've been trying to extricate myself from her. But she's been very hard to get rid of. She's even made threats against my family," he said with a fierce look on his face.

Sophie's mouth fell open in shock. She might have crazy relatives, but Sam had her beat when it came to off-the-wall exes. Blake was looking very normal right now.

"Sam, this is just too freaky. You need a restraining order. Seriously," she said, looking behind her nervously.

Sam frowned and shook his head. "Funny thing. Her dad and my dad were best friends growing up. I haven't even told my parents what she's been up to. If I did, it would ruin my dad's relationship with Rick. My parents and her parents go on little golfing vacations together all the time. If I put a restraining order on Tess, their friendship would be over. I just have to deal with this on my own. I have to come up with a way to get her out of my life for good, without hurting anyone," he said, leaning his head back against the couch and sighing.

Sophie bit her lip, and frowned. Sam was in a huge mess.

"Well, when you tell her you're dating someone new, just be sure and mention you went out with Daphne—not me," she said with a smile, trying to lighten the mood.

Sam closed his eyes and smiled sadly. Wrong time for a joke.

"I just want you to know, Sophie, that I won't let her hurt you. You're too important to me. When I met you at Julie's house, I looked at you and just felt an instant connection. I really need to get to know you now. I think you and I could have something special," he said sitting up and turning toward her.

Sophie blinked and licked her lips. Yikes. "Yeah, um Sam, that sounds great and everything. I really like you too, but honestly, I can't go out with you if you have some crazy girlfriend still hanging on. It's just too dangerous for you and for me. There's no way you can protect me. You can't be with me all day every day. I'm sorry," she said and stood up.

Sam frowned and stood up too. He walked over and grabbed her purse for her.

"Sophie, don't you think some things are worth fighting for? I look at you and it makes me sick to think that you and I could really have something incredible here and we're wasting our chance just because of Tess. Just give me some time. Don't write me off yet. Just give me a chance to get free."

Sophie looked away and brushed the hair out of her eyes. Should she just say good-bye to Sam? Or should she wait until he was totally free of Tess? She remembered seeing Sam for the first time walking toward her with a smile and a handshake. She had definitely felt something. She had felt alive again.

"Sam, I just don't know. I have a lot to think about. But right now, I think you should take me home."

"And there goes my scalp massage," Sam muttered and turned to grab his keys off the table.

They walked silently out to the truck together. Not touching and not talking. He drove down the mountain and pulled up in front of her house. He turned off the truck and got out. She didn't wait for him to open the door for her, but jumped out quickly. He walked her up to her front door with his hands shoved in his pockets and a frown on his face.

Sophie paused on the porch and turned to look at him. "Sam, I felt that connection too. But then, so did Tess. And she's still very connected to you. I don't want to hurt her, and I don't want to hurt you. I don't want to hurt anyone," she said trying to explain her feelings to him.

Sam looked up at her from a few steps down and walked up to stand close to her.

"I know, Sophie. That's why I like you so much. There's something so sweet and gentle and good about you. I can't let you just walk out of my life. Just trust me. Everything's going to work out, I promise," he said, although he turned his head and looked down the street just the same.

Sophie looked too and frowned. Nope, living in fear was no way to start a relationship.

"Well, just the same, let's make it friends until Tess is gone," she said and held her hand out for a polite handshake.

Sam groaned loudly and looked down at her hand. "Oh, come on. Don't do that to me. Friends? Please, Sophie. I just told you how nice and sweet you were. Friends? You're killing me here," he said dramatically.

Sophie laughed and pulled her hand back.

"Fine! We'll leave it at somewhere in between. But if Tess shows up, I'm calling the cops," she said honestly.

Sam smiled and pulled her into a deep hug, resting his head on top of hers.

"It won't come to that. But if it did, then you have my blessing."

Sam pulled back and pushed her hair behind her ears.

"I'll call you tomorrow. By the way, Julie's having a family dinner or something at four o'clock and she wanted me to give you the invitation. She invited me to come with you. She said she didn't want you having to go by yourself," he said and turned to walk away from her.

Sophie watched him go and felt uneasy. She couldn't help the feeling that someone was about to get hurt. She hoped that just this once, it wouldn't be her.

chapter 20

Sophie walked inside her house and threw her keys down on the hallway table.

"Mom?" she called, cocking her ear for an answer. *Nothing.* Her mom was still on her date. She hoped that Candy was having a better time than she'd had. Sophie sighed and went to change out of her clothes and into some comfortable sweats. It was only nine thirty. Still pretty early. Especially for a Saturday night. She went into the family room and turned on the TV. She flipped through all the channels and sighed. It was like the TV people knew everyone was out having fun, so they purposefully put the worst, most boring shows they could think of on. Sophie turned the TV off and leaned her head back on the couch. She should call Jacie. She had promised.

She turned over and grabbed the phone off the coffee table and speed dialed her number. Jacie picked up on the first ring.

"You said you were going to call me. It's almost ten!" Jacie pouted.

Sophie smiled and relaxed against some pillows. Best friends were worth their weight in gold.

"I was on a date, believe it or not," Sophie said, leaning back and feeling the tightness in her head relax.

Jacie coughed into the receiver. "Man, if Blake could see you now. Where did Paul take you?" she asked.

Sophie sighed and twirled a long red curl around her fingers.

"Not Paul. *Sam.* And he took me to Bajio, which is way better than Café Rio—sorry. And then he took me on a tour of his house up in Suncrest," she said, getting up to go find some nail polish. She might as well do her toenails to match her dress for church the next day.

Jacie laughed into the phone. "Yeah right. No one's better than Café Rio. Sorry. You were just mesmerized by your date and didn't notice what you were shoveling in your mouth. Sam, huh? How was it?" she asked.

Sophie grabbed a pale shade of gold and walked back to the family room.

"It was fantastic for a while. He's gorgeous, funny, and fun to be with. He's smart and rich and perfect. Oh, and he has an ex-girlfriend that might want to kill me if she finds out he took me out to dinner," she said all in one breath.

Jacie paused before saying anything. "Run that by me again? That last part about the girlfriend."

Sophie laughed, trying to ignore the pain in her heart. "You heard right. He showed me her picture, Jacie. *Natural* blonde. Gorgeous. They dated for two years, but then he didn't feel like it was right so he broke up with her and she went nuts on him. Picture OJ Simpson in high heels and diamond stud earrings. No joke. I'm buying pepper spray first thing Monday morning," she said honestly.

Jacie hmmmed in the phone. "And you're the brave little lass to win his heart away from the wicked witch. It's interesting, I'll give you that. Good thing you have Paul. I can vouch for him. No crazy ex-girlfriends. And did I mention he's going to be a lawyer?" Jacie said with a pleading voice.

Sophie sighed. "Yeah, yeah. Paul. I like Paul, but there's just something about Sam. I just feel so drawn to him. I can't help it. But you would be proud of me. I told him absolutely that we were just friends until he gets rid of Tess. I'm seeing him tomorrow, though. No way out of it, really. I have to go to some wretched dinner at my father's house tomorrow with him. I don't know what to do. I think this calls for another five-step plan." Sophie said, switching to her other foot.

Jacie laughed into the phone. "How weird is that. We'll both be doing the How to Get Yer Man five-step plan. Well, same results, different steps. Um, I don't know, Sophie. This is a hard one. You don't want some crazed-out hussy to ruin your chances with Prince Charming, but on the other hand, she sounds kind of scary. I don't know if I can help you with that one. You know you could always just go back to Blake. Seriously, you already love his parents; you don't have to get to know him. And he feels so guilty about dumping you at the airport that he's ready to propose right now. No five-step plan needed."

Sophie groaned and told Jacie about the fight that almost happened between Blake and Sam. She thought of Blake and Sam and even Paul and all the other guys out in the world, and she wondered if she wanted Sam. She shook her head to clear all the men out.

"Enough about me," Sophie said. "What about your five-step plan on getting *yer* man back? Did you email him?" Sophie asked, screwing the lid back on the polish.

"I did," Jacie said and left it at that.

Sophie glared at the phone. "Hello! What did you say and has he emailed you back?" she asked.

Jacie laughed. "Duh, he can't write me back until his P-day. I kept it short and sweet. I said something like, 'Hey Bryan, I know you're getting home soon. Just wanted to say hey and that I hope we can get together when you get back.' Just really simple. Nothing mushy, nothing pathetic. What do you think?" Jacie couldn't help herself from asking.

Sophie tilted her head and thought about it.

"Perfect. That way, if he crushes you, it's no big deal. It's not like you're running to the airport with a sign, crying your eyes out and begging him to take you back. Not bad," she said.

Jacie sighed. "Well actually, I am thinking of going to the airport. You'll have to help me design a sign," she said

Sophie's eyes widened in surprise. Jacie was never the aggressor with guys. They always chased her. This was interesting. Jacie was willing to go for it. Maybe she should follow her example. *Or maybe not.*

She finished talking to Jacie and then hung up. She was waddling to the fridge to grab a Fresca when her mom and Clyde walked through the front door, giggling and holding hands. Sophie waved quickly and practically ran to her bedroom and shut the door. She listened as hard as she could. They had obviously gone to the video store and checked out a movie. They couldn't stop laughing. Sophie smiled. Now that was a fun date. Too bad she wasn't cuddled up on the couch watching a movie with Sam, she thought with a frown. Well, there was always next week. She just had to decide if that's where she wanted to be. Friends cuddled, right? Tess wouldn't think so, she was sure.

Sophie groaned and grabbed a magazine. She decided not to think about Tess. But no matter what she did, that's all she could think about. Ugh! She threw the magazine down and stomped over to turn the light off. She'd be asleep by ten o'clock on a Saturday night. Better than staying up and thinking of Sam or Tess, though.

chapter 21

"Now remember, you have to protect me from Daphne. You are my human shield. That woman scares me. She makes me look like a shy little eighth grader," Sam said, pulling up into Sophie's dad's driveway.

Sophie snorted and hopped out of the truck.

"Hey, hold my hand or something. If Daphne sees that, she won't attack me," Sam pleaded.

Sophie shook her head and rolled her eyes. Pathetic. A grown man scared of Daphne. But she grabbed his hand anyway, feeling immediately better herself. It was different showing up there with Sam at her side than showing up all by herself. She didn't feel as tense and stressed as she usually did. Maybe this time wouldn't be so bad.

"Or better yet, you could let me kiss you, and then she'd really get the hint. She called me last night. I told her about you, but I think she thought I was lying. Come on, just a little peck," he said in a teasing voice, trying to get her to smile.

"Holding hands is okay, but let me think about the kissing. If she gets really obnoxious, I'll think about it. Remember, we're just friends." Sophie said, knocking on the door.

Sam grinned and leaned over and kissed her full on the mouth right as the door opened.

"Sophie, dear, that type of behavior is for rated R movies. Not on a respectable person's doorstep," her grandmother said with a cold sniff.

Sophie pushed Sam away, blushing, and walked into the house without saying a word. Her grandmother had never approved of her.

Making excuses wouldn't help at this point.

"Come into the dining room. Julie is just about to serve dinner," she commanded.

Sam and Sophie followed her into the dining room where everyone was already seated. Sam grabbed her hand and pulled her to the two last seats left. Across from Daphne and Farrah. Perfect.

Sophie sat down and pasted her usual fake smile on before glancing at everyone at the table. Her father gave her a quick nod, her aunt surprised her with a real smile, her uncle Lyle ignored her, Farrah looked down her nose at her, and Daphne was downright sneering at her. Sophie's smile slipped a notch as she finally noticed Daphne's hair. Holy. Cow. Holy. Stinkin'. Cow. Daphne had tried downlights. To her utter downfall. Sophie's mouth fell open in dismay as she noticed the greenish tinge to the light ash brown streaks running through Daphne's normally white blonde hair. Sophie had seen this happen before. But that had been in beauty school. And there was that one lady. Sophie'd never forget her. Mom of four, busy, went to the store and grabbed a box of ash brown because she was tired of her bleached out hair and wanted to go natural again. Bright green. Sophie had been able to save the day, three hours later, but this. This was just sad.

"Daphne, I see you've gotten downlights. Do you mind me asking who your stylist is?" Sophie asked politely, trying to hide her horror.

Daphne turned a mottled shade of red and practically hissed at her.

"Mind your own business, Sophie," she said and then looked like she wanted to cry.

"Well, just in case you're wondering, I have an opening early tomorrow morning if you want to come in or something," Sophie offered, trying to be nice.

Daphne threw her napkin down and stomped out of the room. Lexie sighed and shook her head. "Don't mind her, Sophie. Her little friend she always goes to isn't as good as you are. I'll talk to her. If she doesn't want to be mistaken for an alien, she'll show up tomorrow."

Sam laughed and started to make a comment but was interrupted by Julie walking into the room with a large salad bowl in her hands. She placed it in the middle of the table and then removed her apron before sitting down.

"Hi, Sophie. Sam. Thanks for coming," she said, looking across the table at everyone and smiled happily. Sophie smiled back but had to wonder what was going on. From what Julie had told her last week, she was leaving her father, but from her father's expression, nothing had happened yet. Strange. She felt a light pressure on her knee and looked at Sam. He winked at her and grabbed her hand under the table. Sophie smiled back. It was so good to have him here. She should have brought reinforcements a long time ago.

Daphne slunk back into the room with red puffy eyes. Then Sophie's father said the prayer over the food and everyone started dishing up their plates. When everyone was eating and talking, Julie stood up regally and tapped her glass with a fork.

"I'd like to have everyone's attention. I've brought everyone here today to make an announcement. But first, I'd like to make a toast. To the one Reid I truly like and admire. Someone normal and nice. To Sophie," Julie said and raised her glass in her direction.

Sophie's mouth dropped open and she turned to look at Sam, to see if he had heard the same thing she had. He was grinning his head off and lifting his glass to her as well.

"To Sophie," he replied and drank from his glass.

Sophie turned and looked at the rest of her relatives. They all looked as surprised as she was. But unlike Sam, their glasses remained on the table.

"Now that that's done, on to my announcement. I'm leaving Tanner, and I thought since you are all so close, and you were just as much a part of this marriage as I was, that you should all be included in the announcement. And no, I wasn't spring cleaning, Tanner. I have everything packed and gone to my new house on the other side of Alpine. It's actually a block away from Sophie and Candy. It's temporary until we can settle the estate and figure out where all my money has gone. Enjoy dinner, everyone," she said and sat down, picking up her fork and digging into her lasagna as if she hadn't eaten in weeks.

Sophie closed her mouth and took a sip of water.

"Julie, this is insane. What are you talking about? Have you lost your mind? Tanner, what's going on?" Lexie demanded, turning to stare at her brother.

Tanner patted his lips with his napkin and stood. "Julie, I'd like to talk to you in the kitchen, please," he said tonelessly and walked out of the room, assuming Julie would follow. Julie looked longingly at the food on her plate but shrugged and smiled sunnily at everyone before following him.

Sophie felt Sam squeeze her hand comfortingly. He leaned over and whispered in her ear. "We just need to stay until Julie gets in the car and leaves. I want to make sure she's okay and that your dad doesn't try anything," he said.

Sophie nodded and realized he had known what was going to happen. She leaned over and whispered right back in his ear. "You could have warned me!"

Sam shook his head and shrugged before going back to his food. Sophie sighed. The man was addicted to food.

"Well, I bet you're happy," Daphne said maliciously, shooting daggers at her from across the table.

Sophie blinked. "Excuse me? Why would I be happy that my father stole money from his wife and is now getting divorced?" she asked, curious about Daphne's reasoning.

Her grandmother was the one who answered for her, though.

"Because now he'll go back to your mother, of course," she said with utter contempt dripping in her voice.

Sophie tried to bite her tongue but just couldn't. The way her relatives despised her mother had always upset her, but to bring her into this was just plain ridiculous.

"You're all crazy if you think my mother would take him back," she said with her own sniff.

Her grandmother raised her eyebrow in disdain but refused to say another word.

Lexie blew out her breath in exasperation and threw her napkin down. "Mother, if you hadn't pushed and pushed, this would never have happened. He's not a baby anymore! You should have left well enough alone," she said and got up from her chair. She motioned for Daphne, Farrah, and her husband to follow her and walked out the door, leaving their food untouched and Sam and Sophie to face her grandmother by themselves.

"So, I hear you've lived in Alpine all your life. What was it like fifty years ago? Was it the ultra cool, chic place it is now?" Sam asked, shoving green beans in his mouth with the same amount of gusto he'd use if he was eating ice cream. Sophie sighed and nibbled on her bread.

"Young man, I realize you're trying to cover the uncomfortable silence with polite conversation, but this is not the time. My son's life is falling apart," she said sadly and took a sip of water.

Sophie looked up in surprise. She'd never heard her grandmother say anything that completely honest before. All she'd heard from her grandmother her whole life was how wonderful Daphne and Farrah were. Her grandmother loved to fill her in on all the wonderful details of her cousins' lives as if she were trying to explain why she favored them so much. Did she hear how Daphne had won Miss Alpine? Had she heard that Farrah was going to spend a month in Italy? But this was different. Her grandmother was honestly upset.

"Sorry, Mrs. Reid. We could talk about Sophie if you don't want to talk about Alpine. Did you know your granddaughter is a very talented beautician? People I've talked to rave about her skills. You should be very proud of her," he said, grinning at Sophie.

Sophie groaned inwardly and looked down at her plate. The one thing her grandmother was not interested in was her. Bad choice of conversation.

"I've always thought it was a good thing that certain types of people can contribute to society. Even if it is just doing hair. Be the best at what you can do, I always say," she said with an aristocratic tilt of her head.

Sophie's head snapped up at that. "Exactly what type of person am I?" she asked in a strained voice, staring her grandmother in the eyes, not blinking, not wavering.

Her grandmother finally dropped her gaze and dabbed at her mouth unnecessarily.

"Well, Sophie, you know I'm not the kind of person to hold your ancestry against you. It's not your fault your mother's people were nothing but poor, ignorant farmers. If you and your mother can make something of yourselves and contribute to society, then that just goes to prove what America is all about, now doesn't it? Anyone can make a decent, honest living here if they really try hard," she said with a kind smile.

Sophie felt ill. "Now wait a second. You treat me like I'm beneath you because you think my mother's family is poor white trash? Did my father give you that impression, because if so, you have been misinformed. My mother's family might not be wealthy, but they're good, hardworking people who are kind and intelligent and good and loving. Unlike this family," she said, starting to breathe heavy.

Forget it. She put her napkin down and turned to tell Sam it was time they left but froze when she saw Sam's expression. He was royally ticked. He hadn't even looked like this when Blake had tried to pick a fight with him. He looked like he could burst into flames any second.

"Mrs. Reid," Sam said, and then paused and took a breath. "I've never in my life witnessed a grandmother treat her own grandchild with such open contempt. There's no excuse for behavior like that. You owe Sophie an apology," he said coldly.

Sophie's eyebrows shot up. No one ever talked to her grandmother that way. Her own father was still scared to death of her, and he was in his forties.

"Young man, how dare you talk to me like that. I'd like you both to leave now," she said standing up regally and pointing to the door.

Sam stood up too. *The better to intimidate*, Sophie thought. She felt like a bone between two snarling dogs.

"Look, Mrs. Reid, I'll be happy to leave. But I promise you, if I have anything to do with it, Sophie won't be coming back. I don't know why she has if this is the way she's been treated," he said putting his fists on his hips.

Sophie turned to see her grandmother's expression. Her face had gone from red to white. She looked like she had turned to stone.

"My relationship with Sophie is none of your concern. You have no say in what I do or what she does. Now get out!" her grandmother whispered fiercely.

Sam shoved his chair back and reached for Sophie's hand, pulling her up.

"I'll be glad to. But just one last thing. As far as superiority and class, Sophie's the one who got all. Have a good afternoon, Mrs. Reid," he said and pulled Sophie out of the room.

Sophie couldn't help noticing the shocked look on her grandmother's face as they left the room. Her upper class upbringing had never been questioned by anyone before. And she wasn't liking it.

"Sam! Slow down. We can't leave yet. We need to check on Julie and make sure she's okay," Sophie said as Sam reached the front door.

Sam paused and let his breath out. "Right. Man, I can't stand the way she talks to you. No wonder you freaked out when you found out I had money last night. If I had grown up with her as a grandmother, I'd think all rich people were evil too."

Sophie cracked a smile and reached up on her tip toes to put her arms around Sam's neck, hugging him tightly.

"Thanks for sticking up for me. She's not the nicest person in the world. But everyone kind of takes their cues from her. She hates me, so everyone else hates me too. Even my own father. But that felt good. And now, I really never do have to come back here. I can see my brother and sister at Julie's anytime I want," she said, looking on the bright side of things.

Sam hugged her tightly and kissed her sweetly on the cheek. "Look, why don't you come over to my mom and dad's house for dinner? I'm starving to death. I'd like to show you what a real family is supposed to act like. What do you say?" he asked with a smile.

Sophie paused before saying yes. They still hadn't worked out the Tess issue.

"Hey, Sam! Hey, Sophie!" Julie said from the hallway. "I'm taking off now. I've gotta go pick the kids up from Donna's. So everything's okay. Thanks for coming today, Sam. I'll call your mom later. But tell her everything went as expected." Julie already had her purse slung over her shoulder and her car keys in her hand. She looked determined and a little sad—but mostly determined.

Sam let his arms drop from Sophie and walked over to give his aunt a hug.

"Are you sure you're okay?" Sam asked, looking into her face.

Julie smiled and patted Sam's cheek. "I'm better than I've been in a long, long time. I'll see you two later. Now get going," she said, shooing them out the front door.

Sam hugged Julie one last time and then grabbed Sophie's hand, pulling her outside. She felt the warmth of the sun on her face immediately and breathed in the fragrant summer air. It felt good to be outside. It felt great.

She hopped in Sam's truck and buckled her seat belt and wondered if she'd ever hear from her father again. She was turning twenty-one in a few months. She'd be an adult. He would never have to talk to her again if he didn't want to. And it wasn't like he had to try to impress Julie anymore with what a good dad he was. Sophie tried to gauge her own feelings on that. Was she sad about that? Not really. Did that make her a horrible person? Or just normal? She had no clue, but she didn't want to think about it anymore. It was a beautiful day. A day for new beginnings.

"What's going on inside your head, Sophie? You look kind of sad," Sam said, scowling.

Sophie smiled at Sam and patted his hand. "Hey, I'll be okay. And you never know. Maybe someday I'll get a call from my father or my grandmother because they want to talk to me or something. Maybe someday they'll want to get to know me," she said, realizing that someday she might want that.

Sam frowned, causing two lines to appear between his eyes.

"It kills me just thinking about what you had to grow up with. Sorry I said what I did yesterday about how you shouldn't feel sorry for yourself because so many other people have it worse. I guess I didn't have the whole picture. Heck, if I was you, I'd be so full of hate and anger, I'd be miserable. But you're not. You're so nice and kind and full of love. Look at your aunt Lexie. Julie told me how mean she's been to you, but you fixed her hair and now she doesn't look like a vampire anymore. And you even offered to fix Daphne's hair. That's Christlike. I'm really impressed here," Sam said with a half-smile.

"Hey, don't give me qualities I don't have. I wasn't being Christlike when I did Lexie's hair. I just can't stand to see bad hair. That's all," Sophie said, looking away out the window.

Sam laughed and grabbed her hand, holding it on the seat between them.

"Say what you will, but I'm starting to get a picture of the real Sophie. You're pretty amazing," he said simply.

Sophie smiled a little. Nice to know someone thought so.

chapter 22

"Mom, Dad, this is Sophie," Sam said, pushing Sophie toward his parents.

Sophie gulped and held her hand out to shake Sam's dad's hand.

"Hello, Mr. Kellen. It's nice to meet you," she stuttered, becoming so nervous she could barely breathe.

"Call me Stan," he said and pulled her in for a warm hug. Just like the kind Sam gave her.

"Hi, honey. My name is Sue. Come on in and get some dinner. We've already eaten, but there are tons of leftovers since Sam wasn't here," she said, putting her arm around Sophie's shoulders and pulling her toward the kitchen, where four gorgeous people stood, doing dishes and putting food away in the fridge.

"Sam! I didn't know you were coming over today," shouted the man with his hands full of dirty dishes.

Sam grabbed the man in a headlock and kissed him on the top of the head.

"Ah, I can't stay away from you guys too long. You know that," he said and let the man go in order to grab all of his sisters at once in a huge hug, causing them to stop staring at her and giggle and scream.

"Sam! You idiot, let me go," squealed the tallest one, before she gave Sam a kiss on the cheek.

"Sam, stop squeezing me and introduce me to Sophie," the short one commanded, and then hugged him back quickly.

The third girl, kept her arm around Sam protectively and looked at

Sophie measuringly. *Oops.* This one obviously wanted to watch out for her brother's best interests. Sophie'd have to be on her toes. She took in a deep breath for courage and then walked forward.

"Hi, everyone, I'm Sophie, a friend of your brother's," she said, smiling at everyone, even as she felt perspiration pop out on her forehead.

"Hi, Sophie. Sam has told me all about you. I'm Trey, his better looking, younger brother," said the man with a flirtatious smile.

Sophie couldn't help giggling at the young man who looked like a younger, leaner version of Sam, and shook his hand.

"It's a pleasure to meet you," she said, turning to greet the sisters.

"This is Lacie, Casey, and Macie," he said pointing to each one.

Their mom liked to rhyme. *Okay.*

"You guys are even prettier in person," she said, smiling shyly at them.

They all smiled back. "So you're the one who did Aunt Julie's hair, right?" Lacie said, going back to putting dishes in the dishwasher.

Sophie blinked in surprise. Sam had really told his family about her?

"Yeah, that's me."

"I never know what to do with my hair. After you guys are done eating, will you show me how to make it look good? I just need some pointers. All I do is put it up in a ponytail or leave it down straight. I'm just clueless," she said sadly, but with twinkling eyes.

Okay, here she was on steady ground. "Absolutely. It'll be fun," she said.

The sister who hadn't smiled at her as much as the other two, stepped closer, and looked tempted.

"I have a date tomorrow. Could you show me an easy way to do my hair that I could do myself?" she asked through dark thick lashes.

Sophie looked at all three girls. Gorgeous, very athletic, and in need of a good hairdresser. She was in heaven.

"I've got nothing but time on my hands," she said in way of an answer and grabbed the plate Sam shoved in her hands.

Trey gave her a glass to go in her other hand and Sam pushed her toward the kitchen table.

"Hey, Sam, since Sophie's going to be busy doing hair, will you look over a paper I'm writing? You always got A's in philosophy. You're going to have to help me out," he said, giving Sam a quick shoulder massage.

Sam grinned and nodded his head. "Sure, no prob. But only if you promise to help me out next Saturday. I could use some extra muscle," he said, shoveling food in the same way he did every time he was around it.

Trey groaned. "Sam, I told you. My muscles are worth twelve dollars an hour. There's no free lunch, buddy. The sooner you learn that, the happier you'll be," he said, walking backwards and grinning.

Sam turned and glared at Trey. "Did you or did you not just ask me to read your paper?" he demanded.

Trey shrugged. "I bet Sophie would read it for free, wouldn't you, Sophie?"

Sophie paused with her fork halfway to her mouth, horrified.

"Sorry, Trey. I never went to college. I'm not the right person to ask about philosophy," she said apologetically.

Sam glared at Trey and Sophie felt embarrassed.

Trey smiled and brought Sophie a roll. "Listen, Sophie, I just need someone to read it and tell me if it makes sense. I was going to have Sam do it, but obviously, he's just not in the mood to be a good big brother. I understand," he said pathetically.

Sam groaned. "Fine, I won't work you all day long. You can make all my phone calls instead, but it has to be done during the week. I'll give you twenty bucks."

Trey grinned and pumped his fist in the air.

"Love ya, Sam. You know I love ya. Now, when you make the corrections, do it in the margins. Okay?"

Sam frowned and shook his head sadly as Trey ran to get his paper.

"Do you see why I had to move out? I was always checking schoolwork or running errands or taking the girls to meets or this or that or whatever. Big families are big work," he said spearing a tomato from his salad and popping it into his mouth.

Sophie smiled. "A big family like yours seems pretty incredible to me. You should be grateful," she said with a wistful smile.

Sam looked at her oddly but went on eating. They finished just as the girls came in holding gift baskets of makeup and hair products.

"Okay, so here's all of our stuff. We just don't know what to do with it. We get baskets from Aunt Julie every Christmas. She's always giving us stuff like this as a hint," Lacie said.

Sophie pushed her plate away, immediately forgetting about the food. The girls were each holding a large basket—one filled with makeup and one filled with crimpers, curling irons, a blow dryer, and her ever favorite, the ceramic flat iron. And the third basket held miscellaneous things, like nail polish, perfume, boxes of waxing strips and bath oils.

Sophie looked through everything, pulling this and that out.

"Okay, this is junk—don't use this, and just throw this out. But this, now this is the good stuff. Oh, and I love this product. It's *amazing*. I can't believe none of this stuff has been opened. You weren't even tempted?" she asked, staring at the girls in disbelief.

They looked at each other guiltily. Macie crossed her arms defensively and spoke up.

"Well, we're just so busy. Gymnastics is our life. It's practice, school, practice, meet, and then it starts all over again. Now that I'm eighteen, though, I'm cutting back. I'm starting to date and I'm going to go to college next year. I'm majoring in phys ed, but I'm not trying out for the team or anything. So now I've gotta play catch-up," she said, looking hopefully at Sophie.

Sophie smiled brightly at the girls. "Okay, let's do this. Let's start from scratch. Pull those ponytails out and everyone wash your hair. We need to start at the beginning. Now, Casey, how do you feel about bangs, because sweetie, you were made for them. And Macie, I like yours, but with the round shape of your face, why don't we try going without? I think it would really show off your eyes. Lacie, honey, it's all about body with you, and no I'm not talking about your muscles. We need some bounce in your hair. And I'm here to give it to you," she said standing up and grabbing the rubber bands the girls held out to her.

They decided to do everything in the kitchen, so there was room for everyone. Sophie immediately found a pair of scissors in her hand, not the best, but for an emergency they'd do.

"Okay, we'll start out small at first, but next time I do this, we might go all the way. We'll start out with a long sweep to the side, just until you get used to them. Later we can go shorter. You're going to love it," Sophie said, starting to cut.

The other girls got chairs out and started plugging in all the curling irons and blow dryers they had.

Sophie cut Casey some bangs and then dried Casey's hair upside down with mousse on the roots for body. She went straight with Casey's hair, emphasizing the new addition of bangs.

"So easy, so fast, and so dang adorable. Look at the difference, you guys. What do you think?" she asked Lacie and Macie.

The two girls studied their sister intently and then grinned.

"Casey, you have never looked this good. Honestly. What were you thinking?" Lacie said, giggling as Casey ran out of the room to get a mirror.

"Okay, who's the next patient?" Sophie asked turning to see that both girls had already shampooed and conditioned their hair.

"Me!" They both said at once.

Sophie laughed. "Better rock, paper, scissors it," she advised and let them fight it out. Lacie won, and before she knew it, Sophie had her sitting down with her towel wrapped around her shoulders, getting chunky layers cut into her thick, blonde, shoulder-length hair.

"Have you ever thought of some bright, ash blond highlights Lacie? It would be so fun. Especially for a gymnast. I was watching a meet on television a couple months ago between BYU and Utah, and those girls hair were so cool. They had pink and purple streaks, glitter, and everything. Their hair was poppin'," she said, frowning in concentration.

Lacie grinned. "Yeah, everyone goes wild at the meets. You've never seen so much glitter in your life. Too bad it gets everywhere, though. Highlights would be cool," she said nonchalantly. But Sophie knew she'd be getting Sue's permission before she touched these girls' hair with any chemicals.

Sophie grabbed the blow dryer and went to work on Lacie's hair, turning her from lanky and lack luster to the complete opposite.

"Now, if you want me to do your makeup after we're done with your hair, just let me know, and I'll give you guys some quick tips," Sophie offered as she took the towel off Lacie and watched her run from the room just like her sister. Not doing the hair in the bathroom meant they were dying of curiosity.

That left Macie. The one who might not be too sure about her. Sophie'd better do a good job—or else. She studied the girl who sat down nervously in the chair.

"You look kind of unsure, Macie. How about this? I don't cut your hair; I just show you how to do it. Does that sound better?" she said.

Macie looked up and smiled. "I am kind of nervous. I've been dating Mike for a couple months now, and he really likes my hair long," she said.

Sophie frowned, remembering the way she had forced her naturally wavy hair straight for Blake. For over *two* years. And all for nothing.

"Well, what do *you* like Macie? Do you like long hair?" she asked, combing through it.

"Well, it is kind of a pain sometimes, but yeah, I like it long. For now," she said with a nod.

Sophie smiled. "Okay then. Date hair. Get ready for this," she said and started. She blew Macie's hair out straight and then used a clip to put most of the hair up in the back in a sophisticated French twist. She used the rest of the hair to curl making a very soft, romantic look.

She was so used to talking to her customers about everything going on in their lives that she didn't hesitate to ask Macie what she'd been dying to know.

"So, Macie, what's Sam really like? I'm just seeing the courtship Sam. Tell me all his deepest darkest secrets. I won't tell on you, I promise."

Macie laughed and crossed her legs. "Well, to be honest, there's not much difference between courtship Sam and the real guy. What you see is what you get, so if you were expecting anything really exciting, you're out of luck."

Sophie frowned. Dang. She'd been hoping for something juicy.

"He's never done anything naughty? He's been wonderful and nice his whole life?" she asked sounding doubtful.

Macie grinned. "Sorry, but you lucked out. Just think of all the girls out in the world who have to date losers. *You poor thing.*"

Sophie blushed and put the curling iron down to grab the flat iron.

"Hey, I didn't mean to sound disappointed or anything, but it's hard to believe that Sam is so completely amazing. I've never met anyone like him before," she said honestly.

Macie smiled and relaxed. "Well, he is amazing. And I'm not just saying that because I'm his sister. Although he does have a temper. But no one ever sees it unless he gets really mad," she said.

Sophie perked up. A temper, huh? Good to know.

"What do you mean no one sees it?" she asked, her hands busy.

Macie shrugged. "Well, the only time I've ever seen him lose his temper was when I drove to a work site one time last summer to bring him lunch and one of his subs was yelling at this poor little old Hispanic man. I mean, just tearing into the guy. Well, Sam did not like that one bit, and so he threw the guy off his property. And he's never used him again. That's his pet peeve in life, I think. He hates to see people mistreated," she said seriously.

Sophie raised her eyebrows and nodded. She'd be sure not to mistreat anyone in the future. And now that the conversation was done, she was almost done with Macie's do. She used a few bobby pins to pin some of the curls up. Sophie walked slowly around Macie, fixing this and pulling that, until it was perfect. She had been concentrating so hard, she hadn't realized that Sam and his whole family had come back into the kitchen and were staring silently at her as she did Macie's hair. The flash of a camera broke her trance.

She turned and looked at everyone and laughed when they started clapping. Macie walked carefully out of the room to get to the bathroom mirror.

"You took a picture?" she said, looking for a broom to sweep up all the hair.

"Honey, I've never seen my girls look so girly. You are one talented woman. One this family has needed for a long, long time, I might add," Sue said, walking over and hugging her.

Sophie blushed and couldn't help laughing. "Oh this was fun for me. I love doing makeovers. And your daughters are gorgeous. They just needed a little help in the right direction. Ponytails are good for a workout, but after the sports are done, well, there's just so much more to hair," she said, reaching for the broom Sam held out to her.

Macie, Lacie, and Casey ran back into the room together. Lacie and Casey had changed out of their sweats and into cute outfits.

"Mom, you have to take a picture of all of us! For our scrapbooks. This day needs to be remembered forever."

Sue laughed. "Lacie, I already have my camera. Macie, I don't want you ruining your hair, so you can't change. Come out into the living room, and we'll do some glamour shots," she said.

Sophie laughed and followed the whole family into the other room. She watched in delight as all three girls lay on the floor on their stomachs with their chins on their hands. Obviously they were pros at being photographed.

"Uh-uh. Someone's missing. Sophie, you're the star of the show. Get your rear in that picture," Stan said grinning at her.

The girls shouted yes, and Sam pushed her toward the trio. She was supposed to lay on the floor too? Like that? She started to blush and couldn't help it. She was going to end up looking like a ripe strawberry. She crawled onto the floor and propped her chin on her hands just like the girls.

"Now, Sophie, kick your feet up like the girls did. There. Perfect!"

Snap! Flash! Snap! Snap!

Sophie couldn't help giggling as they made her pose in the strangest, goofiest, weirdest poses with them for the next fifteen minutes. She couldn't stop laughing when Sue made them all lay on their back in a circle with their feet up in the air, touching their toes together. She felt like a synchronized swimmer gone bad.

Sam finally rescued her and pulled her up from the floor. He quickly took her outside in the backyard.

"Come on. They won't find us out here," he said and pulled her to the very back of their yard where nestled in amongst some shade trees was a bright white rocker swing.

They sat down while Sophie continued to giggle. "Your family is hilarious. I can't remember the last time I laughed like that. That was fun," she said, grinning at Sam as he pulled her closer to him and put his arm around her.

"Yeah, my family is great. Exhausting, but the greatest blessing in the world. You did good, Sophie. My sisters now look so good that I'm going to have to start worrying when they go on dates. They look like cheerleaders now instead of gymnasts."

Sophie swatted Sam's knee and cuddled into his side. "Oh, Sam. You worry too much. They look fantastic. Every girl needs to feel glamorous and beautiful sometimes. It's good for the soul," she said and sighed as she felt herself start to really relax.

"Then you must have the brightest, shiniest soul in the world, because you're the most glamorous, beautiful woman I know," he said with a gentle smile.

Sophie looked up at him and laughed. "Sam, you are so crazy. No way am *I* glamorous or beautiful. I'm just . . . me," she said, not knowing how to describe herself.

Sam shook his head and grinned. "Modest too. Dang, you're perfect."

Sophie rolled her eyes but couldn't help the glow that was growing around her heart. She'd told Sam she just wanted to be his friend, but what she was starting to feel was different than anything she'd ever felt before.

They swung back and forth for a while without talking, and Sophie realized how late it was. The sun was starting to set. She was finally getting her sunset with Sam.

"Now that's what I'm talking about," Sam whispered and kissed the top of her head.

Sophie smiled and closed her eyes and felt the day's last rays of light settle around her like a blanket of yellow peace.

"I could get used to this," she murmured.

Sam rested his head on the back of the swing and grinned. "Me too. You know, you've completely won over my family, don't you?" he asked.

Sophie opened her eyes, frowning. "How can I win them over if they think Tess is still in the picture?" she said, scooting away from Sam.

Sam opened one eye lazily and pulled her back. "Relax, Sophie. They know I broke up with Tess. I just haven't told them what she's been up to. They haven't mentioned once that they want me to get back together with her. Just let me enjoy this moment. My sisters love you, and my mom loves you for it and my dad is happy all the women in his life are happy. And that means I'm happy," he said, resting his cheek on the top of her head.

Sophie sighed and let it go. "Well, your family seems really, *really* nice. It's like you guys are the perfect family. Perfect, loving mom. Perfect, loving father. Six gorgeous, smart, perfect children. Great house. Not too formal, not too crazy—just right. You guys even have a pool. I just *so* don't fit into this picture," Sophie said, closing her eyes again with a slight frown.

Sam shifted but didn't move his cheek from hers.

"Sophie, come off it. You look at us, but all you see is the outer shell. Life is never perfect. But we do the best we can. Look at my mom. She didn't grow up with a perfect life. Her mom abandoned her when she was nine. She was adopted by an LDS family when she was fourteen. She met my dad when she was working as a waitress and he was going to college. It was love at first sight. My mom doesn't know how to do my sisters' hair because she never learned how. My mom's life now is the complete opposite of what it used to be. She hasn't had the perfect life, but she fits in right where she's supposed to. Here, with us," he said seriously.

Sophie sat up and turned to look at Sam. He was lying back, with his eyes half closed studying her.

"Wow."

Sam laughed. "Yeah, wow. I don't think your grandmother would understand what makes my mom truly the most amazing woman in the world. Her spirit. It's not where you come from. It's what you do with what you have. It's the love you have in your heart. It's the spirit inside. You're a lot like my mom, Sophie. You know that?" he said, pulling her arm so she fell back beside him.

She snuggled into his side again and put her arm around his waist, resting her head on his shoulder.

"That's the nicest thing anyone's ever said to me," she said and felt herself fall just a little bit in love.

They were interrupted by Sam's dad calling them from the deck.

"Come on, you two love birds. Dessert's ready!"

Sam pulled her up regretfully, and they walked back to the house hand in hand. She was so glad Sam had shown her his family. Someday she wanted a family just like his.

They ate homemade ice cream and played a silly game called Apples to Apples. The whole family joined in, giggling and laughing and getting louder and louder every minute.

The phone ringing interrupted the game. Macie jumped up. "I'll get it!" she said and ran out of the room.

She came back a few seconds later with the phone in her hand and a strange expression on her face.

"Uh, Sam. The phone's for you," she said, looking guiltily at Sophie.

Sophie licked her lips and felt weird all of a sudden. The rest of the family exchanged looks, and Sue put her card down.

"Sam, why don't you take that call in the other room?" she said, looking at him pointedly.

Sam shrugged. "Nah. This is okay. Hello?" he said and then slowly put his cards down too.

"Hi, Tess. What's going on?" he said, and glanced at Sophie. Sophie looked away and out the window. She had never felt more uncomfortable in her life.

"Well, right now's not a good time . . . Because I have a guest over . . . No, uh-uh. Her name's Sophie . . . Why? Because I wanted her to meet my family . . . Because, because. Look Tess, I'll call you tomorrow. Okay? . . . Fine, bye," he said and pushed the *end* button.

Sam put the phone down and looked at everyone, who were staring with frowns right back at him.

"That was Tess," he said unnecessarily.

Sue glared at him. "We know, Sam. What did she want?" she asked, looking quickly at Sophie.

Sam looked at Sophie before answering. "She just wanted to come by and hang out. But I told her no."

Lacie shook her head. "Sam, my brother, you have some serious problems." And she put her cards down and got up. "I've got homework. Sophie, it was really great meeting you. Hopefully we'll see you again."

Sophie smiled and nodded at her. Macie and Casey soon followed, stopping by her chair and touching her shoulder before they walked out. Trey all of a sudden had a phone call to make, and Stan got up to refill his glass. Leaving Sue and Sam and her.

Sophie started putting the game back in the box while Sue and Sam stared at each other. Somehow communicating without really talking.

"Well, I've got to put those dishes away. Sophie, you come in and say good-bye before you leave. Okay?" Sue said and walked out. Leaving her alone with Sam.

"I've got work tomorrow morning," Sophie said, looking at her lap. "I should be going."

Sam sighed. "Me too. Go tell my mom good-bye and I'll meet you outside," he said.

Sophie walked quickly to the kitchen, where Sue already had half the dishwasher put away.

"Mrs. Kellen, it was a pleasure to meet you. Thank you so much for dinner and dessert and everything." Sophie said, not surprised when she was hugged again.

"Honey, you come over anytime. You fit right in. Heck, I would love it if you came over every Sunday. We haven't had this much fun in a long time," Sue said and then frowned.

"Sophie, now I don't want you to worry too much about Tess. I'm sure Sam told you she's his ex-girlfriend. To be honest, I don't think he ever loved her. Our family has known her family forever and they kind of grew up together. When Sam graduated from college and started his business, that's when Tess became interested. Tess looked at Sam and saw a good-looking, successful man she thought she could control. And Sam, well, he'd had a crush on her since he was little, so when she went after him, he couldn't believe his good luck. Until he realized that it takes a lot more than good looks and style to make a beautiful heart. And when Sam realized Tess's spirit didn't match her outside, he broke up with her. And then he found you. He's a smart one, my boy. So you don't worry about Tess. She's past history," Sue said with a comforting smile.

Sophie sighed and wondered why she felt like crying.

"I don't know if she's as past as you think. Past history doesn't call and want to come over. Well, anyway, I hope I see you again."

Sue laughed and hugged her tightly. "Oh, there's no doubt about that, honey. We'll be seeing you," she said.

Sophie smiled and found her way to the front door. As she walked outside, she saw that Sam was already by his truck. Talking to a girl. Talking to a tall, beautiful, blond girl. *Tess.*

Sophie didn't know what to do. Should she go back in the house? Nope, they'd both seen her. Sam motioned with his hand for her to come over. Sophie groaned inwardly. She hadn't wanted to meet Tess. Ever. Tess looked like she wanted to scratch her eyes out. *Oh great.* She'd never been a fan of pain. She walked slowly over to Sam and Tess and smiled nervously.

"Hey, Sophie. I'd like to introduce you to Tess. Tess, this is Sophie," he said, not looking uncomfortable at all. He was smiling! *He was crazy.* Sophie stepped forward and clasped Tess's outstretched hand, letting go as soon as she could.

"Nice to meet you," Sophie practically whispered. Her voice had somehow failed her.

"Likewise," Tess said with a frown. She turned back to Sam. "So how long have you two known each other?" she asked, ignoring Sophie altogether.

Sam looked a little worried and licked his lips nervously.

"Not too long. I was just getting ready to take Sophie home. Why don't I call you later and we can talk then?" he said, throwing his keys in the air.

Tess frowned and started tapping her foot in the dirt, sending little puffs of dust into the air. Sophie gulped and looked to Sam. Was she going to go crazy and break the windows of Sam's truck? Would she have a nervous breakdown and try to hurt herself?

Sam winked at her and looked back at Tess.

"Sam, I think you and I need to have a serious talk. Privately. Right now," she said, emphasizing each word with a thrust of her finger into his chest.

Sophie wanted to disappear and looked longingly back at Sam's house. As she glanced back at the house she saw all of Sam's sisters staring out at them from a second-story window. All three of the girls had worried frowns on their faces. When they realized Sophie was staring back at them, they disappeared in a swoosh of curtain. Sophie almost laughed before turning back to see Tess step closer to Sam and put a possessive hand on his arm. Sophie winced and cleared her throat.

"Um, Sam, why don't I wait in the house if you and Tess need to talk?" she said, not wanting to hear what Sam was going to say.

Sam shoved his hands through his hair. He was not as unruffled as he'd like to appear.

"No, Sophie, I need to get you home. Tess, listen, now's just not a good time. I'll talk to you later," he said.

Sophie felt her heart go out to Tess. She knew exactly what it felt like to have your heart broken. Tess must still love Sam. The question was, did she?

Tess blinked a couple times and then smiled brightly. Sophie knew that smile. She'd used it herself so many times. Bright, happy, *fake*.

"Fine, Sam. I'll call you later. Bye, Sophie," Tess said and then walked over to her cream-colored Lexus. She drove away quickly, leaving a trail of dust.

"And that was Tess," Sam said quietly, staring after the car with a perplexed frown.

Sophie leaned her hip against the truck and stared too. "She's just as beautiful as I thought she would be."

Sam jerked his head up, out of his trance. "Yeah, well, pretty is as pretty does. Come on, let's get you home," he said and opened the door for her.

Sophie sighed and hopped up into the truck. As Sam drove her home, he tried to fill the silence with idle chitchat, but Sophie just couldn't. Not after seeing Tess.

"Sam," she finally said. "After what you told me about Tess, how can you act so calm? What if she's back there setting your house on fire, or calling the paper with lies about you, or having a nervous breakdown? What if she follows us and she finds out where I live?" Sophie whispered, grabbing her throat and looking back over her shoulder.

Sam looked at her and tried to grab her hand, but Sophie held away from him.

"Sophie, now let's not get too dramatic here. I think her stopping by and seeing you was the best thing that could have happened. This is a step in the right direction. She's met you and she didn't throw a fit. Actually, she was kind of polite. So now that she knows I've moved on, she'll move on too. This will be great, Sophie. It'll be perfect from now on. No more worries. Tess just needed a little time to get used to the idea of me being with someone else, and now she has. End of story. I'm finally free," he said with a bright, hopeful smile.

Sophie stared at him in surprise. From what she'd seen in Tess's eyes, Tess had not moved on at all. When she had looked into Tess's eyes, Sophie had seen anger, hurt, surprise, and a coldness she had never seen before—not even in her grandmother's eyes. And that was saying something.

"But what if you're wrong, Sam? What if she hasn't moved on? What if you go home and find out she's done something? Where are we then? Look, I'll be honest. After spending the day with you and your family, there's nothing I'd like more than to throw caution to the wind and tell the world I've got myself a new boyfriend. But when I saw Tess today, I don't know. I just felt like this wasn't over by a long shot. Let's give it some time. Let's play it safe and see how Tess handles the idea of me being with you. Okay?" Sophie said, watching Sam's happy smile fade to a thin line.

"I'm just so tired of putting my life on hold because of her, Sophie. After being with you today, there's no way I want to go back to the way things were. You should be with me, Sophie. I don't want to play it safe anymore. I want to be with you," he said passionately.

Sophie reached over and squeezed his hand. "Just for me. Play it safe just a little longer. Be my friend for just a little longer until we know Tess is okay."

Sam frowned. "Friends. Man, I hate that word," he said and pulled into her driveway.

Sophie smiled. "Bye, Sam. Tell your family, I really liked them," she said and shut the door. She walked into her house and burst into tears.

chapter 23

Sophie needed her mom. She walked through the house but gave up and tried Mom's cell phone. After three rings, her mom picked up.

"Mom? Where are you?" Sophie asked, sitting down at the kitchen table, and rested her head on her hands.

"Honey, Clyde invited me over to have dinner with him and his little girl, Kenedy. We're almost done here. I think I'll stay and hang out for a little while, though. Are you okay? You sound kind of sad. What's going on?" Candy asked, sounding concerned.

Sophie paused. If she sounded too upset, she knew her mom would rush home. But she could tell from Candy's voice that she was having a great time. She sounded so happy. No, ruin her mom's night she would not.

"Oh really? I don't know why. I just got home and was wondering where you were. When you get home, I have some incredible gossip for you, though. Julie put on an amazing show this afternoon. Dad will never be the same," she said with a little laugh.

"Ooh. I can't wait. Listen, I gotta go. Clyde's making root beer floats. I should be home around nine or nine thirty."

Sophie sighed. "Okay, Mom. Love ya," she said and hung up.

Great. Now here she was. All alone again. No one to talk to. No boyfriend. No mom. Nobody.

Sophie pushed away from the table and walked into the family room. She flopped on the couch but ignored the remote. She wasn't in the mood to watch *Funniest Home Videos*. She wasn't even in the mood for *Extreme Home Makeover*. She was definitely in the mood for feeling sorry for herself. She took her cell phone out of her pocket. Enter Jacie. The one person she could whine to who wouldn't hold it against her.

"Jacie?" Sophie said into the phone a second later. "Come over. I've got so much complaining to do."

Jacie laughed and hung up without saying a word. Sophie loved that about Jacie. She was a true friend. Fifteen minutes later, they had a package of oreos and a couple of cold Frescas on the floor of Sophie's room.

"Sophie, I told you to go for it. Your feeling sorry for Tess is ruining your social life. I can't guarantee your happiness if you ignore the five basic steps on how to get yer man," Jacie said and shoved two Oreos into her mouth at once.

Sophie glared at her and then stuck her tongue out before she shoved three Oreos into her mouth.

Jacie rolled her eyes and concentrated on not choking.

"So telling Sam that I only want to be friends with him might just be the stupidest thing I've ever done. Life goes on, right?" Sophie said and then whimpered.

Jacie winced for her. "Hey, opposition in all things, my friend. You gotta have it."

Sophie popped the top on her Fresca and took a sip. "Oh well. There's always Blake."

Jacie looked funny and then grabbed another Oreo. "What?" Sophie asked.

Jacie shrugged. "Nothing. I just happened to see Blake down at the park with Bailey this afternoon. It looked like they were having a picnic or something. You might be all out of second chances there too," she said and then laughed at Sophie's tragic expression.

"Oh stop it! Like you even want him. You know you don't," Jacie said, throwing an Oreo at her.

Sophie ducked and then picked the Oreo up off the floor, blowing on it before popping it in her mouth.

"I know. But he was still an option. It's good to have options, and now with Sam firmly in the friend category, I'm just a lonely, single girl with no prospects. It's just kind of depressing," she said honestly.

Jacie lay back on the floor and propped up her head with her arms.

"Well, you know Paul's kind of interested in you. He told me he wants to ask you out. Would you go with him?" she asked.

Sophie shoved the package of Oreos away from her, feeling nauseated and bloated.

"I'd feel kind of lame if I did. I'm so hung up on Sam now. Paul is the nicest guy I've met in forever. I just wish I had met him before Sam," she said.

Jacie turned to her side and looked at her friend.

"Would it have mattered? I mean, say you had been dating Paul and you met Sam. Would you dump Paul for Sam?"

Sophie frowned. "No Tess in the picture?"

Jacie nodded. "No Tess anywhere."

Sophie closed her eyes and sighed. "I'd dump Paul in half a heartbeat to be with Sam. Pathetic, huh?"

Jacie stared at Sophie. "You know what, Sophie? I think you're in love."

Sophie sat up in surprise. "What! Uh-uh. No way. I just met this guy," she said, snorting her vehement disbelief.

Jacie shook her head silently. "Stop overreacting. You're in love. Now, are you just going to sit there and let Tess take yer man?" she demanded.

Sophie groaned. "That's the whole problem! He's not my man. She thinks he's still hers. You know after watching what my mom went through with my dad, I refuse to be the other woman, no matter how crazy Tess is. I'm not blaming Sam. None of this is his fault, but still. I don't want to be the one to push Tess over the edge," she said and then surprised them both by bursting into tears.

Jacie's eyes went wide in horror. "Oh. My. Gosh."

Sophie nodded her head silently. "I know. I'm in trouble."

chapter 24

A whole week passed by and Sophie hadn't heard one word from Sam. He was probably still ticked at being forced into the friendship zone. She tried to stay busy. She had more hair appointments than she knew what to do with. She went to work at seven in the morning and didn't get home until seven thirty at night. She liked it that way, though. No time to drown her sorrows in Oreos. Sophie helped Julie unpack some of her boxes, and when she needed a break, she took her little brother and sister to the park to play. But Julie didn't say one word about Sam. And she didn't ask Sophie about him either. Of course, Julie's mind was probably on more important things, like getting a divorce. But still . . .

Jacie dragged Sophie down to Roberts Crafts so they could get all the materials they'd need to make the best poster any returning missionary had ever seen. She still hadn't heard back from him, but she had hope. She told Sophie that even if he was determined to hate her, after taking one look at her poster, he would know without a shadow of a doubt that her love for him was true and he would forgive her on the spot and she would live happily ever after.

Sophie didn't want to burst her friend's bubble, but her own poster for Blake had been about as perfect as a poster could be. And Blake hadn't even looked at it once. But she was there for Jacie. And if Jacie needed her to glue glitter and beads on a poster, then that's what she'd do. And when Jacie's heart was broken and bleeding on the filthy floor of the airport, she'd be there to drive her home. Where they could both drown their sorrows in Oreos and whatever ice cream they could find. Friends. It's what they did.

On Sunday Sophie went to church, taught her class, and returned home by herself. Candy had been invited to go to church with Clyde at his ward. His daughter, Kenedy, was giving a talk in Primary and had asked Candy to come hear it. Sophie smiled. Her mom had been so pleased. So excited. And Sophie couldn't be happier for her mom.

What she hadn't told her mom was that her dad had called twice for her. She had erased the messages from the machine. She hated to think that her grandmother was right. To think her father thought that he could come back to Candy and that she'd be waiting for him. Nuh-uh. Not if she had anything to say about it. And she actually had a lot to say about it.

Sophie fixed herself a microwave dinner and ate it quickly, before she could taste it much. She threw the gummy cardboard in the garbage and then looked around. Jacie was busy with her family. They had plans to go up to Logan to see her grandma. So Sophie was on her own. Well, she just needed to get used to it was all. Being alone was a blessing. Something to look forward to. A time for contemplation and peace.

Sophie grabbed her keys and left the house. It was that or go crazy. No work, no friends, no mom, no boyfriend. No nothing. So she'd go for a drive. A beautiful Sunday afternoon was the perfect day for a relaxing drive. She didn't know why exactly she was heading toward Draper. Going over the mountain and through Suncrest was just a happy accident. So she liked a pretty view. Who wouldn't?

She drove with music blaring and the window down, pretending her Jeep was a Ferrari. She didn't dare drive into Sam's subdivision. It was a winding, super-secluded subdivision. Too dangerous. Sophie paused though, very tempted. She knew what kind of car Tess drove now. All she had to do was drive past and just see if she was there. If she were Tess, that's where she'd be on a Sunday afternoon.

Sophie stared at the road leading to Sam's house and then drove away. She was just being immature. Only a stalker would drive past a person's house just to see if someone else was there. A stalker she was not. At least she didn't feel like one. She was just curious.

She sighed and turned her music down. It was giving her a headache anyway. She drove down the other side of the mountain and down into Draper. She liked Draper. Well, okay, it was really busy and crowded compared to Alpine, but so what? She just felt like giving Draper an old look-see. *That's no crime,* she thought patting herself on the back.

So what if she just happened to drive toward Sam's parents' neighborhood? There was nothing weird or strange about that. It was a beautiful neighborhood. If anyone asked her why she was there, well, first of all, hello, this is America. Second of all, she was a big fan of architecture and she had noticed last Sunday how all of the homes in that area were very pretty. Someday she might build a house. Okay, maybe someday she'd have Sam build her a house. And all she'd have to say is, "Sam, just like the one by your parents. You know, the one on the left with the, whatever it's called on the roof. Build me that one," she'd say. And it would be done. You had to do your research. You just had to.

Sophie turned down the Kellens' street and slowed down to fifteen miles per hour, creeping toward the cul-de-sac. She could definitely see cars parked in front. Sophie frowned. Were they having a party? Huh. Well, they sure hadn't invited her. She drove closer. She just had to see if Tess's car was there. If it was, then, well, she'd have to think about that. If it wasn't, well, then she could go home and find something to do. *Okay, breathe again.* She missed that feeling. Breathing. She couldn't seem to do it very well when she pictured Sam with Tess. Talking to Tess or hugging Tess or even being in the same state with Tess. Okay, she had to do it.

Sophie drove farther, until she was so far there was no going back. If she could just see beyond that stupid bunch of trees! Sophie bit her lip guiltily. She did not want to get caught. Yet she had to do what she had to do. She pulled her car over to the side of the road and got out. It was hard to miss a car. But she could be sneaky. They'd never see her if she just walked down the sidewalk. Lots of people went for walks on Sundays. Everyone did. Surely people in this neighborhood did too. She'd be completely unnoticeable. She bit her lip. Well, her hair was kind of noticeable. She looked in the back of her car, and on the backseat was an old ball cap. One of Blake's, actually. She used it for days when her hair was a mess but she still had to go to the store for a Fresca and a bag of M&Ms. She grabbed the cap and shoved her hair up into it. Good. No one in their right mind would notice her now and see Sophie Reid. Perfect.

She opened the car door and shut it quietly. She looked around, to see if any neighbors were around, and then walked toward the Kellens' house. See, easy as pie. She walked slower as she heard sounds of people talking and laughing. They were all in the backyard. Sophie frowned.

She had been in that backyard just last week. Man, these people moved on fast. And she'd done their hair too!

Sophie knew she couldn't just walk toward their backyard and peek in like some freak. She stared at the neighbors' yard right next door to the Kellens'. They had a wooden fence between their properties. It didn't look like anyone was home. She could just walk back and peek through a slat. And no one would even know. Then she could leave and go home. Five minutes. There and back. No problem. Sophie looked around nervously one more time and then walked quickly through the side yard of the neighbors' house. She ran toward a large maple tree and hid behind it, putting herself between the tree and the fence.

The sounds of a get-together were really loud now. It was almost obnoxious how loud and happy the Kellens sounded. Sophie frowned and looked through a slat. She could see Lacie and Macie and Casey all lounging on the pool chairs with drinks in their hands and what looked like some of their friends standing by them or sitting by the side of the pool, dipping their feet in. And their hair looked good. Not great, like last Sunday, but oh, so much better than slicked back ponytails.

She switched to a different slat to get a better view and saw Sue and Stan standing by a huge barbecue. It was practically an outdoor kitchen. It was definitely bigger than her kitchen at home. They were flipping burgers and hotdogs and laughing and smiling at each other. They looked so happy. How could that be when she wasn't there?

Sophie frowned even more and switched to another slat. She didn't have the protection of the tree anymore, but she had to see if Sam was there. That was the whole point anyway. She fit her body up against the wooden slats with both hands on either side of her face and stared for all she was worth. She tried to see toward the back of the yard where the swing was. If she got on her tip toes, she could just barely make out a . . . a . . . foot! Yes, a foot! But whose?

Sophie leaned back and sighed. There was no help for it. She had to move closer. She looked up at the large house, looming silent and dark behind her and hoped the people who lived there were gone for the day. It didn't look like anyone was home. She squinched up her face and then made a decision. She'd come this far; there was no going back. She walked toward the back of the yard and found a slat with a gaping hole in it. *All the better to see you with my dear,* Sophie thought feeling slightly wicked.

She pushed her body up against the wood and looked toward the swing. Yep, someone was there. And they weren't alone. But who? She couldn't tell. Was it Trey? Or was it Sam? And who was that girl? Sophie sighed and then just waited. They'd sit up in a minute, and then she'd be able to see their faces. One of them moved. Yes! It was Tess! Oh no. Tess. And she was sitting by . . . not Trey. Sam.

Sophie stood back from the fence and walked quickly back toward her car. Okay, so she had told Sam to break things off with Tess cleanly, and maybe Sam had misheard her and thought she had told him to get back together with her. He was in the same swing he had been in with her, just seven very long days ago. He'd made up his mind. And it was not her.

Sophie reached her car just as a police car parked right behind her. Sophie's head jerked up. Ookaaay. This was so not good. The police man got out of his car and walked toward her with a frown. He looked like some super cop. Tall, dark, and mean.

"Good afternoon. We got a call about a prowler in this area. Would that happen to be you?" he asked in a friendly tone, but with cold steely eyes.

Sophie gulped and crossed her arms across her chest. This was not her day. At all. No boyfriend. Her would have been boyfriend was back with his old girlfriend. She was going to jail. Yep, this was bad.

"Sir, I apologize for looking like a prowler. I was just here to see the Kellens. But it looks like Sam is with another girl. So I just want to go home now," she said brokenly and then ruined her makeup by wiping the tears from her eyes, leaving a trail of black eyeliner smudging down her cheek.

The policeman frowned at her and then looked toward the Kellens' house.

"I know Sam Kellen. You're a friend of his?" he asked skeptically.

Sophie sighed and looked in her pockets for a tissue. None. She sniffed loudly and looked back at the house where loud sounds of voices and laughter and happiness felt like cruel acid in her ears.

"I was. I don't think I am anymore. Look, am I under arrest or anything? I'm sorry if I broke a law or something. But he's sitting in the swing with Tess, and I just want to get out of here," she said, trying hard not to cry.

The policeman shifted his weight to his left leg and studied her.

"The Madisons don't like people walking through their backyard to get a look at their neighbors. I'll give you a warning this time, but trespassing is breaking the law. Remember that next time you want to check on a boyfriend," he said sternly and then walked her to her car door.

Sophie tried to smile at him but just couldn't force her face to move.

"Thanks, officer. Trust me, this is the last time I set foot in Draper. I don't think I'll ever come back here. Even to go to Bajio Grill. I'll stick with Café Rio. Who needs good Mexican food or Sam Kellen?" she asked the police officer.

He stared at her incredulously and shook his head. "Can you drive yourself home, or are you too upset right now?" he asked staring at her in that scary cold way police officers have.

Sophie groaned inwardly and forced her face into a bright, happy smile. It worked for other things beside gynecological visits and relatives. She smiled for all she had at the policeman.

"I'm fine, officer. Super fine. Sorry again. I'll just get out of your hair now," she said and hopped in her car. She had to drive through the cul-de-sac to turn around. There was no help for it. She drove past the Kellens' house and couldn't stop herself from looking wistfully at it. She knew in her heart that she could have been there today. But she had chosen not to be. All because of a little thing called compassion.

As she turned the wheel, she noticed the front door opening and a man coming out on the front porch. She gasped and lowered her head. She still had her baseball hat on. *Please don't be Sam!* she prayed. She whipped her head around and looked quickly back at the porch as she drove out of the cul-de-sac. It was Trey! Yes. Not Sam. She was safe. No one would have to know she had stupidly, embarrassingly been there. As she drove out of the subdivision, she couldn't help noticing that Trey waved the police car down and that the policeman stopped and rolled his window down. She bit her lip and drove the speed limit out of the subdivision and out of Draper. As she went over the mountain and drove back into Utah County, she breathed a sigh a relief. She was not in jail. Sam hadn't seen her, and she could go home. She was lonely, yes, but cell mates weren't exactly the company she had been hoping for. She swore off stalking for the rest of her life.

She pulled into her driveway just as Sam's truck pulled in behind her. She whipped her head around and gasped. No way. No way did

that policeman rat her out! She ripped the hat off her head and got out of the car. She smiled brightly and pushed her hair back, out of her face, as Sam walked toward her. Frowning.

"Hi, Sam!" she said brightly. "What brings you to Alpine?" she asked, knowing exactly what brought him to Alpine.

Sam walked right up to her, standing only two inches away.

"Where've you been, Sophie?" he asked, frowning at her.

Sophie stepped back and bumped up against her car. "Oh, nowhere. What are you doing here?" she asked, looking guiltily over his shoulder. For some reason she just couldn't look him in the eye.

Sam reached up and wiped some of her smeared eyeliner off her cheek.

"It looks like you've been crying. Why are you sad, Sophie?" he asked.

Sophie reached up and wiped her cheek, looking at the evidence on her finger. Black-smeared Maybeline mascara. Perfect.

"Hey, it's Sunday. I always get teary at church. And, well with the divorce and everything, I've been kind of sad," she said, lying as she stared at her shoes.

Sam grabbed her chin and titled her face up. "Sophie, were you in Draper just fifteen minutes ago? Were you at my parents' house? Were you spying on me and my family though our neighbors' fence? Were you crying because you saw Tess there?" he asked gently.

Sophie licked her lips and looked into Sam's eyes. He didn't look mad. He didn't look shocked or disgusted. He actually looked kind of sad too.

"Look, I'm sorry. How was I to know that your neighbors were going to call the cops on me? I just wanted to check to see if Tess was there before I knocked on the door. But she was there. So that settles that. Doesn't it?" she said, although she really hadn't planned on knocking on his family's door. She had been spying plain and simple. Oops.

Sam let his hands fall from her face and stepped back slightly.

"Yeah, she was there. Of course, now she and my parents and my sisters and my brother know that you were spying on us and that you came very close to being arrested for trespassing. Man, Sophie, you are one bent chick," he said with a shake of his head and a very small smile.

Sophie blushed bright red. She had been caught. That police officer had ratted her out to Trey. She would never be able to face them again. She held her hands up to her burning cheeks and walked away from Sam toward her house. This was a bad day. It needed to end.

"So why'd you come by?" Sam asked. "I thought you just wanted to be friends."

Sophie looked back at him. So beautiful, so tall and strong. So perfect.

"You know how it is. I was bored and just went for a drive. I thought I'd satisfy my curiosity and see if you were with Tess. Looks like I'm right. I just wanted proof, but I should have saved myself the gas. I had a feeling you'd be with her," she said, looking to the right of his ear.

Sam frowned and looked down at his shoes.

"Yeah, she wants to get back together. She didn't like the idea of you anywhere near my family. I think she got scared. She's pretty much plastered herself to me ever since Sunday night. I got back home from dropping you off and she was in the family room watching TV with my family. She says she's been going to counseling and that she's a lot better now. She wants me to give her another chance," he said almost forlornly.

Sophie quit looking at her neighbors' house and stared at Sam. He sounded so sad. Not at all like a man who wanted to get back together with his ex-girlfriend.

"So do you believe her? Do you think she's really getting some help?" she couldn't help asking.

Sam winced and nodded his head. "Yes, I believe her. But that doesn't change anything. I mean, I'm glad she's seeing a counselor, but that doesn't mean I'm in love with her. I don't want to get back together with her. She told me that her counselor said that any strong emotions like sadness or anger could really send her over the edge right now. According to Tess, he says she has to stay calm and happy and to her, that means she needs to be with me. I feel like I'm being blackmailed into being with her. If I don't do what she wants, then she'll have some psychotic episode and blame it all on me. And you told me that I had to make sure she was okay before I could be with you. So I don't know what to do," he said, clearly upset.

Sophie frowned and kicked her shoe in the dirt. Now what?

"Oh, Sam, what a mess. I'm so sorry. I guess I did say that. I didn't think this would happen, though. I seriously thought you'd just have a talk with her and then it would all work out. Now you're even more stuck than you were before. Maybe you should call her counselor and ask him for some advice too," she said, not knowing really what to say.

"Yeah, I guess. This last week has just exhausted me. I feel like I'm walking on eggshells. I want to move on with my life, but she won't let me and you won't let me," he said, with his eyebrows drawn together.

Sophie frowned back at him. "Hey, now that's not fair. You know I would love to be with you. You can't blame this on me. Can't you see that if I get between you and Tess that everything would just be worse? Look, I don't think you should have to babysit Tess's fragile psyche the rest of your life, but I do think there's got to be a solution that will work for everyone. Don't you?" she pleaded with him.

Sam shoved his hands in his pockets and looked up at the sky. When he looked back down at her, he looked defeated. "If there is a solution, then I don't know what it is. Right now, she's back at my house waiting for me. She knows I came after you; everyone does. Who knows what I'll find when I get home? Will she be okay? Will she have thrown a fit? I don't know. Maybe the best solution for everyone is if I just take off and move away. I've gotten offers from other builders to buy me out. I could just pick up and move and start over. That might be the only way to be free," he said, staring off into space.

Sophie's mouth fell open. Move? Leave? She'd never see him again.

"Okay, that might be a little extreme, don't you think? I mean, wouldn't you miss your family? Wouldn't you miss me?" she asked, stepping closer to him and grabbing his hand.

Sam stared down at their hands clasped together.

"Remember? We're just friends," he said, and let her hand go.

Sophie rubbed her shoulders as she watched him walk to his truck and get in. She suddenly felt cold. Had she been cruel to insist that they just be friends? What she was, was completely stupid. And now, yet again, she was alone. And this time, it was hopeless. Sam was gone.

chapter 25

Sophie woke up the next morning determined to be happy. Determined to be the same ole, happy Sophie that everyone knew and loved. She would not let anyone affect her happiness. How dumb would that be? It was completely anti-feminist to allow a man to turn her world upside down, shake it, shatter it, and then leave it for her to clean up. Nope, she wasn't going to stand for it. No Sam, no big deal. Life was moving on without him. And she'd be just fine, thank you.

She pushed through the front door of the salon and threw her bag down in her chair.

"What's wrong with you?" Cathie asked, frowning at her. "You look like your dog just died," she said, still staring at her.

Sophie groaned and couldn't even find the strength to paste on a fake smile for everyone's comfort and enjoyment.

"It's no big deal. I just had the chance to be with the most awesome guy in the world, and I turned him down. No big deal. I'll be back in the saddle by the weekend," she said, shrugging.

Cathie raised an eyebrow and tsked but thankfully didn't say another thing.

"Well, some girl has been calling like every five minutes for you. I told her that you didn't have an appointment until ten and that she could come on down. I hope that was okay."

Sophie glanced at the clock. It was only eight thirty. She'd planned on doing some cleaning and organizing, but what the heck. Money was good too. "What was her name, Cathie?" she asked, walking to the front desk to grab the messages.

Cathie grabbed a paper off the counter and handed it to her. "Some silly name. Oh yeah—Daphne. Who'd ever name a kid that?" she said and walked back to her station.

Sophie couldn't help grinning. Daphne. Her little cousin. She'd expected her a week ago, but it would take a little humility to walk through the salon doors and ask her for help. And Daphne was as far away from humble as you could get.

The doorbell clanged and Sophie turned around and was not surprised to see her cousin. She was surprised to see her hair. Gone were the subtle green streaks. Daphne's hair was now a strange mottled color closer to moss than blonde.

"You little idiot," she muttered under her breath. "Daphne, come on in. Let's get started. I have an appointment at ten, and this is going to take a while. Why don't you come sit down over here and tell me what's been going on," Sophie said, gesturing to her chair.

Daphne looked miserable, so Sophie decided not to rub it in too much. She looked completely deflated, not to mention horrible. The ultra blonde hair, although very Baywatch, had been a good look for her. Moss green, not so flattering.

Daphne sat down gingerly in the seat and stared miserably into the mirror.

"My mom is so mad at me. She's been yelling at me for over a week to come see you and get this fixed. I thought Jen could fix it, but she just made it worse," Daphne whispered, trying not to whimper. "I have a date this Friday with Eric. He wants me to meet his parents. How can I meet anyone's parents with hair like this?" she asked with a shaky voice.

Sophie couldn't help smiling, but she did pat Daphne on the shoulder. "Well, let's just focus on getting you looking normal. Forget about Eric, forget about parents. Let's just focus on you for a while. Okay? Now I'm going to be honest with you. What you've done to your hair has really damaged it. Let me guess—after I saw you that Sunday, you tried to bleach out the downlights, right?" Sophie asked, fingering Daphne's hair that now felt like straw.

Daphne nodded, looking guiltily down in her lap.

Sophie sighed. "Okay, and when that didn't work, your friend tried to cover it with a light brown all over, right?" Sophie asked, hoping she would be able to fix her cousin's hair.

Daphne nodded again. "I'm never speaking to Jen again! I can't believe she did this to me. And we're like best friends. I always knew she was jealous of me, but ruining my hair! She went way too far," Daphne said, turning red in the face and clenching her fists.

Sophie blinked a couple times and decided to let that go. "Well, I'm going to be honest with you, Daphne. You have completely trashed your hair. Your hair is so damaged, it's deader than straw. It's totally stripped. We're going to have to cut half your hair off, condition it for an hour, and you're going to have to do deep conditioning treatments weekly, which means the color we're going to put on will fade faster. Now, tell me. Do you want to go back to blonde? Or do you want to try a light brown? An all-over color would be gentler on your hair right now. I could add some silicone to give it the shine that normal healthy hair has. What do you think?" Sophie asked, hoping her cousin wouldn't demand something insane and impossible.

Daphne looked at herself in the mirror and tilted her head to the side as if she were studying a Picasso. "I've really been thinking about my hair lately. When Mom came home after you fixed her hair, it was like she was a totally different person. I think you are your hair. When she had that horrible black hair, she was like that. All severe and sarcastic and depressing, you know. And now that she's back to her natural hair color, she's so much more relaxed. And so I started to think about my hair and how blonde it was. I mean, it was fine for high school, but now that I'm older and I'm dating successful men, I need to look successful too, you know. So that's why I had Jen add the downlights. But, you know how that turned out. So why don't we go with maybe a light ash brown. But if we do that, you have to give me some blonde highlights around the face. I mean, I can't go completely blonde-free. I'd just die," Daphne said, looking completely serious.

Sophie studied her cousin and thought about what she had said. Daphne might actually have a point. And what did that say about her, with her reddish brown, crazy wavy hair? Probably nothing good.

"Okay, let's do it. Now about the cut. You've had the same hairstyle for the past five years. Super long, super straight blonde hair. I'm going to cut to just under your chin. I know this will be a shock, but we just don't have a choice here, Daphne. I'll give you a fun cut with some layers, and I'll style it for you. I think you'll like it," Sophie said reassuringly.

Daphne swallowed but nodded. "Do what you have to do. And my mom's paying. I've got her credit card. So the sky's the limit. Take all day. Move mountains. Just get this green crap off my head and let me look normal again," she said pleadingly.

Sophie smiled and put the drape around her cousin's tense shoulders.

"Moving mountains is what I do. Just relax. Cathie, will you call my ten o'clock and reschedule? I've got a mountain in my way right now," she said and went to work.

Three long, tedious hours later, Sophie put her flat iron down and turned Daphne's chair so that she could look at her straight on. She moved a lock of hair into place and then smiled. She was an artist. Before her sat a new woman. Gone was the ex-cheerleader. Gone was the Martian from outer space. Now, in their place was a modern, chic, beautiful woman. With beautiful hair. Sophie had outdone herself. Daphne's hair was cut into an ultra-sophisticated hairstyle. Models would be begging for her advice on hair after this. The layers she had cut were curled and waved around her face, setting off the glossy tones of her silky light ash brown hair. The subtle blonde highlights surrounding her face looked natural. Buh-bye Pamela Anderson. Hello, Jennifer Aniston. Thank heavens.

Sophie turned Daphne's chair back around so she could see the mirror and watched her cousin's reaction. She didn't care too much what Daphne thought. For herself, she knew she had worked a miracle.

Daphne took a deep breath and let it out slowly. A small, relieved smile bloomed on her face.

"It doesn't even look like me at all does it?" she asked, not expecting an answer. "I guess now I have to take back all those mean things I've said to you, huh?" Daphne said, glancing at Sophie, and then back at her beloved reflection.

Sophie snorted. "Why? You meant them. Just because you don't look like a freak anymore, doesn't mean we're best friends," Sophie said and undid the drape from her cousin's shoulders.

Daphne frowned and stood up, turning to look at Sophie.

"Yeah, well, now that you've helped me out, it won't be so much fun making fun of you," she said honestly.

Sophie's eyes went wide and she nodded. "Well, sorry to take all the fun out of your life," she said and walked toward the cash register.

Daphne glared at her back and followed her. "You know, it's not like you've ever given me and Farrah a chance anyway. You were determined to hate us from the very beginning. We just obliged you and tortured you, because that's what you expected," Daphne said with a flip of her newly cut hair.

Sophie raised one eyebrow and rang up the transaction. "Rationalize your behavior all you want to, Daphne. Picking on me constantly, making fun of my clothes and my hair and my mom and my house and choice in career and on and on and on and on. You did all that just because you thought that's what I wanted you to do? Daphne, look, I'm glad I could help you out this time. I mean, no one should have to look like that. But I'm really booked. All of my regular customers are taking up every second I have. So tell Jen hi for me," Sophie said and then told her cousin how much she owed her.

Daphne didn't even blink at the exorbitant figure, just handed her Lexie's credit card.

"You know I can't go back to Jen! She already ruined my hair once. You have to take me on. Look, I'm sorry for all the crap we dished out on you. I'm sorry. Now can we move on?" she asked, impatiently tapping her foot on the tile floor.

Sophie stared at her cousin in disbelief. The nerve!

"No," she said and handed her cousin the receipt.

Daphne ripped the receipt out of her hand and flounced out of the salon. Sophie watched her go and shook her head. Okay, so maybe she was being unforgiving, but there were limits. And Daphne was hers.

Cathie walked up and patted her on the shoulder. "You've got a kinder heart than I do. I would have dyed her hair purple," she said, laughing.

Sophie laughed too. She had to admit after especially awful family get-togethers she'd dreamed of doing horrible things to Daphne's hair. But she felt good about what she had done. She'd helped her cousin, but now that her cousin knew how good she was, every hair dresser Daphne went to would pale in comparison. Daphne would be tortured by the hair she could have had.

Sophie giggled. "Ah, just seeing her happy face is my reward," she said.

Cathie burst out laughing. "Honey, you crack me up," she said and picked up the phone.

Sophie spent the rest of the week working and thinking of Sam. And Tess.

Friday afternoon found her at the airport with Jacie, holding up posters and trying not to look at the frowning faces of his family standing on the other side of the aisle.

"Why don't you at least just go and say hi to his mom?" Sophie prodded.

Jacie looked at her shoe and shook her head. "The woman hates me. There's no way I'm going to say hi. She'd punch me in the nose," she muttered.

Sophie sighed and set her sign down by her feet. "Well, can I just sit down in a chair? I've been on my feet all day," she complained.

Jacie glared at her and tugged on her arm. "No! I want him to see these signs before he sees theirs. He'll know as soon as he sees these signs how much I love him," she said, nodding her head almost violently.

Sophie glanced at the signs she and Jacie had spent way too much time making and honestly couldn't see how all the glitter and beads added up to love. But maybe she was wrong. Maybe that had been her problem. Maybe Blake had taken one look at her sign and seen no love. Maybe it had shouted friendship.

Sophie frowned and held up her sign again, even though her arms were starting to ache.

"Look! Some people are walking off. He'll be out any second. Hold it higher!" Jacie said excitedly.

Sophie hoisted her sign even higher and promised herself a gym membership. Her arms must be the wimpiest things in the world. She was dying!

Jacie started to breathe quickly, and her face was turning red in excitement. And her hair, well, her hair looked fantastic. If anything said love—forget the poster—it was the hair. Sophie smiled, pleased at the job she had done. Jacie had never looked better.

"Oh my gosh, Sophie! He's coming!" Jacie screeched in her ear.

Sophie looked around her sign and saw a tall, dark-haired man in a suit with a name tag walk toward them, holding a carry-on. He was grinning and looking at everyone all at once.

"Mom! Dad!" Bryan shouted and dropped his bag, before running to his family. He must not have seen Jacie, or their sign.

Sophie lowered her sign just a little bit so she could watch. She glanced at Jacie and was relieved to see she wasn't crushed by the fact he hadn't noticed her yet. Jacie was glowing as she watched him. She was staring at him as if she were memorizing his face. She loved him. Sophie's mouth hung open in surprise. Okay, yeah, Jacie had said how much she loved him and on and on, but Sophie had to admit that she wasn't really sure she believed her. Jacie was always so cool and self-assured, and nothing ever really got to her. But looking at Jacie now was like seeing the real her, for the first time. There was no façade. No pretense. No walls. Just a girl in love with a boy.

Sophie looked back at Bryan and watched as he hugged one family member after another. He looked good. He'd gotten taller, and his face looked a little different. He looked more like a man and less like the boy she had seen two years ago. He was so happy. He let go of one of his sisters as his mom reached up and whispered in his ear and pointed in their direction. He frowned and looked over his shoulder at the two girls staring at him with garish, bright signs.

Sophie gulped and felt nervous all of a sudden. She couldn't imagine what Jacie was feeling. She looked quickly at her friend and couldn't believe the glowing smile on Jacie's face. Crazy.

Bryan walked up to Jacie, completely ignoring Sophie, and shoved his hands in his pockets. He was not smiling.

"Hi, Jacie. Thanks for your email," he said quietly, although his eyes were blazing furiously.

"Hi, Bryan. I know we haven't kept in touch, but I just wanted to welcome you home," she said, still smiling brightly at him. Sophie wondered how Bryan couldn't see radiant beams of love shooting from her eyes.

"So what about the last two years? You wrote me once in the MTC to tell me that you were going to date everyone else while I was gone, and then I get an email last week saying hi. I'm sorry, but I just don't get it," he said stonily.

Jacie lost a little bit of her glow but didn't give up. She stepped closer to Bryan and grabbed his hand, letting her sign fall to the side.

"I made a mistake. I made a huge mistake. I love you, Bryan. I love you so much. I've loved you for the last two years. Every day I've loved you," she said, staring up into his furious face.

Bryan groaned and pulled his hands away. "You loved me when you went out with all of those other guys? You loved me then?" he asked, his voice getting louder.

Sophie glanced at Bryan's parents, who were staring at him with worried frowns on their faces. Sophie gulped and hoped Jacie knew what she was doing. This could go so wrong in so many ways.

"Yes, Bryan. On every single date I went on, I wondered what you were doing and what you were feeling and if you ever thought of me. I thought of you every day, every morning, and every night. I can't live without thinking of you," she said, grabbing his hand again with both of hers.

Bryan used his free hand to run it through his painfully short hair. He looked away from Jacie and closed his eyes.

"And you just expect me to forget about all of that? It's been two years. Do you expect us to just pick up where we left off? You're crazy!" he said through his teeth, and tried again unsuccessfully to pull his hand free.

Jacie suddenly realized that things weren't going the way she wanted them to and let go. She took a breath and pushed her hair behind her ears.

"I can't take back what I did," she told him. "But I'll tell you one thing. The only thing that matters. I love you. I might have gone on a few dates while you were gone. I might have gone to the dances. But I loved you every minute of the last two years. And I love you now. If you never want to see me again, then that's your decision and I'll understand. If you want to go out with other girls, I'll understand. If you want to yell and scream at me, I'll understand. You do what you have to do. But I love you," she said simply, staring up at him with pleading eyes.

Bryan let his shoulders fall and looked at his feet. He took a breath and looked over Jacie's head and then back down at her.

"Jacie," he said, and then stopped. He shook his head again and then looked right at her. He reached up and wiped a tear off her cheek and then stepped back.

"I love you too. But man, are you going to make it up to me," he said with a sudden grin.

Jacie covered her face with her hands and started to cry. He reached over and then let his hands fall.

"Look, knock it off. I'm not released yet. I can't hug you or anything. Just come over to my house tonight. My parents are having an open house. Okay?" he said, tilting her chin up gently.

Jacie sniffed and then smiled back at him.

"Of course I'll be there," she said and looked like she wanted to launch herself at him, but stopped at the last second.

He grinned down at her and then noticed her sign on the floor.

"Cool sign. Hey, Sophie," he said and then walked back toward his frowning family. He talked to them for a few minutes, and their frowns disappeared quickly.

They all turned and waved at Jacie and Sophie and then walked as a large group to the walkway leading toward the luggage.

Sophie put her arm around her friend's shoulders and wasn't surprised to feel her trembling.

"Sophie, he's going to give me another chance," Jacie whispered.

Sophie laughed and hugged her. "Of course he is! He loves you," she said, and the girls danced around in a circle in the middle of the airport, not caring who was watching or who was laughing at them.

They ran with their signs, giggling and laughing back toward the parking lot.

"Sophie, thanks for coming with me. You're the bestest best friend in the whole world," Jacie said, glowing and giggling in happiness.

Sophie opened the door for Jacie and pushed her in. "I know. Now let's go redo your makeup and get something yummy at the bakery to take to his house. You must not go empty-handed. And as we both know, you can't cook anything but macaroni and cheese," she said wisely.

Jacie nodded absently. "You're coming with me, though, right?"

Sophie got in the driver's side and shook her head. "Nah, you're on your own now. Besides, I'd just be in the way. He wants to see you, not me."

Jacie frowned. "Yeah, but no matter what Bryan says, I bet his family still hates me," she said worriedly.

Sophie shrugged. "Well, if their son loves you, then they'll just have to accept it. All his parents want is for him to be happy. If you make him happy, then that's that."

Jacie nodded but still looked worried.

Sophie shook her head. "Hey, dope, stop looking for things to worry about. Bryan is home and he wants to see you! I saw his face. He was furious with you, but he was happy you were there," she said, feeling a small painful prick in her heart.

Jacie smiled and laughed. "You're right. That's all that matters right now. He's giving me another chance."

They drove back to Alpine, planning everything from Jacie's wedding reception to the names of their future children. Life was back on track.

chapter 26

Sophie finished Jacie's makeup and hair and gave her a quick hug before taking off. Jacie had to run to the bakery, and Sophie had to admit she needed a little break from happily ever after. It was giving her a headache. Yeah, she was happy for Jacie, but it just would have been nicer if they both had gorgeous, wonderful men in love with them at the same time. Sophie grinned. She knew she was being a brat. She was completely and totally happy for Jacie. She just needed a little break. Nothing bitter or dark. Just a nice hour or two with a good book and a carton of Ben and Jerry's.

Sophie pulled into her driveway and noticed a car parked along the street. She frowned, not recognizing the car. It was an old Accord. A sad, tan little thing. *Who in the world?* she wondered and watched as her father got out of the car and walked toward her.

Sophie shut her door and waited for him. This was the first time he'd come to her house. Ever. She watched as he approached and noticed how nervous he looked. He was actually going to speak to her. No sister or mother around. No cousins to cushion the awkwardness. He was on his own. She wondered what he had to say that would bring him here.

"Um, hi, Sophie. Is your mom here?" he asked, looking away from her as soon as their eyes met.

Of course. He was here to see her mom.

"Sorry, she's working until seven tonight. You can reach her at the salon," she said and turned around to walk in.

"Wait, Sophie," he said.

Sophie turned around, curious by the nervousness in his voice.

"Well, I was just wondering," he said, and then paused before going on. "I was just wondering why your mom won't return my calls. I've left messages, but she's acting like she doesn't want to talk to me," he said, sounding slightly insulted.

Sophie blinked a couple times. Brother.

"Yeah, well, listen Dad. This is the deal. Now that you and Julie are getting a divorce, it doesn't mean that Mom is waiting to take up where you two left off. She doesn't want to get back together with you. Don't you remember? You left her. You almost destroyed her. You really can't understand why she doesn't want to talk to you?" she asked, stunned.

Tanner breathed out slowly and put his hands behind his back, looking down dejectedly.

"I don't know. I just thought that maybe, now that Julie left me, that maybe your mom and I could work things out. Maybe we could go back to being a family. The three of us," he said and looked up at her hopefully.

Sophie's mouth fell open a fraction. Her grandmother had hinted at it, but this was unreal.

"You have a new family. Well, you did. Remember your two children Carter and Callie? Maybe you should call Julie and see if you can work things out," she said and frowned at him.

Tanner's face fell, and he looked even more pathetic.

"Sophie, you're a young girl. You just don't understand about life and love and relationships yet. I messed things up with Julie. Really, just a silly misunderstanding, but she has it in her head that she never wants to see me again. And Carter and Callie are fine. I've never been good with children anyway. So, I was just thinking that now would be the perfect opportunity to allow Candice back into my life. She was always so kind and understanding. I could use somebody like that right now."

Sophie's eyebrows rose an inch, and she felt her heart turn to stone. "Um, I believe that the key word in that sentence was *use*. That was the verb you chose. *Use*. Believe it or not, I understand more than you think I do. I'm not ten anymore, and Mom isn't that same woman you used to know. She's strong now. After you left she started her own business, she raised me single-handedly, and she's happy now. She's even dating. I don't think you should try to pull her back into your life just because you can use her. That's just selfish," she said, feeling the blood start to hum in her veins. This was the longest conversation she'd had with her dad in, well, ever, and instead of the wonderful, touching moment of love shared between a father and daughter, she felt like reading him the riot act. This wasn't going well.

Tanner stared at her for a moment and then shook his head to clear anything she had tried to tell him out.

"Just tell her that I still love her. Okay? I've gotta run. I need to see my lawyer about some details to do with the divorce. I'm staying with your grandmother for a while until we can figure out what goes to whom. So tell Candice to call me there," he said and walked back to his car, confident that Sophie would do as she was told.

Sophie stared as her father drove away, and felt completely powerless. He hadn't understood one thing she had said. That or she was so utterly beneath him that anything she said had to be ignored based on the fact that a young woman knew nothing of value.

Sophie sat down on her front porch step and rested her chin on her hands, letting her hair fall forward, covering her face. And at that moment, it all hit her at once. She was tired. She was tired of men. Did she love them? Did they love her? Did any of it matter anyway?

She sighed and thought about going into the house and changing into a pair of shorts, but she couldn't find the energy to move. She heard a car drive up and tilted her head to the side to see who it was. Great. Blake. Just when she thought her day couldn't get any more irritating.

"Hey, Sophie!" Blake said cheerfully and walked over and sat down next to her.

She lifted her head and brushed her hair out of her eyes. He looked good. He looked happy. Wow. She caught herself smiling back at him.

"Hey, Blake. What's going on?" she asked, scooting away from him.

He smiled and scooted closer. "I just saw you sitting on your porch and thought I'd stop and say hi. How's it going?" he asked, pushing a curl out of her eyes.

Sophie frowned and scooted again. "Oh, it's going. So what are you doing in town? I thought since you've moved in with your buddies that you'd be busy getting ready for school and getting a job and all that fun stuff," she said, trying to make polite conversation.

Blake grinned. "I am. I was picking up some of my stuff. I took your advice. I called Bailey and asked her out on a date, just like you said."

Sophie smiled back at him and patted his shoulder. "There you go! So did you have fun?" she asked.

He took her hand and started playing with her rings, twisting them and pulling them. Sophie sighed but didn't pull her hand away. Blake used to do that all the time when they dated in high school. It was as natural for him as breathing and didn't mean anything.

"I did. I took her on a picnic at the park. We had a good time," he said, pulling one ring off and putting it on a different finger.

Sophie smiled at him and let him scoot closer. "Oh, that's fantastic, Blake. See? Now you feel better, don't you? You look great. You look happy. Dating is just what you needed," she said, and felt a bit of peace settle inside. Blake was going to be okay.

Blake looked up at her and frowned slightly. "Sophie, don't you see? I went on that date with Bailey just to see if you were right. I even kissed her good night. And there was nothing. Seriously, nothing. I mean, writing to her was great, and I loved writing to her, but being with her is a different story. Sophie, I'm not in love with Bailey!" he said, grabbing both her hands and leaning toward her as he talked.

Sophie leaned back and tried to pull her hands away. "Wait! What is going on here? So why do you look so happy?" she asked, confused now.

Blake kept one hand firmly clasping one of hers and put one hand on her knee.

"I'm happy because now you'll believe me. We should be together," he said and leaned down to kiss her.

Sophie blinked and then jumped up, pushing Blake back. Blake was so caught offguard, he fell backward into the flowerbed, crushing all of her mom's impatiens.

"Blake! You idiot! What do you think you're doing?" Sophie yelled at him.

Blake groaned and sat up, coming slowly to his feet.

"Dang, Sophie. What's the matter with you? I think I landed on a rock or something," he said, rubbing his back and looking sad.

Sophie sighed and put her hands on her hips.

"Blake, this is it. I'm sorry you got hurt, but honestly, I'm going to the Humane Society and getting a dog tomorrow, and if you ever try to pull a stunt like that again, my dog is going to put a hole in your rear end. Got it?" she said, feeling smoke rise from ears.

"What's wrong with kissing?" Blake yelled back at her, getting mad too.

Sophie shook her head in irritation.

"Kissing is great, Blake. As a matter of fact, I just discovered lately that I like kissing. I just don't happen to like kissing you. And I'm sorry, but I just don't want to be with you anymore," she said, more gently.

Blake's shoulders sagged, and he bent over to try to fix some of the flowers. "My mom was sure if I kissed you that you'd come to your senses. I didn't believe her, but my dad said I should go for it. They really love you and miss you, Sophie. I miss you too, but you're right. We never did get that kissing stuff right. Don't worry about getting the dog. I can take a hint. I might have been slow this time, but I just figured, if you could wait for me for two years, then you'd be willing to give me one more chance," he said, looking at her sincerely confused.

Sophie frowned and then shrugged. "I don't know, Blake. I don't even know if I can explain it. I probably should have given you one more chance. You're right—I did wait for you for two years. I thought I loved you. I thought we would get married and have a big happy family and live down the street from our parents. But when you came back and I saw you again, I just knew deep in my heart that you weren't meant for me. Eternity is such a long time, Blake. Being with the wrong person for eternity can't be heaven," she said sadly, sitting back down on the porch.

Blake sat down next to her and grabbed her hand. This time, it was a comforting gesture.

"I completely know what you mean. Sorry again for trying to kiss you. Forgive me?" he asked with his old charming smile back in place.

Sophie grinned at him and hugged him.

"Of course. I love ya, Blake," she said with a tear in her eye.

Blake winced. "As a friend," he said with a dramatic sigh and stood up. "Well, I'm off to break the news to my parents. They'll take it hard, but they'll get over it eventually. Just be patient with them," he said and walked away.

Sophie sat where she was and watched him go. She thought of how Jacie had refused to wait for Bryan while all the time being completely in love with him. And how she had waited faithfully for Blake for two long years, and she hadn't even been close to being madly in love. Why? Why had she chosen to wait for someone she wasn't truly in love with? Was it for the attention? Had she done it just so people would ask her about her missionary, because some of that specialness rubbed off on her? Or did she do it because it was safe? Because she would have two years all to herself, no pressure, no men? She sighed and stood up. Maybe she'd never know why she did it. All she knew now was that recess was over and real life had begun.

chapter 27

Sophie fixed her mom a plate of grilled oriental chicken salad and put it in front of her. Candy looked tired tonight. Happy but tired.

"So, Mom, how was work?" she asked, sitting down opposite her mom and pushing a napkin toward her.

Candy smiled at her and took a bite. "Mmm! This is good, hon. Oh, work was fine. Same ole, same ole. Cathie had to do Sister Martin's hair today, though. Holy cow, I don't know how Cathie does it, but she held her tongue and didn't say one word. She just nodded and smiled the whole time."

Sophie grinned and then gave up and laughed a little. Sister Martin was a local yoga teacher, and, well, Cathie was about twenty pounds overweight. Sister Martin always asked for Cathie to do her hair and then gave her advice on nutrition and exercise the entire time she was getting her dark brown roots done. Cathie was a saint.

"Poor Cathie. What she won't say for a good tip," she said and picked a piece of chicken out of her mom's salad and nibbled on it.

Candy laughed and took another bite. "Julie stopped in and bought some shampoo and conditioner. She really is so sweet. I can't believe I've hated her all these years. She was telling me about the divorce. Sounds like your dad is going to be a free man very soon," Candy said, looking down at her plate.

Sophie frowned and played with the salt and pepper shakers on the table.

"Yeah, about that Mom. You're not thinking of getting back together with Dad, are you? Because Clyde seems like such a nice guy,"

Sophie said, wondering what she would do or say or think or even feel if her mom did want to get back together with her dad.

Candy stared at her for a second and then burst out laughing so hard, Sophie looked up in shock.

"Sophie!" Candy gasped and then laughed harder. "Sophie, you little idiot!" she said between giggles.

Sophie sighed in relief and grabbed her mom's fork and took the biggest piece of chicken and ate it. Life was okay again.

"I can't believe you would even think such a thing," Candy finally said when her face turned back to its normal color and she was able to breathe again.

Sophie smiled. "Well, I saw Dad today, and he mentioned how he had been trying to get in touch with you," she mumbled, looking down at the floor.

Candy snorted and speared a piece of cabbage. "Poor man. Poor, poor man. But on to something more interesting. Clyde is taking me out to dinner on Friday. I want you to help me pick out something to wear. And you have to do my hair and makeup and everything. He's taking me somewhere really fancy up in Park City. I think he's going to kiss me," she said, blushing.

Sophie stared at her mother in shock. "You mean he hasn't been kissing you all this time?" she asked

Candy giggled. "Well, of course not! We haven't been on that many dates," she said going back to her salad.

Sophie blinked, still stunned. Wow. Sam had kissed her barely half an hour after she had met him. Men could so different.

"Mom, come on, you've been out together like at least five times now. No kissing at all? What about that time he came over and watched a movie with you? No cuddling? No making out?"

Candy frowned and looked at her daughter carefully. "Honey, you've got to understand something. I guess we should have had this talk a lot sooner. I just thought you understood."

Sophie started to blush and held up her hands to interrupt her mom. "Hold on! Hold on, Mom. I know all about the birds and the bees. Please, let's not go there," Sophie begged

Candy laughed and shook her head. "No, you goof ball. I'm not talking about sex. I'm talking about kissing and cuddling with someone, you know, making out. Sophie, I haven't been kissing Clyde and he hasn't been kissing me because we both know where kissing leads. Your dad was the only man I've ever kissed. Did you know that?" she asked.

Sophie shook her head, horrified for her mother.

"You see, when women start kissing and cuddling with the men they're involved with, feelings of love naturally follow. Men are so different. They just like kissing because it feels good and they don't jump to the next level like we do. We equate physical intimacy with love, and we zoom on ahead to commitment and marriage and children. I've been down that road. I know where it leads. And so does Clyde. He doesn't want to get hurt again, and I sure don't want my heart broken again. Taking things slow, physically, is the smartest thing you can do. It saves you a lot of misery. Sophie, as your mother, one of the most important piece of advice I could give you is to protect your heart."

Sophie felt a big *aaahhhh* form in her head and just barely stopped herself from saying it out loud.

"Well, so you're ready to kiss him this Friday, huh?" Sophie asked, snagging another piece of her mom's salad.

Candy blushed and nodded. "Yes, I think so. I know you haven't had a chance to get to know him very well, but Clyde is wonderful. I'm thinking of inviting him over for Sunday dinner so you two can get to know each other better. He's such a good father, so open and loving and affectionate. And he's been the perfect gentleman. I really like him, Sophie," she said with a grin.

Sophie grinned back and nodded. "Then I like him too. As long as he treats you good, then I'm all for this."

Candy sparkled at her. "So you'll hook me up and make me look ten years younger, ten pounds lighter, and ten times more wonderful than I am?"

Sophie got up and hugged her mom. "Impossible, Mom. You're already perfect. But I'll be happy to get you ready for your date. I even have a new outfit that will look amazing on you. Don't worry about a thing. Just have Cathie do your nails, though, okay?"

Candy laughed and hugged her daughter back.

"You got it, hon. Thanks."

Sophie's cell phone rang and she answered it. "Hello?" she said, not recognizing the number on the screen.

"Hey, Sophie. This is Paul. Do you remember me?" he said.

Sophie smiled and leaned back in her chair. "Of course I do! The defender of all hair stylists. What's going on?" she asked while her mom looked at her curiously.

"I'm doing great. I was just wondering if you had any plans this Friday. I'd love to take you out to dinner and a movie or something."

Sophie paused for a second before saying yes. She couldn't help thinking of Sam. What would he be doing this Friday night? Hopefully he wasn't moving. But if he wasn't, then she knew he'd probably be with Tess. And, yes, maybe part of that was her fault. If she'd been more heartless, she could have told Sam to get rid of Tess as quickly as possible and forget the consequences. But she wasn't. So here she was, not exactly dating Sam. So did that mean she should stay home Friday night? Or not?

"Paul, I'd love to," she said and concentrated on not thinking of Sam.

Candy watched her daughter talk on the phone while she finished her salad.

Sophie shut her cell phone and slipped it into her pocket. She looked up to find her mother watching her with a frown.

"What?" Sophie asked.

Candy smiled and pushed her plate away. "I was just wondering why you looked so grim when you said yes to that boy. And what ever happened to Sam? I thought he was getting rid of his ex so he could be with you. I thought you really liked him. Julie told me that his whole family is in love with you," Candy said, raising an eyebrow.

Sophie sighed and leaned her head back. "It's complicated, Mom. His ex has a nervous breakdown anytime she thinks of him with another girl. And her counselor thinks that her being with Sam right now is the healthiest thing she could do. So Sam is stuck. And while he's stuck, I'm at home waiting. And you know I've done my share of waiting. So hello Paul. He's really nice too, Mom. You'll like him. He's going to be a lawyer," she said and laughed at her mom's expression.

"A lawyer, huh? This could be interesting," Candy said and got up to put her plate in the sink.

Sophie frowned. Interesting. Just what she didn't need right now.

chapter 28

Sophie saw her mom off on her date and was pleased to see that Clyde had brought a huge bouquet of roses for Candy. He was on the right track, and Sophie couldn't be happier. Her dad had called again that day, but thank heavens for caller ID. The best invention a girl ever had. She watched Clyde's car pull away and waved at her mom. Candy had looked fantastic. She didn't look a day over thirty-five. She was glowing. She was beautiful and as excited as any sixteen-year-old going out on a date. Sophie sighed in happiness and put the roses in a large vase. With Clyde around, they were going to have to invest in nicer vases.

She thought about Clyde being with her mom and didn't feel any nervousness or unease. She knew instinctively that Clyde was the type of man who would take care of her mom and love her faithfully. She couldn't help thinking forward to the wedding. What would her mom wear? Where would they get married? And more important, where would she live? With them? In an apartment?

Sophie frowned for the first time and shook her head. Details. Details she didn't even need to worry about until way down the road. Heck, her mom hadn't even kissed the guy yet. But still. She shook her head and smiled. Flowers. She was taking care of flowers. Focus! Too bad she couldn't call Jacie on the phone and talk over this new development. She was on her first real date with Bryan. They were driving up to Salt Lake to walk around Temple Square. The perfect date for a newly returned missionary. She had helped Jacie think of it. Jacie was firmly in the throes of happiness, and nothing was budging her.

Sophie finished taking care of the roses and glanced at the clock. Paul would be there shortly, but until then, she didn't have anything to do or anyone to talk to. She walked listlessly through the house. She was dressed and ready, since she and her mom had gotten ready at the same time. Her hair was perfect—curly ringlets pulled up into a soft twist with wisps of waves framing her face. She knew she looked good. But she just wasn't excited for some reason. She didn't know why she wasn't looking forward to her date with Paul. Poor Paul. First, going out with Jacie who was hung up on Bryan, and now her. Paul deserved a girl who was excited to be with him.

Sophie frowned and grabbed a magazine off the counter and flopped down in a big overstuffed chair in the family room. She flipped through the magazine quickly and threw it on the floor. Well, if it killed her, she would do the best she could to make sure Paul had a good time. She didn't want him to wonder for even a second if she was excited to be with him.

She flipped her tan legs over the arm of the chair and tried to relax. She thought of all the new styles she wanted to try out on her clients for next week. She had just gotten a new hairstyle magazine in the mail, and she studied it like a doctor would study a medical journal. She jerked up when she heard the doorbell and glanced at her watch. Paul was fifteen minutes early. She walked quickly to the door and opened it.

Paul was standing on her front porch with a small bouquet of daisies in his hand.

Sophie didn't have to fake the grin spreading on her face.

"Paul! How did you know I love daisies more than anything?" she exclaimed, taking the bouquet and feeling a sweet happiness settle around her.

"Hey, if there's one thing I've learned in college, it's to do my homework. I called Jacie yesterday and asked her," he said shyly.

Sophie smiled at him, completely charmed. "Come on in so I can put these in water," she said and scooted back so he could walk in.

"This will just take a second," she said while he followed her into the kitchen.

"Whoa! Looks like someone got here before me," Paul said frowning at the large bouquet of different colored roses sitting in the middle of the kitchen table.

Sophie laughed and reached for a vase underneath the sink. "Nah, those are my mom's. She's on a date tonight with a really wonderful man. He came prepared, just like you."

Paul visibly relaxed and sat down while Sophie arranged the flowers and filled the vase with water.

"So where are we off to tonight?" she asked, setting her bouquet next to her mom's. It didn't matter to her that her bouquet was smaller and less flashy. She was a daisy girl through and through. Roses would never have touched her heart like the daisies had. Paul was off to a good start.

"There's this cool restaurant up in Salt Lake called Boca de Pepe's. It's authentic Italian where they bring out the most amazing food on these huge platters everyone shares from. You'll love it," he assured her getting up from the table.

Sophie grinned at him and grabbed her purse and cell phone. "I'm sure I will," she said and followed Paul out to his car.

On the drive up to Salt Lake, they chatted about music and friends they both knew. And Paul was right—the food at Boca de Pepe's was the most incredible food she'd ever had. She gorged herself on antipasto, bread, and enough carbohydrates to keep her going for the next year.

Paul didn't seem to care, because he was doing the same thing. Sophie smiled to herself when she realized that she wasn't faking anything. She was having a really nice time. Paul was good-looking, smart, kind, and an attentive date.

"So tell me about Jacie. How's her love life now?" Paul said while reaching for more bread.

Sophie looked at Paul carefully. Was he really just friends with Jacie? Had he just asked her out to make Jacie jealous? Hmm. Why would he be interested in that?

"Well, you know, her missionary just got back in town. She's been looking forward to seeing him again," she said, patting her mouth with her napkin.

Paul nodded, but she couldn't help but notice a slight frown line between his eyes.

"She mentioned that on the phone the other day. Do you think it's serious, or is she just being nice to him?" he asked, still looking grim.

Sophie paused and thought about it. Paul seemed a little sad about Jacie and Bryan. Maybe she shouldn't feel too bad about thinking once or twice, okay, a hundred times about Sam on their date.

"Well, to be honest, I think it might be serious. They've been together almost every day since he's been home," she said softly, hoping she wasn't causing him too much pain.

Paul gave her a half-smile and shook his head. "I'm happy for her. Jacie and I were always really good friends," he said, although Sophie realized that Jacie was the one who had just wanted to be friends with Paul. Paul might have had other ideas.

"Jacie's an amazing person. Beautiful, fun, and smart. I can see why you'd be sad," Sophie said, breaking through the unsaid words.

Paul looked her straight in the eyes and his shoulders fell. "Hey, I'm sorry. I didn't mean to make you feel bad. I really like you. It's just hard to get back into the social thing when you're still hung up on someone who never saw you as anything other than a friend. I'm just being an idiot, torturing myself. How about this? I shut up about Jacie, and we keep having a good time?" he asked, grabbing her hand and smiling at her again.

Sophie smiled back, her heart breaking a little for him and knowing exactly how he felt.

"I sort of know what you feel like. I'm sorry," she said.

Paul shrugged and reached for more of the Italian sausage and noodles.

"No big deal. Broken hearts heal every day. It just takes a little time, a little space, and a gorgeous woman to take your mind off of it," he said.

Sophie smiled. "You might be right," she said and then choked on a mushroom when she saw Sam walk into the restaurant with Tess on his arm. She turned her body quickly to hide her face, and pretended she dropped something on the floor.

"Sophie? Are you okay?" Paul asked.

"Oh yeah, just dropped my napkin," she muttered. With her head still down by her feet, she turned her head and saw the waitress lead Sam and Tess to a table just two down from theirs. Sam seemed so wrapped up in Tess, though, that she doubted he would notice them. Paul was almost done. All they had to do was pay and leave without being noticed. Easy.

She sat up and put her napkin over her plate and smiled brightly at Paul.

"I'm ready to go, how about you?" she asked, scooting back in her chair.

"I don't think I can move. Give me just a minute." Paul said with a laugh. "Besides, we haven't decided what we want to do now. Did you want to go to a movie? Or would you rather come back to my place?" he said with a comically lecherous grin.

Sophie couldn't help laughing but quickly turned her chair away from Sam and Tess. If Sam looked over, he would see a girl with reddish hair, but he wouldn't necessarily recognize her.

"Oh, I don't know. Is anything good playing?" she asked, nervous now, and not caring what they did as long as they just left. Seeing Sam tonight was the worst thing possible.

"It's still pretty early. Why don't we drive back and hit the theaters at Thanksgiving Point? I don't really want to say good night to you yet," he said.

Sophie couldn't help smiling at that. Paul was a charmer. Yeah, he was hung up on her best friend, but he was still fun to be with.

"Sounds good. Let's go see what's playing," she said and picked up her purse and stood up.

Paul grabbed her hand and pulled her back down.

"Sophie, hold up! We haven't even gotten the check. And what about dessert? Is something wrong? You're acting kind of jumpy all of a sudden," he said, looking concerned.

Sophie sat back down and sighed. She opened her mouth to speak but was interrupted.

"Paul! My future lawyer. Out on a date, I see," a warm, masculine voice said from right behind her.

Sophie turned slowly and looked way, way up to see Sam standing right behind her, looking down at her with an unreadable expression.

Paul stood up, grinning, and shook Sam's hand.

"Sam! My future client. Good to see you. Looks like you have the same taste in restaurants as I do," he said, sitting back down.

Sam smiled at Paul and then turned and frowned at her again. Sophie swallowed and took a drink of water. He had no right to frown at her like that!

"I think we have the same taste in a lot of things," Sam said, glancing at Sophie.

"Hi, Sophie. How are you doing?" Sam said.

Sophie cleared her throat and glanced up at Sam quickly. "Great. Just great, Sam. Nice to see you again," she said, her voice squeaking slightly.

Paul looked over at Tess. "So you're here on a date, huh?"

Sam looked back at Tess, who was frowning at Sophie and tapping her long, elegant fingers on the table.

"Oh, Tess is just a friend. Now you. You two are definitely on a date," he said, resting his hand on Sophie's shoulder and squeezing.

Sophie gulped and looked at Paul, who had no clue what was really going on.

"Yep. I was surprised when Sophie agreed to go out with me. A gorgeous redhead like her. I thought I'd have to beat the men out of the way to even get in line," he said with a wink at her.

"Yeah, well, looks like you lucked out tonight, Paul," Sam said grimly.

Paul laughed, completely clueless. "That's me. The luckiest man on earth. Hey, I have a great idea! We still haven't even ordered dessert. Why don't you and your date join us? We'd love the company, right Sophie?" Paul said, beaming over at Tess.

Sophie glanced over at Tess and blinked when she saw Tess smiling back at Paul. This could not be good.

"Really, Paul? Um, I thought we were going to skip dessert and go to the movies," she said, folding her napkin nervously in her hand.

Paul shook his head quickly and stood up, motioning for the waiter. As he directed the waiter to move their tables together, he smiled reassuringly at her. "No worries, Sophie, there's nothing good playing anyway."

Sophie moved her chair back into place and glanced at Sam to gauge his feelings on this new situation. He looked strangely pleased. And Tess looked to be in her element. Paul was being the perfect gentleman and held her chair out for her. Sophie frowned. The way he was looking at Tess, she had a feeling Paul would be getting over Jacie a little faster than he thought he would. After everyone was settled and Sam and Tess had ordered, they all looked at each other. Sophie studiously looked anywhere but at Tess. Tess had no problem looking at her, though.

"So, Sophie, I hear you're completely in love with Sam and that the reason you were almost arrested last week was because you were stalking him. That can't be right . . . can it?" she asked with a laugh and a flip of her long blonde hair.

Paul's eyes narrowed, and his gaze jerked back to her face. "Really? What's going on, Sophie? I didn't know you were involved with Sam. You should have said something when I called you," he said, looking hurt and confused.

Sophie blew the hair out of her eyes and looked down into her lap. What to say to that? She opened her mouth to deny it but then shut it again. Tess was right. About everything. She had no excuse and she refused to lie.

Sam cleared his throat and gave Tess a warning look. "You're completely exaggerating as usual, Tess. And you shouldn't believe everything my little sisters tell you. Everything is romantic and overly dramatic to them. They were probably just teasing you," he said with a look of warning to Tess.

Paul studied Sophie and then put his napkin on his plate and turned to pierce Sam with eyes that were suddenly grim and all business. "Okay, but you and Sophie have been together? You've been dating? I must be missing something here because if you two are involved, then why are you here with Tess?" he asked going into lawyer mode.

Sophie sighed again and felt a migraine coming on. She refused to say anything. Sam was on his own. She had no idea how to explain it so that it didn't sound crazy.

Sam took a sip of water and stared at Tess. Tess smiled back.

"Oh, I can answer this one," Tess said. "Let me, Sam. First of all, I was just joking around with Sophie. I guess they know each other because Sam's aunt is Sophie's stepmother or something really weird. Of course, Sam isn't involved with Sophie. Why would he be involved with her, when he has me?" she said and laid a possessive hand on Sam's arm and leaned over to kiss him on the cheek.

"Sam and I have been together forever, haven't we, honey? We've had our ups and downs as most couples have, but honestly, when it really comes down to it, Sam and I both know that there's really no one else for us. Sure we've dated other people off and on, but we always get back together. We were meant for each other. Now, if I'm not mistaken, you and Sophie have that couple look too. Better watch out, Paul, or you and Sam will be shopping for engagement rings together. I was just telling Sam yesterday about this fantastic sale on diamonds Jared is having. It wouldn't hurt to look, would it?" she said and smiled as the waiter walked up with their food.

Sophie's usually upturned mouth set into a grim, thin line as she watched Tess and Sam get their food. She looked at Sam and saw his eyes on her, pleading for her not to say anything. Pleading with her to just go along with Tess. Sophie felt steam rise from her ears. Tess was out of control. And no one wanted to do anything about it.

Sophie opened her mouth to say something but was interrupted by the arrival of their desserts. Paul didn't look happy, but he didn't look as upset as he had, either. But he was willing to put on a happy face for the sake of polite society. Sophie took a deep breath and tried to do the same.

"Well, Tess, I think it's obvious why Sam is with you," Paul said. "You're exquisite. No need to convince me. But as far as shopping for rings, this is my first date with Sophie," he said, and didn't have to say what he probably wanted to, that this was also their last.

Sophie felt miserable. She and dating did not do well together. Yet another disaster to tell her grandchildren about. All she had to do was get through her dessert as quickly as possible and then she could leave. With Paul, who was no longer looking at her, but ignoring her completely. He was mad. He probably felt used, and he had every right to. She should never have agreed to go out with him when she had feelings for Sam. But it was her pride that had made her say yes. She didn't want to be sitting at home, pathetically waiting for the phone to ring. And she would have waited a long time. Because Sam was here with Tess. Not her.

Sophie's mouth fell open as she watched Tess feed Sam with her fork, and then wipe his mouth with her napkin, all the while doing a really bad impression of Marilynn Monroe. Sophie snapped. She didn't care about polite society; she didn't care that Paul was furious with her. She could not sit there and watch Tess get gooey all over Sam. And the worst part, Sam was just sitting there, letting her do it.

"So, Tess, how are the counseling sessions going? Are you making any headway with those temper tantrums of yours? I hear the Super Nanny is in town if you need any pointers on controlling your anger and control issues," Sophie said sweetly as she slipped a mouthful of chocolate mousse between her lips.

Tess turned and glared at her, and Sam closed his eyes and tilted his head back in defeat.

"I don't know what you've heard, Sophie, but you must have been grossly misinformed. You shouldn't listen to petty gossip. It's so tacky," Tess said with a sneer and bright red cheeks.

Sophie smiled in fake confusion but didn't retreat. "Well, isn't that the real reason you're with Sam tonight? Because he's scared to death you'll hurt yourself if he doesn't bend over backward for you?" she said and daintily patted her lips with her napkin. She'd learned a lot from watching her grandmother over the years. She could play this game with the best of them.

"Sophie, that's enough," Paul said through tight lips. He stood up and threw some money down on the table and held his hand out for her. "I think we'll call it a night. Tess, Sam," he said and then pulled her out of the restaurant.

Sophie had a hard time keeping up with Paul's long strides. He opened the car door for her without saying a word and then walked around to get in. She felt horrible. Why hadn't she shut her mouth? Why couldn't she have just sat there and taken it? Because she couldn't stand seeing Sam with Tess. That's why. She had snapped, and now she was lucky Paul wasn't making her walk home. Who knew what Sam thought of her now? He was probably furious with her.

Paul drove down the road and got on the freeway before speaking. "Okay, I want the whole story, Sophie. I think I deserve that much," he said, still not looking at her.

Sophie knotted her hands together nervously and stared at the side of Paul's face. It couldn't hurt. He was already furious with her. "Well, remember when we met? At that Italian restaurant. Well, Sam came in to get a haircut the next day and asked me out. Later he told me that he wanted to be with me but that he felt torn because of his ex-girlfriend, Tess. He had broken up with her a while ago, but every time she saw him with another girl or even heard about it, she would go crazy and trash his house or threaten his family. She even threatened to commit suicide. Well, so I told him I'd just be friends with him until he got his Tess situation under control. She came over one night when I was at his family's house and just lost it, I guess. She told him that she was seeing a counselor and that the healthiest thing for her right now was to be with him. And he felt so guilty about her that he went along with it. I think she's just manipulating him, though. At first I felt so sorry for her. The way he talked about her, I got the impression she was fragile, and I didn't want to be the reason she hurt herself. But after seeing her tonight, I know it's all a bunch of crap. She's just using him, Paul. She's just using him," she said furiously, kicking herself for being the good guy and stepping aside for her.

Paul frowned and glanced at her. He was silent for a few minutes, making Sophie even more nervous.

"Okay, I believe you. Tess is flat-out gorgeous, but I did get this cold vibe from her. Like she could be cruel. But that still doesn't answer why you said yes to me when I called and asked you out. All you had to say was, 'Sorry, Paul, but I have feelings for someone else. Thanks but no thanks,' " he said, frowning again.

Sophie sighed and turned in her seat to face him.

"Paul, I do apologize, but I didn't say yes to hurt you. Besides, I like you, and I thought we could have some fun tonight. You're right, though. I do have feelings for Sam. But then again, you still have feelings for Jacie. So neither one of us is innocent," she said, smiling placatingly at Paul.

Paul grimaced and pulled into the Iceberg parking lot.

"Well, it's too late for a movie now. How about I treat you to a shake since you didn't get to finish your dessert? Friends?" he asked and held his hand out to shake.

Sophie grinned back at him and ignored his hand to give him a hug.

"Definitely friends, Paul," she said and hopped out of the car to follow him in.

They spent the next hour talking over their milk shakes and trying to figure out their love lives. Sophie felt as comfortable talking to Paul as she did talking to Jacie. And Paul had great advice from a guy's perspective. She could have used a friend like Paul years ago. He thought she should play it cool with Sam. It was good that he had seen that she wasn't waiting at home for him. Men, whether they wanted to admit it or not, always loved a challenge, and knowing a girl was waiting at home by the phone for them was always a bit boring. And as far as Tess, he was intrigued. Enough to call her up and ask her out. He promised to tell her if anything came up about Sam or any devious plots to snare him. Sophie couldn't wait. She loved the idea of having a spy in enemy territory. But would it even matter? After watching her tonight, Sam probably wouldn't be calling her anytime soon.

chapter 29

Sophie watched as Paul drove away in his car, and wasn't surprised to see Sam get out of his truck that was parked on the opposite side of the street. She'd seen Sam's truck when Paul had dropped her off but hadn't mentioned it to him. Now she was in for it. She'd come clean with Paul and they were still on good terms, but Sam was a different story. He was here to tell her he never wanted to see her again. She knew it. She watched him get closer and straightened her shoulders and lifted her chin. She'd never been dumped before—oops, okay, well, she had, but never in this type of situation. Blake had just let her meet her replacement. But this, this could get ugly. But she was ready. She would apologize, and if he still never wanted to see her again, well, then, that was just his loss. There were plenty of other guys she could date. Well, actually, now that Paul was strictly just a friend, that wasn't quite true. But she would prevail. She would survive.

Forget it—she would beg him to reconsider.

Sam walked up to her, not smiling, with his hands shoved in his pockets. Sophie opened her mouth to say she was sorry but then stopped. Sam had beaten her to it.

"Sophie, before you say anything, I just had to come here tonight and tell you how sorry I am. I know when you saw me walk in the restaurant with Tess that you were thinking all sorts of horrible things about me. You probably thought I wasn't serious about getting Tess out of my life and that I was just messing with your emotions. So please, just let me explain. Will you let me do that much?" he pleaded with her, taking his hands out of his pockets and grabbing her hands so she couldn't run away.

Sophie blinked and played catch-up. He was here to apologize to her. Okay, this sounded better than getting yelled at and dumped.

"Okay, Sam, I'll listen," she said soberly.

Sam led her onto her porch where there were two old rocking chairs and motioned for her to sit down. Sophie sat down and folded her hands solemnly in her lap and then looked at Sam. He really looked horrible. Completely miserable. He had bags under his eyes, as if he hadn't been sleeping, and there was a long line between his eyes from stress. So maybe this last week hadn't been so fun for him either.

"Sophie, there's a logical explanation for why I was at that restaurant with Tess," he said, looking at her pleadingly.

Sophie frowned and looked away, not making it easy on him.

"A logical reason, huh? Boca De Pepe's is a really amazing restaurant. It's not like you took her to McDonald's, Sam. Why would you take your ex-girlfriend out to such a cool place?" she asked, still looking away.

Sam sighed and scooted his chair closer to hers.

"It's not what you're thinking, Sophie. Honestly. Her dad owns a car lot on State Street, and he has tons of coupons for free dinners for restaurants all over Utah. Well, I wasn't even planning on being with Tess tonight. I've been up since five this morning. We had a cement pour, and then I was running like crazy the whole rest of the day. But I get this call from Tess saying how her dad gave her these coupons for dinner and how she just wanted to say thank you for being such a good friend to her. So I agreed because on the phone she sounded really healthy and strong. And I thought tonight would be the perfect time to tell her that from now on, I didn't want to see her, even as friends. My life is too complicated right now and too busy. It's hard enough making a relationship work without the added complication of an ex-girlfriend. So I said yes, and that's why you saw us there tonight. And after the way she hurt your feelings and the things she said about us being a couple, well, I'd just had it. After you and Paul left, I told Tess that I never want to see her again. She stormed out of the restaurant and I came here. And so here I am," he said, looking at her hopefully.

Sophie looked at Sam carefully. He was telling the truth. Wow. "You really did tell her you never want to see her again? Seriously?" she asked hopefully.

Sam nodded his head twice. "Yes, and I meant every word. I still haven't told my parents everything she's done, but if she tries to mess things up between you and me, then I will. What you and I have is too special to let anyone ruin. Will you promise to have faith in me, Sophie? Will you believe me when I tell you that I'll do anything to be with you?" he asked as he rubbed his thumb back and forth over her knuckles.

Sophie smiled and turned her body toward Sam.

"I will. And I'm sorry too, Sam. I shouldn't have been there with Paul, but you didn't call me all week, and the way you left the last time I saw you, I wasn't sure if you ever would," she said quickly, wanting to come clean too.

Sam smiled. "Well, I have to admit when I saw you with Paul, I was really caught off guard, but then I realized what a hypocrite I was being. I'm so sorry, Sophie. I'm sorry for not calling you this last week. I've been so busy at work, and I've been going crazy trying to solve my problem with Tess, just like you said to. I didn't want to call you and tell you that I had no idea what to do. How lame would that be? But tonight I realized that sometimes, the best solution is just the truth. No more walking on eggshells for me," he said with obvious relief in his voice.

Sophie grinned at him. "Oh, I am so glad to hear you say that. You know, when I saw your truck, I just knew for sure you came over to tell me that you never wanted to see me again. But I had decided to beg you to reconsider. I couldn't imagine not being with you, Sam," she said honestly.

Sam grinned back at her, and his face changed. He didn't look exhausted and stressed out anymore. He looked like he always did. Perfect.

"Well, listen, it's late and I have to work tomorrow, so I better get going. I know it's asking a lot, considering how this night started, but would you mind if I kissed you good night?" Sam asked, standing up.

Sophie smiled and stood up but paused as the lights of a car pulling into the driveway shined over the two of them.

Sophie stepped back from Sam as her mom and Clyde got out of the car and walked up the sidewalk toward them.

"Hi, Mom. Hi, Clyde," Sophie said, blushing slightly.

Her mom was frowning and Clyde was looking very stern. Almost fatherly. Yikes.

"Hi, sweetie. This must be Paul," she said walking up the steps.

Sophie laughed nervously. "Um, no. Paul just dropped me off. This is Sam. He was kind of waiting for me. He just wanted to talk to me about something," she said as her mom and Clyde stopped right in front of her and Sam.

"Sam, huh?" Clyde said soberly.

Sam cleared his throat and thrust his hand out. "Yes, sir. My name is Sam Kellen. Pleased to meet you," he said.

Clyde looked down at Sam's hand and then back to his face, measuring him. He finally shook Sam's hand, but from Sam's expression, he was shaking rather firmly. Sophie glanced at her mom and saw a surprised expression, and then a look of amusement, on her face. Candy put her hand on Clyde's shoulder.

"Clyde, why don't we go on in and let Sophie finish telling Sam good-bye. Okay? It was nice meeting you, Sam," she said and then opened the door and practically dragged Clyde inside.

Sophie laughed softly. "Well, that was interesting."

Sam massaged his hand and gave her a half-smile. "Hey, if I found my daughter on the front porch getting ready to kiss some guy, I'd do more than break a few fingers. Dang, that man has the grip of a farmer."

Sophie laughed and took Sam's hand in hers, massaging it for him.

"And he's not even my dad. Yet. Now where were we?" she asked, looking up at him.

Sam grinned and faster than she thought possible, had her in his arms again and was leaning down to kiss her. She was expecting something long and passionate but was surprised when he kissed her softly and quickly before gently letting her go.

"Now, no begging for more. Clyde might be watching and I need my hands. Tomorrow I've gotta get up early and run down to St. George for the weekend. There's a builders seminar I signed up for a long time ago. But I'll call you when I get back. And you've got my cell phone if you need me for anything. Okay?" he said and hugged her one last time before walking across the street to his truck.

She couldn't help smiling as she watched him go. Sam was hers. He was really hers. No matter how much Tess wanted him, he was hers. She felt amazing, exhilarated, and free all of a sudden. She ran in the house but then remembered Clyde was there. She couldn't jump up and down and scream with her mom in front of company. It would be too alarming for someone who wasn't used to their happy dances. She walked quietly to her room and then waited half an hour before she heard Clyde leave.

Sophie found her mom in the bathroom washing her face.

"Sam is finally free, Mom. He's mine forever!" she said quickly and sat down on the edge of the bathtub.

Candy laughed and kept scrubbing. "Well, of course he is. Why wouldn't he be? He told you he was going to get rid of his ex-girlfriend. Sometimes you just have to trust people," she said and rinsed her face.

Sophie grinned and picked some flaking nail polish off her fingernail. "I guess you're right. So what's the deal with Clyde and the handshake from Hades?" she asked, raising her eyebrow at her mom.

Candy laughed and grabbed her moisturizer and started to apply the yellowish cream all over her face and neck.

"That was kind of funny, huh? I hope Sam wasn't mad about it. Isn't Clyde cute? He was going all dad on you, and he doesn't even know you very well yet. Where was he three years ago, when you started dating? If he had just given Blake a handshake like that once, I guarantee Blake would have never even thought about writing that other girl," Candy said as she put toothpaste on her brush.

Sophie grimaced, not wanting to even think about Blake.

"Well, just tell Clyde that I'm very flattered that he was as menacing as possible, but that I can handle things from here on out, okay?"

Candy laughed and spit in the sink before answering. "Too late. I already had a little talk with him about it. He's kind of embarrassed. He hopes you're not mad at him, because he really wants to start off on the right foot with you. His fatherly instincts just went into overdrive when he saw my daughter on the front porch with a man who looked like he was getting ready to kiss her," she said, eyeing her daughter mischievously.

Sophie laughed and pointed at her mom. "Oh no, we're not talking about my good night kiss. I want to know about your good night kiss. Did he finally kiss you?" she asked, leaning forward and grinning.

Candy looked at her and giggled helplessly. "Well, yes. He did. He kissed me once at the restaurant, and he kissed me again right before he left. He wants me to spend more time with his daughter. And, now don't freak out, he wants to spend some time with you. Now don't look like that! I know you don't like men very much, older men anyway, and that's your father's fault, but I really think you'll like Clyde. He talked about the future. He talked about commitment and how if things keep going the way they are, that maybe marriage would be down the road. And he wanted to know what I thought about helping him raise his daughter. She's just a young little thing. She needs a mom so badly. And get this, Sophie. He asked me if I would be willing to have more children," Candy said in a whisper.

Sophie's mouth fell open. "Mom! You know, you are still so young. You could have like three more kids if you wanted to. Do you want to?" she asked, thinking of the changes that would be happening soon in her life. A new dad. A new little sister. Her mom having a baby? Holy cow. Life was moving very fast all of a sudden.

Candy turned and leaned against the counter and looked at her daughter.

"Well, you know you turned out so incredible. And I have always wondered what having a little boy would be like. He'd probably look like Clyde. Can you imagine? A little blond boy running around with skinned knees and dirty hands," Candy said, her voice going soft and her eyes all dreamy.

Sophie smiled, got up, and gave her mom a hug. "If that's what you want, then that's what you should have, Mom. If you want a dirty little kid hanging around breaking windows and getting into everything, then by all means, let's call Clyde right now and tell him to get a move on," she said, laughing at her mom's expression. "No, I'm serious. If you're wondering if I would be okay with Clyde, then yes. Any man willing to go up against Sam for me is someone I would be proud to call stepfather or whatever," she said with a half-smile.

Candy laughed and hugged her daughter tightly.

"Mom! I can't breathe!" Sophie yelped, pulling away, gasping.

Candy kissed her on the cheek and floated out of the room. Sophie grinned and followed her. They read their scriptures together and prayed, and then they both went their separate ways.

Tomorrow was a new day. But with her mom happy and with Sophie on her way, she felt a new energy. Anything was possible. Maybe even Sam.

chapter 30

As Sophie put her pajamas on, she heard the phone ring. She glanced at the clock and wondered who in the world would call at eleven o'clock at night. She ran to grab it since her mom was already in bed. She got it on the third ring.

"Hello?" she asked, not even bothering to look at the caller ID. She just wanted to stop the ringing.

"I guess you think you've won, don't you, Sophie?" asked a furious, feminine voice.

Sophie shook her head in confusion. "Excuse me? Who is this?" she demanded.

"If you go near him even one more time, I'll know. And that's when you'll pay. I know all about your mom's tacky little beauty salon. Hope she has good insurance because fire damage can just ruin a good career," she said and hung up.

Sophie's mouth fell open, and she stared at the phone in her hand. She quickly checked the caller ID, but it said Unknown Caller. She slowly replaced the phone and realized who it was. Tess. It wouldn't have been hard for her to get her phone number. Her mom was listed in the phone book. Along with the address of their salon. Sophie felt a frisson of fear run down her spine. She felt like calling Sam but grabbed her hand back just in time. No way would she give him another excuse to talk to Tess.

Sophie walked slowly back to her room and shut the door, but she was no longer tired. She lay on her bed and cradled her head in her hands. Should she call the police? That would be the wisest thing

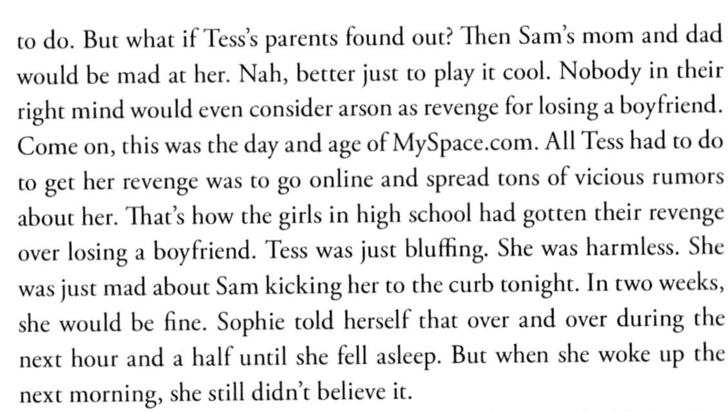

to do. But what if Tess's parents found out? Then Sam's mom and dad would be mad at her. Nah, better just to play it cool. Nobody in their right mind would even consider arson as revenge for losing a boyfriend. Come on, this was the day and age of MySpace.com. All Tess had to do to get her revenge was to go online and spread tons of vicious rumors about her. That's how the girls in high school had gotten their revenge over losing a boyfriend. Tess was just bluffing. She was harmless. She was just mad about Sam kicking her to the curb tonight. In two weeks, she would be fine. Sophie told herself that over and over during the next hour and a half until she fell asleep. But when she woke up the next morning, she still didn't believe it.

Since it was Saturday, Sophie met Jacie down at the Timberline track. They had made it a habit ever since they were sophomores at Lone Peak to run most Saturdays. That way they didn't have to feel guilty about all the pizza and Oreos they ate during the week.

"Sophie, that is so wild. Did you know that if you got married now too, that you and your mom could be pregnant at the same time? Your kid's uncle could be younger than him. Or her. Only in Utah," she said with a breathless giggle.

Sophie was too tired to laugh, and stopped to catch her breath.

"Hey, no stopping. We've only done two and a half laps. We stop at three, and if we feel like doing one more than we get Maggie Moo's tonight," Jacie reminded her as she gasped for air.

"Sorry, I'm just so tired. Going on a date with a man still hung up on my best friend and then dealing with Sam and my mom's near proposal kept me up all night," she said, leaning over to catch her breath.

Jacie laughed while leaning down to stretch her muscles out.

"Sorry about Paul. I thought he was over me a long time ago. Oops," she said with a grin.

Sophie walked over to her water bottle and took a sip before collapsing on the grass. "Yeah right. You knew he was still hung up on you. He's such a nice guy. Too bad," she said.

Jacie shook her head. "Poor Paul indeed. I can't believe he wants to be set up with Tess. And to think I thought he had good taste in women," she said with a sneer.

Sophie shrugged. "Actually, I hope he does go out with her—and soon. She called me last night. She threatened to burn down my mom's salon if I go out with Sam. If Paul goes out with her, then maybe he can find out what's going on behind that exquisite psycho façade of hers."

Jacie gave up and flopped down on the grass, lying down and spreading her hands out.

"You should have called the cops and you know it, Sophie. This woman is playing hardball, and you need all the ammo you can get. What if she goes ahead with it? What then?" she asked.

Sophie sat down next to her and leaned forward to stretch her calves.

"She won't. She's all talk. But I swear, if she hurts my mom, there will be no mercy for her. Forget Sam's parents and their best friends and all their future golfing trips. If Tess is determined to come between me and Sam, then she doesn't know who she's messing with," Sophie said, frowning at her knee caps.

Jacie snorted. "No offense, but you're the nicest person I know. That's the only reason we're best friends. No one else would put up with me," she said with a wink.

Sophie rolled her eyes. "Whatever. I don't think I'm the only who can stand your company. It looks like Bryan likes you hanging around. A lot," she said with a raised eyebrow.

Jacie grinned. "Yeah, and no crazy ex-girlfriend around to burn my house down either. He's the perfect boyfriend."

Sophie glared at Jacie and threw a handful of grass into her face. She laughed as Jacie sputtered and spit out grass.

"Hey! You could have waited until my mouth was closed, you brat," Jacie said, sitting up and using her water bottle to rinse out her mouth.

"That's what you get for being so cocky," Sophie said, still laughing.

Jacie splattered Sophie with water from her bottle, and they were even for a moment.

"There's no telling what some dog did on that grass, you know," Jacie said, still glaring at her.

Sophie rolled her eyes and turned onto her stomach. "Yeah yeah, cry me a river."

Jacie laughed and copied her friend. "Well, there is one way you could make it up to me. You could come to this bridal show down in American Fork with me. It's at the Noni building. Come on! Don't look like that. It won't be that bad. Besides, you could get a lot of ideas for your own wedding. Well, you know, if that ever happens," she said with a smirk.

Sophie groaned and laid her chin on her crossed arms. "You've got to be kidding me. You're not even engaged to Bryan yet! If Bryan found out what you were doing, he'd run back to Russia faster than you can say eternal commitment."

Jacie shrugged and took the rubber band out of her hair, letting it fall around her shoulders.

"He's the one who brought it up on our date when we went to Temple Square. His mission president thinks it's a good idea for returned missionaries to get married as soon as they find the right person. No putting it off for school or money or anything like that. He told me that I'm the right person," Jacie said, blushing and looking away.

Sophie gasped and grabbed Jacie's hand. "Are you serious? You are? Oh my heck, you're going to be engaged as soon as he can dig up a few dollars for a ring."

Jacie grinned and sighed in happiness. "He told me he's been looking on e-bay ever since the night he got home. He's dead serious," she said, sounding completely happy about the turn of events.

Sophie shook her head in awe. Some men knew what they wanted and went for it, while some men . . .

"Fine, I'll go to the bridal show with you. But on one condition. You help me out with my life. I need a new five-step plan. The last one on how to get yer man was great, but now I need a plan on how to get Tess out of our lives. I can't get excited about my relationship with Sam until she's moved on. And trust me, she's still very much in the picture. Whether Sam wants to believe it or not," she said miserably.

Jacie frowned and thought about it. "Hmmm. A new five-step plan. You know what, I might need some more info on this situation. What do you say we go spying tonight and turn things around on Tess?"

Sophie blinked in surprise. She'd already been caught spying once. But with Jacie with her, she might be able to pull it off this time.

"Well, I know she's an interior decorator. I should be able find out where she'll be tonight. Hey! I bet Julie would help me. She's friends with Tess's parents too. She can give us some background info. You know, this just might work," she said.

Jacie rolled her eyes. "Hello! I'm the master, remember? Of course it will work. We'll find out what's really going on, and then I can make a real five-step program to fit your needs. No more guessing. I need the facts before you get the plan. And honestly, Sophie, if we find out she's up to no good, are you going to be woman enough to do something about it?" she asked, looking at her friend with a frown.

Sophie sighed and covered her eyes with her wrist.

"I haven't even been girl enough, let alone woman enough. But it's time to grow up. Sam is worth fighting for. I really want this relationship to work, Jacie," she said honestly.

Jacie got up and reached her hand down to help Sophie to her feet.

"Okay, then, let's go get changed and you get on the phone to Julie. Get the scoop and then we'll plan our strategy for tonight," she said.

"Won't Bryan want to be with you tonight?"

Jacie shook her head. "Nah, he's helping his uncle finish his basement today. Something about sheet rocking. I'm free. What about you? Now that Sam thinks he's free, won't he want to be with you?"

Sophie shook her head. "He told me last night that he's going to be out of town for a few days at some builders conference in St. George. It's mostly just golfing, but he says he has to be there. So I'm free. Let's do it."

Jacie nodded and they shook hands. But Sophie was worried. If she and Jacie did go out spying tonight, and she was caught, not only would she look like an idiot, not only would she be humiliated beyond anything, Sam would find out. He'd already gotten rid of one crazy girlfriend. What would stop him from getting rid of another?

An hour later after a hot shower, Sophie lay on her bed and dialed Julie's number. She almost hoped Julie wasn't—

"Hello?"

Sophie sighed and played with the yarn knots on her quilt.

"Yeah, hi, Julie. This is Sophie. How's it going?" she asked.

"Oh, you know, as good as can be expected for having your life in complete chaos. But other than that, really great. What about you? How are you doing?"

Sophie took a deep breath. Could she really ask Julie about Tess? Why was she so embarrassed?

"Good, good. We're all good. So about the divorce, were you able to find all that money dad took?" she asked, trying to put off the inevitable.

Julie sighed on the other line before answering. "Actually, yes and no. Tanner took the money so he could invest in this insane real estate deal down in St. George. He thought it would make him millions.

I guess having everyone know his wife was the one with the money didn't sit too well with his ego. I think he was just trying to impress his mother. He wanted to prove himself or something. Instead, he proved what a . . . well, anyway. The money is long gone, but that's okay. Me and the kids have plenty to live off of. We'll be fine. I'm kind of worried about your dad, though. After the divorce, he's going to need to get a job. He hasn't worked in ten years. I don't know what he'll do," she sad worriedly.

Sophie frowned. "You've got to be kidding me. He hasn't had a job this whole time? What did he do all day?" she asked, stunned.

Julie laughed. "Golf, of course. Anyways, listen, I'm glad you called. I've got a favor to ask you. I kind of need a babysitter next Wednesday. I have to see my lawyer, and the kids are out for a professional day at school. Do you think you can change your schedule around to watch the kids for a couple hours?" she asked, sounding very nervous and very shy about it.

Sophie smiled. "No problem. Me and the boss get along pretty good. She usually gives me whatever hours I want. But on one condition," she said, grateful that Julie had given her the perfect opening.

"What? You name it—anything. I'm desperate," she said.

Sophie took a deep breath and closed her eyes tightly. "I want some information on Tess, and I need your help. She's been kind of threatening to me and Sam lately, and I just want to check up on her tonight. I know you and Sam's mom and dad are close with her family. Would you find out where she'll be tonight?" she asked and waited for Julie to say something. Anything.

"Julie?"

"Oh, I'm here. I was just thinking. You know, I was talking to Sue last night. She's kind of worried about Sam, actually. I think she found a letter from Tess to Sam in a pair of pants she was washing, and I guess it was really vindictive and threatening. And she really likes you, by the way."

Sophie let out a sigh of relief. "She does? Oh, I'm so glad. After getting caught by the cops for spying on them, I thought she'd think I was a real psycho."

Julie laughed. "I heard about that. What were you thinking? Anyway, yeah, Sam has been trying to break up with her for almost six months now, and she just won't let go. Sue was so happy when Sam met you. You're so down to earth and funny and nice. Tess is just—well, she's just so controlling and cold. She's very possessive. And Sam is such a softie. He can't stand hurting anyone. And she plays him like a fiddle. Constant guilt trips. Sue doesn't know everything, but she knows more than Sam thinks. She tries to stay out of Sam's personal life, but it's been tearing her to pieces."

Sophie's eyes widened. Maybe Sam should give his parents a little more credit. Interesting.

"Well then, you won't mind me asking you if you'll find out where she's going to be tonight," Sophie said. "Don't let her or her parents know I'm asking, though. She called me last night and made some serious threats. I just want to see what she's up to. This is just between you and me. Find out what her plans are tonight and then call me back. Okay?" she said.

Julie paused but then agreed. "Okay. It feels kind of snoopy, but if it helps get Sam away from Tess, then I'll do it. And for the babysitting, of course."

Sophie laughed and hung up a minute later. Perfect! And Sam's mom liked her! Even better.

chapter 31

Sophie and Jacie snuck around to the back of Sam's house. She had been completely shocked when Julie had called her back and told her that Tess was having a dinner party at Sam's house while he was down in St. George. It had been set up months ago, and Sam didn't care, as long as he wasn't there. Tess had been the one to decorate Sam's house, and she used it to show off to her future clients. That and the view from his balcony was the best in Suncrest. There were five cars parked in front of Sam's house—two Mercedes, a Hummer, and two BMWs. Sophie had parked far down the road, but as she and Jacie snuck past the cars, she started getting huge butterflies in her stomach. Just the image of that cop who had caught her the last time was enough to send her running back down the hill. But with Jacie dragging her quickly toward the back of the house, she had no choice. Jacie was having too much fun.

Sam's yard wasn't fenced, and the landscape was almost completely natural because of the slope of the yard. His house was sitting on the edge of a cliff. Great view, but scary if you were trying snoop. It was still light outside. It wouldn't be sunset for another hour, so Sophie and Jacie had to be really careful. Jacie had borrowed army fatigues from Bryan so they'd mesh in with the trees and rocks. Sophie had to roll up the pants like twenty times and use an old belt to cinch in the pants. They looked ridiculous. But they did blend in.

"We should have painted black lines under our eyes like Rambo or something," Jacie whispered.

Sophie rolled her eyes. "This is bad enough. Really. Now be quiet.

No more talking," she said and slipped under Sam's deck. No one could resist his view for long. All she had to do was wait.

Jacie joined her, and they laid on their stomachs, trying to ignore the ants and other interesting bugs crawling through the dirt and leaves.

"It's almost ninety-five degrees. She better hurry and come out here before I bake to death," Jacie muttered.

Sophie blew on Jacie's face to cool her off.

"Dude, gum first if you're going to be the air conditioning," Jacie said, waving her hands in front of her face.

Sophie cracked up but put her hand over her mouth as they heard the French doors above them open.

"Marrissa, you have to see this view. It's horrible for my complexion, but it's the best money can buy," Tess said with a cultured laugh.

The two women walked to the edge of the deck. Sophie could feel every footfall.

"So tell me, Tess, when am I going to be getting your wedding announcement? Last time we went to lunch, you told me Sam was seconds from proposing. Don't tell me he's getting cold feet now," the woman said in a high-pitched, annoying voice.

Sophie and Jacie exchanged looks. Tess was completely deluded.

"Oh, Marrissa, you wouldn't believe what I've been through lately. Sam took me to Boca de Pepe's last night, and I was hoping he was going to finally ask me. But instead he told me he had met this other woman and that he's confused now about his feelings for me. I just don't know what to do. You've dealt with this situation before, Marrissa. Give me some advice. If I don't do something right now, this house will never be mine. And you know how hard I've worked for this relationship. I've done everything but handcuff him and drag him to the church. I even got Daddy's golfing buddy Mac to call Sam and tell him that I'm so fragile right now that the best thing for me is a strong, stable, loving relationship. But it's not working," Tess said sounding very put out.

Marrissa laughed and moved farther down the deck. Jacie and Sophie had to crawl on their stomachs to follow the conversation.

"Honey, I know just what you mean. My second marriage was almost ruined by a trashy little gold digger. It was his secretary if you can believe that. Robert almost proposed to a secretary instead of me. I had to nip that in the bud quickly. It takes power, Tess. You have to be forceful. Don't put up with excuses or second best. If you want Sam, and obviously you do, then don't let anyone get in your way. You rule your own destiny, darling. Don't be afraid to intimidate people. There are two classes of people in this world. The powerful and the weak. The powerful get what they want and the weak don't. Which class are you, Tess?" the woman asked.

Tess paused before answering. "Marrissa, you know the answer to that. I wouldn't be standing here with you if I was weak. I'd be a secretary at my dad's car lot. You're right. I've come too far to be defeated now. You know I did call his little girlfriend last night and told her to back off. But she seems really dim. I don't think she understands who she's up against."

Marrissa laughed and took a sip of her drink. "Then show her you mean business, Tess. Tell me about her. What's this girl like?" she asked.

Tess sighed. "You think a secretary is trashy. You haven't seen trashy. This girl Sam's been blinded by is a poor little beautician. Her father left her and her mother when she was a little girl. She's never even been to college. She works at this dump on Main Street in Alpine. And you should see her, Marrissa. She has the ugliest color of hair you've ever seen. Bright orange. I'm not kidding. And you would not believe how many freckles she has. I don't even think she knows what sunscreen is. Seriously, I can't even imagine any sane man looking twice at her, but to pick her over me? Sometimes I wonder if Sam is blind. She was on a date with another guy last night, which excuse me, but how tacky is that? She's supposed to be in love with Sam and she's already cheating on him. So the guy she's with can't even take his eyes off me, and get this. He called me up this afternoon and asked me out. I said yes, of course. He might be able to give me some dirt on her. I can't wait. I'm even thinking of asking Uncle Edward to audit them. It pays to have an uncle who works for the IRS. I would love to see the look on her face when she opens up the letter telling her they're auctioning off their salon to pay for back taxes. Now that would make me feel better," Tess said with a smile in her voice.

Marrissa laughed, a loud and unpleasant sound full of cruelty and glee.

"Tess, you are one woman I would not want to mess with. Seriously, though, if you want this view? Get your view, honey. I've known you and Sam too long. You two were made for each other. You'll be the premier couple of Draper. It makes me jealous just thinking of it. And talk about rich. With your skills and the houses he builds, no one will be able to touch you. I know the editor of *Salt Lake Magazine.* I'm not going to promise you anything, but if you can pull this off, I don't see why you couldn't get the cover. Just imagine it. Tess Kellen, the Style Star of Draper. I'll be expecting a wedding announcement in my mail within the month. If I don't, then I'll be very surprised. And disappointed," she added and then left Tess alone on the deck to rejoin the party inside.

Sophie let her breath out in an audible woosh of air. Jacie glared at her and held her finger to her mouth. Tess was obviously making a call.

"Hi, Mommy? It's Tess . . . Yeah, the party's going fine. I'm just still upset over Sam . . . I know, he'll come back to me, but I'm worried this time. What if he doesn't? Marrissa just promised me the cover of *Salt Lake Magazine* if Sam and I get engaged . . . I know, Mom. Don't you think I've tried? I called her last night . . . Oh, I don't know. Do you think I should? . . . Hmm. Well, he got so mad last time I threatened to have his sisters taken off the team. He hates it when I threaten his family . . . But, Mom! I like Trey . . . Well, okay. If we do get him kicked out of BYU, he can always go to the U . . . Okay. I love you too, Mommy," Tess said and hung up. She quickly walked to the doors and reentered the house.

Sophie and Jacie exchanged horrified looks. They scrambled back up the steep slope and practically ran down the road. They jumped into Jacie's car and drove quickly away without saying anything.

As soon as their tires hit Alpine, they both breathed a sigh of relief. "Honey, you're on your own," Jacie said. "There is no five-step program I know of to help you. Besides, you're not up against just one crazy woman. You're up against her whole crazy family," Jacie said, shaking her head.

Sophie sighed and slumped lower in her seat. "So now that it's hard, you're going to leave me hanging? I thought you said you were the master," Sophie said with a half-smile.

Jacie frowned and pulled into Sophie's driveway. "Give me a lovesick girl or boy any day, and poof, problem solved. Give me a family of psychos, well, everyone has their limits. What you need is a restraining order. Not a five-step plan. Man, why didn't we bring a tape recorder? No five steps needed. Just a long jail sentence," she said, getting out and walking toward the house.

Sophie joined her and they walked in to find Candy sitting at the kitchen table, crying softly. Sophie rushed to her mom's side.

"What is going on, Mom? Are you okay?" Sophie demanded, kneeling in front of her mom.

Candy lifted her head up and stared at her daughter, not even taking in the camouflage pants and shirt.

"Hey, sweetie. Sorry. I just never have known how to get along with your dad's side of the family. It's no big deal. So what have you girls been up to?" she said, grabbing a tissue and blowing her nose.

Sophie's eyebrows snapped together, and she sat down next to her mom, with Jacie doing the same.

"Who was it? What did they say and where are they?" Sophie asked in a soft, strangely kind voice.

Candy shook her head and tried to laugh. "Oh, it's nothing, Sophie. Don't mind me. You know what a baby I am. I'm the type who cries at commercials, you know. I always overreact. Just forget it," she said and moved to get up.

Sophie grabbed her mom's hand and shook her head. "No. Now, please sit down, and tell me why you're crying," she asked again more firmly this time.

Candy sighed and pushed her hair out of her face and looked at her daughter and Jacie. "Fine. I just ran into your grandmother at Kohlers. She was furious with me. She says I've poisoned you against their family and that you won't even do Daphne's hair. She says I'm a poor example of a mother and that if I loved you, I'd encourage you to treat your family with more respect and gratitude for all they've done for you. And then she told me that she wanted a hair appointment with you at nine o'clock sharp on Monday morning. And that if you wouldn't do her hair, then she would know who to blame. And then she walked off with her nose in the air as if I were so far beneath her. Ooh, I hate the way she's always made me feel like nothing. I thought once Tanner left me, I'd be done with his family. But surprisingly, they still have the ability to make me feel like an insecure little eighteen-year-old."

Sophie looked down at her hands and tried so hard, so incredibly hard, not to blow up. It would just scare her mother and make her feel worse. She composed her features and then smiled. She took a breath and hoped the smile would hold.

"Well, Mom, you know that's your own dang fault. You can't let the way they treat you or feel about you affect you. Everyone knows how amazing and wonderful you are. If they're determined to be evil and horrible every chance they get, then that's their problem. Not ours. I say we just laugh it off," Sophie said and then laughed heartily.

Candy looked up in surprise and relief. "Oh, you're so right, Sophie. They are just crazy, aren't they? And I'm so glad you're not mad. I'd hate for you to rush over there and yell at them or something. You are really an amazingly mature person, Sophie. I think Liz Reid is wrong. I am a great mother. Just look at you," she said and smiled.

Sophie smiled back and glanced at Jacie. Jacie had one eyebrow raised and a smirk on her mouth. She had fooled her mom. Jacie wasn't buying it, though.

"So will you do your grandmother's hair on Monday? I'm sure it's just a trim and a rinse, nothing big. Really elementary stuff. I bet you could be done with her in less than an hour," Candy said, getting up and going to the fridge to get Frescas for each of them.

Sophie licked her lips and smiled. "Oh, Mom, of course I'll do her hair. I can't wait," she said as she and Jacie took their drinks and walked out of the room.

Jacie shut the door to Sophie's room and stood staring at her friend. "What evil lurks within your soul right now, Sophie Reid? What are you planning?"

Sophie smiled to herself and kicked off her shoes before doing a belly flop onto her bed. She picked up a hair magazine and thumbed through before answering.

"Jacie, do you remember Sister Anderson? She died two years ago, but she loved loved loved that blue dye my mom would put in her hair. She was the most darling lady. Do we still have any?" she asked innocently.

Jacie walked over to Sophie's window seat and sat down gingerly on the cushion and took a sip of her Fresca while she thought about it.

"You know why we're best friends, Sophie?" she asked, not expecting a reply. "Because you are the only one I know who would even consider dying their own grandmother's hair blue," she said with a slight laugh.

Sophie turned over on her back and sighed. "I know she goes to this really high-priced salon up in Salt Lake. She has fantastic hair. Simple, chin-length cut, beautiful ash blonde highlights. Not a hint of gray anywhere. She has the hair of a soap opera queen. But I'll tell you something. After I'm done with her, I promise you, she'll never say one mean thing to my mother again."

Jacie snorted and picked up a magazine. "That or she'll sue you."

Sophie shook her head. "Nope, it's all about family with her. She'd never tarnish the family name by dragging me through the courts. My mother yes, me no. She'll just have to take it. Daphne must have cried loud and hard on her shoulder to have her use her authority like this. She probably ran to her mom too, but Lexie doesn't want to give up her new look. So Grandmother came to the rescue."

Jacie turned the page of the magazine. "So what, does that make you the fire breathing dragon?"

Sophie laughed and took the rubber band out of her hair. "Yep. It definitely does."

Jacie glanced quickly through the magazine and threw it on the floor by the other ones before walking over to sit on the edge of Sophie's bed.

"Okay, so we're set to take care of your grandmother. But what about Tess? What are you going to do? The IRS will make your grandmother look like a saint."

Sophie sat up and turned to face her friend. "I know. But honestly, I just don't know what to do. I don't think knocking on her door and asking her to stop will work. What would you do? Forget the five steps thing. Just tell me what I should do," Sophie said.

Jacie took another sip of Fresca and tilted her head to think about it.

"If it were me, and you're not, but if you were, I'd tell his mom. If Sam's mom knew what this girl was doing to her darling baby boy, she'd snatch that girl bald. It's the mother bear syndrome. No one's more protective than a mother."

Sophie frowned and reached over and grabbed her Fresca from the table. "I don't know. That kind of sounds like tattling to me."

Jacie laughed and crushed her can, throwing it in Sophie's wastebasket with a perfect swish.

"And here I thought you had turned to the dark side. No, I don't think you should tattle. But I know someone who will," she said grinning.

Sophie frowned and studied her friend. "Okay, now I know you're scheming something. You have that delighted-with-yourself look. What's the plan?"

Jacie jumped on the bed excitedly.

"I think we should invite Sam's mom and his sisters to the salon for a complimentary haircut. You do the sisters, and I'll do the mom. And Sam can't get mad at you for telling on Tess," Jacie said.

Sophie frowned and took another sip. "Hmmm. Well, it is tempting. And we're just trying to help. Sam wouldn't want Trey kicked out of school," she said, trying to convince herself that they should do it.

Jacie hopped off the bed and pulled open Sophie's closet.

"I'm going to have to borrow an outfit, though, for payment for services rendered. I love this dress. It would look darling on me. You know Bryan's homecoming talk is tomorrow in church. Please?" Jacie asked in a whiny, wheedling voice any three-year-old would be jealous of.

Sophie giggled and gave in. "Okay, on the condition that you bring me back the last two outfits you borrowed last month. And that when you tell Sam's mom what's been going on, that you're very subtle about it. Don't just blurt it out like that's the reason she's there or something. Do it with tact. Do it like she's the one who pulled the information out of you against your will. Something like that."

Jacie took the dress off the hanger and laid it on a chair.

"Well, duh. Dang, Sophie, who do you take me for? One of your relatives? This is me we're talking about. Give me some credit."

Sophie sighed and silently bid farewell to her dress as Jacie left. If only Jacie were right. Maybe Sam's mom could fix this mess. Sophie sighed and walked into her bathroom. She felt like taking a long, hot bubble bath. The perfect medium to imagine blue hair and her grandmother's face. But as she lay amidst the bubbles, it wasn't her grandmother's face she saw. It was Sam's.

chapter 32

Sophie dressed very carefully Monday morning. She wanted to put her grandmother at ease, so she wore her Liz Claiborne pantsuit her mother had bought her last Christmas. She had never dreamed of wearing it to work before. An accidental splat of bleach on the pale gray linen would torture her, but it was for a good cause. Her grandmother could spot a Wal-Mart brand from twenty paces. She could still remember the time she had been invited over to a Christmas Eve dinner at her grandmother's house and had gone shopping with her mother for the perfect outfit. She thought if she looked nice enough, her dad would notice her. Together they had picked a beautiful red velvet dress. And yes, it had been from Wal-Mart. But instead of saying hi or giving her a welcoming hug, her grandmother had told her that Dillards had sales occasionally and that even with her mother's low income, she should at least try and have some pride in the way she looked. Sophie had been devastated. Ahh. The memories.

She got to work early and had Jacie mix up the color for her grandmother. She didn't want any tell-tale color on her hands, or on her clothes for that matter. She wanted her grandmother completely clueless as to what lay ahead. At nine o'clock sharp, Sophie stood at the front door, ready to open it for Liz when she arrived. And she was right on time.

"Good morning, Grandmother. Why don't you come over here, and have a seat," Sophie said, smiling in a friendly, non-threatening way.

Liz Reid frowned at her and walked confidently toward her.

"I want you to know that this horrible attitude you have toward your cousins will not be tolerated. I expect you to call Daphne this afternoon and apologize to her. And her color has already begun to fade. She needs a touch-up and another conditioning treatment. I want you to fit her in tomorrow at the latest," Liz said as she sat down and got comfortable.

Sophie ground her teeth but didn't let her smile drop. "Hmmm. So what would you like done today?" she asked, not responding to her grandmother's command.

Liz stared in the mirror at herself and smiled.

"Well, I have to admit, everyone's been coming to you for these amazing transformations. I honestly don't think you can do anything to improve upon what I already have. But then, Lexie thought she looked good for years, the poor thing. Maybe I'm not seeing what other people are. So I'm going to do what Lexie and Daphne have done and put myself in your hands. Change is always refreshing for the soul," she said with a wise smile.

Sophie nodded her head in complete agreement.

"You know, you're right," Sophie said. "And as it just so happens, there's a look I've been thinking of for you for a long time. I think it would really fit your personality. Should we go for it?" she asked, just to make sure she had her grandmother's complete agreement.

Liz flicked her hand. "Yes, yes, just get on with it. The Daughters of the Pioneers are meeting for lunch at one. I can't wait to see their faces."

Sophie smiled. Neither could she. "Grandmother, let's make this even more exciting, like a real makeover. Why don't we go over to the last station over there. There isn't a mirror. You won't get to see yourself until you're completely done. What do you say? Are you up for a surprise?" she asked, smiling brightly.

Liz frowned, not liking it at all, but nodded her head in agreement.

"Fine, fine. Whatever you'd like," she said and moved to the station Sophie directed her to.

She picked up her scissors and cut two inches off the length of her grandmother's hair and layered it all over. It was almost exactly the same haircut she gave Bishop Tomlinson when he came in. Liz's expression didn't change at all from the serene look she always had. The only difference was a strained look around the eyes as she saw more hair fall on the floor than she was expecting. Sophie smiled brightly and kept going.

Sophie smiled and patted Grandmother on the shoulders. "Just let me go and get the color and I'll be right back," she said and then walked quickly to the back of the salon where Jacie was already waiting for her. She handed Sophie the solution, already made up, and shook her head.

"I can't believe you're really going through with it. Impressive," Jacie said and then walked back to her own client.

Sophie took in a deep breath. She'd already cut her grandmother's hair ruthlessly short. Should she go ahead with the color? The cut alone would make her point. She stood still, undecided. She glanced on the wall, where her mother had hung photographs of all the nail techs and hairstylists. The one in the very center was of Candy. She was busy cutting Martha Johansen's hair. Candy was smiling and beautiful and completely in her element. And her grandmother had crushed her Saturday. Nope, someone had to stop her grandmother. Her father never had. He'd just stood there while he watched his wife be insulted. Well, Sophie was nothing like her father, and this would prove it once and for all.

Sophie walked back toward her grandmother with a bright smile on her face.

"Can I get you a magazine while I do this part? You must be bored," she said.

Liz sniffed and glanced at the magazines Sophie held out to her. She grabbed a *Time* magazine and opened it.

Sophie was grateful. Sure, most grandmothers would take the time to talk to their granddaughter. Not Liz Reid. Wrong granddaughter.

Sophie went to work and brushed the semi-permanent color all over her grandmother's hair. She wrapped her grandmother's head in plastic and led her to a dryer to let her sit for twenty minutes. She went to the back to grab a drink and get away from her grandmother.

Jacie joined her seconds later. "Dude, how much of that stuff did you use? It's not Halloween, you know," she said, worriedly.

Sophie shrugged. "She wants me to call Daphne and apologize to her this afternoon. She won't put up with my bad attitude," she said in reply.

Jacie's mouth fell open. "I take it back."

"Well, I hope the place is cleared when she realizes what I've done. I've never seen her scream, but this could do it. I know I would. This will be bad for our reputation. She might not sue, but she sure as heck will tell all of her friends not to go near our salon," Sophie said frowning.

Jacie shrugged. "We have a very loyal clientele. All of her friends go somewhere else anyway. She's already told everyone to stay away because she hates your mom so much. Seriously, she won't be able to do anything."

"Who won't be able to do anything?" Candy said, putting her purse down and looking suspiciously at Sophie and Jacie.

Sophie blushed immediately, and Jacie's face went pale.

"Mom! What are you doing here? You know she's here. I told you to stay away until eleven."

Candy shrugged, a strained frown on her face. "What kind of coward would that make me, sending my daughter in alone to face her? I just want you to know that I'm here if you need me. If she doesn't like the style you give her, then I won't let her treat you badly. Everyone has let her get away with saying anything she wants. But I won't let her put you down or make you feel like you aren't the amazing hairstylist that you are. You're my daughter," Candy said and walked out of the room with a determined lift of her shoulders.

"See what I mean about mothers?" Jacie said and walked out.

Sophie groaned. Her mom was going to be furious with her now because there was no way that her grandmother was going to be happy with her new do.

Sophie forced herself to walk back out and over to her grandmother. Her mother was over at the cash register, completely ignoring her ex-mother-in-law. Good.

"Okay, we're finished. Let's walk over to the sinks and rinse your hair," Sophie said and lifted the hair dryer up.

As Sophie rinsed her grandmother's hair, she cringed inwardly at the eerily bright blue hair now covering her grandmother's head. She was feeling huge amounts of remorse and guilt. Why'd she do it? Too late now. She led her grandmother over to her station. Sophie picked up the hair dryer and started blowing her grandmother's hair dry. It only took a few minutes since there wasn't much left. She then used a very small curling iron to roll tiny rows of curls all over her head. She picked them out to form a soft afro-like style and then sprayed the entire creation with the stiffest hairspray science had created.

"Ta da!" Sophie said and took the drape off her grandmother's shoulders. She helped her grandmother up out of her chair and then walked her over to an adjacent mirror. Sophie stood behind her grandmother, staring stoically as Liz sat down weakly in the chair.

"My hair! What have you done, Sophie Reid?" her grandmother whispered, lifting her hands shakily to her hair.

"That will be a hundred and fifty dollars," she said and turned her back on Liz Reid to walk toward the cash register, not even looking back to see if her grandmother followed.

She rang up the sale and looked up as the check for the amount requested was handed her.

"Why? How could you do this to me?" her grandmother asked in a faltering, shocked voice.

Sophie looked up and handed her the receipt. "No one's ever stood up to you before, have they? Every time you look in the mirror and see your beautiful blue hair, I want you to remember all the horrible, mean, nasty, spiteful, vicious, cruel things you've said and done to my mother. You're through bullying me, and you're through bullying my mom. From now on, you leave us alone. I know it's beyond you to feel remorse for the way you've treated us, but you're not allowed to even look at my mom the wrong way. And if I ever hear of you making her cry again, there's just no telling what I'll do. And as far as calling Daphne this afternoon, don't plan on it," Sophie said and walked away toward the back of the salon, leaving her grandmother standing in horrified shock.

Sophie walked to the back of the salon where her mother stood, waiting for her, looking pale and extremely upset.

"Sophie Reid! Young lady, you are in huge trouble. As of right now, you are suspended from doing hair in this salon. I've never been so ashamed of you in all my life," Candy sputtered, so furious she could barely talk.

Sophie hesitated, never having seen her mother mad at her before. "What do you mean? Are you serious?" she asked, stunned.

Candy went to the back door and opened it. "Out. I will talk to you later," she said, holding the door open for her.

Sophie felt ill all of a sudden. "But, Mom, I did it for you. She deserved it; you know she did! She's a complete witch. Now she won't hurt your feelings anymore," Sophie said, pleading with her mom to understand.

Candy shook her head, her cheeks turning bright red. "How could you do that to your own grandmother, Sophie?" she said, looking away from her in disappointment.

Sophie picked up her purse and walked out of the salon. She couldn't believe it. She was out of a job.

chapter 33

Sophie went home because she didn't know where else to go. She changed out of her pant suit and into some jean shorts and a T-shirt. She wandered around the house looking for something to do, but her mom had already done the dishes and there was no laundry waiting to be folded. She sat down at the kitchen table and rested her head on her arms. She had really messed up. Now her mom was mad at her. She could never remember her mom being mad at her, ever. Candy was the most laid back, kind-hearted, generous person in the world. But today, Candy looked like she wanted to spank her. Sophie shuddered at the memory. What if her mom kicked her out? She already had to find a new job. What if she had to find an apartment too?

What was that quote? Revenge is mine, saith the Lord? She should have paid more attention in Seminary. Because from where she was sitting, revenge wasn't as fun as she thought it would be. It was actually pretty miserable. And lonely.

Her cell phone rang, and she quickly flipped it open. Jacie!

"Hey," Sophie said quickly, just grateful that someone was still talking to her.

"Holy crap, Sophie. You're mom is so mad. I have never seen her like this before. Right after you left, she ran out and grabbed your grandma and made her come back. She tore up the check she wrote out to you, and she's trying to fix her hair for free. Your mom is doing your grandmother's hair, Sophie. It is just too surreal. Oops! Gotta go. Here she comes," Jacie said and hung up on her before she had a chance to even react.

Sophie shut her cell phone and stared at it, horrified. Things had just gone from bad to incredibly horrible. She had been sticking up for her mom and now her mom was stuck trying to fix her mess. Sophie bit her lip and pushed away from the table. She had to do something. How could she make this up to her mom? She paced the small kitchen, kicked the table a few times, and then sat down again. There was no way she could fix this. Right now her mom was in the company of the one person on earth who hated her for reasons unknown. And it was all Sophie's fault. She could just imagine the scathing comments her mom was hearing every few seconds.

Sophie started to cry at the realization that she was the one who had caused her mom all the pain and hurt this time. She'd turned the other cheek for her relatives her whole life. Why couldn't she have turned it just one last time?

Sophie grabbed her purse and ran out to her car. She drove to Kohlers and bought all the ingredients for her mom's favorite meal. Why her mom loved meat loaf was beyond her, and just the thought of squishing raw hamburger through her fingers made her want to hurl, but this was not about her. She stopped by Peppermint Place just to be safe and bought a half pound of her mom's favorite. Chocolate covered potato chips. She thought about getting her mom some flowers, but Clyde's bouquet was still on the table. There just wasn't room. What else could she do? Sophie sat in the parking lot and banged her head on the wheel. What could she possibly get her mom to make her forget how mad she was?

Sophie started the car and drove back to Family Video. She'd buy her one of those LDS self-help books. There had to be one on divorced women getting remarried. They had one for every subject. Then she'd get her a DVD. She'd rent her favorite, *Napoleon Dynamite*. Her mom would have to forgive her now.

Sophie ran through Family Video, going almost crazy with the need to buy her mom whatever it was that would make her happy again. She ended up getting two books, since she couldn't decide, and, well, they were having a sale. She got the DVD and even a card. Family Video was like the one-stop shopping place for everything to do with Christlike gift-giving. Exactly what she needed.

Sophie hurried home and started on the meat loaf. Her mom wouldn't be home until four, so that gave her two hours to get everything ready. She chopped, peeled, sliced, and diced. She even got out the potatoes to make homemade mashed potatoes. This would be the meal of the century.

One and a half hours later, after cleaning the kitchen and taking a shower, she set two plates on the table. One for her. One for her mom. The mom who might still love her after all of her hard work.

The meat loaf had another twenty minutes to cook, the rolls were already done and cooling on the counter, and the pot of salty water was boiling, just waiting for all of the diced potatoes she had already cut. She dumped them into the water, and fifteen minutes later, strained the water from them and poured them into a large bowl, where she added onion soup mix and cream cheese. She added a little milk and then whipped until they were perfect. She turned the oven off and slipped the bowl of mashed potatoes in next to the meat loaf to stay warm until her mom got home. Now all she had to do was wait.

She took off her apron and dialed Jacie's number. Jacie answered on the second ring.

"Wait a second," Jacie said.

Sophie sighed and waited a long, long minute until Jacie's voice came back on.

"She just left. Expect her in three minutes. Man, Sophie. You are going to get it. It took her three hours to get rid of all that blue. She had to cancel all of her appointments. She looks completely exhausted. I would not want to be you," Jacie said.

Sophie winced and stared at her toe. "So what about my grandmother? Is she still in shock? Does she look normal?" Sophie couldn't help asking.

Jacie laughed. "Well, with that haircut you gave her, she definitely looks like a little ole granny lady. There wasn't anything your mom could do about that. But when your grandmother walked out of here, she finally looked okay. She didn't have that horrified, I'm-going-to-keel-over in shock look anymore. She almost looked, well, kind of peaceful. It was weird. But anyway, what are you going to do? Your mom's almost home, I bet. If you want to call me later, I'll be at Bryan's house. Call me if you need me. Okay?" Jacie said.

Sophie sighed. "Thanks, Jacie. Whatever happens, I'll call you and let you know if I have to move out tomorrow. I already have to find a new job."

Jacie snorted. "Yeah right. You're a gold mine. Your mom's not going to let you go."

Sophie frowned and remembered her mom's face. "Yeah. Well, bye, Jacie."

Sophie hung up the phone just as her mom pulled into the driveway. She hurried and took the meat loaf and the mashed potatoes out of the oven and placed them on the hot pads on the table. As she slipped the oven mitts off her hands, the front door opened. She quickly placed a plate of rolls in the middle of the table and stood back.

Candy walked into the kitchen a second later and stood still as she looked at her daughter and the loaded table without expression.

"Hey, Mom. Um, I feel really bad about what happened today, so I made your favorite meal. I even got you a video for later, also, your favorite. And for dessert, chocolate covered potato chips. Everything you could ever want," Sophie added lamely, noticing how exhausted her mother looked.

Candy glanced away from all the food and sighed. She didn't look very hungry. She didn't look very interested in the movie either.

"Oh, and I just happened to be at Family Video and picked you up a couple books on dating after divorce and second marriages for the LDS woman. You might find them interesting," Sophie said, holding the books up.

Candy sighed and sat down at the table, moaning as she lifted her feet up to rest on the chair opposite her. But she still didn't say anything.

Sophie felt her shoulders sag in defeat. Nothing she had done had softened her mother's heart. Her mom hated her now. She sat down by her mom and picked up her feet and gave her a foot massage. She should run to the bathroom and grab that chocolate scented lotion her mom loved so much, but she didn't want Candy to hurry to her room and lock the door on her. There could be no forgiveness if there was no communication.

"Hard day, huh?" Sophie said quietly.

Candy looked up from her lap and looked at her daughter without smiling. "You could say that," she said, talking for the first time since walking in the house

"Do you hate me?" Sophie whispered, looking down at her mom's sore toes and biting her lip to stop the trembling.

Candy sighed yet again and leaned over and hugged her daughter. "Of course I don't hate you. Why don't you load me up a plate and we'll see how good this tastes?" she said, trying to sound interested in the food.

Sophie dropped her mom's feet and got up to wash her hands before putting small portions of everything on her mom's plate. She pushed it toward her mother and waited for her mom to say a blessing on the food.

Candy mumbled a quick prayer and then took a small bite of the meat loaf. She then took a very small bite of the potatoes and then an even smaller bite of the roll. "It's very good. Thank you," she said politely.

Sophie grimaced and then took all the food off the table. She started getting Tupperware bowls out to put all the leftovers away. They had enough food to last them a week now.

"Your grandmother says hi, by the way," Candy said.

Sophie continued putting the food away and didn't look around. "Yeah right."

Candy shifted her weight and repositioned her feet on top of the chair again. "She wanted me to tell you how sorry she was for the way she's treated you and me and that she hopes that someday you'll forgive her," Candy said softly.

Sophie turned slowly to face her mom. "She did not say that. After what I did? She's probably calling her lawyer right now," she said shakily.

Candy shrugged and pushed her potatoes around her plate with her fork.

"She really said it. And after spending three endless hours in her company, I think she means it. She and I sort of had a coming together. We talked about the past and how maybe we could put aside our differences and try to get along," she said.

Sophie shook her head in disbelief. "Yeah, but what have you ever done to her? You've never done one mean thing to her. What is she talking about?" Sophie demanded, mad all over again.

Candy held up a tired hand. "Simmer down, Sophie. I'm not completely innocent. Your grandmother had the perception that I had stolen her son away from her. She's resented me ever since. She admits that she never thought I was good enough for her son, but has lately come to the realization that she could have been wrong. She's willing to let today go, if you'll let the past go," Candy said, finally putting her fork down and reaching for the chocolate covered potato chips.

Sophie sniffed and opened the fridge to get her mom a Fresca. You couldn't eat potato chips without a Fresca. Chocolate covered or not.

Candy smiled her thanks and popped the top as she crunched down on a decadent, salty, sweet slice of heaven.

"I'm supposed to let a whole lifetime of cruelty just go. Geez, one bad dye job and now I have to forgive her?" Sophie demanded.

Candy raised an eyebrow, and Sophie blushed. That one little dye job had been about as bad as you could get. It might actually be a fair trade.

"If you ever want to work at the salon again, you will. There will on no account be any more revenge dye jobs or haircuts for that matter, ever again. Do I make myself clear?" Candy asked in a quiet voice that was nonetheless full of steel.

Sophie gulped and nodded her head humbly. "Okay, Mom. Do you forgive me?" she asked sadly.

Candy sighed. "Of course I do. But that doesn't make me a push-over. You're still suspended for the whole week. And after hours, you have to go in and clean the bathrooms and mop the floors and wash the windows. And no complaining," Candy said, grabbing another chip.

Sophie's mouth fell open in horror. "Come on, Mom! Admit it. Liz Reid with blue granny hair was the best thing you've ever seen in your life. How many times have you fantasized about doing that yourself?" Sophie demanded, her hand on her hip.

Candy looked away and finally smiled. "Okay, maybe I have fantasized about doing just that. But I didn't. You did. Now you get to pay up. But maybe I won't make you do the windows. Everything else though," she said sternly.

Sophie smiled and nodded her head. "Okay, Mom. One week suspension and floors and bathrooms."

Candy smiled and offered her daughter a chip. Sophie sat down gratefully and took one.

"I love you, Mom," she whispered, so happy to have her mom still smile at her.

Candy grinned and got up and gave her daughter a hard hug. "I know you do, you little idiot. I know. And by the way, you are meeting your grandmother tomorrow afternoon for lunch at McGrath's in

Sandy for lunch at one o'clock sharp. You will be expected to apologize and have a nice, civilized conversation with her."

Sophie pulled away from her mom and groaned. "What good will that do? She knows I can't stand her now. What's the point? Fine, I'll call and apologize. I'll send a card. But one on one with her? Please, anything but that," Sophie begged.

Candy laughed and put her plate in the sink. "You wicked, wicked girl. Did you really think you could dye your grandmother's hair blue and get away with it? I bet you get a call from your dad tonight too," she said, shaking her head and chuckling softly.

Sophie sighed and leaned her head back against the chair. "Yeah right. He hasn't called me in over ten years. I doubt I'll hear from him," she said.

Candy started doing the dishes and ignored her. The doorbell rang and Sophie got up to get the door. *Please don't be a relative. Please, please please,* she murmured all the way to the door. She opened it up to see Clyde standing on the front porch, smiling.

"Hey, Sophie! Is your mom here? I got done at work early and thought I'd stop by," he said hopefully.

Sophie smiled and opened the door wider to let him in. "She's in the kitchen. Are you hungry? We have meat loaf and mashed potatoes and rolls," she said, leading the way into the kitchen.

Sophie watched as her mom turned and saw Clyde. All of the exhaustion and upset of the day immediately disappeared. Sophie stared in amazement at the look on her mom's face. She'd never seen it before. She was glowing. It was more than happy. It was more than excitement at seeing a boyfriend. Sophie gulped. Her mom was seriously in love. She glanced at Clyde and saw the same thing. Yikes.

She left the two of them in the kitchen and walked down the hallway toward her bedroom, and the doorbell rang again. She ran to the door, before her mom had to leave Clyde. *Please don't be a relative. Please don't be a relative.*

She opened the door and stared in surprise. Sam. Sam was on her front porch. Sam with the psycho girlfriend that wanted to take her and her mom down. Sam, the man she was halfway in love with.

"Hey, Sam, I didn't know you were back in town," she said, looking past Sam down the road to the left and the right just in case Tess was right behind him with an IRS agent.

"Hey, Sophie. I told you I was going to call you, but I figured I'd rather just see you in person instead," he said, staring at her with a tired smile on his face. He was wearing work clothes, and he looked exhausted.

"You look hungry," she said and opened the door for him to come in. She led the way into the kitchen once again, to find her mother locked in a passionate kiss with Clyde.

Sophie blushed down to her collarbone and cleared her throat loudly. Her mom sprang apart from Clyde quickly, and laughed in embarrassment. Clyde was blushing almost as brightly as she was. Sophie caught her mother's eye and burst out laughing.

"I told you kissing was fun, didn't I?" she said. "Hey, Sam stopped by. It's a good we have tons of food and that someone didn't eat any of it," she muttered just for her mother to hear.

"Come on in, Sam. You've met Clyde. Have a seat and we'll have this reheated in no time," Candy said, motioning for Sam to sit down opposite Clyde.

Sam and Clyde looked at each other measuringly before shaking hands politely. Sophie smiled when Clyde didn't squish Sam's bones together. Progress.

She and Candy had steaming plates of meat loaf and potatoes out in front of the men within minutes. It had barely had time to even cool off.

Candy and Sophie joined the men at the table and picked off their plates as both Sam and Clyde devoured everything in sight. After thirds and fourths, they both sat back, stuffed and content. Sophie and Candy weren't used to having men over for dinner. Neither one of them could believe how much food had disappeared.

"Candy, those were the best mashed potatoes I've ever had in my life. Honey, you have got to be the best cook in Alpine," Clyde said, staring at her adoringly.

Sophie didn't say a word, just raised one eyebrow. She was totally fine letting her mom take all the credit. If it got her back in her mom's good graces, she'd do anything.

Candy cleared her throat and shifted in her seat. "Well, Clyde, actually, Sophie was the chef today."

Clyde's face fell, while Sam grinned and pumped his fist in the air. "Yeah baby! You can cook and do hair. Life just looks better and better," he said, laughing at Clyde.

Clyde glared at Sam and turned back to Candy. "I bet you are a great cook, though, Candy. Right?" he asked, looking at her hopefully.

Candy laughed. "Well, of course. Who do you think taught Sophie?" she said and took his plate to the sink.

Clyde smiled easily and looked triumphantly back at Sam. "Well, then. Everything's good. So what's a hardworking girl like you doing home in the middle of the day cooking up a storm?" Clyde asked.

Sophie blushed and looked down at her lap. She didn't want to lie, but she in no way wanted Sam to know what she had done. He'd think she was horrible. Worse, he'd think she was like Tess. She looked to her mom for help, but Candy had turned her back to her.

Sophie looked up and met Sam's eyes before she looked at Clyde. Well, fine then. No big deal. The truth would set her free.

"Mom sent me home today because she suspended me from working at the salon for a week. She got really mad at me when I dyed a client's hair blue and chopped most of her hair off," she said in a non-emotional voice.

Sam's eyes went wide, and Clyde sat up and stared at her.

"What? You dyed someone's hair blue? Are you serious?" Clyde sputtered, not believing it. "But your mom says you're the best stylist she has. You would never do anything like that. Unless you did it on purpose," he said slowly as it dawned on him.

Sam nodded his head and crossed her arms across his chest as he leaned back in the chair. "Would this someone you chopped and dyed happen to be related to you, Sophie?" he asked in a kind voice.

Sophie couldn't look at him. She stared at her lap and nodded mutely.

"Did this person do or say something to you or to someone you care about that maybe upset you?" Sam asked gently.

Sophie nodded again.

Clyde leaned his elbows on the table and leaned toward her. "What did they say, Sophie?" he asked.

Sophie glanced toward her mom, who was still turned away from her. She sighed and gripped her hands together.

"She was mean to Mom. She made her cry. She always makes Mom feel like dirt, and I was sick of it. She demanded I do her hair, and so I did. And I'm not even sorry."

Candy whipped her head around and Sophie gulped. "I mean, I am. Very sorry, that I handled it the way I did. But I'm not sorry for sticking up for my mom," she said, slightly defiant.

Candy sniffed and turned back to the dishes.

Clyde frowned. "This person made your mom cry? And all you did was dye her hair blue? Sounds good to me," he said and leaned back with a smile on his face.

Candy whirled around again. "Clyde! What in the world?"

Clyde laughed and got up to put his arms around Candy's waist. "Honey, if I ever saw anyone make you cry, there's no telling what I'd do. You can't blame Sophie for doing what she did. It's natural to protect the people you love. I'd have been ashamed of her if she hadn't dyed this person's hair blue," he said and swooped down to kiss Candy on the cheek.

Candy laughed and hugged Clyde back. Sophie marveled at the change in her mom. She had been cold and angry when she had gotten home. Now she was giggling about it. Sophie liked Clyde. He would make a great stepfather.

She grinned and looked at Sam, who wasn't looking at Clyde and her mom, but right at her with a half-smile on his face.

"It was your grandmother, wasn't it?" he asked quietly.

Sophie nodded and got up from her chair. "Come on, let's leave these lovebirds to the dishes. Let's go out in the backyard," she said and took his hand.

They went out the sliding glass door and out into the small backyard. It was nothing like his family's large, acre-and-a-half park, but it was well maintained and filled with colorful flower beds of zinnias, snapdragons, and roses. She and Candy loved to spend their spare time planting flowers and digging out weeds. And it showed.

"It's beautiful out here, Sophie," Sam said and followed her over to two large deck chairs that she and Candy had bought at DI a few years back. They'd sanded and refinished them together.

Sam and Sophie sat down and reached for each other's hand at the same time. Sam smiled over at her, and Sophie felt herself blushing for some reason. It wasn't like she hadn't held a boy's hand before, but ever since Sam had come over and told her that Tess was out of his life for good, did that mean she was his girlfriend now?

"What in the world are you thinking, Sophie Reid? You have the strangest look on your face, like you can't believe we're in your backyard holding hands," Sam said with a laugh in his voice.

Sophie blushed brighter and couldn't help giggling. "I don't know. It's just strange to have you here with me. I've got you all to myself for once. No Tess, no Daphne, no one but you and me. It's kind of nice," she said, smiling at him.

Sam grinned at her and kissed her hand before leaning back and closing his eyes to the sun.

"Get used to it. From here on out, sweetheart, it's just you and me. I have a feeling we'll be doing this fifty years from now. Holding hands and sitting out in the yard. You'll be complaining that I haven't done as much weeding as I should, and I'll be nagging you to go in the house and make me some cookies. It'll be great."

Sophie closed her eyes too and let their hands swing between the chairs.

"What are you saying? I'm the complaining type? And exactly how much do you think you're going to weigh in fifty years, if you don't mind my asking?" she asked with a faint smile.

Sam immediately sucked in his stomach and puffed out his chest. "If I don't still have a six-pack in fifty years, I'll take you to Hawaii for a month."

Sophie snorted and shifted her hair out from under her.

"You better buy those tickets now, buddy, because men who can eat that much mashed potatoes and meat loaf don't have six-packs unless they're carrying them in their hands," she said with a laugh.

Sam grunted but didn't say anything back for a while. He really did look tired. Almost exhausted in a way she'd never seen before. It worried her and she squeezed his hand.

"By the way, Mom and Dad want you to come over to the house for dinner tomorrow night. We're having a big family dinner and they want you there," Sam said with a frown.

Sophie sat up and shifted in her seat. "What's going on, Sam? Is there a problem?" she asked, shading her eyes from the sun.

Sam didn't open his eyes, but the line between his eyes grew more pronounced. "We just found out this morning that Trey is getting kicked out of BYU. He's so upset. He drove home last night and hasn't spoken to anyone. Dad finally dragged it out of him. I've never seen him look so devastated. Some anonymous tipster told his professor that he's selling term papers online for two hundred dollars apiece. They had proof, they had receipts, they had some of his old papers. Everything. I just don't get it, Sophie. Trey's not the type to do something like that. He doesn't need the money. There's no motive. He's so busy with school and dating, he barely has time to write his own term papers, let alone someone else's. Mom and Dad are totally crushed. They figure if the whole family gets together tomorrow at dinner, then we can figure out what to do. Trey needs us right now. All of us," Sam said, opening his eyes and looking at her sadly.

Sophie felt so many emotions at once, she didn't know what to say or think. His mom and dad wanted her at a family dinner? They thought she was as good as family? Wait a sec . . . Trey!

"Sam, look, I think I know what this is all about. But before I tell you how I know, I want you to promise not to be mad at me," she pleaded, sitting up and throwing her feet over the side of the wooden chair to face him.

Sam's eyes narrowed and he sat up too. "What are you saying, Sophie? You know about Trey getting kicked out? How could you know? What's going on?" Sam asked, frowning darkly.

Sophie held up her hands. "Don't jump to any conclusions, Sam. Just let me explain. Remember when you were out of town last Saturday? Well, Jacie and I were goofing off, and I told her I needed to get Tess out of our lives, and well, Jacie thought it would be a good idea if we checked up on her. Julie told us Tess was having a party at your house, so we snuck over there and hid under the deck. Well, Tess and this lady she called Marrissa came out, and she promised Tess the cover of some Salt Lake magazine if she got engaged to you. She thought you two would make the most glamorous couple in Draper," Sophie said and paused to take a breath.

Sam blinked his eyes in confusion but motioned for her to continue.

"Well, so after Marrissa went in the house, Tess stayed out and called her mom and told her how upset she was about you wanting to be with me and what should she do, blah, blah, blah, and then her mom talked, which I couldn't hear of course, but then Tess said, 'Well, I like Trey,' and something about how he could at least go to the U. Sam, I think Tess's mom and dad are behind Trey getting kicked out. I bet you a million dollars that Tess calls you up and tells you that she can fix this for Trey, as long as you get back together with her," Sophie said and then took a deep breath.

She watched as Sam's eyebrows snapped down and his hands clenched in his lap. He looked furious.

"I've gotten three messages to call Tess today on my phone, but I haven't called her back. I just figured it was more of the same. I guess I'll be returning her call after all," he said and reached for his phone. "Wait a minute. What else did Tess say? Did she say anything else?" he asked, gripping his phone hard enough to break it.

Sophie licked her lips and looked down in her lap. Should she tell him everything? She looked back up at him and wondered why not. Tess's parents didn't need protection if they were the type of people to go after their best friend's son.

"Okay, but . . . okay. Well, Tess said something to Marrissa about how her dad had one of his golfing buddies call you and pretend to be Tess's counselor just so you wouldn't leave her. And Tess kind of laughed about it. And then she said she was going to have her uncle who works for the IRS come after me and my mom and take our salon away," she said and shifted her feet nervously as she watched Sam's expression go from dark to dangerous.

"She's been playing me this whole time," Sam said. "She must think I'm a complete idiot. I can't believe I wasted two years of my life on someone so cold and heartless," he said quietly and then stood up. He shoved his hands in his pockets and paced around her small backyard before flipping his phone open and pushing a few buttons.

"Hey, Dad. It's Sam. We need to talk. Where are you? Okay, I'll be there in fifteen minutes. Bye," he said and then walked over to her as he shoved his phone in his pocket.

Sophie stood up and looked up into Sam's face. He looked so angry. She remembered what his sister had said about how he never lost his temper unless someone else was being hurt. Then watch out. Poor Tess didn't know what she had gotten herself into.

"Sophie, I've gotta take off. It looks like I need to take care of some family business right now. Dinner's tomorrow at six o'clock at my parents' house. I really need you there," he said and leaned down and kissed her on the cheek.

Sophie smiled and grabbed his hand. "I'll walk you to your truck," she said and led him around the side yard to the front. He was so upset, he probably wasn't up to saying good-bye to her mom and Clyde.

When they arrived at his truck, Sam put his sunglasses on and turned to look at her. "Sophie, why didn't you call me Saturday night? You have my cell number. Were you ever planning on telling me any of this?" he asked in a soft voice.

Sophie cleared her throat nervously and looked away from the hard reflection of Sam's sunglasses.

"I guess I didn't think she'd really do it. I mean, who would hurt the brother of the man you're supposed to be in love with? And that stuff about her dad setting you up . . . I don't know. I thought I could spare you the pain. I mean, these people were supposed to be your friends. I'm sorry, Sam. If I had realized that she was serious about going after Trey, I would have driven straight to your house and told your mom and dad. But how crazy would that look? I mean, I was almost arrested once for spying, and there I was doing it again, although in my defense, it was Jacie's idea this time. You already got rid of one crazy girlfriend. I didn't want you to think I was like Tess," she said, finally looking up and meeting his eyes.

Sam smiled faintly at her and put his arms around her to give her a big hug.

"You could never be like Tess," he said pulling away and taking out his keys from his pocket. "And thanks. I'm going over to tell my mom and dad everything right now. I'll have to tell them about the spying. I hope you don't mind," he said, opening the door and jumping up into the truck.

Sophie looked up at him, frowning slightly. "Oh, Sam, what will your parents think of me?" she asked, crossing her arms over her chest, miserably.

Sam grinned down at her. "I already know what they think of you. They think you're the best thing to ever happen to me. Spying aside, you're perfect," he said, and shut the door.

She waved at him as he drove away, and went back in the house. She'd find out soon enough what they thought. She would be going to their house for dinner tomorrow. She swore right then that she would never spy, ever again. But then thoughts of having teenaged children entered her head. Oh, forget it. It was like Sam said. She was bent. Not too crazy, but just a little bent. Now if only his parents didn't take out a restraining order on her. Sophie stayed in her room until Clyde left, but was out in the kitchen waiting when her mom walked back in. They walked wordlessly into the family room and collapsed on the couch, side by side.

"You know, Clyde really likes you, Sophie. Especially after today. He said he hopes his daughter turns out just like you. Can you believe that?" Candy said, shaking her head.

Sophie threw a pillow at her mom. "Hey! Like that's such a bad thing. One hair disaster does not make me a criminal, you know."

Candy laughed. "Well, almost. But tonight was good. It felt great to have you and Sam and Clyde sitting around our little table. It just felt right."

Sophie sighed happily. "It did. I really like Clyde. Anyone who thinks I'm cool for dyeing my grandmother's hair blue is the stepfather for me. Sign me up," she said.

Candy laughed. "Honey, you've been signed up for two weeks now. I really think this is going to happen. I have the strongest feeling that Clyde is going to propose to me soon. Are you okay with that?" she asked softly.

Sophie nodded her head slowly. "I am."

Candy sighed and went on. "You know, you don't have to worry. If I do get married, you can stay here in this house as long as you want. It's paid for. I'll move in with Clyde and Kenedy. Or if you want to, you can move in with us. It's whatever you want to do," Candy said, looking at her daughter anxiously.

Sophie's eyebrows raised an inch. "You and Clyde already have it worked out?"

Candy nodded. "Clyde is a very practical man. It's better to get all the details worked out now, before the wedding, so there's no stress or pressure on me. He wants to make everything perfect for me. He doesn't want me to worry about you. He said he'd take care of everything," she said.

Sophie's took a deep breath. She felt like she was at the top of a roller coaster. Life was getting ready to throw some death defying spins at her.

"Well, thanks, Mom. It might be weird for me to move in with you and Clyde, though. You'll be newlyweds and everything, and it will be a hard enough adjustment for his little girl to make as it is. I think I would just complicate things. Besides, you'll be pregnant by Christmas anyway. So yeah, I can stay here. I'm practically twenty-one. No big deal. I'm a big girl," she said, smiling for her mom's sake as she cringed inwardly. She'd never been alone in her life. Even when she had gone to girls camp, she'd been horribly homesick. What would it be like living in the house all by herself? It looked like she was going to find out very soon.

Sophie frowned. "Wait just one second. Don't you think you and Clyde are moving kind of fast? You two haven't known each other very long. What's wrong with dating for a few more months, just to make sure you're making the right decision? What's the rush?" Sophie asked worriedly.

Candy smiled and nodded her head. "You're right. What's the rush? Except, I just know Clyde is the man I've been waiting for my whole life. I think I fell in love with him on our first date. And he feels the same way. He's a good man, Sophie. I've been praying about it, and I just have this warm, happy glow in my heart. I feel good about this. I know that Clyde will love me and take good care of me and protect me. But if you don't feel good about it, then I'll wait. I don't want this to upset you."

Sophie smiled reassuringly at her mom, even as she whimpered on the inside. Even if she wasn't ready, her mom obviously was. Time to grow up.

"Go for it, Mom. You deserve this."

Candy smiled in relief. "Oh, you're the best, Sophie. I knew this would be okay. And what about you and Sam? How are things going between you two?" Candy asked.

Sophie licked her lips and shrugged. "Well, his mom and dad want me to come over for dinner tomorrow night. They're having a family dinner and think I should be there," she said with a nervous smile.

Candy laughed. "Wow. You do work fast. Family dinners are big stuff. Maybe I'm not the only one moving fast, huh?" she said with a wiggle of her eyebrows.

Sophie laughed and got up. "Hey, I'm not the one talking marriage here. Anyway, I've got to get going. I have a salon to clean tonight," she said and walked down the hall as her mom giggled after her.

As she grabbed cleaning supplies out of the hall closet, she couldn't stop thinking of Trey. Sam had said he was devastated. She could only imagine how sad he was right then. She walked outside and threw the spray bottles and paper towels in the front seat of her Jeep and drove to the salon. She didn't want to underestimate

Sam and his family, but honestly, what could they do? Tess and her parents were determined to manipulate everybody and everything. She hoped somewhere there was a solution, but from where she was standing, it didn't look good.

chapter 34

Sophie didn't hear from Sam until ten o'clock that night. She was already in bed, reading a magazine, when he finally called. He sounded even more tired, if that were possible.

"So what did your dad say? Does he believe me?" Sophie asked as she nibbled nervously on her fingernail.

"He called Bert, and they're meeting up on Wednesday for lunch. I want to go with him, but my dad thinks he'll be able to get the truth out of him if it's one-on-one. My mom's ballistic, though. She wants to drive over there right now and tear them apart," he said with a chuckle.

Sophie smiled faintly. At least he hadn't lost his sense of humor. Yet.

"But what about Trey? Is he okay?" she asked working on another fingernail.

"Well, I told him everything you said, and he's having a hard time believing it. He's always had a thing for Tess. And she always flirted with him constantly. He can't believe that she would do this to him just to get to me. But at least he's coming out of his room now and he's talking to everybody. He's been on the phone with BYU, and he's requesting a meeting for tomorrow afternoon. I really think he'll be able to go back to school soon. We're hoping anyway," he said, not sounding very sure.

Sophie frowned and switched hands, moving the phone to her other ear. "And what about Tess? Did you call her?" she asked, closing her eyes.

Sam paused before answering. Uh-oh.

"Well, yeah. She denied everything, of course. She called you a psychopathic liar and suggested that you get some serious help, fast. She thinks you're trying to ruin her life. She says she's scared that you'll come after her and hurt her or something. She told me she's applying for a restraining order tomorrow against you. Oh, and she told me to tell you that if you come within a hundred feet of her, she'll be forced to sue you for stalking," he said.

Sophie's mouth fell open, and she stared at her phone. "You have got to be kidding me," she said faintly, feeling her heart beat quickly in her chest. Life was getting too surreal, even for her.

Sam laughed. "Oh, you're just not used to Tess yet. She's very dramatic. I wouldn't take it to heart. She's put restraining orders on tons of people. She keeps her family's lawyer very busy. Trust me," he said in a bored voice.

Sophie gulped and felt her skin go clammy. Tess was getting a restraining order against her? She'd never hurt anyone! Okay, well, besides dyeing her grandmother's hair blue. But still, a restraining order?

"Okay. Well, umm . . . so you never answered my question. Do your mom and dad believe me?" she asked, wondering what she would do if he said no.

"Of course they do. Why wouldn't they?" he asked.

Sophie talked to him for a few more minutes but had to hang up and get some Tylenol. Her head was suddenly pounding and her stomach felt upset. She took a sip of water and wondered what would happen next as she popped one of the pills in her mouth and swallowed. Would Tess ever stop? Would they be looking over their shoulders the rest of their lives? She trudged back down the hall toward her bedroom and massaged her temples. There just had to be a solution to this. Unfortunately she had no clue what that was.

The next day, Sophie dressed carefully for her lunch date with her grandmother. A modest white, calf-length denim skirt and a simple scooped-neck pale lime green silk shirt. She pulled her hair back in a French braid and used very little cosmetics. Simple and refined. The perfect outfit to get chewed out in.

She drove to McGrath's and walked in at two minutes to one. Right on time. She saw her grandmother sitting on the long bench,

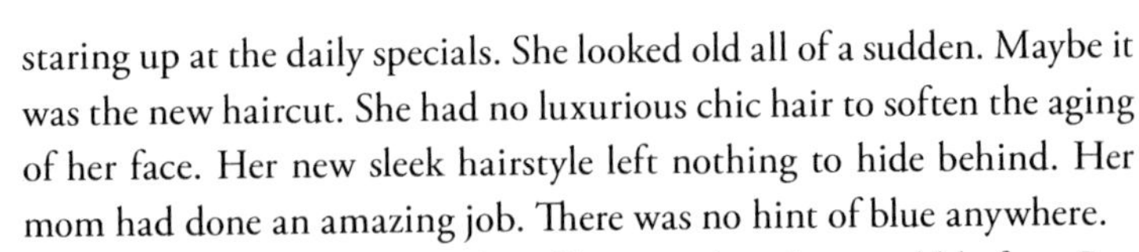

staring up at the daily specials. She looked old all of a sudden. Maybe it was the new haircut. She had no luxurious chic hair to soften the aging of her face. Her new sleek hairstyle left nothing to hide behind. Her mom had done an amazing job. There was no hint of blue anywhere.

Sophie had never thought of her grandmother as old before. But today, sitting there by herself, she looked almost fragile. *Fragile* was not a word Sophie'd ever used in connection with her grandmother. She'd ruled her family with sarcasm and cruelty. How could someone like that be fragile? Sophie must be imagining things.

Sophie sighed and squared her shoulders. She walked up and stood to the side of her grandmother. "Hello," she said, not knowing what else to say.

Liz looked up at her granddaughter and nodded.

"Sophie. You're right on time. Our table is ready for us," she said and led the way through the dining room to a small table by the window. As they sat down, their waitress handed them their menus and left to get their drinks.

Sophie adjusted her skirt and then looked across the table at her grandmother, since there was nothing else she could do.

"Thank you for meeting me for lunch today. It looks like there are some things that you and I need to deal with," her grandmother said, turning the page of her menu.

Sophie rolled her eyes and opened her menu. What an understatement. "Looks like it. What would you like to talk about?" she asked.

Her grandmother looked up and raised one perfectly tweezed brow. Sophie had the grace to blush.

"Well, of course why you felt you had to humiliate me. Your mother tried to explain how you've felt all these years, and I just couldn't believe it. I had to hear it from your own lips. How in the world could you not feel like you're a part of our family? You have my blood running through your veins. You look almost exactly like my Aunt Giselle. You are a Reid through and through. Why in the world would you feel this way?" she asked in exasperation.

Sophie pushed her menu away and folded her hands in her lap before staring in her grandmother's eyes. Truth time.

"How would you feel? Your father leaves your mother when you're ten years old. From that time forward, it's like its open season on my mother. A mother who did nothing to deserve being abandoned, by the way. A woman I look up to more than any other person in this world. Every dinner, every family get-together, you and Lexie and even my own father have to make it a point to say insulting things about my mother in front of me. How did you think I would feel? Did you think if you put her down enough, I'd agree with you? She's my mother. I love her. She's the one person in this world who has never let me down. Unlike your son. And not only was she the target of all of your brilliant sarcasm, but I was too. Nothing I ever did was up to the Reid standards. I was constantly compared to my cousins. And never in a positive way. How would you expect me to feel? Loved? Nurtured? Accepted? I used to feel anger and hate, but lately I've just felt empty inside when I think of you all. That is until you made my mom cry at Kohlers. All those years of insults, all the tears my mother cried, it finally hit me that you were never going to stop. My mother would never be able to atone for marrying your son. You would never let her. And I realized that I was going to have to be the one to stop it."

Sophie paused and took a sip of water. The waitress showed up with her pad of paper in hand and a questioning look on her face. Sophie glanced at her grandmother. She looked pale but determined.

"Yes, fine. We'll order now. It takes forever to get the food anyway. I'll have the shrimp linguine with the rice and a cup of chowder. And you, Sophie?" she asked in a shaky voice.

Sophie picked up the menu and glanced at it for a second. She just wasn't hungry. But she should at least order something. That way she could take it home and her mom could reheat it later for dinner since they had no leftovers now.

"Um, I'll have the cajun salmon, blackened, with a salad and the red potatoes," she said and handed the waitress her menu.

After the young girl had walked away, she looked at her grandmother expectantly. Did she have a comeback? Did she have any rationalizations for her behavior? Sophie was actually curious. Her grandmother didn't look like she knew what to say.

"Oh, and I formally apologize for dyeing your hair blue. It was immature and needlessly cruel of me," Sophie said as an afterthought. There. Now her mom would be happy.

"Why apologize? You meant it. You were glad you did it," Liz said with a half-smile.

Sophie took another sip of water so she didn't have to answer.

"Well, I guess I've been put in my place," Liz said. "I see now that what I've thought of as constructive criticism was taken for just plain criticism. That would be a mistake on your part," she said finally.

Sophie raised her own eyebrow at that, in almost the same way her grandmother had. "Constructive criticism. Is that what they call emotional and verbal abuse now? I hadn't heard," she murmured.

Liz blew out her cheeks in outrage and sat up straighter.

"You listen here, young lady. Don't you play the victim with me," she said, her face turning red.

Sophie stared coldly across the table at her grandmother.

"Then you don't play the concerned but loving grandparent with me. We both know what a lie that is. If you want to pretend that our relationship is something it's not, then go ahead. But since we're here, face to face, why not just be honest with each other? Hmmm? Let's just lay it all down on the table for once. I have no interest in being a part of the Reid family. As a small child I yearned for my father's attention. Well, I've grown up and realize that his faults and failings aren't my faults and failings. I'm through being your family's verbal punching bag. No more dinners, no more mandatory monthly family get-togethers. I'm moving on without you, and I have to say, good riddance," she said angrily, her voice getting louder and louder.

Her grandmother held her hand up in a plea for an end to the barrage of angry words.

"I see now that what you really need is counseling. How could you twist everything around so selfishly? Everything is not about you, Sophie. I'm sorry you got your feelings hurt on occasion. Well, toughen up. The world is a tough place. If you can't take a few dinners with your family, well, then, you're a wimp," she said bluntly.

Sophie nodded her head. "You could be right. I might be a wimp. But if the world is such a horrible, tough place, then wouldn't it be nice to have a family that is a comfort and a refuge against such a hurtful place? I can see that you're determined to believe what you want to believe, and I'm just as determined to stay as far away from my father and you and the rest of my relatives. So it looks like this lunch is a failure," Sophie said, almost sadly. She had been hoping that her grandmother would try to reach out to her. She must have been insane.

Sophie flagged down her waitress. "Excuse me, but could you box up my lunch to go? It looks like I'm going to have to cut my lunch date with my grandmother short today," she said, smiling at the waitress.

As the girl hurried off to see to the changes, Sophie glanced at her grandmother as she picked up her purse. She was shocked to see a single tear running down her grandmothers' cheek.

Sophie felt a spurt of guilt. She really hadn't wanted to make her grandmother cry.

"Well, I guess I'll be seeing you," Sophie said and stood up.

"Wait. Just wait a second. Give me five more minutes. Please," Liz asked, looking up at her granddaughter.

Sophie sat down hesitantly and nodded her head for her grandmother to go ahead.

"I'm sorry for the way you never felt accepted or good enough in our family. I guess I am to blame for some of that. I think, though, that I was trying to punish your father, and instead punished you. I did spend all my money and affection on your cousins. Your Aunt Lexie married the man I wanted her to. She did everything I wanted her to. Your father disobeyed me and married your mother. I had a beautiful young woman from a very fine family picked out for him, but he took one look at your mother and ignored everything I said. He married your mother without a single thought to his future. And I've been punishing him ever since. Maybe all the comments and the insults were meant to prove a point to your father. That see, if he had just done what I had told him to, then his daughter would have been dressed like a princess. If he had just done as he was told, his family could be going to Disneyland with me. I'm sorry, Sophie. You're right; you were being punished all this time for your father's failings."

Sophie blinked, surprised by the honesty. "So did it work? Was my father punished enough for his disobedience?" she asked, curious.

Her grandmother sniffed and played with her napkin. "If he had cared about someone besides himself, he might have been. I honestly thought that with his marriage to Julie, he would finally be the man I had envisioned for him to be. But that hasn't happened. It's taken me twenty-three years, but I finally realize that your mother was not the downfall of my son. My son was his own downfall," she said and took a long sip of water.

Sophie licked her lips and sat back against the chair. Well, then.

"I appreciate you saying that. I know that was hard for you," Sophie finally said, not knowing what else to say.

Her grandmother nodded. "It's always hard to admit one's failures."

Sophie smiled. "So this whole picking your children's spouses? That seems really odd. Did you really think it would work?" she had to ask.

Liz looked up and frowned. "Well, it's not as bad as you think. But your father had many wonderful choices from a certain group of families. He had plenty of opportunities to make an appropriate selection. He just picked the exact opposite of everything I wanted for him. I wanted him to marry a college graduate. He choose a beauty school graduate. I wanted him to marry a woman from a family with education, class, and of good society. He chose a young woman from a small farming town. It wasn't your mother so much as it was the absolute defiance of his choices. I raised my son a certain way, and I expected him to continue in the way he was brought up. He let me down. And I just . . . I just couldn't get over it," she admitted.

Sophie sighed and shook her head. "There's this little thing called agency. It's an amazing idea, really. I think it would solve a lot of your hang-ups," she offered.

Her grandmother's eyes narrowed dangerously. "I didn't come here to be preached to, young lady," she said stiffly.

Sophie smiled. "What exactly did you expect to happen today, if you don't mind my asking?" she asked as the waitress brought her lunch in a take-out bag.

Liz paused and reached for her spoon.

"Why, I came to explain to you why you should be grateful to be a Reid and that although your recent behavior is understandable, that your future respect and devotion to this family is expected and deserved," she said coolly.

Sophie closed her eyes and smiled a little bit sadly. "How about this? If you ever deal with your issues with my father, then we'll talk. Until then, I refuse to be the family's whipping boy any longer. I suggest counseling," she said as she picked up her bag and stood to leave.

"Sophie!" her grandmother called out.

Sophie paused and turned around.

"Your mother did a good job on my hair, of course, but in the future, I would like to come to you. If you're willing to take me on?" she said with that fragile look again.

Sophie frowned and looked down at her shoes. Should she? She would basically be agreeing to one-on-one time with her grandmother on a somewhat monthly schedule. Well, it was better than the dinners with all the relatives. It was a good trade. And she had to face it. She did owe it to her.

"Okay. I'll do it," Sophie said and gave her grandmother a real smile. Her grandmother smiled back. It was a first.

Sophie turned and walked away and felt lighter somehow. She'd done it. She'd finally had it out with her grandmother. It was amazing what a little honesty could do.

She got in her car and drove out of the parking lot. She headed toward home and didn't even see the cream-colored Lexus following right behind her.

chapter 35

Sophie decided to stop at the Iceberg connected to the gas station just off the Lehi exit and splurge on an order of onion rings. She deserved a treat after her head-to-head with her grandmother. Well, that and she hadn't eaten anything. She hopped out of the car and went in to order. But she couldn't decide whether she'd been good enough to order a shake. She'd made her grandmother cry, and she was still feeling kind of bad about that. Sophie frowned. Okay, just the onion rings.

"Excuse me, but is that your red Jeep outside?" a tall man with a John Deere hat said after tapping her on the shoulder.

"Yes?" she asked, turning to look at him.

"Because there's a young lady out there letting the air out of all your tires. Pretty pointless since you're right where you can pump them all up again," he said, shaking his head at the stupidity.

Sophie gasped and ran back outside. She saw the long blonde hair and long tan legs walking away from her saggy-looking Jeep and knew exactly who it was.

"Hey! Wait a second, Barbie! You can't just pull a stunt like that and walk away. Who do you think you are?" Sophie yelled, while pulling her cell phone out of her pocket.

Tess turned around and smiled innocently at her. Sophie scowled.

"Sophie, is that you? I would recognize that orange hair anywhere," Tess said sympathetically.

Sophie ignored her and spoke into her cell phone. "Yes, I'm here at the Iceberg off the freeway in Lehi. A woman named Tess just let the air out of my tires. I have a witness, and I'd like to press charges against her," she said, watching Tess's expression turn from coolly amused to horrified.

Tess put her hands on her hips and stamped her foot.

"You have a lot of nerve, you little tramp!" Tess shouted at her.

Sophie laughed in her face. She'd just gone up against her grandmother. She could handle a spoiled brat any day.

"Look, blondie, I know all about your plans to sic an IRS agent on my mom and how you got Sam's brother kicked out of BYU. You're not the only one who can apply for a restraining order. And now that I have proof of your intent, I'll have it on record. You're going down, you psycho," Sophie yelled right back, oblivious to the crowd of truckers now surrounding them from a distance.

Tess stepped closer to her and shoved a finger in her face. "Sam doesn't want you. He might want a little taste of independence, but he doesn't want you. He wants me! Now you either take the hint and stay out of this, or you will pay, you trashy little hick," she said with scorn dripping off her tongue.

Sophie snorted. That was all she had?

"Honey, if I'm trashy, what do you call a woman who can't get it through her head that her ex-boyfriend wants nothing to do with her? He's been trying to dump you for over half a year now and you're so desperate, you keep hanging on. Have a little pride. Just take your little color swatches and your carpet samples and go find another home builder you can be the most awesome couple in Draper with," Sophie said with a saccharin sweet smile.

Tess gasped and then hauled off and backhanded Sophie across the face, cutting open her cheek with one of her diamond rings.

Sophie grabbed her cheek, horrified at the feeling of blood dripping down her face. She looked down at her white skirt and knew the bright red polka dots were her blood. A police car pulled up to the two women, and a police officer got out and walked right over to her. He reached down and talked into his radio.

"Send an ambulance to the Iceberg in Lehi. We have an injured woman here," he said and put his radio down.

Tess looked guilty but smiled brightly and walked up to the officer.

"Officer, we were just having a private conversation when I was gesturing with my hand and accidentally cut her face. It was all very innocent," she assured him.

Sophie gasped and lurched forward to contradict her. The trucker who told her about her tires got there first.

"Officer, I've been here since the very beginning. This blonde woman followed the redhead here in, and while she was inside let the air out of all her tires. Then she started yelling at her about some boyfriend that doesn't want her anymore and then backhanded her as hard as she could. I'm a witness and my buddies over there are witnesses too," he said, pointing to three men standing to the side.

The officer frowned and nodded. "I'll need to get their statements in a minute," he said and turned back to Sophie. "Do you want to press charges, young lady?" he asked.

Sophie stared at Tess's innocent expression and beautiful face and nodded.

"Yes, officer. I want to press charges," she said.

The officer immediately turned and took out his handcuffs and motioned for Tess to follow him. Sophie watched in awe as the officer cuffed Tess and put her in the back of his car.

"It looks like you're going to need stitches," he said as the ambulance roared into the parking lot. Sophie shook her head in shock. Everything was happening too fast. It felt like she was watching herself in a movie as she sat in the ambulance and the EMTs told her that she needed a plastic surgeon. They drove her to the hospital, where she finally remembered to call her mom.

The officer showed up later and told her that Tess was being processed but that she'd most likely make bail within the hour. He quickly took down all of her information and then left without a backward glance. She looked down at her watch and realized that it was already six o'clock. She had just stood up Sam and his family. Her first family council and she had missed it.

She was put in a room, where Dr. Sanders joined her. He was the plastic surgeon on call, he told her as he walked through what he was going to do.

"Is it going to be really ugly? The scar?" she couldn't help asking.

Dr. Sanders smiled and patted her shoulder.

"Nah. This is a cakewalk. Yesterday I had to put a hand back together. Your face is going to look red for a while, but I have some ointment I'll give you. If you're a good girl and put it on a few times a day, you'll barely be able to see it. Hey, relax! I'm the best. Now just lay back and pretend you're on a beach in Hawaii. And from now on, stay away from ex-girlfriends," he said, chuckling as he pricked her cheek with a local anesthetic. Sophie tried not to cry but couldn't help the tears that ran down her face. Dr. Sanders paused and asked her if she wanted to wait for her mom to get there, but Sophie shook her head. If her mom saw her cheek torn up, she'd be too upset to drive her home.

It took longer than she had expected. Her mom had sewn up skirts faster than this guy, but maybe there was a little bit of a difference.

When he was done, he wiped the blood off her cheek and told the nurse to get her a drink of water. She must have looked a little dehydrated from all the crying.

Candy walked in just as the nurse walked out. Sophie took one look at her mom and sniffed back her last tear. It wouldn't help to upset her mom any more than she already was. Candy looked white as a sheet and every one of her birthdays.

"Oh, honey! Look what she did to you. A silly little ring did this?" she asked in a whisper as she set her purse down and drew a chair up to the side of Sophie's bed.

Sophie's face was still numb, but she nodded her head. She'd asked the nurse for a mirror and had been shocked by the teeny little stitches zigzagging across her upper cheek.

"The doctor said it was a good thing it was a diamond ring. It could have been even more jagged."

Candy winced. "The reason it took me so long to get here is because Sam was at the house looking for you. He wanted to give you a ride to his mom and dad's house since he was working in the area. He's just outside. He really wants to see you," she said, picking up Sophie's hand and holding it tightly.

Sophie groaned. "I don't want him to see me like this. I can barely keep from slobbering, for pete's sake," Sophie grouched.

Candy surprised her and laughed. "Well, I don't think he'll care. I got your call, and I'm afraid he heard pretty much everything. He seems really upset."

Sophie winced and looked away. "Well, okay. But if he breaks up with me because I'm ugly now, then I want Clyde to beat him up."

Candy snorted and stood up. "Well, I have to go fill out all your paperwork before I can take you home. So you just sit here and rest while you talk to Sam," Candy said and kissed her on her good cheek before walking out.

As soon as Candy disappeared, Sam walked in, holding a huge bouquet of flowers with a grim expression on his face.

Sophie watched him as he placed the flowers carefully on the table and sat in Candy's vacated seat.

"No need to have Clyde beat me up, Sophie. You're still the most beautiful woman in the world. No scratch could make me think anything else," he said and gently took her hand and laid his cheek on it.

Sophie felt one more tear slip out and she sniffed. How sweet.

"Well, I guess if your parents didn't believe me before, they will now. Tess is one crazy woman," she said as Sam put a tissue in her hand.

Sam frowned and looked at his feet. "Honey, there was no doubt you were telling the truth. I swear, Sophie, I had no idea she was capable of hurting you like this. I'm so sorry," he said and looked up to meet her eyes.

Sophie tried smiling at him, but her face was too numb.

"I don't blame you, Sam. You shouldn't feel responsible for anything Tess does. I still can't believe you dated her for two years, though. How could you choose to be with a woman like her and then turn around and choose to be with me?" she asked with a frown.

Sam had the grace to blush and sat back in his chair. "Yeah, well, people grow up. Remember, our families kind of grew up together. We were always thrown together at social events. I had a crush on her since I was in the eighth grade. But she never even looked at me until I got back from my mission. I would ask her out all the time, but she would never say yes. She'd always somehow give me hope, though, that someday I might be worthy of her. And then a year after I graduated and closed on my first deal, she showed up at the house one night and asked me out. I was in heaven. After that, she introduced me to all her friends. It was a completely different world than I was used to. Parties in Park City. Trips to Las Vegas. It was all the glitz and glamour and social life that anyone could dream of. It was the life I always thought I wanted. And then one night, we were at this party, and I looked over at Tess, and I thought, wow, I must be the luckiest man on earth to have her. Out of all the guys here, she picked me. Well, halfway through the party, I looked at her again and saw her flirting with this guy I used to know in college. Super wealthy, very successful, but very nice. And

I saw the expression on his face. He was stunned that she was talking to him. He looked like a little puppy dog, so happy to have the attention of this gorgeous woman. And I suddenly realized. That was me. A stupid little grateful puppy," he said with a sneer.

Sam shifted in his chair and looked up at the ceiling before going on.

"After that party, I started to really think about Tess and what I wanted out of a relationship, and I realized, in all honesty, I didn't need or even want all the parties and the constant fun. I wanted somebody who loved me. I wanted someone who had a kind heart. Someone I could trust. Someone I could spend my life with, raising kids and playing in the backyard. I wanted what my parents had. And so I broke up with Tess. And that's when the beautiful façade crumbled. Everything fell away, and what was left was a cruel, vicious woman who would do anything to get her way. I'm sorry you had to get involved with this mess. But I promise you, I'll never let her hurt you again. I love you, Sophie," he said and looked up to meet her eyes.

Sophie felt her mouth open in surprise. He had said it. He had said it! She watched as Sam reached out his hand. She thought he was going to caress her cheek or something, but instead he wiped some slobber off her chin.

"Sorry there, but you're making a puddle," he said with a smile.

Sophie blushed and felt her chin.

"So are you going to say anything?" he asked, still smiling at her.

Sophie looked up and met his beautiful, kind eyes and smiled.

"I bet you're expecting me to say I love you back," she said and watched as his smile slipped a notch. "I bet you're expecting me to say something, like I would love to spend my life with you, raising kids and being happy," she said, still smiling, as Sam started to frown and sit up straighter in his chair. "I bet you're even expecting me to jump out of this bed and kiss you," she said.

Sam frowned at her and crossed his arms over his chest. "So what are you going to do?" he asked stiffly.

Sophie flung her blanket aside and hopped out of bed. She plopped herself on Sam's lap and threw her arms around his neck.

"I'm going to tell you that I would love to be loved by you. I love you, Sam," she said and bent down and gave him a slobbery kiss on the cheek.

Sam grinned and looked like he was going to kiss her back, but changed his mind at the last second. He grabbed a tissue from the bedside table and gently wiped her chin.

"Sophie, you are a stinker. But I love that about you," he said and laughed happily.

"Hey now! What's this? This young lady's been through the ringer and you're acting like you're on a date," Stan Kellen said from the doorway.

Sophie jumped off Sam's lap and back into bed as Sue and Stan and Lacie, Macie, Casey, and Trey all fell into the room, carrying bouquet after bouquet of flowers. They all grinned at her, obviously having witnessed the whole touching scene between her and Sam.

"I hope you don't mind, Sophie. I called my family on the way over." Sam, although not a redhead, was blushing bright red nonetheless. She was hugged and kissed by every member of the Kellen family. Her mom came in seconds later, with Clyde in tow, and there were introductions for everyone. Sam and Sophie exchanged looks of bewilderment and shock at how her hospital room had turned into a festive family get-together.

"Well now, I bet you thought you were getting out of our family dinner, just because of bodily injury, but it just doesn't work that way in our family," Stan said, smiling down at her.

Sophie laughed and fixed her blanket over her legs. "Trust me, I'd much rather have been at your house than getting attacked by Tess," she said, bringing everyone's smiles to a crashing stop. Everywhere she looked, there were dark, fierce frowns.

"Honey, now you just leave everything to us. We're taking on Tess now. You and Sam, just focus on you and Sam," Sue said, locking eyes with her husband.

Stan looked grim but sad at the same time. Sophie couldn't help feeling sad for his ruined relationship with Tess's parents.

Sam stood up and held his hands up for everyone's attention. Everyone quieted down immediately and waited to hear what he had to say.

"Now listen up, everyone. I know Tess has done some horrible things. Trey, I know you're feeling a lot of anger right now, but just so everyone is clear, I'm the one who's going to take care of Tess. I know how you are. You all want to go find her and do your worst. But I'm the one who brought these troubles into our family, and I'll be the one to get them out. Agreed?" he said and looked everyone in the eye until they nodded.

Stan and Sue looked at each other before shaking their heads at Sam. Stan faced down his son.

"Look, Sam, I know how you feel, but to be honest, Bert and June were our friends first. We trusted them. From what I'm hearing, they're the ones who put Tess up to a lot of this. You're welcome to have it out with Tess, but we'll be dealing with her parents," he said, staring his son down.

Sam stood still and thought about it for a moment before conceding. "Okay, that's fair, Dad. And I know it doesn't help, but for all it's worth, I'm sorry. If I hadn't gotten involved with Tess, you'd still have your friends," he said, shifting his feet uncomfortably.

Sue shook her head fiercely. "They weren't our friends. They never were. Anyone who could scheme to ruin my son's reputation just to blackmail my other son is no one I'd want to be with. So you stop feeling guilty right now. Your dad and I are feeling enough for all of us. Especially now that our little Sophie got hurt," she said and walked over to grasp Sophie's hand in hers.

Sophie smiled and squeezed her hand back. "Well, I will say that this is one interesting family. I had a feeling when I met Sam that he wouldn't be boring," she said with a laugh.

Everyone laughed, easing the tension in the room. Ten minutes later Sam's family left with promises of future family dinners. Candy and Clyde remained with Sam, looking slightly confused. Sophie hadn't told her mom everything about Tess, because she hadn't wanted to worry her about the IRS, but now, she and Clyde were playing catch-up and didn't look very happy about it.

"Sophie, I should spank your britches. What are you thinking not telling me about Tess threatening us?" Candy said, with sparks flying from her eyes.

Sophie sighed and closed her eyes. What was it about parents that made them want to take on the world for their children? Whatever it was, her mom had gotten two servings of it. Sam tried to ease things over with her mom, but Sophie could tell she was in for it as soon as she got home. Clyde didn't look that much happier.

"Now, honey, I know you don't know me very well, but you've got to know that I'm here for you. I'm the man to protect you now. You can come to me for anything, and you know I'll do whatever I can to help you. I know we haven't talked about it, but I'm planning on being your dad soon. I just want you to know that I'm serious about being your father, the same way I'm Kenedy's father. And that means trusting me to take care of you," he said with a hurt expression in his eyes.

Sophie looked at him in awe. Her own father had never cared one way or the other about her. It was so strange to have someone jumping at the chance. She shocked everyone by bursting into tears. Clyde gave her a hug and patted her on the back, until she stopped sniffling. She looked up to blow her nose and saw her mom, crying on Sam's shoulder. Candy hurried over and hugged Sophie on the other side.

"Sorry, babe, but the two of you hugging is the sweetest thing I've ever seen," Candy said, looking at Clyde with so much love in her eyes, Sophie felt embarrassed being in the same room with them. Sophie looked up at Clyde and saw the same emotion mirrored in his eyes.

Sam cleared his throat. "Um, well, Sophie. Listen, I've got to get going. I know you're in good hands here with Clyde and your mom. I'll call you tonight, probably pretty late, but I'll come by first thing tomorrow to check on you. Okay?" he said.

Clyde actually smiled at Sam and didn't even try and shake his hand. Candy ran around the bed to give Sam a quick hug. And Sophie waited until Sam bent down and gave her a quick peck on the cheek.

"Okay, Sam. I guess I'll see you tomorrow then," she said a little sadly. She didn't want him to go. But it was obvious he had something important to do.

"Well, I guess that's that," she said to no one in particular.

"Hey, no frowning now. The doctor said it's not good for your stitches," Candy said with a shake of her finger

Sophie shook her head and smiled. "Mom, you just made that up."

Candy laughed. "Maybe I did, but at least you're smiling now."

Candy and Clyde helped her into the wheelchair and wheeled her out to Candy's car. Clyde was meeting his brother at the Iceberg to pick up her Jeep.

The pain pills were starting to kick in, and as soon as she got home, she went right to bed and fell asleep. She didn't even hear the phone ring three hours later. She didn't even think of Sam until the next day.

chapter 36

Sophie woke up the next morning to someone gently tapping her on the shoulder. She blinked her bleary eyes open and screamed when she saw the blonde hair.

"No!" she screamed and held her hands up in front of her face.

"Hey, wacko. What is this? Post-traumatic stress disorder? It's me, your best friend, doofus," Jacie said, offended.

Sophie sat up, still gasping from fear.

"Sorry, it's your blonde hair. You looked like Tess for a second," she said, leaning back against the pillows.

Jacie sat next to her and handed her a Fresca. Sophie didn't even have to ask for a straw. Mmmm. The perfect drink for a dry throat.

"I'll forgive you for mistaking me for some wacked out psycho, but first you have to tell me everything. Don't you dare leave anything out," Jacie commanded.

Sophie's face was sore, and she didn't feel like talking. Candy walked in just then and handed her three pills to take.

"Hey, Jacie. Just give her a second while she takes some pills. She's gotta take this antibiotic and something for the pain," Candy murmured.

Jacie winced and looked away from the stitches. "Yeah, I can see why. I can wait a few seconds, but I'm about to die here from lack of knowledge. All you said on the phone was that Tess had hurt her and she had to go to the hospital. Details. I need lots of details," she pleaded.

Candy sat down on the other side of Sophie and held her hand as she talked and talked and talked. Sophie would add a nod here and there and a grunt occasionally, but Candy pretty much said everything she would have. Jacie sat back in anger and disgust.

"What some women will do to get a ring on their finger," she said, and then stared at her own finger with a faint smile.

Candy and Sophie exchanged a look. "What about you, Jacie? Your finger is looking a little bare," Candy said with a raised eyebrow.

Jacie did something completely out of character and blushed. "Well, to be honest, it won't be for long. I have a sneaking suspicion that Bryan might propose this Saturday night. He's taking me up to Snow Bird to ride the tram and take me to dinner up there somewhere. He told me to dress in my nicest dress," she said, giggling.

Sophie forgot about herself for a moment and clapped her hands joyfully for her friend.

"I'm so happy for you, Jacie. You guys are going to make an awesome couple. When do you think you'll get married?" she asked.

Jacie smiled and crossed her fingers. "If everything goes the way it should, I want to get married in early October. It's not too hot, not too cold. Just perfect."

Candy and Jacie talked about wedding plans for the next hour, while Sophie was content to just sit back and listen. The doorbell had Candy popping up and smiling at Sophie. "I bet I know who that is," she said with a wink.

Sophie frowned and ran her fingers through her hair. She had wanted to get up and take a shower before Sam got there. She hadn't even had breakfast yet.

Candy walked back in Sophie's room with a shocked look on her face. "Sophie, honey. Your, um, family is here to see you," she said. "Jacie, why don't you come in the kitchen with me and we'll throw together some pancakes for breakfast while Sophie has a nice visit," she said and moved aside for Jacie to walk past her.

Sophie sat up to see who it was. Her eyes went big when she saw her father standing uncomfortably next to her grandmother and her aunt Lexie and Daphne and Farrah. She could not believe it.

The relatives walked further into her bedroom. Daphne and Farrah sat down in her window seat while everyone else stood around her bed.

"Your mom called and told us how you got hurt. We wanted to come by and see if you needed anything," her father said in a scratchy, nervous voice.

Her grandmother took a box of chocolates from her purse and laid them on her side table. "These are for when you feel better."

Sophie nodded her gratitude and looked over at Lexie and Daphne and Farrah, who looked very out of place in her bedroom. Probably because they'd never been there before.

"You're lucky it's not worse. I've heard of angry ex-girlfriends running down people with their cars. At least you had a good plastic surgeon. I hear Dr. Sanders is the best," Lexie said, nodding her head sympathetically.

Daphne and Farrah didn't say anything, but they didn't look scornful either. It was a nice change.

"Um, well, thanks for coming over. As you can see, I'm doing fine. Mom and Jacie are here if I need anything. But it was . . . nice of you to stop by and check on me," she said finally, not knowing what else to say.

Her father cleared his throat and shifted his feet. "Well, we won't keep you. I know you haven't had your breakfast yet," he said and took his mother by the elbow. Her relatives said their farewells and disappeared quickly. Sophie was left staring at the empty room, surprised and strangely touched.

Jacie left soon after breakfast to go to work. With Sophie and her mom not there, everyone else was needed at the salon. Sam finally called at eleven o'clock and sounded really strange. He told her he was coming over and that he was bringing someone with him. Before hanging up, he asked her if she was still drooling.

Sophie frowned and went to shower and brush her teeth, and well, to check her chin too. What a thing to ask. As if she'd always had a drooling problem. She combed through her wet hair and added a little foundation under her eyes but kept it at that since she didn't want to get any makeup near her stitches.

She put on some shorts and a T-shirt and was just getting ready to get another Fresca when Sam knocked on the door. As she opened the door, her eyes went big and round and her mouth fell open. Sam was standing next to Ruth Todd, her favorite newswoman.

"Hi," she said faintly as Sam grinned at her.

"Hey, Sophie. This is Ruth Todd. I've been on the phone with her producers, and they're dong a segment on dangerous relationships. We think it's a good idea to show that women can be just as abusive as men sometimes. Do you mind if Ruth comes in and asks you a few questions?" he asked, smiling appealingly at her.

Sophie nodded dumbly and moved aside to let them in. Ruth patted her on the shoulder. "That looks so painful. If this is a bad time, I can always come back," she said kindly.

Candy walked down the hall. "Sam? Is that . . . Ruth Todd! Oh my gosh, you're Ruth Todd!" Candy squeaked.

Sophie came out of her trance and smiled at her mom. They were both huge fans.

"Mom, Ruth is here to do an interview about abusive relationships. She's just going to ask me a few questions," she said and showed Ruth and Sam into the family room where they all sat down.

"My camera man is outside. I thought I'd ask you first if you wanted to be on film or not. We could shade your face if you feel more comfortable with that," she said, looking kindly at her.

Sophie blushed and looked at Sam. He really wanted her to go on the ten o'clock news and talk about everything Tess had done? He gave her a small smile and a nod. Yep, he really did.

"Well, okay. You can have your camera man come inside. You don't have to shade my face or anything. I don't have anything to be ashamed of," she said.

Ruth went back outside and had the cameraman come in with her. They set up the room with lights and got the microphone hooked to her shirt and Sam's shirt. Candy stayed way, way in the background.

"Sam, when did you get the feeling that you were in an abusive relationship?" Ruth asked sympathetically.

Sam looked uncomfortable but looked straight at the camera.

"I don't know if I ever considered it an abusive relationship. But looking back on it now, I realize I was manipulated and controlled from the very beginning. She didn't want me to be with my friends or my family. She wanted to control everything I did. Where I went, who I talked to, even what I thought."

Ruth nodded her head and looked at Sophie. "Sophie, when you and Sam started seeing each other, were you ever scared that Sam's ex-girlfriend would hurt you?" she asked, as the camera man zoomed in on her stitches.

Sophie cleared her throat and looked down before replying. "Well, yes, actually. She called me up once and threatened to burn down our hair salon. She even threatened to have her uncle, who is an IRS agent, take away the salon. I was scared, but I never thought she'd be physically violent," she said honestly.

Ruth motioned for the camera to turn toward her. "Statistics show that verbal abuse is a precursor to physical abuse. Sam, how did you feel when you found out that your ex-girlfriend had assaulted Sophie?"

Sam took a deep breath and shook his head. "I've never been so scared in my life when I found out Sophie was in the hospital. At first I didn't know what had happened or how hurt she was. We were lucky this time. There's no telling what she's capable of," he said, looking angry.

Ruth continued to question Sam for a while and then asked, "So what steps can you take to protect yourself from this happening again?" Ruth asked as the cameraman turned to Sophie's face once more.

Sam reached over and took Sophie's hand before answering. "Ruth, I think doing what we're doing right now is the first important step. Talking about it and getting it out in the open is one of the best ways to make the abuse stop. There are always restraining orders, but I think education about what is healthy and what is not is the first step in the right direction," he said and then smiled.

Ruth talked for a few more minutes and then ended the interview. She stood up and shook both of their hands before leaving. Candy ran to the front window and watched their news van drive away.

Sophie sat on the couch, still in shock, just staring at Sam.

"I cannot believe what just happened. Sam, what just happened?" she asked.

Sam laughed and moved to sit by her on the couch.

"I'm doing what I told you I would. I'm taking care of Tess. We never mentioned her name once, but everyone who knows me knows her. She's not getting away with this. She'll be humiliated that everyone knows what she did. Her parents have let her get away with being spoiled rotten, but life is getting ready to catch up with her. And by the way, Trey was reinstated at BYU this morning. All charges have been dropped against him. My dad's lawyer has been busy all morning. It looks like Tess will plea bargain out of any jail time, but if we're lucky, she'll be forced to take anger management classes," he said with a grin.

Sophie took a deep breath and let it out. It was finally over. No more Tess hanging over their heads. No more threats, no more guilt. They were finally free.

Candy came back into the room, with her hands on her hips and a perplexed look on her face.

"Sam, why didn't you call and warn us? If you had just given us even five minutes heads up, Sophie could have at least put on a little eye makeup or done something with her hair," she said, staring at her daughter with a frown.

Sam grinned and put his arm around Sophie's shoulders.

"Exactly. I know who I'm dealing with. You two are the queens of beauty. I thought it would make more of a visual statement to see Sophie bare bones. The viewing audience probably wouldn't feel as sorry for someone who looked as fabulous as Sophie always does. Nope, I had to keep it a secret. Sorry, Candy," he said, looking charmingly apologetic.

Candy sniffed and then smiled. "Okay, you're probably right. But still. Sophie's one chance to be on the news, and she looked like a sad little waif."

Sophie smiled and shook her head. Sam had thought of every angle.

"I'm almost starting to feel sorry for Tess," she said, running her fingers through her still damp, wavy hair.

Sam's smile disappeared, and she wished she hadn't brought up her name.

"Well, don't," he said quietly as he looked at her hurt cheek.

Candy and Sophie glanced at each other before jumping into a conversation about Trey and how he got back into the Y. Sam relaxed again, and he left later with a smile on his face. Sophie spent the day being lazy and getting phone calls from friends who had heard what had happened. Working at a salon meant you didn't have any secrets, especially with Jacie telling everyone she could think of what had happened. The only annoying thing was, everyone kept asking her when she and Sam were getting married. She was going to have a BIG talk with Jacie later. She had to constantly remind everyone that it was Jacie getting married. Not her. By the end of the day, she felt like putting a sign around her neck, saying, "No, I'm not engaged." Candy just laughed at her.

With her mom and her best friend thinking of weddings nonstop, it was a little weird. And sometimes, when she was all by herself, she couldn't help picturing herself walking out of the Timpanogos Temple with Sam, smiling at friends and family. But then she'd catch herself and think of other things. Life was too short to daydream about future weddings. But then again . . .

chapter 37

The next month passed by quickly. Sophie's face started to heal, and Dr. Sanders was right—if you looked closely, you could see a faint red line, but with a little makeup, she was good as new. Sam promised he could barely see it. He said that she had so many freckles, her scar was camouflaged. She chose to believe him.

Sam had been right about Tess, too. She had plea bargained down to attempted assault and never saw the inside of a jail cell. She did have twenty hours of community service, though. She had to go to all of the local high schools and talk about abusive relationships and how to recognize when you were in one. Sophie had kind of been looking forward to a trial where she could point out Tess to the jury and cry and sob and watch as they sent her away for a year in prison. But hey, community service was okay too.

And according to Stan, his and Bert's last lunch together was something not to be forgotten. Stan never told Sam what had been said, but within three weeks, Tess and her parents had decided to relocate to Las Vegas. Something about the social circles in Utah being stagnant and boring. Sophie didn't care one way or the other. She didn't plan on doing much gambling, so she crossed her fingers that she'd never have to run into Tess again.

In the meantime, Sophie stayed busy at work. Her grandmother's blue fiasco hadn't affected her schedule at all. She actually seemed busier than usual. And her grandmother made a habit of coming to the salon once a week. She came for her nails, for an eyebrow waxing, for a manicure and pedicure, and for a touch-up on her color. Sophie actually started to look forward to her weekly hour with her grandmother at the salon. It just so happened that her grandmother was a very interesting person, and with the claws retracted, Sophie had to admit, she really liked her. Anyone brave enough to go back to someone who had dyed their hair blue was not only incredibly courageous, but trusting. And Sophie swore that from then on, her grandmother would have the most stylish hair in Alpine—well, besides her and her mother, of course.

And when Sophie wasn't working, Jacie had her rushing all over Utah looking for the perfect wedding dress. Bryan had proposed that Saturday night and had placed a large marquis cut diamond on Jacie's finger. Sophie had been shocked at the size. Bryan was not rich by any means, but he knew how to shop e-bay. And Jacie didn't care where the ring came from, as long as it was on her finger.

Jacie had already set the date for October third and had the stake center reserved for the reception. She couldn't make up her mind whether to do a Cinderella theme or an ultra-sophisticated modern reception. Sophie had to admit, planning a wedding was kind of fun. And if on occasion she tortured Sam with all the details, then that was okay too. A few hundred hints couldn't hurt. And she wasn't half as bad as Sam's sisters and his mom. Sue had bought all the available wedding magazines and placed them blatantly around the house. But his sisters were the worst. Every time Sophie went to dinner at his parents' house, every other word was about when she and Sam were married, or how cute their children would be. Sam would just smile and ignore everyone, but Sophie could tell he was slowly being driven crazy.

It wasn't just her with marriage on the brain, though. It seemed like everyone in Alpine was getting engaged. She'd received Blake's wedding announcement in the mail. She opened the card in surprise to find a glossy picture of Blake with his arms around the cutest little blonde she'd ever seen. Blake looked so handsome and happy. They looked good together. Sophie paused to see if there was any pain in her heart. She smiled in relief when there wasn't. She put the invitation on the fridge with three magnets. She couldn't wait to go and dance at Blake's wedding.

She called up Dorie and got all the details. Blake had met Jen on a blind date, and they had fallen in love immediately. Dorie insisted that she and Jack adored her, and Sophie was glad to hear the truth in her voice. Sophie couldn't help asking about Bailey, though. Dorie paused and chuckled.

"Well, from what Blake has told me, and he hasn't told me much, it turns out that she's engaged to get married soon too. So all's well that ends well," she said laughing.

Sophie laughed and hung the phone up soon after. She leaned against the kitchen counter and stared out the window. Everything was ending well for everyone. Especially her mom. Candy couldn't stop smiling if her life depended on it. Tonight was the night. Clyde had let her in on all the details. He was going to take Candy to the temple, where they would do some sealings and then afterward, they were going to walk around the grounds, where he would propose. Sophie thought about sneaking to the temple and hiding behind a bush with a camera to get the exact moment caught on film, but with her luck, she'd get caught by security and spend the night in jail. Nah, this moment was her mom's and Clyde's. She would stay home and wait for the announcement when her mom got home. She'd have to practice looking surprised, though.

Sam was coming over after work to keep her company. They were planning on grilling some steaks in the backyard and watching a video. Very laid back, very relaxing. Very . . . boring.

Sophie sighed. She was trying really really hard not to be jealous of everyone getting engaged, but it was starting to get to her. Sam was so laid back, he was going to be thirty before he even thought about asking her. And after his big speech in the hospital about wanting someone to raise kids with, nothing had happened. Not one more mention of kids. He had probably just been feeling guilty about her getting hurt, so he had thrown that in to make her feel better. Well, it wasn't working anymore. Sophie frowned and got stuff out of the fridge to make a salad. If she wasn't careful, she was going to be in a very bad mood by the time Sam arrived. She looked at the clock and frowned deeper. He should have been to her house five minutes ago. And that was another thing. Things were always coming up with him. He was never on time to anything. Yeah yeah, building inspectors and meetings with clients. Well, what about her? Wasn't she as important as some old building inspector or client?

Sophie glared at the clock and threw the last cherry tomato on top of the salad. Okay, it was official. She was in a rotten mood. She got the steaks out of the fridge, where they had been marinating, and let them sit on the counter so they could be room temperature before she grilled them.

She grabbed a Fresca, kicked the fridge door shut, and walked out on the front porch to wait for Sam. She sat down in a huff and popped the top of her soda. She glared at all the cars and trucks driving by. Not one of them was Sam. Fifteen *long* minutes later, Sam finally pulled up with a smile on his face.

Well, he's in a good mood, she thought darkly, as she stood to greet him.

"Hey, beautiful! What's a gorgeous girl like you doing home on a Friday night?" Sam asked.

Sophie sniffed and looked away from him. "I have no idea," she said grumpily and tilted her face up for a very quick, little kiss. She turned her face at the last moment, and he ended up kissing her on the cheek. She almost smiled at his frown. Ha!

"Well, come on in. The steaks are ready for grilling," she said and walked in the house.

"Is everything okay, Sophie? You seem a little different today," Sam said, smiling again, for some really annoying reason.

Sophie rolled her eyes. "Oh no, not me. I'm never in a bad mood. Everything's fine," she said breezily and grabbed the plate of steaks and walked out the door to the patio. Sam followed her a moment later and sat down in one of the patio chairs as she went to work.

"So tonight's the big night, huh?" Sam said, leaning back and closing his eyes tiredly.

Sophie smiled slightly. "Yeah, it's hilarious. My mom has no idea he's asking her tonight. How could you not know? I mean, Clyde was standing there, just grinning his head off at her, and all she could do was complain about some broken clasp on her temple bag. She is going to be so surprised," she said, as she closed the lid to the barbecue and sat next to Sam.

Sam looked over at her and laughed. Sophie frowned. "What is the matter with you? You're too happy," she said grouchily and looked away. It was hard looking at happy people when she was in a bad mood. It was just too irritating.

"Sophie, honey, what's the matter? You can tell me," Sam said and grabbed her hand.

Sophie pulled her hand away and glared at him. "Nothing! Everything is perfect!" she said, maybe a little more loudly than she should have.

Sam just laughed, making it worse. His phone rang and he stood up to answer it, walking toward the back of the yard to talk. As if she cared what his little sub contractor wanted to say to him.

She checked the steaks and brought their plates out, putting the salad on the table and getting everything ready.

Sam said good-bye and shut his phone as he walked up to her and put his arms around her, hugging her tightly.

"Sweetie, I'm sorry you're not in the best mood tonight. But hey, we're together. Right? You and me. What could be better than that?" he asked, staring deeply into her eyes.

Sophie sighed and hugged him back. He was right. Sort of.

"Sorry, for some reason today, I'm just a little out of sorts. Don't mind me," she said and reached up and kissed him on the cheek.

As she put the steaks on their plates and handed one to Sam, he glanced at his watch.

"Sophie, you don't mind if I watch the five o'clock news, do you?" he asked, opening the door and walking back into the house.

Sophie stared after him, not believing it. She made him dinner, and the thanks she got was being ignored for the sports scores on TV. Unbelievable. She grabbed her plate and walked into the house to join Sam. He was already on her couch with the TV on. He glanced up and patted the seat next to him.

"Have a seat. You've been on your feet all day," he said and then turned to stare at the screen lovingly.

Sophie glared at him but sat down anyway. He turned the volume up and then set his plate down on the coffee table.

Sophie got up to grab her drink, but Sam grabbed her wrist and pulled her back down.

"Wait a second. Don't go anywhere," he said, kind of tensely.

Sophie stared at him in surprise. He was acting kind of strange all of a sudden. Almost nervous. And he had broken out in a sweat. Maybe he was sick. She glanced at the TV and saw Ruth Todd. He was stressing out about Ruth?

"What's going on? Is she going to do another segment on abusive relationships?" Sophie asked, leaning forward in interest.

"Okay, everyone," Ruth Todd said, "we never do this, but we're going to a take a little break from the hard news to do something kind of fun. Sam Kellen has asked us to do him a little favor. Sophie? Sam loves you more than anything in the world. And he really wants to know if you'll marry him," she said with a bright smile.

Sophie's mouth dropped open, and she turned and stared at Sam. He was already down on his knees with a gorgeous diamond ring in his hands.

"What do you say?" he asked, grinning at her.

Sophie jumped up and down. "Yes! Yes! Yes!" she screamed and then threw herself at Sam, knocking him backward into the couch. He laughed and sat up.

"Let me just put this on your finger before I lose it," he said quickly, slipping it on her finger. But then, instead of cherishing the moment of a lifetime, he ran to the front of the house and opened the front door, yelling outside.

"Okay, everyone, she said yes!" he yelled and stepped aside for her mom and Clyde and Jacie and Bryan and his mom and dad and his sisters and Trey to come in.

Everyone stopped by and gave her a hug and kiss and exclaimed over the ring.

Sophie was still in shock. "Mom! What are you doing here? This is your big night," she said, staring at Clyde in confusion.

"Nah, this is your big night. Clyde just made up all that stuff to put you off the scent. Sam didn't want you to suspect a thing. We've been planning this forever," she said, hugging her daughter.

Sophie laughed. "I can't believe this. I was so mad at him too. Everyone I know is engaged, and here I was, sitting at home on a Friday night, watching the news," she said, shaking her head at Sam, who was across the room, still grinning at her. Sam patted Trey on the back and hurried to Sophie's side, putting his arm around her shoulders.

"Everything happened so fast. What do you think, Sophie? Are you happy? Do you like the ring?" he asked, smiling down at her sweetly.

Sophie grinned and looked down at her ring and then gasped in surprise.

"Sam! Oh my heck. How many carats are in my ring?" she asked, feeling slightly dizzy. Her ring was huge. A large square cut diamond set in platinum. She'd never seen anything like it before.

Sam grinned and took her hand in his so he could see it in the light.

"Custom made, Sophie. And look on the inside. It's inscribed," he said, blushing slightly and staring at her.

Sophie tilted the ring and brought it closer so she could read it.

Sam and Sophie. A love made in heaven.

"Ooooohhh," she said, and felt a little tear slip out. "That's so sweet, Sam. I love you," she told him and hugged him tightly.

Sam hugged her back and then did something very strange.

"I love you too, babe. Now watch this, because you don't want to miss it," he said and then turned her around to see Clyde standing in the middle of the family room, clapping his hands to get everyone's attention.

Candy exchanged confused looks with her, and they listened to hear what he was saying.

"Everyone! Everyone! If I could just get your attention. I know we're all ecstatic for Sam and Sophie, and I would never want to steal their spotlight, but this is something that just can't wait another second. Candy, my darling, my love. Will you be my wife?" he asked, staring at her across the room.

Candy flung her hands up to her face and stared in shock at Clyde. She turned and looked to Sophie for confirmation that this was really happening.

Sophie laughed and pushed her toward Clyde. "You are not dreaming, Mom."

Candy walked slowly toward Clyde as everyone watched in silence.

"Honey, this is the part where you actually have to say yes or no," Clyde said, coloring slightly.

Candy took his outstretched hands. "Yes, Clyde, I would love to marry you," she said to shouts of congratulations.

Clyde picked her up and threw her in the air. And then the party really started. Sam and Sophie's steaks were long forgotten, so they ordered pizzas from Dimetri's. Trey had to leave for a date, and Sam's sisters left to go to a friend's house. Everyone else spilled out into the backyard and stayed up late into the night, talking about weddings and honeymoons. Sophie sat back in her chair smiling happily as she held Sam's hand and looked up at the stars.

"Is this really happening, Sam?" she asked as he raised her hand and kissed it.

Sam smiled just as happily.

"Of course it is. You and me forever, Sophie. It was meant to be. The first time I laid eyes on you, I had the most amazing feeling inside. It was like someone was standing at my shoulder whispering to me, 'Look at her, Sam. Look at your future. Look at your happiness. Look at the rest of your life,' " he said, staring at her seriously.

Sophie sighed happily. "That's so beautiful, Sam. I wish I could say I heard something when I met you. All I could think was, 'Holy cow, that man is beautiful,' " she said, laughing.

Sam grinned. "That works too. I love you, Sophie," he said.

Sophie looked at their clasped hands and felt a burst of happiness inside her that she'd never experienced before. This really was happening.

"I love you too, Sam," she said and knew she had just entered the next phase of her life.

chapter 38

TWO YEARS LATER

Sophie stared at the back of her grandmother's head and nodded her approval. Perfection. She turned off the hairdryer and massaged Liz's back.

"What do you think?" Sophie asked and stepped to the side to see her grandmother's expression.

Liz Reid studied herself with a half-smile. Gone was the short boyish hairstyle. She now had the same hairstyle as Barbara Walters. It worked for her. She looked ten years younger since switching to Sophie. Not including the first month, of course.

"Dear, you always do it just the way I like it. I love it," Liz said, and smiled at her granddaughter. "But I have to insist that you stop working. I know everyone loves the way you do their hair, but that baby's due any minute now, and you need to put your feet up. I don't think you're resting nearly as much as you should be," she said, sounding worried.

Sophie took the drape off her grandmother's shoulders and held out her hand to help her up.

"Grandma, you worry too much. The doctor says I'm fine. And I have the best OB in Utah. He should know," she said, smiling.

Liz sniffed. "Well, yes, Dr. Brown is very highly recommended, but still. Your due date's in two weeks. You should get as much rest as you can right now, because after that little one gets here, you won't rest for twenty years," she said, shaking her head.

Sophie laughed and walked her grandmother to the door. "Okay, okay. I'll take it easy. Mom is just as bad as you are. I only came in today to do your hair. I'm only doing one or two clients a day now. And next week, I'm not coming in at all. So see? Nothing to worry about."

Her grandmother put on her jacket and studied her granddaughter's face carefully.

"Well, then, I'm glad you have some sense. Now listen, I know you're doing Daphne's hair tomorrow. That girl has such a mouth on her, but whatever she says, just take it with a grain of salt and don't do anything drastic. Please?" she said.

Sophie laughed and opened the door. "Grandma, you have my promise that all the blue dye has been thrown out of the salon. No more revenge for me. I've repented."

Her grandmother leaned up and kissed Sophie on the cheek. "Haven't we all. I love you, dear. Call me if you need anything, or if the baby comes. Okay?"

Sophie assured her she would and watched as her grandmother walked away.

She waddled to the back of the salon, where Jacie was already there with her feet up on the stool. They couldn't tell who was bigger. They both looked like they were twenty months pregnant.

"Did you save me any of that cake?" Sophie asked, looking all around for the cake a client had brought in just that morning.

Jacie looked guilty and patted her stomach. "Um, there wasn't that much left. Honestly. It's lunchtime anyway. How about I take you to Subway? My doctor told me to cut down on the French fries and hamburgers. I'm on the Jared diet now."

Sophie frowned. She had been looking forward to that cake. Darn Jacie.

"Fine, but I want a footlong, you stinker," she said pouting.

Sophie heard the sound of water and looked around. "Who left the faucet on?" she asked as she massaged her back.

Jacie laughed and pointed at the floor. "Dude, you did."

Sophie stared at the ground in front of her at the large puddle of fluid on the floor and gasped in shock.

"My water broke! Call Sam for me! I'm going to the hospital!" Sophie yelled and grabbed her purse.

Jacie pushed herself up off the couch and shook her head. "Uh-uh.

I'm driving you to the hospital, and you call Sam on your cell. He can meet us there. Call your mom too. She's at Dr. Brown right now getting an ultrasound. She's just minutes away from the hospital," Jacie said as she ran to put the closed sign on the front door.

Sophie waddled as fast as she could toward Jacie's car. Jacie stopped her, though, and wouldn't let her sit down until she had gone back for a drape and put it over the seat.

"No way are you dripping on my car. Love ya, but not that much," she said.

They reached the hospital the same time Sam and his parents did. Within five minutes, her mom and Clyde were there. Her father showed up twenty minutes later, followed by her grandmother and Lexie. And after two very long hours of pushing, she had her son to show them.

After the measuring and the cleaning and the diapering, the announcement was finally made. "Everyone, please meet Adam Samuel Kellen," Sam said, holding his son up proudly in the nursery for all to see.

That night as Sophie lay in bed, exhausted, elated, and really in a lot of pain, she realized she was happier than she'd ever been. She had the love of her life, a gorgeous, healthy new son, and her family. All of them, together. She couldn't help thinking what an incredible makeover her life had been given.

She turned on her other side and watched with a tender smile on her face as Sam walked into the room, carrying a large bouquet of bright white daisies. Life was so strange sometimes. Sometimes it was really pretty great.

Here's an excerpt from

soul searching,

also by
Shannon Guymon

chapter one

Micah sat down in the back row with her two roommates, Lisa and April. She smoothed her long linen skirt over her knees and concentrated on not crossing her legs. She tucked the blond wisps of hair that had come loose from her clip behind her ears and took a deep, calming breath as she looked out over the large congregation of beautiful people. She hated going to church.

She felt her body tense up as it always did and concentrated on the perfection of her fingernails. She might have her problems, but at least there were no chips in her fingernails. *That has to count for something,* she thought. She'd had the lady at the nail salon paint them a light shade of mauve. Not too bright, not too pale. Her father would surely approve.

Micah looked up as the opening song ended and waited for the bishop to approach the podium. She liked Bishop Nielson. He was always polite and courteous to her. And as long as he didn't call her in for any kind of interview, she would like him a lot.

Testimony meeting. Great. Micah felt her stomach clench into an even tighter ball of nerves and automatically reached for her purse. If she didn't have a roll of Tums, then she might as well lie down and die. Her fingers searched the bottom of her purse and finally clutched around the half-eaten tube of comfort—the only comfort she would be getting that morning anyway. Her father had told her just last week that he was expecting her to bear her testimony soon. He was disappointed that she hadn't been given a calling yet. *Embarrassed* was the word he had used. He had gently suggested that by bearing her testimony, she would give the bishop a good impression of her.

She hated bearing her testimony. What was a testimony anyway, except people getting up and crying about how wonderful their roommates were, or how hard going to school was but they made it through because they worked so hard? *Blah, blah, blah.* And today it would be her. She felt all cold and clammy inside at the thought. She always wondered how these girls could get up every fast and testimony meeting and cry their eyes out about the dumbest things. Every time the bishop got up and talked about how strong the Spirit had been in a certain meeting, she felt so confused. Couldn't he hear how pointless they all sounded?

If her father hadn't been expecting her for lunch today, she would have gotten up and walked out right then. Using the excuse of feeling ill and staying home could only be used so often though. *I could always lie.* She could tell her father she had borne her testimony and he would never know. Except her father had a bad habit of always checking up on her—accidentally running into her bishop at the bank or calling up Brother Harris, the first counselor, for tax advice.

Her father wasn't stupid. He'd just pack on the guilt until she cracked. Until she'd do anything for him to stop—stop what? What was it exactly he did? She paused and thought about it as the bread was passed to her. He sucked the life out of her. That's what he did. She frowned at the disloyal thought. Surely, a loving, dutiful, and grateful daughter wouldn't think something so awful of her father. Would she?

Micah threw all thoughts of her father out of her mind and focused on her game plan: getting through the next hour. What could she bear her testimony about? What? Think, think, think. What would impress the bishop so much that he would have no choice but to make her the next Relief Society president? *As if.* But her father just wouldn't give up hoping. He kept reminding her that if she would just mention the fact that her great-great uncle had been a General Authority, she would see some results. What her father didn't seem to understand though, was that Bishop Nielson had a way of looking right through you. He didn't see all of the superficial stuff she had been throwing at him. He saw her soul. She, Bishop Nielson, and God all knew there wasn't much there worth talking about. Too bad her dad didn't understand that.

She looked around desperately, wishing for any kind of inspiration. But all she could see were perfect, happy people. It made her sick. She couldn't imagine being one of them. She always felt as if she were outside looking in. Or to be more exact, inside looking out—inside a prison and looking out into a world where people were happy. Where it was possible to be somebody wonderful. Where you didn't always feel so . . . broken.

If she could just steal a little bit from each person. Not much, just a little. If she could just take a little of Erin's confidence, snatch a small portion of Julie's glow, or take a teeny bit of Carly's sense of humor, then she'd be okay. She would be normal then. Okay, so she would be some kind of soul snatcher and would go to hell, but for just one day, wouldn't it be worth it? All of these girls in her ward had something that she didn't have. She wasn't sure exactly what that was, but she knew it, just like she knew her own name. They had this inner glow that made people swarm to them. People wanted to be near them. People *enjoyed* being with them. Micah winced as she realized that there was no one swarming to be anywhere near her.

Micah glanced over at her roommates and smiled gratefully. At least she had two roommates to sit by. And these two girls were actually nice. They weren't exactly girls approved of by her father, definitely no one she could bring home for dinner. But still they tried hard to include her, even when she had spent the better part of the summer trying to ignore their existence. They always insisted on dragging her to ward activities or to the movies. She had to admit it was kind of nice. She almost felt normal when it was just the three of them. Too bad Lisa was at least twenty pounds overweight. Her father was very critical of people who were even slightly overweight. And April. She *really* liked April, but she could just imagine her father's comments about her. Micah thought April was so cool. She had ultra-black hair and super-thin plucked eyebrows, and her choice of makeup was, well . . . interesting. She was very much into the primary colors. Her T-shirts and jeans looked like she purchased them from garage sales. Yep, her dad would have a field day with April. Better to leave well enough alone.

Every time her dad questioned her about her roommates, she would act as if she despised them and the only reason she was staying was so she could set a good example for them. Her father would always beam at her approvingly when she would say stupid things like that. And she knew her secret was safe. She was happy in her little apartment with her unlikely roommates. And no one would ever have to know.

About the Author

Shannon Guymon lives in Alpine, Utah, with her husband and six children. She enjoys spending time in the mountains, gardening, being with her family, and, of course, writing. She is the author of *Never Letting Go of Hope*, *A Trusting Heart*, *Justifiable Means*, *Forever Friends*, and *Soul Searching*.

0 26575 70817 2